URSULA K. LE GUIN'S
AWARD-WINNING SAGA OF
TWO PLANETS
AND THE VISIONARY MAN
WHO TRIED TO UNITE THEM

D0885372

MARVIN ATCHLEY

THE DISPOSSESSED

URSULA K. Le GUIN

`74

AVON
PUBLISHERS OF BARD, CAMELOT AND DISCUS BOOKS

AVON BOOKS
A division of
The Hearst Corporation
959 Eighth Avenue
New York, New York 10019

First Avon Printing, July, 1975
Tenth Printing

Printed in the U.S.A.

For the partner

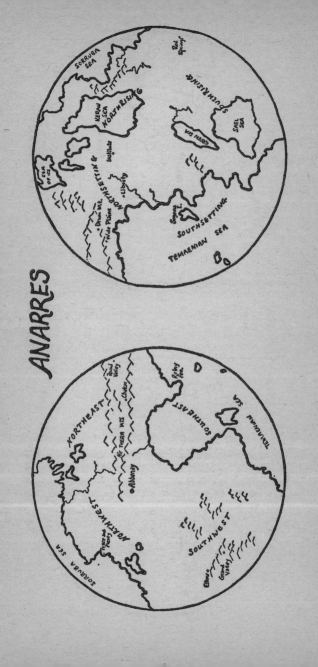

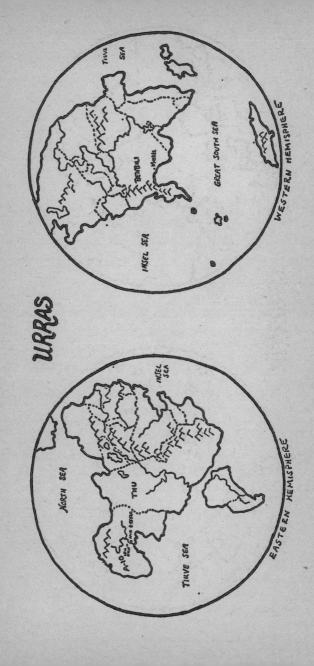

Chapter 1

There was a wall. It did not look important. It was built of
uncut rocks roughly mortared. An adult could look right
over it, and even a child could climb it. Where it crossed
the roadway, instead of having a gate it degenerated into
mere geometry, a line, an idea of boundary. But the idea
was real. It was important. For seven generations there
had been nothing in the world more important than that
wall.

Like all walls it was ambiguous, two-faced. What was
inside it and what was outside it depended upon which
side of it you were on.

Looked at from one side, the wall enclosed a barren
sixty-acre field called the Port of Anarres. On the field
there were a couple of large gantry cranes, a rocket pad,
three warehouses, a truck garage, and a dormitory. The
dormitory looked durable, grimy, and mournful; it had no
gardens, no children; plainly nobody lived there or was
even meant to stay there long. It was in fact a quarantine.
The wall shut in not only the landing field but also the
ships that came down out of space, and the men that came
on the ships, and the worlds they came from, and the rest

1

of the universe. It enclosed the universe, leaving Anarres outside, free.

Looked at from the other side, the wall enclosed Anarres: the whole planet was inside it, a great prison camp, cut off from other worlds and other men, in quarantine.

A number of people were coming along the road towards the landing field, or standing around where the road cut through the wall.

People often came out from the nearby city of Abbenay in hopes of seeing a spaceship, or simply to see the wall. After all, it was the only boundary wall on their world. Nowhere else could they see a sign that said No Trespassing. Adolescents, particularly, were drawn to it. They came up to the wall; they sat on it. There might be a gang to watch, offloading crates from track trucks at the warehouses. There might even be a freighter on the pad. Freighters came down only eight times a year, unannounced except to syndics actually working at the Port, so when the spectators were lucky enough to see one they were excited, at first. But there they sat, and there it sat, a squat black tower in a mess of movable cranes, away off across the field. And then a woman came over from one of the warehouse crews and said, "We're shutting down for today, brothers." She was wearing the Defense armband, a sight almost as rare as a spaceship. That was a bit of a thrill. But though her tone was mild, it was final. She was the foreman of this gang, and if provoked would be backed up by her syndics. And anyhow there wasn't anything to see. The aliens, the off-worlders, stayed hiding in their ship. No show.

It was a dull show for the Defense crew, too. Sometimes the foreman wished that somebody would just try to cross the wall, an alien crewman jumping ship, or a kid from Abbenay trying to sneak in for a closer look at the freighter. But it never happened. Nothing ever happened. When something did happen she wasn't ready for it.

The captain of the freighter *Mindful* said to her, "Is that mob after my ship?"

The foreman looked and saw that in fact there was a real crowd around the gate, a hundred or more people. They were standing around, just standing, the way people had stood at produce-train stations during the Famine. It gave the foreman a scare.

2

"No. They, ah, protest," she said in her slow and limited Iotic. "Protest the, ah, you know. Passenger?"

"You mean they're after this bastard we're supposed to take? Are they going to try to stop him, or us?"

The word "bastard," untranslatable in the foreman's language, meant nothing to her except some kind of foreign term for her people, but she had never liked the sound of it, or the captain's tone, or the captain. "Can you look after you?" she asked briefly.

"Hell, yes. You just get the rest of this cargo onloaded, quick. And get this passenger bastard on board. No mob of Oddies is about to give *us* any trouble." He patted the thing he wore on his belt, a metal object like a deformed penis, and looked patronizingly at the unarmed woman.

She gave the phallic object, which she knew was a weapon, a cold glance. "Ship will be loaded by fourteen hours," she said. "Keep crew on board safe. Liftoff at fourteen hours forty. If you need help, leave message on tape at Ground Control." She strode off before the captain could one-up her. Anger made her more forceful with her crew and the crowd. "Clear the road there!" she ordered as she neared the wall. "Trucks are coming through, somebody's going to get hurt. Clear aside!"

The men and women in the crowd argued with her and with one another. They kept crossing the road, and some came inside the wall. Yet they did more or less clear the way. If the foreman had no experience in bossing a mob, they had no experience in being one. Members of a community, not elements of a collectivity, they were not moved by mass feeling; there were as many emotions there as there were people. And they did not expect commands to be arbitrary, so they had no practice in disobeying them. Their inexperience saved the passenger's life.

Some of them had come there to kill a traitor. Others had come to prevent him from leaving, or to yell insults at him, or just to look at him; and all these others obstructed the sheer brief path of the assassins. None of them had firearms, though a couple had knives. Assault to them meant bodily assault; they wanted to take the traitor into their own hands. They expected him to come guarded, in a vehicle. While they were trying to inspect a goods truck and arguing with its outraged driver, the man they wanted came walking up the road, alone. When they recognized

3

him he was already halfway across the field, with five Defense syndics following him. Those who had wanted to kill him resorted to pursuit, too late, and to rock throwing, not quite too late. They barely winged the man they wanted, just as he got to the ship, but a two-pound flint caught one of the Defense crew on the side of the head and killed him on the spot.

The hatches of the ship closed. The Defense crew turned back, carrying their dead companion; they made no effort to stop the leaders of the crowd who came racing towards the ship, though the foreman, white with shock and rage, cursed them to hell as they ran past, and they swerved to avoid her. Once at the ship, the vanguard of the crowd scattered and stood irresolute. The silence of the ship, the abrupt movements of the huge skeletal gantries, the strange burned look of the ground, the absence of anything in human scale, disoriented them. A blast of steam or gas from something connected with the ship made some of them start; they looked up uneasily at the rockets, vast black tunnels overhead. A siren whooped in warning, far across the field. First one person and then another started back towards the gate. Nobody stopped them. Within ten minutes the field was clear, the crowd scattered out along the road to Abbenay. Nothing appeared to have happened, after all.

Inside the *Mindful* a great deal was happening. Since Ground Control had pushed launch time up, all routines had to be rushed through in double time. The captain had ordered that the passenger be strapped down and locked in, in the crew lounge, along with the doctor, to get them out from underfoot. There was a screen in there, they could watch the liftoff if they liked.

The passenger watched. He saw the field, and the wall around the field, and far outside the wall the distant slopes of the Ne Theras, speckled with scrub holum and sparse, silvery moonthorn.

All this suddenly rushed dazzling down the screen. The passenger felt his head pressed back against the padded rest. It was like a dentist's examination, the head pressed back, the jaw forced open. He could not get his breath, he felt sick, he felt his bowels loosen with fear. His whole body cried out to the enormous forces that had taken hold of him, *Not now, not yet, wait!*

4

His eyes saved him. What they insisted on seeing and reporting to him took him out of the autism of terror. For on the screen now was a strange sight, a great pallid plain of stone. It was the desert seen from the mountains above Grand Valley. How had he got back to Grand Valley? He tried to tell himself that he was in an airship. No, in a spaceship. The edge of the plain flashed with the brightness of light on water, light across a distant sea. There was no water in those deserts. What was he seeing, then? The stone plain was no longer plane but hollow, like a huge bowl full of sunlight. As he watched in wonder it grew shallower, spilling out its light. All at once a line broke across it, abstract, geometric, the perfect section of a circle. Beyond that arc was blackness. This blackness reversed the whole picture, made it negative. The real, the stone part of it was no longer concave and full of light but convex, reflecting, rejecting light. It was not a plain or a bowl but a sphere, a ball of white stone falling down in blackness, falling away. It was his world.

"I don't understand," he said aloud.

Someone answered him. For a while he failed to comprehend that the person standing by his chair was speaking to him, answering him, for he no longer understood what an answer is. He was clearly aware of only one thing, his own total isolation. The world had fallen out from under him, and he was left alone.

He had always feared that this would happen, more than he had ever feared death. To die is to lose the self and rejoin the rest. He had kept himself, and lost the rest.

He was able at last to look up at the man standing beside him. It was a stranger, of course. From now on there would be only strangers. He was speaking in a foreign language: Iotic. The words made sense. All the little things made sense; only the whole thing did not. The man was saying something about the straps that held him into the chair. He fumbled at them. The chair swung upright, and he nearly fell out of it, being giddy and off balance. The man kept asking if someone had been hurt. Who was he talking about? "Is he sure he didn't get hurt?" The polite form of direct address in Iotic was in the third person. The man meant him, himself. He did not know why he should have been hurt; the man kept saying something about throwing rocks. But the rock will never hit, he

5

thought. He looked back at the screen for the rock, the white stone falling down in darkness, but the screen had gone blank.

"I am well," he said at last, at random.

It did not appease the man. "Please come with me. I'm a doctor."

"I am well."

"Please come with me, Dr. Shevek!"

"You are a doctor," Shevek said after a pause. "I am not. I am called Shevek."

The doctor, a short, fair, bald man, grimaced with anxiety. "You should be in your cabin, sir—danger of infection—you weren't to be in contact with anybody but me, I've been through two weeks of disinfection for nothing, God damn that captain! Please come with me, sir. I'll be held responsible—"

Shevek perceived that the little man was upset. He felt no compunction, no sympathy; but even where he was, in absolute solitude, the one law held, the one law he had ever acknowledged. "All right," he said, and stood up.

He still felt dizzy, and his right shoulder hurt. He knew the ship must be moving, but there was no sense of motion; there was only a silence, an awful, utter silence, just outside the walls. The doctor led him through silent metal corridors to a room.

It was a very small room, with seamed, blank walls. It repelled Shevek, reminding him of a place he did not want to remember. He stopped in the doorway. But the doctor urged and pleaded, and he went on in.

He sat down on the shelf-like bed, still feeling light-headed and lethargic, and watched the doctor incuriously. He felt he ought to be curious; this man was the first Urrasti he had ever seen. But he was too tired. He could have lain back and gone straight to sleep.

He had been up all the night before, going through his papers. Three days ago he had seen Takver and the children off to Peace-and-Plenty, and ever since then he had been busy, running out to the radio tower to exchange last-minute messages with people on Urras, discussing plans and possibilities with Bedap and the others. All through those hurried days, ever since Takver left, he had felt not that he was doing all the things he did, but that they were doing him. He had been in other people's hands.

6

His own will had not acted. It had had no need to act. It was his own will that had started it all, that had created this moment and these walls about him now. How long ago? Years. Five years ago, in the silence of night in Chakar in the mountains, when he had said to Takver, "I will go to Abbenay and unbuild walls." Before then, even; long before, in the Dust, in the years of famine and despair, when he had promised himself that he would never act again but by his own free choice. And following that promise he had brought himself here: to this moment without time, this place without an earth, this little room, this prison.

The doctor had examined his bruised shoulder (the bruise puzzled Shevek; he had been too tense and hurried to realize what had been going on at the landing field, and had never felt the rock strike him). Now he turned to him holding a hypodermic needle.

"I do not want that," Shevek said. His spoken Iotic was slow, and, as he knew from the radio exchanges, badly pronounced, but it was grammatical enough; he had more difficulty understanding than speaking.

"This is measles vaccine," said the doctor, professionally deaf.

"No," Shevek said.

The doctor chewed his lip for a moment and said, "Do you know what measles is, sir?"

"No."

"A disease. Contagious. Often severe in adults. You don't have it on Anarres; prophylactic measures kept it out when the planet was settled. It's common on Urras. It could kill you. So could a dozen other common viral infections. You have no resistance. Are you right-handed, sir?"

Shevek automatically shook his head. With the grace of a prestidigitator the doctor slid the needle into his right arm. Shevek submitted to this and other injections in silence. He had no right to suspicion or protest. He had yielded himself up to these people; he had given up his birthright of decision. It was gone, fallen away from him along with his world, the world of the Promise, the barren stone.

The doctor spoke again, but he did not listen.

For hours or days he existed in a vacancy, a dry and

7

wretched void without past or future. The walls stood tight about him. Outside them was the silence. His arms and buttocks ached from injections; he ran a fever that never quite heightened to delirium but left him in a limbo between reason and unreason, no man's land. Time did not pass. There was no time. He was time: he only. He was the river, the arrow, the stone. But he did not move. The thrown rock hung still at midpoint. There was no day or night. Sometimes the doctor switched the light off, or on. There was a clock set in the wall by the bed; its pointer moved from one to another of the twenty figures of the dial, meaningless.

He woke after long, deep sleep, and since he was facing the clock, studied it sleepily. Its pointer stood at a little after 15, which, if the dial was read from midnight like the 24-hour Anarresti clock, should mean that it was midafternoon. But how could it be midafternoon in space between two worlds? Well, the ship would keep its own time, after all. Figuring all this out heartened him immensely. He sat up and did not feel giddy. He got out of bed and tested his balance: satisfactory, though he felt that the soles of his feet were not quite firmly in contact with the floor. The ship's gravity field must be rather weak. He did not much like the feeling; what he needed was steadiness, solidity, firm fact. In search of these he began methodically to investigate the little room.

The blank walls were full of surprises, all ready to reveal themselves at a touch on the panel: washstand, shitstool, mirror, desk, chair, closet, shelves. There were several completely mysterious electrical devices connected with the washstand, and the water valve did not cut off when you released the faucet but kept pouring out until shut off—a sign, Shevek thought, either of great faith in human nature, or of great quantities of hot water. Assuming the latter, he washed all over, and finding no towel, dried himself with one of the mysterious devices, which emitted a pleasant tickling blast of warm air. Not finding his own clothes, he put back on those he had found himself wearing when he woke up: loose tied trousers and a shapeless tunic, both bright yellow with small blue spots. He looked at himself in the mirror. He thought the effect unfortunate. Was this how they dressed on Urras? He

8

searched in vain for a comb, made do by braiding back his hair, and so groomed made to leave the room.

He could not. The door was locked.

Shevek's first incredulity turned to rage, a kind of rage, a blind will to violence, which he had never felt before in his life. He wrenched at the immovable door handle, slammed his hands against the slick metal of the door, then turned and jabbed the call button, which the doctor had told him to use at need. Nothing happened. There were a lot of other little numbered buttons of different colors on the intercom panel; he hit his hand across the whole lot of them. The wall speaker began to babble, "Who the hell yes coming right away out clear what from twenty-two—"

Shevek drowned them all out: "Unlock the door!"

The door slid open, the doctor looked in. At the sight of his bald, anxious, yellowish face Shevek's wrath cooled and retreated into an inward darkness. He said, "The door was locked."

"I'm sorry, Dr. Shevek—a precaution—contagion—keeping the others out—"

"To lock out, to lock in, the same act," Shevek said looking down at the doctor with light, remote eyes.

"Safety—"

"Safety? Must I be kept in a box?"

"The officers' lounge," the doctor offered hurriedly, appeasingly. "Are you hungry, sir? Perhaps you'd like to get dressed and we'll go to the lounge."

Shevek looked at the doctor's clothing: tight blue trousers tucked into boots that looked as smooth and fine as cloth themselves; a violet tunic open down the front and reclosed with silver frogs; and under that, showing only at neck and wrists, a knit shirt of dazzling white.

"I am not dressed?" Shevek inquired at last.

"Oh, pajamas will do, by all means. No formalities on a freighter!"

"Pajamas?"

"What you're wearing. Sleeping clothes."

"Clothes to wear while sleeping?"

"Yes."

Shevek blinked. He made no comment. He asked, "Where are the clothes I wore?"

"Your clothes? I had them cleaned—sterilization. I hope you don't mind, sir—" He investigated a wall panel Shevek

9

had not discovered and brought out a packet wrapped in pale-green paper. He unwrapped Shevek's old suit, which looked very clean and somewhat reduced in size, wadded up the green paper, activated another panel, tossed the paper into the bin that opened, and smiled uncertainly. "There you are, Dr. Shevek."

"What happens to the paper?"

"The paper?"

"The green paper."

"Oh, I put it in the trash."

"Trash?"

"Disposal. It gets burned up."

"You burn paper?"

"Perhaps it just gets dropped out into space, I don't know. I'm no space medic, Dr. Shevek. I was given the honor of attending you because of my experience with other visitors from offworld, the ambassadors from Terra and from Hain. I run the decontamination and habituation procedure for all aliens arriving in A-Io. Not that you're exactly an alien in the same sense, of course." He looked timidly at Shevek, who could not follow all he said, but did discern the anxious, diffident, well-meaning nature beneath the words.

"No," Shevek assured him, "maybe I have the same grandmother as you, two hundred years ago, on Urras." He was putting on his old clothes, and as he pulled the shirt over his head he saw the doctor stuff the blue and yellow "sleeping clothes" into the "trash" bin. Shevek paused, the collar still over his nose. He emerged fully, knelt, and opened the bin. It was empty.

"The clothes are burned?"

"Oh, those are cheap pajamas, service issue—wear 'em and throw 'em away, it costs less than cleaning."

"It costs less," Shevek repeated meditatively. He said the words the way a paleontologist looks at a fossil, the fossil that dates a whole stratum.

"I'm afraid your luggage must have got lost in that final rush for the ship. I hope there was nothing important in it."

"I brought nothing," Shevek said. Though his suit had been bleached almost to white and had shrunk a bit, it still fit, and the harsh familiar touch of holum-fiber cloth was pleasant. He felt like himself again. He sat down on the bed facing the doctor and said, "You see, I know you don't take things, as we do. In your world, in Urras, one must buy things. I come to your world, I have no money, I cannot buy, therefore I should bring. But how much can I bring? Clothing, yes, I might bring two suits. But food? How can I bring food enough? I cannot buy, I cannot bring. If I am to be kept alive, you must give it to me. I am an Anarresti, I make the Urrasti behave like Anarresti: to give, not to sell. If you like. Of course, it is not necessary to keep me alive! I am the Beggarman, you see."

"Oh, not at all, sir, no, no. You're a very honored guest. Please don't judge us by the crew of this ship, they're very ignorant, limited men—you have no idea of the welcome you'll get on Urras. After all you're a world-famous —a galactically famous scientist! And our first visitor from Anarres! I assure you, things will be very different when we come into Peier Field."

"I do not doubt they will be different," Shevek said.

The Moon Run normally took four and a half days each way, but this time five days of habituation time for the passenger were added to the return trip. Shevek and Dr. Kimoe spent them in vaccinations and conversations. The captain of the *Mindful* spent them in maintaining orbit around Urras, and swearing. When he had to speak to Shevek, he did so with uneasy disrespect. The doctor, who was ready to explain everything, had his analysis ready: "He's used to looking on all foreigners as inferior, as less than fully human."

"The creation of pseudo-species, Odo called it. Yes. I thought that perhaps on Urras people no longer thought that way, since you have there so many languages and nations, and even visitors from other solar systems."

"Very few of those, since interstellar travel is so costly and so slow. Perhaps it won't always be so," Dr. Kimoe added, evidently with an intent to flatter Shevek or to draw him out, which Shevek ignored.

"The Second Officer," he said, "seems to be afraid of me."

"Oh, with him it's religious bigotry. He's a strict-interpretation Epiphanist. Recites the Primes every night. A totally rigid mind."

"So he sees me—how?"

11

"As a dangerous atheist."

"An atheist! Why?"

"Why, because you're an Odonian from Anarres—there's no religion on Anarres."

"No religion? Are we stones, on Anarres?"

"I mean established religion—churches, creeds—" Kimoe flustered easily. He had the physician's brisk self-assurance, but Shevek continually upset it. All his explanations ended up, after two or three of Shevek's questions, in floundering. Each took for granted certain relationships that the other could not even see. For instance, this curious matter of superiority and inferiority. Shevek knew that the concept of superiority, of relative height, was important to the Urrasti; they often used the word "higher" as a synonym for "better" in their writings, where an Anarresti would use "more central." But what did being higher have to do with being foreign? It was one puzzle among hundreds.

"I see," he said now, another puzzle coming clear. "You admit no religion outside the churches, just as you admit no morality outside the laws. You know, I had not ever understood that, in all my reading of Urrasti books."

"Well, these days any enlightened person would admit—"

"The vocabulary makes it difficult," Shevek said, pursuing his discovery. "In Pravic the word *religion* is seldom. No, what do you say—rare. Not often used. Of course, it is one of the Categories: the Fourth Mode. Few people learn to practice all the Modes. But the Modes are built of the natural capacities of the mind, you could not seriously believe that we had no religious capacity? That we could do physics while we were cut off from the profoundest relationship man has with the cosmos?"

"Oh, no, not at all—"

"That would be to make a pseudo-species of us indeed!"

"Educated men certainly would understand that, these officers are ignorant."

"But is it only bigots, then, who are allowed to go out into the cosmos?"

All their conversations were like this, exhausting to the doctor and unsatisfying to Shevek, yet intensely interesting to both. They were Shevek's only means of exploring the new world that awaited him. The ship itself, and

Kimoe's mind, were his microcosm. There were no books aboard the *Mindful*, the officers avoided Shevek, and the crewmen were kept strictly out of his way. As for the doctor's mind, though intelligent and certainly well-meaning, it was a jumble of intellectual artifacts even more confusing than all the gadgets, appliances, and conveniences that filled the ship. These latter Shevek found entertaining; everything was so lavish, stylish, and inventive; but the furniture of Kimoe's intellect he did not find so comfortable. Kimoe's ideas never seemed to be able to go in a straight line; they had to walk around this and avoid that, and then they ended up smack against a wall. There were walls around all his thoughts, and he seemed utterly unaware of them, though he was perpetually hiding behind them. Only once did Shevek see them breached, in all their days of conversation between the worlds.

He had asked why there were no women on the ship, and Kimoe had replied that running a space freighter was not women's work. History courses and his knowledge of Odo's writings gave Shevek a context in which to understand this tautological answer, and he said no more. But the doctor asked a question in return, a question about Anarres. "Is it true, Dr. Shevek, that women in your society are treated exactly like men?"

"That would be a waste of good equipment," said Shevek with a laugh, and then a second laugh as the full ridiculousness of the idea grew upon him.

The doctor hesitated, evidently picking his way around one of the obstacles in his mind, then looked flustered, and said, "Oh, no, I didn't mean sexually—obviously you—they . . . I meant in the matter of their social status."

"*Status* is the same as *class?*"

Kimoe tried to explain status, failed, and went back to the first topic. "Is there really no distinction between men's work and women's work?"

"Well, no, it seems a very mechanical basis for the division of labor, doesn't it? A person chooses work according to interest, talent, strength—what has the sex to do with that?"

"Men are physically stronger," the doctor asserted with professional finality.

"Yes, often, and larger, but what does that matter when we have machines? And even when we don't have ma-

13

chines, when we must dig with the shovel or carry on the back, the men maybe work faster—the big ones—but the women work longer. . . . Often I have wished I was as tough as a woman."

Kimoe stared at him, shocked out of politeness. "But the loss of—of everything feminine—of delicacy—and the loss of masculine self-respect— You can't pretend, surely, in *your* work, that women are your *equals?* In physics, in mathematics, in the intellect? You can't pretend to lower yourself constantly to their level?"

Shevek sat in the cushioned, comfortable chair and looked around the officers' lounge. On the viewscreen the brilliant curve of Urras hung still against black space, like a blue-green opal. That lovely sight, and the lounge, had become familiar to Shevek these last days, but now the bright colors, the curvilinear chairs, the hidden lighting, the game tables and television screens and soft carpeting, all of it seemed as alien as it had the first time he saw it.

"I don't think I pretend very much, Kimoe," he said.

"Of course, I have known highly intelligent women, women who could think just like a man," the doctor said, hurriedly, aware that he had been almost shouting—that he had, Shevek thought, been pounding his hands against the locked door and shouting. . . .

Shevek turned the conversation, but he went on thinking about it. This matter of superiority and inferiority must be a central one in Urrasti social life. If to respect himself Kimoe had to consider half the human race as inferior to him, how then did women manage to respect themselves—did they consider men inferior? And how did all that affect their sex lives? He knew from Odo's writings that two hundred years ago the main Urrasti sexual institutions had been "marriage," a partnership authorized and enforced by legal and economic sanctions, and "prostitution," which seemed merely to be a wider term, copulation in the economic mode. Odo had condemned them both, and yet Odo had been "married." And anyhow the institutions might have changed greatly in two hundred years. If he was going to live on Urras and with the Urrasti, he had better find out.

It was strange that even sex, the source of so much solace, delight, and joy for so many years, could overnight become an unknown territory where he must tread care-

14

fully and know his ignorance; yet it was so. He was warned not only by Kimoe's queer burst of scorn and anger, but by a previously vague impression which that episode brought into focus. When first aboard the ship, in those long hours of fever and despair, he had been distracted, sometimes pleased and sometimes irritated, by a grossly simple sensation: the softness of the bed. Though only a bunk, its mattress gave under his weight with caressing suppleness. It yielded to him, yielded so insistently that he was, still, always conscious of it while falling asleep. Both the pleasure and the irritation it produced in him were decidedly erotic. There was also the hot-air-nozzle-towel device: the same kind of effect. A tickling. And the design of the furniture in the officers' lounge, the smooth plastic curves into which stubborn wood and steel had been forced, the smoothness and delicacy of surfaces and textures: were these not also faintly, pervasively erotic? He knew himself well enough to be sure that a few days without Takver, even under great stress, should not get him so worked up that he felt a woman in every table top. Not unless the woman was really there.

Were Urrasti cabinetmakers all celibate?

He gave it up; he would find out, soon enough, on Urras.

Just before they strapped in for descent the doctor came to his cabin to check the progress of the various immunizations, the last of which, a plague inoculation, had made Shevek sick and groggy. Kimoe gave him a new pill. "That'll pep you up for the landing," he said. Stoic, Shevek swallowed the thing. The doctor fussed with his medical kit and suddenly began to speak very fast: "Dr. Shevek, I don't expect I'll be allowed to attend you again, though perhaps, but if not I wanted to tell you that, that I, that it has been a great privilege to me. Not because—but because I have come to respect—to appreciate—that simply as a human being, your kindness, real kindness—"

No more adequate response occurring to Shevek through his headache, he reached out and took Kimoe's hand, saying, "Then let's meet again, brother!" Kimoe gave his hand a nervous shake, Urrasti style, and hurried out. After he was gone Shevek realized he had spoken to him in Pravic, called him *ammar*, brother, in a language Kimoe did not understand.

The wall speaker was blatting orders. Strapped into the bunk, Shevek listened, feeling hazy and detached. The sensations of entry thickened the haze; he was conscious of little but a profound hope he would not have to vomit. He did not know they had landed till Kimoe came hurrying in again and rushed him out to the officers' lounge. The viewscreen where Urras had hung cloud-coiled and luminous so long was blank. The room was full of people. Where had they all come from? He was surprised and pleased by his ability to stand up, walk, and shake hands. He concentrated on that much, and let meaning pass him by. Voices, smiles, hands, words, names. His name again and again: Dr. Shevek, Dr. Shevek. . . . Now he and all the strangers around him were going down a covered ramp, all the voices very loud, words echoing off the walls. The clatter of voices thinned. A strange air touched his face.

He looked up, and as he stepped off the ramp onto the level ground he stumbled and nearly fell. He thought of death, in that gap between the beginning of a step and its completion, and at the end of the step he stood on a new earth.

A broad, grey evening was around him. Blue lights, mist-blurred, burned far away across a foggy field. The air on his face and hands, in his nostrils and throat and lungs, was cool, damp, many-scented, mild. It was not strange. It was the air of the world from which his race had come, it was the air of home.

Someone had taken his arm when he stumbled. Lights flashed on him. Photographers were filming the scene for the news: The First Man from the Moon: a tall, frail figure in a crowd of dignitaries and professors and security agents, the fine shaggy head held very erect (so that the photographers could catch every feature) as if he were trying to look above the floodlights into the sky, the broad sky of fog that hid the stars, the Moon, all other worlds. Journalists tried to crowd through the rings of policemen: "Will you give us a statement, Dr. Shevek, in this historic moment?" They were forced back again at once. The men around him urged him forward. He was borne off to the waiting limousine, eminently photographable to the last because of his height, his long hair, and the strange look of grief and recognition on his face.

The towers of the city went up into mist, great ladders of blurred light. Trains passed overhead, bright shrieking streaks. Massive walls of stone and glass fronted the streets above the race of cars and trolleys. Stone, steel, glass, electric light. No faces.

"This is Nio Esseia, Dr. Shevek. But it was decided it would be better to keep you out of the city crowds just at first. We're going straight on to the University."

There were five men with him in the dark, softly padded body of the car. They pointed out landmarks, but in the fog he could not tell which great, vague, fleeting building was the High Court and which the National Museum, which the Directorate and which the Senate. They crossed a river or estuary; the million lights of Nio Esseia, fog-diffused, trembled on dark water, behind them. The road darkened, the fog thickened, the driver slowed the vehicle's pace. Its lights shone on the mist ahead as if on a wall that kept retreating before them. Shevek sat leaning forward a little, gazing out. His eyes were not focused, nor was his mind, but he looked aloof and grave, and the other men talked quietly, respecting his silence.

What was the thicker darkness that flowed along endlessly by the road? Trees? Could they have been driving, ever since they left the city, among trees? The Iotic word came into his mind: "forest." They would not come out suddenly into the desert. The trees went on and on, on the next hillside and the next and the next, standing in the sweet chill of the fog, endless, a forest all over the world, a still striving interplay of lives, a dark movement of leaves in the night. Then as Shevek sat marveling as the car came up out of the fog of the river valley into clearer air, there looked at him from the darkness under the roadside foliage, for one instant, a face.

It was not like any human face. It was as long as his arm, and ghastly white. Breath jetted in vapor from what must be nostrils, and terrible, unmistakable, there was an eye. A large, dark eye, mournful, perhpas cynical? gone in the flash of the car's lights.

"What was that?"

"Donkey, wasn't it?"

"An animal?"

"Yes, an animal. By God, that's right! You have no large animals on Anarres, have you?"

17

"A donkey's a kind of horse," said another of the men, and another, in a firm, elderly voice, "That *was* a horse. Donkeys don't come that size." They wanted to talk with him, but Shevek was not listening again. He was thinking of Takver. He wondered what that deep, dry, dark gaze out of the darkness would have meant to Takver. She had always known that all lives are in common, rejoicing in her kinship to the fish in the tanks of her laboratories, seeking the experience of existences outside the human boundary. Takver would have known how to look back at that eye in the darkness under the trees.

"There's Ieu Eun ahead. There's quite a crowd waiting to meet you, Dr. Shevek; the President, and several Directors, and the Chancellor, of course, all kinds of bigwigs. But if you're tired we'll get the amenities over with as soon as possible."

The amenities lasted several hours. He never could remember them clearly afterward. He was propelled from the small dark box of the car into a huge bright box full of people—hundreds of people, under a golden ceiling hung with crystal lights. He was introduced to all the people. They were all shorter than he was, and bald. The few women there were bald even on their heads; he realized at last that they must shave off all their hair, the very fine, soft, short body hair of his race, and the head hair as well. But they replaced it with marvelous clothing, gorgeous in cut and color, the women in full gowns that swept the floor, their breasts bare, their waists and necks and heads adorned with jewelry and lace and gauze, the men in trousers and coats or tunics of red, blue, violet, gold, green, with slashed sleeves and cascades of lace, or long gowns of crimson or dark green or black that parted at the knee to show the white stockings, silver-gartered. Another Iotic word floated into Shevek's head, one he had never had a referent for, though he liked the sound of it: "splendor." These people had splendor. Speeches were made. The President of the Senate of the Nation of A-Io, a man with strange, cold eyes, proposed a toast: "To the new era of brotherhood between the Twin Planets, and to the harbinger of that new era, our distinguished and most welcome guest, Dr. Shevek of Anarres!" The Chancellor of the University talked to him charmingly, the First Director of the nation talked to him seriously, he was introduced to ambassadors, astronauts, physicists, politicians, dozens of people, all of whom had long titles and honorifics both before and after their names, and they talked to him, and he answered them, but he had no memory later of what anyone had said, least of all himself. Very late at night he found himself with a small group of men walking in the warm rain across a large park or square. There was the springy feeling of live grass underfoot; he recognized it from having walked in the Triangle Park in Abbenay. That vivid memory and the cool vast touch of the night wind awakened him. His soul came out of hiding.

His escorts took him into a building and to a room which, they explained, was "his."

It was large, about ten meters long, and evidently a common room, as there were no divisions or sleeping platforms; the three men still with him must be his roommates. It was a very beautiful common room, with one whole wall a series of windows, each divided by a slender column that rose treelike to form a double arch at the top. The floor was carpeted with crimson, and at the far end of the room a fire burned in an open hearth. Shevek crossed the room and stood in front of the fire. He had never seen wood burned for warmth, but he was beyond wonder. He held out his hands to the pleasant heat, and sat down on a seat of polished marble by the hearth.

The youngest of the men who had come with him sat down across the hearth from him. The other two were still talking. They were talking physics, but Shevek did not try to follow what they said. The young man spoke quietly. "I wonder how you must feel, Dr. Shevek."

Shevek stretched out his legs and leaned forward to catch the warmth of the fire on his face. "I feel heavy."

"Heavy?"

"Perhaps the gravity. Or I am tired."

He looked at the other man, but through the hearth glow the face was not clear, only the glint of a gold chain and the deep jewel red of the robe.

"I don't know your name."

"Saio Pae."

"Oh, Pae, yes. I know your articles on Paradox."

He spoke heavily, dreamily.

"There'll be a bar here, Senior Faculty rooms always

19

have a liquor cabinet. Would you care for something to drink?"

"Water, yes."

The young man reappeared with a glass of water as the other two came to join them at the hearth, Shevek drank off the water thirstily and sat looking down at the glass in his hand, a fragile, finely shaped piece that caught the gleam of the fire on its rim of gold. He was aware of the three men, of their attitudes as they sat or stood near him, protective, respectful, proprietary.

He looked up at them, one face after the other. They all looked at him, expectant. "Well, you have me," he said. He smiled. "You have your anarchist. What are you going to do with him?"

Chapter 2

ANARRES

In a square window in a white wall is the clear, bare sky. In the center of the sky is the sun.

There are eleven babies in the room, most of them cooped up in large, padded pen-cots in pairs or trios, and settling down, with commotion and elocution, into their naps. The two eldest remain at large, a fat active one dismembering a pegboard and a knobby one sitting in the square of yellow sunlight from the window, staring up the sunbeam with an earnest and stupid expression.

In the anteroom, a matron, a one-eyed woman with grey hair, confers with a tall, sad-looking man of thirty. "The mother's been posted to Abbenay," the man says. "She wants him to stay here."

"Shall we take him into the nursery full-time, then, Palat?"

"Yes. I'll be moving back into a dorm."

"Don't worry, he knows us all here! But surely Divlab will send you along after Rulag soon? Since you're partners, and both engineers?"

"Yes, but she's . . . It's the Central Institute of Engineering that wants her, see. I'm not that good. Rulag has a great work to do."

21

The matron nodded, and sighed. "Even so—!" she said with energy, and did not say anything else.

The father's gaze was on the knobby infant, who had not noticed his presence in the anteroom, being preoccupied with light. The fat infant was at this moment coming towards the knobby one rapidly, though with a peculiar squatting gait caused by a damp and sagging diaper. He approached out of boredom or sociability, but once in the square of sunlight he discovered it was warm there. He sat down heavily beside the knobby one, crowding him into the shade.

The knobby one's blank rapture gave place at once to a scowl of rage. He pushed the fat one, shouting, "Go 'way!"

The matron was there at once. She righted the fat one. "Shev, you aren't to push other people."

The knobby baby stood up. His face was a glare of sunlight and anger. His diapers were about to fall off. "Mine!" he said in a high, ringing voice. "Mine sun!"

"It is not yours," the one-eyed woman said with the mildness of utter certainty. "Nothing is yours. It is to use. It is to share. If you will not share it, you cannot use it." And she picked the knobby baby up with gentle inexorable hands and set him aside, out of the square of sunlight.

The fat baby sat staring, indifferent. The knobby one shook all over, screamed, "Mine sun!" and burst into tears of rage.

The father picked him up and held him. "There, now, Shev," he said. "Come on, you know you can't have things. What's wrong with you?" His voice was soft, and shook as if he also was not far from tears. The thin, long, light child in his arms wept passionately.

"There are some just can't take life easy," the one-eyed woman said, watching with sympathy.

"I'll take him for a dom visit now. The mother's leaving tonight, you see."

"Go on. I hope you get posted together soon," said the matron, hoisting the fat child like a sack of grain onto her hip, her face melancholy and her good eye squinting. "Byebye, Shev, little heart. Tomorrow, listen, tomorrow we'll play truck-and-driver."

The baby did not forgive her yet. He sobbed, clutching his father's neck, and hid his face in the darkness of the lost sun.

The Orchestra needed all the benches that morning for rehearsal, and the dance group was thumping around in the big room of the learning center, so the kids who were working on Speaking-and-Listening sat in a circle on the foamstone floor of the workshop. The first volunteer, a lanky eight-year-old with long hands and feet, stood up. He stood very erect, as healthy children do; his slightly fuzzy face was pale at first, then turned red as he waited for the other children to listen. "Go on, Shevek," the group director said.

"Well, I had an idea."

"Louder," said the director, a heavy-set man in his early twenties.

The boy smiled with embarrassment. "Well, see, I was thinking, let's say you throw a rock at something. At a tree. You throw it, and it goes through the air and hits the tree. Right? But it can't. Because—can I have the slate? Look, here's you throwing the rock, and here's the tree," he scribbled on the slate, "that's supposed to be a tree, and here's the rock, see, halfway in between." The children giggled at his portrayal of a holum tree, and he smiled. "To get from you to the tree, the rock has to be halfway in between you and the tree, doesn't it. And then it has to be halfway between halfway and the tree. And then it has to be halfway between *that* and the tree. It doesn't matter how far it's gone, there's always a place, only it's a time really, that's halfway between the last place it was and the tree—"

"Do you think this is interesting?" the director interrupted, speaking to the other children.

"*Why* can't it reach the tree?" said a girl of ten.

"Because it always has to go half of the way that's left to go," said Shevek, "and there's always half of the way left to go—see?"

"Shall we just say you aimed the rock badly?" the director said with a tight smile.

"It doesn't matter how you aim it. It *can't reach the tree*."

"Who told you this idea?"

"Nobody. I sort of saw it. I think I see how the rock actually does—"

"That's enough."

Some of the other children had been talking, but they

23

stopped as if struck dumb. The little boy with the slate stood there in the silence. He looked frightened, and scowled.

"Speech is sharing—a cooperative art. You're not sharing, merely egoizing."

The thin, vigorous harmonies of the orchestra sounded down the hall.

"You didn't see that for yourself, it wasn't spontaneous. I've read something very like it in a book."

Shevek stared at the director. "What book? Is there one here?"

The director stood up. He was about twice as tall and three times as heavy as his opponent, and it was clear in his face that he disliked the child intensely; but there was no threat of physical violence in his stance, only an assertion of authority, a little weakened by his irritable response to the child's odd question. "No! And stop egoizing!" Then he resumed his melodious pedantic tone: "This kind of thing is really directly contrary to what we're after in a Speaking-and-Listening group. Speech is a two-way function. Shevek isn't ready to understand that yet, as most of you are, and so his presence is disruptive to the group. You feel that yourself, don't you, Shevek? I'd suggest that you find another group working on your level."

Nobody else said anything. The silence and the loud thin music went on while the boy handed back the slate and made his way out of the circle. He went off into the corridor and stood there. The group he had left began, under the director's guidance, a group story, taking turns. Shevek listened to their subdued voices and to his heart still beating fast. There was a singing in his ears which was not the orchestra but the noise that came when you kept yourself from crying; he had observed this singing noise several times before. He did not like listening to it, and he did not want to think about the rock and the tree, so he turned his mind to the Square. It was made of numbers, and numbers were always cool and solid; when he was at fault he could turn to them, for they had no fault. He had seen the Square in his mind a while ago, a design in space like the designs music made in time: a square of the first nine integers with 5 in the center. However you added up the rows they came out the same, all inequality

24

balanced out; it was pleasant to look at. If only he could make a group that liked to talk about things like that; but there were only a couple of the older boys and girls who did, and they were busy. What about the book the director had spoken of? Would it be a book of numbers? Would it show how the rock got to the tree? He had been stupid to tell the joke about the rock and the tree, nobody else even saw it was a joke, the director was right. His head ached. He looked inward, inward to the calm patterns.

If a book were written all in numbers, it would be true. It would be just. Nothing said in words ever came out quite even. Things in words got twisted and ran together, instead of staying straight and fitting together. But underneath the words, at the center, like the center of the Square, it all came out even. Everything could change, yet nothing would be lost. If you saw the numbers you could see that, the balance, the pattern. You saw the foundations of the world. And they were solid.

Shevek had learned how to wait. He was good at it, an expert. He had first learned the skill waiting for his mother Rulag to come back, though that was so long ago he didn't remember it; and he had perfected it waiting for his turn, waiting to share, waiting for a share. At the age of eight he asked why and how and what if, but he seldom asked when.

He waited till his father came to take him for a dom visit. It was a long wait: six decads. Palat had taken a short posting in maintenance in the Water Reclamation Plant in Drum Mountain, and after that he was going to take a decad at the beach in Malennin, where he would swim, and rest, and copulate with a woman named Pipar. He had explained all this to his son. Shevek trusted him, and he deserved trust. At the end of sixty days he came by the children's dormitories in Wide Plains, a long, thin man with a sadder look than ever. Copulating was not really what he wanted. Rulag was. When he saw the boy, he smiled and his forehead wrinkled in pain.

They took pleasure in each other's company.

"Palat, did you ever see any books with all numbers in them?"

"What do you mean, mathematics?"

"I guess so."

"Like this?"

Palat took from his overtunic pocket a book. It was small, meant to be carried in a pocket, and like most books was bound in green with the Circle of Life stamped on the cover. It was printed very full, with small characters and narrow margins, because paper is a substance that takes a lot of holum trees and a lot of human labor to make, as the supplies dispenser at the learning center always remarked when you botched a page and went to get a new one. Palat held the book out open to Shevek. The double page was a series of columns of numbers. There they were, as he had imagined them. Into his hands he received the covenant of eternal justice. Logarithmic Tables, Bases 10 and 12, said the title on the cover above the Circle of Life.

The little boy studied the first page for some while. "What are they for?" he asked, for evidently these patterns were presented not only for their beauty. The engineer, sitting on a hard couch beside him in the cold, poorly lit common room of the domicile, undertook to explain logarithms to him. Two old men at the other end of the room cackled over their game of "Top 'Em." An adolescent couple came in and asked if the single room was free tonight and went off to it. Rain hit hard on the metal roofing of the one-storey domicile, and ceased. It never rained for long. Palat got out his slide rule and showed Shevek its operation; in return Shevek showed him the Square and the principle of its arrangement. It was very late when they realized it was late. They ran through the marvelously rain-scented, muddy dark to the children's dormitory, and got a perfunctory scolding from the vigil-keeper. They kissed quickly, both shaking with laughter, and Shevek ran to the big sleeping room, to the window, from which he could see his father going back down the single street of Wide Plains in the wet, electric dark.

The boy went to bed muddy-legged, and dreamed. He dreamed he was on a road through a bare land. Far ahead across the road he saw a line. As he approached it across the plain he saw that it was a wall. It went from horizon to horizon across the barren land. It was dense, dark, and very high. The road ran up to it and was stopped.

He must go on, and he could not go on. The wall stopped him. A painful, angry fear rose up in him. He had to go on or he could never come home again. But the wall stood there. There was no way.

He beat at the smooth surface with his hands and yelled at it. His voice came out wordless and cawing. Frightened by the sound of it he cowered down, and then he heard another voice saying, "Look." It was his father's voice. He had an idea his mother Rulag was there too, though he did not see her (he had no memory of her face). It seemed to him that she and Palat were both on all fours in the darkness under the wall, and that they were bulkier than human beings and shaped differently. They were pointing, showing him something there on the ground, the sour dirt where nothing grew. A stone lay there. It was dark like the wall, but on it, or inside it, there was a number; a 5 he thought at first, then took it for 1, then understood what it was—the primal number, that was both unity and plurality. "That is the cornerstone," said a voice of dear familiarity, and Shevek was pierced through with joy. There was no wall in the shadows, and he knew that he had come back, that he was home.

Later he could not recall the details of this dream, but that rush of piercing joy he did not forget. He had never known anything like it; so certain was its assurance of permanence, like one glimpse of a light that shines steadily, that he never thought of it as unreal though it had been experienced in dream. Only, however reliably *there*, he could not reattain it either by longing for it or by the act of will. He could only remember it, waking. When he dreamed of the wall again, as he sometimes did, the dreams were sullen and without resolution.

They had picked up the idea of "prisons" from episodes in the *Life of Odo*, which all of them who had elected to work on History were reading. There were many obscurities in the book, and Wide Plains had nobody who knew enough history to explain them; but by the time they got to Odo's years in the Fort in Drio, the concept "prison" had become self-explanatory. And when a circuit history teacher came through the town he expounded the subject, with the reluctance of a decent adult forced to explain an obscenity to children. Yes, he said, a prison was a place where a State put people who disobeyed its Laws.

27

But why didn't they just leave the place? They couldn't leave, the doors were locked. Locked? Like the doors on a moving truck, so you don't fall out, stupid! But what did they *do* inside one room all the time? Nothing. There was nothing to do. You've seen pictures of Odo in the prison cell in Drio, haven't you? Image of defiant patience, bowed grey head, clenched hands, motionless in encroaching shadows. Sometimes prisoners were sentenced to work. Sentenced? Well, that means a judge, a person given power by the Law, ordered them to do some kind of physical labor. Ordered them? What if they didn't want to do it? Well, they were forced to do it; if they didn't work, they were beaten. A thrill of tension went through the children listening, eleven- and twelve-year-olds, none of whom had ever been struck, or seen any person struck, except in immediate personal anger.

Tirin asked the question that was in all their minds: "You mean, a lot of people would beat up one person?"

"Yes."

"Why didn't the others stop them?"

"The guards had weapons. The prisoners did not," the teacher said. He spoke with the violence of one forced to say the detestable, and embarrassed by it.

The simple lure of perversity brought Tirin, Shevek, and three other boys together. Girls were eliminated from their company, they could not have said why. Tirin had found an ideal prison, under the west wing of the learning center. It was a space just big enough to hold one person sitting or lying down, formed by three concrete foundation walls and the underside of the floor above; the foundations being part of a concrete form, the floor of it was continuous with the walls, and a heavy slab of foamstone siding would close it off completely. But the door had to be locked. Experimenting, they found that two props wedged between a facing wall and the slab shut it with awesome finality. Nobody inside could get that door open.

"What about light?"

"No light," Tirin said. He spoke with authority about things like this, because his imagination put him straight into them. What facts he had, he used, but it was not fact that lent him his certainty. "They let prisoners sit in the dark, in the Fort in Drio. For years."

"Air, though," Shevek said. "That door fits like a vacuum coupling. It's got to have a hole in it."

"It'll take hours to bore through foamstone. Anyhow, who's going to stay in that box long enough to run out of air!"

Chorus of volunteers and claimants.

Tirin looked at them, derisive. "You're all crazy. Who wants to actually get locked into a place like that? What for?" Making the prison had been his idea, and it sufficed him; he never realized that imagination does not suffice some people, they must get into the cell, they must try to open the unopenable door.

"I want to see what it's like," said Kadagv, a broad-chested, serious, domineering twelve-year-old.

"Use your head!" Tirin jeered, but the others backed Kadagv. Shevek got a drill from the workshop, and they bored a two-centimeter hole through the "door" at nose height. It took nearly an hour, as Tirin had predicted.

"How long you want to stay in, Kad? An hour?"

"Look," Kadagv said, "if I'm the prisoner, I can't decide. I'm not free. You have to decide when to let me out."

"That's right," said Shevek, unnerved by this logic.

"You can't stay in too long, Kad. I want a turn!" said the youngest of them, Gibesh. The prisoner deigned no reply. He entered the cell. The door was raised and set in place with a bang, and the props wedged against it, all four jailers hammering them into place with enthusiasm. They all crowded to the air hole to see their prisoner, but since there was no light inside the prison except from the air hole, they saw nothing.

"Don't suck all the poor fart's air out!"

"Blow him in some."

"Fart him in some!"

"How long'll we give him?"

"An hour."

"Three minutes."

"Five years!"

"It's four hours till lights-out. That ought to do it."

"But I want a turn!"

"All right, we'll leave you in all night."

"Well, I meant tomorrow."

Four hours later they knocked the props away and

29

released Kadagv. He emerged as a dominant of the situation as when he had entered, and said he was hungry, and it was nothing; he'd just slept mostly.

"Would you do it again?" Tirin challenged him.

"Sure."

"No, I want second turn—"

"Shut up, Gib. Now, Kad? Would you walk right back in there now, without knowing when we'll let you out?"

"Sure."

"Without food?"

"They fed prisoners," Shevek said. "That's what's so weird about the whole thing."

Kadagv shrugged. His attitude of lofty endurance was intolerable.

"Look," Shevek said to the two youngest boys, "go ask at the kitchen for leftovers, and pick up a bottle or something full of water, too." He turned to Kadagv. "We'll give you a whole sack of stuff, so you can stay in that hole as long as you like."

"As long as *you* like," Kadagv corrected.

"All right. Get in there!" Kadagv's self-assurance brought out Tirin's satirical, play-acting vein. "You're a prisoner. You don't talk back. Understand? Turn around. Put your hands on your head."

"What for?"

"You want to quit?"

Kadagv faced him sullenly.

"You can't ask why. Because if you do we can beat you, and you have to just take it, and nobody will help you. Because we can kick you in the balls and you can't kick back. Because you are *not free*. Now, do you want to go through with it?"

"Sure. Hit me."

Tirin, Shevek, and the prisoner stood facing one another in a strange, stiff group around the lantern, in the darkness, among the heavy foundation walls of the building.

Tirin smiled arrogantly, luxuriously. "Don't tell me what to do, you profiteer. Shut up and get into that cell!" And as Kadagv turned to obey, Tirin pushed him straight-arm in the back so that he fell sprawling. He gave a sharp grunt of surprise or pain, and sat up nursing a finger that had been scraped or sprained against the back

30

wall of the cell. Shevek and Tirin did not speak. They stood motionless, their faces without expression, in their role as guards. They were not playing the role now, it was playing them. The younger boys returned with some holum bread, a melon, and a bottle of water. They were talking as they came, but the curious silence at the cell got into them at once. The food and water was shoved in, the door raised and braced. Kadagv was alone in the dark. The others gathered around the lantern. Gibesh whispered, "Where'll he piss?"

"In his bed," Tirin replied with sardonic clarity.

"What if he has to crap?" Gibesh asked, and suddenly went off into a peal of high laughter.

"What's so funny about crapping?"

"I thought—what if he can't see—in the dark—" Gibesh could not explain his humorous fancy fully. They all began to laugh without explanation, whooping till they were breathless. All were aware that the boy locked inside the cell could hear them laughing.

It was past lights-out in the children's dormitory, and many adults were already in bed, though lights were on here and there in the domiciles. The street was empty. The boys careened down it laughing and calling to one another, wild with the pleasure of sharing a secret, of disturbing others, of compounding wickednesses. They woke up half the children in the dormitory with games of tag down the halls and among the beds. No adult interfered; the tumult died down presently.

Tirin and Shevek sat up whispering together for a long time on Tirin's bed. They decided that Kadagv had asked for it, and would get two full nights in prison.

Their group met in the afternoon at the lumber recycling workshop, and the foreman asked where Kadagv was. Shevek exchanged a glance with Tirin. He felt clever, he felt a sense of power, in not replying. Yet when Tirin replied coolly that he must have joined another group for the day, Shevek was shocked by the lie. His sense of secret power suddenly made him uncomfortable: his legs itched, his ears felt hot. When the foreman spoke to him he jumped with alarm, or fear, or some such feeling, a feeling he had never had before, something like embarrassment but worse than that: inward, and vile. He kept thinking about Kadagv, as he plugged and sanded nail

31

holes in three-ply holum boards and sanded the boards back to silky smoothness. Every time he looked into his mind there was Kadagv in it. It was disgusting.

Gibesh, who had been standing guard duty, came to Tirin and Shevek after dinner, looking uneasy. "I thought I heard Kad saying something in there. In a sort of funny voice."

There was a pause. "We'll let him out," Shevek said.

Tirin turned on him. "Come on, Shev, don't go mushy on us. Don't get altruistic! Let him finish it out and respect himself at the end of it."

"Altruistic, hell. I want to respect myself," Shevek said, and set off for the learning center. Tirin knew him; he wasted no more time arguing with him, but followed. The eleven-year-olds trailed along behind. They crawled under the building to the cell. Shevek knocked one wedge free, Tirin the other. The door of the prison fell outward with a flat thump.

Kadagv was lying on the ground, curled up on his side. He sat up, then got up very slowly and came out. He stooped more than necessary under the low roof, and blinked a lot in the light of the lantern, but looked no different from usual. The smell that came out with him was unbelievable. He had suffered, from whatever cause, from diarrhea. There was a mess in the cell, and smears of yellow fecal stuff on his shirt. When he saw this in the lantern light he made an effort to hide it with his hand. Nobody said anything much.

When they had crawled out from under the building and were heading around to the dormitory, Kadagv asked, "How long was it?"

"About thirty hours, counting the first four."

"Pretty long," Kadagv said without conviction.

After getting him to the baths to clean up, Shevek went off at a run to the latrine. There he leaned over a bowl and vomited. The spasms did not leave him for a quarter of an hour. He was shaky and exhausted when they passed. He went to the dormitory common room, read some physics, and went to bed early. None of the five boys ever went back to the prison under the learning center. None of them ever mentioned the episode, except Gibesh, who boasted about it once to some older boys and girls; but they did not understand, and he dropped the subject.

The Moon stood high over the Northsetting Regional Institute of the Noble and Material Sciences. Four boys of fifteen or sixteen sat on a hilltop between patches of scratchy ground-holum and looked down at the Regional Institute and up at the Moon.

"Peculiar," said Tirin. "I never thought before . . ."

Comments from the other three on the self-evidence of this remark.

"I never thought before," said Tirin unruffled, "of the fact that there are people sitting on a hill, up there, on Urras, looking at Anarres, at us, and saying, 'Look, there's the Moon.' Our earth is their Moon; our Moon is their earth."

"Where, then, is Truth?" declaimed Bedap, and yawned.

"In the hill one happens to be sitting on," said Tirin.

They all went on staring up at the brilliant, blurry turquoise, which was not quite round, a day past its full. The northern ice cap was dazzling. "It's clear in the north," Shevek said. "Sunny. That's A-Io, that brownish bulge there."

"They're all lying around naked in the sun," said Kvetur, "with jewels in their navels, and no hair."

There was a silence.

They had come up to the hilltop for masculine company. The presence of females was oppressive to them all. It seemed to them that lately the world was full of girls. Everywhere they looked, waking or asleep, they saw girls. They had all tried copulating with girls; some of them in despair had also tried not copulating with girls. It made no difference. The girls were there.

Three days ago in a class on the History of the Odonian Movement they had all seen the same visual lesson, and the image of iridescent jewels in the smooth hollow of women's oiled, brown bellies had since recurred to all of them, privately.

They had also seen the corpses of children, hairy like themselves, stacked up like scrap metal, stiff and rusty, on a beach, and men pouring oil over the children and lighting it. "A famine in Bachifoil Province in the Nation of Thu," the commenter's voice had said. "Bodies of children dead of starvation and disease are burned on the beaches. On the beaches of Tius, seven hundred kilometers away in the Nation of A-Io (and here came the jeweled navels), women kept for the sexual use of male members of the *propertied class* (the Iotic words were used, as there was no equivalent for either word in Pravic) lie on the sand all day until dinner is served to them by people of the *unpropertied class*." A close-up of dinnertime: soft mouths champing and smiling, smooth hands reaching out for delicacies wetly mounded in silver bowls. Then a switch back to the blind, blunt face of a dead child, mouth open, empty, black, dry. "Side by side," the quiet voice had said.

But the image that had risen like an oily iridescent bubble in the boys' minds was all the same.

"How old are those films?" said Tirin. "Are they from before the Settlement, or are they contemporary? They never say."

"What does it matter?" Kvetur said. "They were living like that on Urras before the Odonian Revolution. The Odonians all got out and came here to Anarres. So probably nothing's changed—they're still at it, there." He pointed to the great blue-green Moon.

"How do we know they are?"

"What do you mean, Tir?" asked Shevek.

"If those pictures are a hundred and fifty years old, things could be entirely different now on Urras. I don't say they are, but if they were, how would we know it? We don't go there, we don't talk, there's no communication. We really have no idea what life's like on Urras now."

"People in PDC do. They talk to the Urrasti that man the freighters that come in at Port of Anarres. They keep informed. They have to, so we can keep up trade with Urras, and know how much of a threat they pose to us, too." Bedap spoke reasonably, but Tirin's reply was sharp: "Then PDC may be informed, but we're not."

"Informed!" Kvetur said. "I've heard about Urras ever since nursery! I don't care if I never see another picture of foul Urrasti cities and greasy Urrasti bodies!"

"That's just it," said Tirin with the glee of one following logic. "All the material on Urras available to students is the same. Disgusting, immoral, excremental. But look. If it was that bad when the Settlers left, how has it kept on going for a hundred and fifty years? If they were so sick, why aren't they dead? Why haven't their propertarian societies collapsed? What are we so afraid of?"

34

"Infection," said Bedap.

"Are we so feeble we can't withstand a little exposure? Anyhow, they can't *all* be sick. No matter what their society's like, some of them must be decent. People vary here, don't they? Are we all perfect Odonians? Look at that snotball Pesus!"

"But in a sick organism, even a healthy cell is doomed," said Bedap.

"Oh, you can prove anything using the Analogy, and you know it. Anyhow, how do we actually know their society is sick?"

Bedap gnawed on his thumbnail. "You're saying that PDC and the educational supplies syndicate are lying to us about Urras."

"No; I said we only know what we're told. And do you know what we're told?" Tirin's dark, snub-nosed face, clear in the bright bluish moonlight, turned to them. "Kvet said it, a minute ago. He's got the message. You heard it: detest Urras, hate Urras, fear Urras."

"Why not?" Kvetur demanded. "Look how they treated us Odonians!"

"They gave us their Moon, didn't they?"

"Yes, to keep us from wrecking their profiteering states and setting up the just society there. And as soon as they got rid of us, I'll bet they started building up governments and armies faster than ever, because nobody was left to stop them. If we opened the Port to them, you think they'd come like friends and brothers? A thousand million of them, and twenty million of us? They'd wipe us out, or make us all what do you call it, what's the word, slaves, to work the mines for them!"

"All right. I agree that it's probably wise to fear Urras. But why hate? Hate's not functional; why are we taught it? Could it be that if we knew what Urras was really like, we'd like it—some of it—some of us? That what PDC wants to prevent is not just some of them coming here, but some of us wanting to go there?"

"Go to Urras?" Shevek said, startled.

The argued because they liked argument, liked the swift run of the unfettered mind along the paths of possibility, liked to question what was not questioned. They were intelligent, their minds were already disciplined to the clarity of science, and they were sixteen years old. But at

35

this point the pleasure of the argument ceased for Shevek, as it had earlier for Kvetur. He was disturbed. "Who'd ever want to go to Urras?" he demanded. "What for?"

"To find out what another world's like. To see what a 'horse' is!"

"That's childish," Kvetur said. "There's life on some other star systems," and he waved a hand at the moon-washed sky, "so they say. What of it? We had the luck to be born here!"

"If we're better than any other human society," said Tirin, "then we ought to be helping them. But we're forbidden to."

"Forbidden? Nonorganic word. Who forbids? You're externalizing the integrative function itself," Shevek said, leaning forward and speaking with intensity. "Order is not 'orders.' We don't leave Anarres, because we *are* Anarres. Being Tirin, you can't leave Tirin's skin. You might like to try being somebody else to see what it's like, but you can't. But are you kept from it by force? Are we kept here by force? What force—what laws, governments, police? None. Simply our own being, our nature as Odonians. It's your nature to be Tirin, and my nature to be Shevek, and our common nature to be Odonians, responsible to one another. And that responsibility is our freedom. To avoid it, would be to lose our freedom. Would you really like to live in a society where you have no responsibility and no freedom, no choice, only the false option of obedience to the law, or disobedience followed by punishment? Would you really want to go live in a prison?"

"Oh, hell, no. Can't I talk? The trouble with you, Shev, is you don't say anything till you've saved up a whole truckload of damned heavy brick arguments, and then you dump them all out and never look at the bleeding body mangled beneath the heap—"

Shevek sat back, looking vindicated.

But Bedap, a heavy-set, square-faced fellow, chewed on his thumbnail and said, "All the same, Tir's point remains. It would be good to know that we knew all the truth about Urras."

"Who do you think is lying to us?" Shevek demanded.

"Placid, Bedap met his gaze. "Who, brother? Who but ourselves?"

The sister planet shone down upon them, serene and brilliant, a beautiful example of the improbability of the real.

The afforestation of the West Temaenian Littoral was one of the great undertakings of the fifteenth decad of the Settlement on Anarres, employing nearly eighteen thousand people over a period of two years.

Though the long beaches of Southeast were fertile, supporting many fishing and farming communities, the arable area was a mere strip along the sea. Inland and westward clear across the vast plains of Southwest the land was uninhabited except for a few isolated mining towns. It was the region called the Dust.

In the previous geological era the Dust had been an immense forest of holums, the ubiquitous, dominant plant genus of Anarres. The current climate was hotter and drier. Millennia of drought had killed the trees and dried the soil to a fine grey dust that now rose up on every wind, forming hills as pure of line and barren as any sand dune. The Anarresti hoped to restore the fertility of that restless earth by replanting the forest. This was, Shevek thought, in accordance with the principle of Causative Reversibility, ignored by the Sequency school of physics currently respectable on Anarres, but still an intimate, tacit element of Odonian thought. He would like to write a paper showing the relationship of Odo's ideas to the ideas of temporal physics, and particularly the influence of Causative Reversibility on her handling of the problem of ends and means. But at eighteen he didn't know enough to write such a paper, and he never would know enough if he didn't get back to physics soon and out of the damned Dust.

At night in the project camps everybody coughed. In the daytime they coughed less; they were too busy to cough. The dust was their enemy, the fine dry stuff that clogged the throat and lungs; their enemy and their charge, their hope. Once that dust had lain rich and dark in the shade of trees. After their long work, it might do so again.

She brings the green leaf from the stone,
From heart of rock clear water running. ...

Gimar was always humming the tune, and now in the hot evening returning to camp over the plain she sang the words aloud.

"Who does? Who's 'she'?" asked Shevek.

Gimar smiled. Her broad, silky face was smeared and caked with dust, her hair was full of dust, she smelled strongly and agreeably of sweat.

"I grew up in Southrising," she said. "Where the miners are. It's a miner song."

"What miners?"

"Don't you know? People who were already here when the Settlers came. Some of them stayed and joined the solidarity. Goldminers, tinminers. They still have some feast days and songs of their own. The *tadde** was a miner, he used to sing me that when I was little."

"Well, then, who's 'she'?"

"I don't know, it's just what the song says. Isn't it what we're doing here? Bringing green leaves out of stones!"

"Sounds like religion."

"You and your fancy book-words. It's just a song. Oh, I wish we were back at the other camp and could have a swim. I stink!"

"I stink."

"We all stink."

"In solidarity . . ."

But this camp was fifteen kilos from the beaches of the Temae, and there was only dust to swim in.

There was a man in camp whose name, spoken, sounded like Shevek's: Shevet. When one was called the other answered. Shevek felt a kind of affinity for the man, a relation more particular than that of brotherhood, because of this random similarity. A couple of times he saw Shevet eyeing him. They did not speak to each other yet.

Shevek's first decads in the afforestation project had been spent in silent resentment and exhaustion. People who had chosen to work in centrally functional fields such

---

*Papa. A small child may call any adult *mamme* or *tadde*. Gimar's *tadde* may have been her father, an uncle, or an unrelated adult who showed her parental or grandparental responsibility and affection. She may have called several people *tadde* or *mamme,* but the word has a more specific use than *ammar* (brother/sister), which may be used to anybody.

as physics should not be called upon for these projects and special levies. Wasn't it immoral to do work you didn't enjoy? The work needed doing, but a lot of people didn't care what they were posted to and changed jobs all the time; they should have volunteered. Any fool could do this work. In fact, a lot of them could do it better than he could. He had been proud of his strength, and had always volunteered for the "heavies" on tenth-day rotational duty; but here it was day after day, eight hours a day, in dust and heat. All day he would look forward to evening when he could be alone and think, and the instant he got to the sleeping tent after supper his head flopped down and he slept like a stone till dawn, and never a thought crossed his mind.

He found the workmates dull and loutish, and even those younger than himself treated him like a boy. Scornful and resentful, he took pleasure only in writing to his friends Tirin and Rovab in a code they had worked out at the Institute, a set of verbal equivalents to the special symbols of temporal physics. Written out, these seemed to make sense as a message, but were in fact nonsense, except for the equation or philosophical formula they masked. Shevek's and Rovab's equations were genuine. Tirin's letters were very funny and would have convinced anyone that they referred to real emotions and events, but the physics in them was dubious. Shevek sent off one of these puzzles often, once he found that he could work them out in his head while he was digging holes in rock with a dull shovel in a dust storm. Tirin answered several times, Rovab only once. She was a cold girl, he knew she was cold. But none of them at the Institute knew how wretched he was. They hadn't been posted, just as they were beginning independent research, to a damned tree-planting project. Their central function wasn't being wasted. They were working: doing what they wanted to do. He was not working. He was being worked.

Yet it was queer how proud you felt of what you got done this way—all together—what satisfaction it gave. And some of the workmates were really extraordinary people. Gimar, for instance. At first her muscular beauty had rather awed him, but now he was strong enough to desire her.

"Come with me tonight, Gimar."

39

"Oh, no," she said, and looked at him with so much surprise that he said, with some dignity of pain, "I thought we were friends."

"We are."

"Then—"

"I'm partnered. He's back home."

"You might have said," Shevek said, going red.

"Well, it didn't occur to me I ought to. I'm sorry, Shev." She looked so regretfully at him that he said, with some hope, "You don't think—"

"No. You can't work a partnership that way, some bits for him and some bits for others."

"Life partnership is really against the Odonian ethic, I think," Shevek said, harsh and pedantic.

"Shit," said Gimar in her mild voice. "Having's wrong; sharing's right. What more can you share than your whole self, your whole life, all the nights and all the days?"

He sat with his hands between his knees, his head bowed, a long boy, rawboned, disconsolate, unfinished. "I'm not up to that," he said after a while.

"You?"

"I haven't really ever known anybody. You see how I didn't understand you. I'm cut off. Can't get in. Never will. It would be silly for me to think about a partnership. That sort of thing is for . . . for human beings. . . ."

With timidity, not a sexual coyness but the shyness of respect, Gimar put her hand on his shoulder. She did not reassure him. She did not tell him he was like everybody else. She said, "I'll never know anyone like you again, Shev. I never will forget you."

All the same, a rejection is a rejection. For all her gentleness he went from her with a lame soul, and angry.

The weather was very hot. There was no coolness except in the hour before dawn.

The man named Shevet came up to Shevek one night after supper. He was a stocky, handsome fellow of thirty. "I'm tired of getting mixed up with you," he said. "Call yourself something else."

The surly aggressiveness would have puzzled Shevek earlier. Now he simply responded in kind. "Change your own name if you don't like it," he said.

"You're one of those little profiteers who goes to school

to keep his hands clean," the man said. "I've always wanted to knock the shit out of one of you."

"Don't call me profiteer!" Shevek said, but this wasn't a verbal battle. Shevet knocked him double. He got in several return blows, having long arms and more temper than his opponent expected: but he was outmatched. Several people paused to watch, saw that it was a fair fight but not an interesting one, and went on. They were neither offended nor attracted by simple violence. Shevek did not call for help, so it was nobody's business but his own. When he came to he was lying on his back on the dark ground between two tents.

He had a ringing in his right ear for a couple of days, and a split lip that took long to heal because of the dust, which irritated all sores. He and Shevet never spoke again. He saw the man at a distance, at other cookfires, without animosity. Shevet had given him what he had to give, and he had accepted the gift, though for a long time he never weighed it or considered its nature. By the time he did so there was no distinguishing it from another gift, another epoch in his growing up. A girl, one who had recently joined his work gang, came up to him just as Shevet had in the darkness as he left the cookfire, and his lip wasn't healed yet. . . . He never could remember what she said; she had teased him; again he responded simply. They went out into the plain in the night, and there she gave him the freedom of the flesh. That was her gift, and he accepted it. Like all children of Anarres he had had sexual experience freely with both boys and girls, but he and they had been children; he had never got further than the pleasure he assumed was all there was to it. Beshun, expert in delight, took him into the heart of sexuality, where there is no rancor and no ineptitude, where the two bodies striving to join each other annihilate the moment in their striving, and transcend the self, and transcend time.

It was all easy now, so easy, and lovely, out in the warm dust, in the starlight. And the days were long, and hot, and bright, and the dust smelled like Beshun's body.

He worked now in the planting crew. The trucks had come down from Northeast full of tiny trees, thousands of seedlings raised in the Green Mountains, where it rained

41

up to forty inches a year, the rain belt. They planted the little trees in the dust.

When they were done, the fifty crews who had worked the second year of the project drove away in the flatbed trucks, and they looked back as they went. They saw what they had done. There was a mist of green, very faint, on the pallid curves and terraces of the desert. On the dead land lay, very lightly, a veil of life. They cheered, sang, shouted from truck to truck. Tears came into Shevek's eyes. He thought, *She brings the green leaf from the stone.* . . . Gimar had been posted back to Southrising a long time ago. "What are you making faces about?" Beshum asked him, squeezing next to him, as the truck jounced and running her hand up and down his hard, dust-whitened arm.

"Women," Vokep said, in the truck depot in Tin Ore, Southwest. "Women think they own you. No woman can really be an Odonian."

"Odo herself—?"

"Theory. And no sex life after Asieo was killed, right? Anyhow there're always exceptions. But most women, their only relationship to a man is *having*. Either owning or being owned."

"You think they're different from men there?"

"I know it. What a man wants is freedom. What a woman wants is property. She'll only let you go if she can trade you for something else. All women are propertarians."

"That's a hell of a thing to say about half the human race," said Shevek, wondering if the man was right. Beshun had cried herself sick when he got posted back to Northwest, had raged and wept and tried to make him tell her he couldn't live without her and insisted she couldn't live without him and they must be partners. Partners, as if she could have stayed with any one man for half a year!

The language Shevek spoke, the only one he knew, lacked any proprietary idioms for the sexual act. In Pravic it made no sense for a man to say that he had "had" a woman. The word which came closest in meaning to "fuck," and had a similar secondary usage as a curse, was specific: it meant rape. The usual verb, taking only a plural subject, can be translated only by a neutral word like copulate. It meant something two people did, not something one person did, or had. This frame of words could not contain the totality of experience any more than any other, and Shevek was aware of the area left out, though he wasn't quite sure what it was. Certainly he had felt that he owned Beshun, possessed her, on some of those starlit nights in the Dust. And she had thought she owned him. But they had both been wrong; and Beshun, despite her sentimentality, knew it; she had kissed him goodbye at last smiling, and let him go. She had not owned him. His own body had, in its first outburst of adult sexual passion, possessed him indeed—and her. But it was over with. It had happened. It would never (he thought, eighteen years old, sitting with a traveling-acquaintance in the truck depot of Tin Ore at midnight over a glass of sticky sweet fruit drink, waiting to hitch a ride on a convoy going north), it could never happen again. Much would yet happen, but he would not be taken off guard a second time, knocked down, defeated. Defeat, surrender, had its raptures. Beshun herself might never want any joy beyond them. And why should she? It was she, in her freedom, who had set him free.

"You know, I don't agree," he said to long-faced Vokep, an agricultural chemist traveling to Abbenay. "I think men mostly have to learn to be anarchists. Women don't have to learn."

Vokep shook his head grimly. "It's the kids," he said. "Having babies. Makes 'em propertarians. They won't let go." He sighed. "Touch and go, brother, that's the rule. Don't ever let yourself be owned."

Shevek smiled and drank his fruit juice. "I won't," he said.

It was a joy to him to come back to the Regional Institute, to see the low hills patchy with bronze-leaved scrub holum, the kitchen gardens, domiciles, dormitories, workshops, classrooms, laboratories, where he had lived since he was thirteen. He would always be one for whom the return was as important as the voyage out. To go was not enough for him, only half enough; he must come back. In such a tendency was already foreshadowed, perhaps, the nature of the immense exploration he was to undertake into the extremes of the comprehensible. He would most

43

likely not have embarked on that years-long enterprise
had he not had profound assurance that return was possible, even though he himself might not return; that indeed
the very nature of the voyage, like a circumnavigation of
the globe, implied return. You shall not go down twice
to the same river, nor can you go home again. That he
knew; indeed it was the basis of his view of the world.
Yet from that acceptance of transience he evolved his vast
theory, wherein what is most changeable is shown to be
fullest of eternity, and your relationship to the river, and
the river's relationship to you and to itself, turns out to
be at once more complex and more reassuring than a
mere lack of identity. You *can* go home again, the
General Temporal Theory asserts, so long as you understand that home is a place where you have never been.

He was glad, then, to get back to what was as close to a
home as he had or wanted. But he found his friends there
rather callow. He had grown up a good deal, this past
year. Some of the girls had kept up with him, or passed
him; they had become women. He kept clear, however, of
anything but casual contact with the girls, because he really didn't want another big binge of sex just yet; he had
some other things to do. He saw that the brightest of the
girls, like Rovab, were equally casual and wary; in the
labs and work crews or in the dormitory common rooms,
they behaved as good comrades and nothing else. The
girls wanted to complete their training and start their research or find a post they liked, before they bore a child;
but they were no longer satisfied with adolescent sexual
experimentation. They wanted a mature relationship, not
a sterile one; but not yet, not quite yet.

These girls were good companions, friendly and independent. The boys Shevek's age seemed stuck in the end of
a childishness that was running a bit thin and dry. They
were overintellectual. They didn't seem to want to com-
mit themselves either to work or to sex. To hear Tirin talk
he was the man who invented copulation, but all his affairs
were with girls of fifteen or sixteen; he shied away from
the ones his own age. Bedap, never very energetic sexually,
accepted the homage of a younger boy who had a homo-
sexual-idealistic crush on him, and let that suffice him. He
seemed to take nothing seriously; he had become ironical
and secretive. Shevek felt cut out from his friendship. No

friendship held; even Tirin was too self-centered, and late-ly too moody, to reassert the old bond—if Shevek had wanted it. In fact, he did not. He welcomed isolation with all his heart. It never occurred to him that the re-serve he met in Bedap and Tirin might be a response; that his gentle but already formidably hermetic character might form its own ambience, which only great strength, or great devotion, could withstand. All he noticed, really, was that he had plenty of time to work at last.

Down in Southeast, after he had got used to the steady physical labor, and had stopped wasting his brain on code messages and his semen on wet dreams, he had begun to have some ideas. Now he was free to work these ideas out, to see if there was anything in them.

The senior physicist at the Institute was named Mitis. She was not at present directing the physics curriculum, as all administrative jobs rotated annually among the twenty permanent postings, but she had been at the place thirty years, and had the best mind among them. There was always a kind of psychological clear space around Mitis, like the lack of crowds around the peak of a mountain. The absence of all enhancements and enforcements of au-thority left the real thing plain. There are people of in-herent authority; some emperors actually have new clothes.

"I sent that paper you did on Relative Frequency to Sabul, in Abbenay," she said to Shevek, in her abrupt, companionable way. "Want to see the answer?"

She pushed across the table a ragged bit of paper, evi-dently a corner torn off a larger piece. On it in tiny scrib-bled characters was one equation:

$$\frac{ts}{2}(R) = 0$$

Shevek put his weight on his hands on the table and looked down at the bit of paper with a steady gaze. His eyes were light, and the light from the window filled them so they seemed clear as water. He was nineteen, Mitis fifty-five. She watched him with compassion and admiration.

"That's what's missing," he said. His hand had found a pencil on the table. He began scribbling on the fragment of paper. As he wrote, his colorless face, silvered with fine short hair, became flushed, and his ears turned red.

45

Mitis moved surreptitiously around behind the table to sit down. She had circulatory trouble in her legs, and needed to sit down. Her movement, however, disturbed Shevek. He looked up with a cold annoyed stare.

"I can finish this in a day or two," he said.

"Sabul wants to see the results when you've worked it out."

There was a pause. Shevek's color returned to normal, and he became aware again of the presence of Mitis, whom he loved. "Why did you send the paper to Sabul?" he asked. "With that big hole in it!" He smiled; the pleasure of patching the hole in his thinking made him radiant.

"I thought he might see where you went wrong. I couldn't. Also I wanted him to see what you were after. . . . He'll want you to come there, to Abbenay, you know."

The young man did not answer.

"Do you want to go?"

"Not yet."

"So I judged. But you must go. For the books, and for the minds you'll meet there. You will not waste that mind in a desert!" Mitis spoke with sudden passion. "It's your duty to seek out the best, Shevek. Don't let false egalitarianism ever trick you. You'll work with Sabul, he's good, he'll work you hard. But you should be free to find the line you want to follow. Stay here one more quarter, then go. And take care, in Abbenay. Keep free. Power inheres in a center. You're going to the center. I don't know Sabul well; I know nothing against him; but keep this in mind: you will be his man."

The singular forms of the possessive pronoun in Pravic were used mostly for emphasis; idiom avoided them. Little children might say "my mother," but very soon they learned to say "the mother." Instead of "my hand hurts," it was "the hand hurts me," and so on; to say "this one is mine and that's yours" in Pravic, one said. "I use this one and you use that." Mitis's statement, "You will be *his man*," had a strange sound to it. Shevek looked at her blankly.

"There's work for you to do," Mitis said. She had black eyes, they flashed as if with anger. "Do it!" Then she went out, for a group was waiting for her in the lab. Confused, Shevek looked down at the bit of scribbled paper. He thought Mitis had been telling him to hurry up and correct his equations. It was not till much later that he understood what she had been telling him.

The night before he left for Abbenay his fellow students gave a party for him. Parties were frequent, on slight pretexts, but Shevek was surprised by the energy that went into this one, and wondered why it was such a fine one. Uninfluenced by others, he never knew he influenced them; he had no idea they liked him.

Many of them must have saved up daily allowances for the party for days before. There were incredible amounts of food. The order for pastries was so large that the refectory baker had let his fancy loose and produced hitherto unknown delights: spiced wafers, little peppered squares to go with the smoked fish, sweet fried cakes, succulently greasy. There were fruit drinks, preserved fruit from the Keran Sea region, tiny salt shrimp, piles of crisp sweet-potato chips. The rich plentiful food was intoxicating. Everybody got very merry, and a few got sick.

There were skits and entertainments, rehearsed and impromptu. Tirin got himself up in a collection of rags from the recycle bin and wandered among them as the Poor Urrasti, the Beggarman—one of the Iotic words everybody had learned in history. "Give me *money*," he whined, shaking his hand under their noses. *"Money! Money!* Why don't you give me any *money?* You haven't got any? Liars! Filthy propertarians! Profiteers! Look at all that food, how did you get it if you haven't any *money?"* He then offered himself for sale. "Bay me, bay me, for just a little *money*," he wheedled.

"It isn't *bay*, it's *buy*," Rovab corrected him.

"Bay me, buy me, who cares, look, what a beautiful body, don't you want it?" Tirin crooned, wagging his slender hips and batting his eyes. He was at last publicly executed with a fish knife and reappeared in normal clothing. There were skillful harp players and singers among them, and there was plenty of music and dancing, but more talk. They all talked as if they were to be struck dumb tomorrow.

As the night went on young lovers wandered off to copulate, seeking the single rooms; others got sleepy and went off to the dormitories; at last a small group was left amid the empty cups, the fishbones, and the pastry crumbs, which they would have to clean up before morning. But it was hours yet till morning. They talked. They nibbled on this and that as they talked. Bedap and Tirin and Shevek were there, a couple of other boys, three girls. They talked about the spatial representation of time as rhythm, and the connection of the ancient theories of the Numerical Harmonies with modern temporal physics. They talked about the best stroke for long-distance swimming. They talked about whether their childhoods had been happy. They talked about what happiness was.

"Suffering is a misunderstanding," Shevek said, leaning forward, his eyes wide and light. He was still lanky, with big hands, protruding ears, and angular joints, but in the perfect health and strength of early manhood he was very beautiful. His dun-colored hair, like the others', was fine and straight, worn at its full length and kept off the forehead with a band. Only one of them wore her hair differently, a girl with high cheekbones and a flat nose; she had cut her dark hair to a shiny cap all round. She was watching Shevek with a steady, serious gaze. Her lips were greasy from eating fried cakes, and there was a crumb on her chin.

"It exists," Shevek said, spreading out his hands. "It's real. I can call it a misunderstanding, but I can't pretend that it doesn't exist, or will ever cease to exist. Suffering is the condition on which we live. And when it comes, you know it. You know it as the truth. Of course it's right to cure diseases, to prevent hunger and injustice, as the social organism does. But no society can change the nature of existence. We can't prevent suffering. This pain and that pain, yes, but not Pain. A society can only relieve social suffering, unnecessary suffering. The rest remains. The root, the reality. All of us here are going to know grief; if we live fifty years, we'll have known pain for fifty years. And in the end we'll die. That's the condition we're born on. I'm afraid of life! There are times I—I am very frightened. Any happiness seems trivial. And yet, I wonder if it isn't all a misunderstanding—this grasping after happiness, this fear of pain. . . . If instead of fearing it and running from it, one could . . . get through it, go beyond it. There is something beyond it. It's the self that suffers, and there's a place where the self—ceases. I don't know how to say it. But I believe that the reality—the truth that I recognize in suffering as I don't in comfort and happiness—that the reality of pain is not pain. If you can get through it. If you can endure it all the way."

"The reality of our life is in love, in solidarity," said a tall, soft-eyed girl. "Love is the true condition of human life."

Bedap shook his head. "No. Shev's right," he said. "Love's just one of the ways through, and it can go wrong, and miss. Pain never misses. But therefore we don't have much choice about enduring it! We will, whether we want to or not."

The girl with short hair shook her head vehemently. "But we won't! One in a hundred, one in a thousand, goes all the way, all the way through. The rest of us keep pretending we're happy, or else just go numb. We suffer, but not enough. And so we suffer for nothing."

"What are we supposed to do," said Tirin, "go hit our heads with hammers for an hour every day to make sure we suffer enough?"

"You're making a cult of pain," another said. "An Odonian's goal is positive, not negative. Suffering is dysfunctional, except as a bodily warning against danger. Psychologically and socially it's merely destructive."

"What motivated Odo but an exceptional sensitivity to suffering—her own and others'?" Bedap retorted.

"But the whole principal of mutual aid is designed to *prevent* suffering!"

Shevek was sitting on the table, his long legs dangling, his face intense and quiet. "Have you ever seen anybody die?" he asked the others. Most of them had, in a domicile or on volunteer hospital duty. All but one had helped at one time or another to bury the dead.

"There was a man when I was in camp in Southeast. It was the first time I saw anything like this. There was some defect in the aircar engine, it crashed lifting off and caught fire. They got him out burned all over. He lived about two hours. He couldn't have been saved; there was no reason for him to live that long, no justification for those two hours. We were waiting for them to fly in anesthetics from the coast. I stayed with him, along with a couple of girls. We'd been there loading the plane. There wasn't a doctor. You couldn't do anything for him, except

49

just stay there, be with him. He was in shock but mostly conscious. He was in terrible pain, mostly from his hands. I don't think he knew the rest of his body was all charred, he felt it mostly in his hands. You couldn't touch him to comfort him, the skin and flesh would come away at your touch, and he'd scream. You couldn't do anything for him. There was no aid to give. Maybe he knew we were there, I don't know. It didn't do him any good. You couldn't do anything for him. Then I saw . . . you see . . . I saw that you can't do anything for anybody. We can't save each other. Or ourselves."

"What have you left, then? Isolation and despair! You're denying brotherhood, Shevek!" the tall girl cried.

"No—no, I'm not. I'm trying to say what I think brotherhood really is. It begins—it begins in shared pain."

"Then where does it end?"

"I don't know. I don't know yet."

Chapter 3

URRAS

When Shevek woke, having slept straight through his first morning on Urras, his nose was stuffy, his throat was sore, and he coughed a lot. He thought he had a cold—even Odonian hygiene had not outwitted the common cold—but the doctor who was waiting to check him over, a dignified, elderly man, said it was more likely a massive hay-fever, an allergic reaction to the foreign dusts and pollens of Urras. He issued pills and a shot, which Shevek accepted patiently, and a tray of lunch, which Shevek accepted hungrily. The doctor asked him to stay in his apartment, and left him. As soon as he had finished eating, he commenced his exploration of Urras, room by room.

The bed, a massive bed on four legs, with a mattress far softer than that of the bunk on the *Mindful*, and complex bedclothes, some silky and some warm and thick, and a lot of pillows like cumulus clouds, had a room all to itself. The floor was covered with springy carpeting; there was a chest of drawers of beautifully carved and polished wood, and a closet big enough to hold the clothing of a ten-man dormitory. Then there was the great common room with the fireplace, which he had seen last night; and a third room, which contained a bathtub, a washstand, and an elaborate shitstool. This room was

51

evidently for his sole use, as it opened off the bedroom, and contained only one of each kind of fixture, though each was of a sensuous luxury that far surpassed mere eroticism and partook, in Shevek's view, of a kind of ultimate apotheosis of the excremental. He spent nearly an hour in this third room, employing all the fixtures in turn, and getting very clean in the process. The deployment of water was wonderful. Faucets stayed on till turned off; the bathtub must hold sixty liters, and the stool used at least five liters in flushing. This was really not surprising. The surface of Urras was five-sixths water. Even its deserts were deserts of ice, at the poles. No need to economize; no drought. . . . But what became of the shit? He brooded over this, kneeling by the stool after investigating its mechanism. They must filter it out of the water at a manure plant. There were seaside communities on Anarres that used such a system for reclamation. He intended to ask about this, but never got around to it. There were many questions he never did ask on Urras.

Despite his stuffy head he felt well, and restless. The rooms were so warm that he put off getting dressed, and stalked about them naked. He went to the windows of the big room and stood looking out. The room was high. He was startled at first and drew back, unused to being in a building of more than one storey. It was like looking down from a dirigible; one felt detached from the ground, dominant, uninvolved. The windows looked right over a grove of trees to a white building with a graceful square tower. Beyond this building the land fell away to a broad valley. All of it was farmed, for the innumerable patches of green that colored it were rectangular. Even where the green faded into blue distance, the dark lines of lanes, hedgerows, or trees could still be made out, a network as fine as the nervous system of a living body. At last hills rose up bordering the valley, blue fold behind blue fold, soft and dark under the even, pale grey of the sky.

It was the most beautiful view Shevek had ever seen. The tenderness and vitality of the colors, the mixture of rectilinear human design and powerful, proliferate natural contours, the variety and harmony of the elements, gave an impression of complex wholeness such as he had never seen, except, perhaps, foreshadowed on a small scale in certain serene and thoughtful human faces.

Compared to this, every scene Anarres could offer, even the Plain of Abbenay and the gorges of the Ne Theras, was meager: barren, arid, and inchoate. The deserts of Southwest had a vast beauty, but it was hostile, and timeless. Even where men farmed Anarres most closely, their landscape was like a crude sketch in yellow chalk compared with this fulfilled magnificence of life, rich in the sense of history and of seasons to come, inexhaustible.

This is what a world is supposed to look like, Shevek thought.

And somewhere, out in that blue and green splendor, something was singing: a small voice, high up, starting and ceasing, incredibly sweet. What was it? A little, sweet, wild voice, a music in midair.

He listened, and his breath caught in his throat.

There was a knock at the door. Turning naked and wondering from the window, Shevek said, "Come in!"

A man entered, carrying packages. He stopped just inside the door. Shevek crossed the room, saying his own name, Anarresti-style, and, Urrasti-style, holding out his hand.

The man, who was fifty or so, with a lined, worn face, said something Shevek did not understand a word of, and did not shake hands. Perhaps he was prevented by the packages, but he made no effort to shift them and free his hand. His face was extremely grave. It was possible that he was embarrassed.

Shevek, who thought he had at least mastered Urrasti customs of greeting, was nonplused. "Come on in," he repeated, and then added, since the Urrasti were forever using titles and honorifics, "sir!"

The man went off into another unintelligible speech, sidling meantime towards the bedroom. Shevek caught several words of Iotic this time, but could make no sense of the rest. He let the fellow go, since he seemed to want to get to the bedroom. Perhaps he was a roommate? But there was only one bed. Shevek gave him up and went back to the window, and the man scuttled on into the bedroom and thumped around in it for a few minutes. Just as Shevek had decided that he was a night worker who used the bedroom days, an arrangement sometimes made in temporarily overcrowded domiciles, he came out again. He said something—"There you are, sir," perhaps?—and ducked his head in a curious fashion, as if he thought that Shevek, five meters away, was about to hit him in the face. He left, Shevek stood by the windows, slowly realizing that he had for the first time in his life been bowed to.

He went into the bedroom and discovered that the bed had been made.

Slowly, thoughtfully, he got dressed. He was putting on his shoes when the next knock came.

A group entered, in a different manner; in a normal manner, it seemed to Shevek, as if they had a right to be there, or anywhere they chose to be. The man with the packages had been hesitant, he had almost slunk in. And yet his face, and his hands, and his clothing, had come closer to Shevek's notion of a normal human being's appearance than did those of the new visitors. The slinking man had behaved strangely, but he had looked like an Anarresti. These four behaved like Anarresti, but looked, with their shaven faces and gorgeous clothes, like creatures of an alien species.

Shevek managed to recognize one of them as Pae, and the others as men who had been with him all last evening. He explained that he had not caught their names, and they reintroduced themselves, smiling: Dr. Chifoilisk, Dr. Oiie, and Dr. Atro.

"Oh, by damn!" Shevek said. "Atro! I am glad to meet you!" He put his hands on the old man's shoulders and kissed his cheek, before thinking that this brotherly greeting, common enough on Anarres, might not be acceptable here.

Atro, however, embraced him heartily in return, and looked up into his face with filmy grey eyes. Shevek realized that he was nearly blind. "My dear Shevek," he said, "welcome to A-Io—welcome to Urras—welcome home!"

"So many years we have written letters, destroyed each other's theories!"

"You were always the better destroyer. Here, hold on, I've got something for you." The old man felt about in his pockets. Under his velvet university gown he wore a jacket, under that a vest, under that a shirt, and probably another layer under that. All of these garments, and his trousers, contained pockets. Shevek watched quite fascinated as Atro went through six or seven pockets, all containing

54

belongings, before he came up with a small cube of yellow metal mounted on a bit of polished wood. "There," he said, peering at it. "Your award. The Seo Oen prize, you know. The cash is in your account. Here. Nine years late, but better late than never." His hands trembled as he handed the thing to Shevek.

It was heavy; the yellow cube was solid gold. Shevek stood motionless, holding it.

"I don't know about you young men," said Atro, "but I'm going to sit down." They all sat down in the deep, soft chairs, which Shevek had already examined, puzzled by the material with which they were covered, a nonwoven brown stuff that felt like skin. "How old were you nine years ago, Shevek?"

Atro was the foremost living physicist on Urras. There was about him not only the dignity of age but also the blunt self-assurance of one accustomed to respect. This was nothing new to Shevek. Atro had precisely the one kind of authority that Shevek recognized. Also, it gave him pleasure to be addressed at last simply by his name.

"I was twenty-nine when I finished the *Principles,* Atro."

"Twenty-nine? Good God. That makes you the youngest recipient of the Seo Oen for a century or so. Didn't get around to giving me mine till I was sixty or so. . . . How old were you, then, when you first wrote me?"

"About twenty."

Atro snorted. "Took you for a man of forty then!"

"What about Sabul?" Oiie inquired. Oiie was even shorter than most Urrasti, who all seemed short to Shevek; he had a flat, bland face and oval, jet-black eyes. "There was a period of six or eight years when you never wrote, and Sabul kept in touch with us; but he never has talked on your radio link-up with us. We've wondered what your relationship is."

"Sabul is the senior member of the Abbenay Institute in physics," said Shevek. "I used to work with him."

"An older rival; jealous; meddled with your books; been clear enough. We hardly need an explanation, Oiie," said the fourth man, Chifoilisk, in a harsh voice. He was middle-aged, a swarthy, stocky man with the fine hands of a desk worker. He was the only one of them whose face was not completely shaven: he had left the chin

55

bristling to match his short, iron-grey head hair. "No need to pretend that all you Odonian brothers are full of brotherly love," he said. "Human nature is human nature."

Shevek's lack of response was saved from seeming significant by a volley of sneezes. "I do not have a handkerchief," he apologized, wiping his eyes.

"Take mine," said Atro, and produced a snowy handkerchief from one of his many pockets. Shevek took it, and as he did so an importunate memory wrung his heart. He thought of his daughter Sadik, a little dark-eyed girl, saying, "You can share the handkerchief I use." That memory, which was very dear to him, was unbearably painful now. Trying to escape it, he smiled at random and said, "I am allergic to your planet. The doctor says this."

"Good God, you won't be sneezing like that permanently?" old Atro asked, peering at him.

"Hasn't your man been in yet?" said Pae.

"My man?"

"The servant. He was supposed to bring you some things. Handkerchiefs included. Just enough to tide you over till you can shop for yourself. Nothing choice—I'm afraid there's very little choice in ready-made clothes for a man your height!"

When Shevek had sorted this out (Pae spoke in a rapid drawl, which matched with his soft, handsome features), he said, "That is kind of you. I feel—" He looked at Atro. "I am, you know the Beggarman," he said to the old man, as he had said to Dr. Kimoe on the *Mindful*. "I could not bring money, we do not use it. I could not bring gifts, we use nothing that you lack. So I come, like a good Odonian, 'with empty hands.' "

Atro and Pae assured him that he was a guest, there was no question of payment, it was their privilege. "Besides," Chifoilisk said in his sour voice, "the Ioti Government foots the bill."

Pae gave him a sharp glance, but Chifoilisk, instead of returning it, looked straight at Shevek. On his swarthy face was an expression that he made no effort to hide, but which Shevek could not interpret: warning, or complicity?

"There speaks the unregenerate Thuvian," old Atro said

with his snort. "But you mean to say, Shevek, that you brought nothing at all with you—no papers, no new work? I was looking forward to a book. Another revolution in physics. See these pushy young fellows stood on their heads, the way you stood me with the *Principles*. What have you been working on?"

"Well, I have been reading Pae—Dr. Pae's paper on the block universe, on Paradox and Relativity."

"All very well. Saio's our current star, no doubt of that. Least of all in his own mind, eh, Saio? But what's that to do with the price of cheese? Where's your General Temporal Theory?"

"In my head," said Shevek with a broad, genial smile. There was a very little pause.

Oiie asked him if he had seen the work on relativity theory by an alien physicist, Ainsetain of Terra. Shevek had not. They were intensely interested in it, except for Atro, who had outlived intensity. Pae ran off to his room to get Shevek a copy of the translation. "It's several hundred years old, but there's fresh ideas in it for us," he said.

"Maybe," said Atro, "but none of these offworlders can follow *our* physics. The Hainish call it materialism, and the Terrans call it mysticism, and then they both give up. Don't let this fad for everything alien sidetrack you, Shevek. They've got nothing for us. Dig your own pigweed, as my father used to say." He gave his senile snort and levered himself up out of the chair. "Come on out for a turn in the Grove with me. No wonder you're stuffy, cooped up in here."

"The doctor says I'm to stay in this room three days. I might be—infected? Infectious?"

"Never pay any attention to doctors, my dear fellow."

"Perhaps in this case, though, Dr. Atro," Pae suggested in his easy, conciliating voice.

"After all, the doctor's from the Government, isn't he?" said Chifoilisk, with evident malice.

"Best man they could find, I'm sure," Atro said unsmiling, and took his leave without urging Shevek further. Chifoilisk went with him. The two younger men stayed with Shevek, talking physics, for a long time.

With immense pleasure, and with that same sense of profound recognition, of finding something the way it was

57

meant to be, Shevek discovered for the first time in his life the conversation of his equals.

Mitis, though a splendid teacher, had never been able to follow him into the new areas of theory that he had, with her encouragement, begun to explore. Gvarab was the only person he had met whose training and ability were comparable to his own, and he and Gvarab had met too late, at the very end of her life. Since those days Shevek had worked with many people of talent, but because he had never been a full-time member of the Abbenay Institute, he had never been able to take them far enough; they remained bogged down in the old problems, the classical Sequency physics. He had had no equals. Here, in the realm of inequity, he met them at last.

It was a revelation, a liberation, Physicists, mathematicians, astronomers, logicians, biologists, all were here at the University, and they came to him or he went to them, and they talked, and new worlds were born of their talking. It is of the nature of idea to be communicated: written, spoken, done. The idea is like grass, It craves light, likes crowds, thrives on crossbreeding, grows better for being stepped on.

Even on that first afternoon at the University, with Oiie and Pae, he knew he had found something he had longed for ever since, as boys and on a boyish level, he and Tirin and Bedap had used to talk half the night, teasing and daring each other into always bolder flights of mind. He vividly remembered some of those nights. He saw Tirin, Tirin saying, "If we knew what Urras was really like, maybe some of us would want to go there." And he had been so shocked by the idea that he had jumped all over Tirin, and Tir had backed down at once; he had always backed down, poor damned soul, and he had always been right.

Conversation had stopped. Pae and Oiie were silent.

"I'm sorry," he said. "The head is heavy."

"How's the gravity?" Pae asked, with the charming smile of a man who, like a bright child, counts on his charm.

"I don't notice," Shevek said. "Only in the, what is this?"

"Knees—knee joints."

"Yes, knees. Function is impaired. But I will get accustomed." He looked at Pae, then at Oiie. "There is a question. But I don't wish to give offense."

"Never fear, sir!" Pae said.

Oiie said, "I'm not sure you know how." Oiie was not a likable fellow, like Pae. Even talking physics he had an evasive, secretive style. And yet beneath the style, there was something, Shevek felt, to trust; whereas beneath Pae's charm, what was there? Well, no matter. He had to trust them all, and would. "Where are women?"

Pae laughed. Oiie smiled and asked, "In what sense?"

"All senses. I met women at the party last night—five, ten—hundreds of men. None were scientists, I think. Who were they?"

"Wives. One of them was my wife, in fact," Oiie said with his secretive smile.

"Where are other women?"

"Oh, no difficulty at all there, sir," Pae said promptly. "Just tell us your preferences, and nothing could be simpler to provide."

"One does hear some picturesque speculations about Anarresti customs, but I rather think we can come up with almost anything you had in mind," said Oiie.

Shevek had no idea what they were talking about. He scratched his head. "Are all the scientists here men, then?"

"Scientists?" Oiie asked, incredulous.

Pae coughed. "Scientists. Oh, yes, certainly, they're all men. There are some female teachers in the girls' schools, of course. But they never get past Certificate level."

"Why not?"

"Can't do the math; no head for abstract thought; don't belong. You know how it is, what women call thinking is done with the uterus! Of course, there's always a few exceptions, Godawful brainy women with vaginal atrophy."

"You Odonians let women study science?" Oiie inquired.

"Well, they are in the sciences, yes."

"Not many, I hope."

"Well, about half."

"I've always said," said Pae, "that girl technicians properly handled could take a good deal of the load off the men in any laboratory situation. They're actually defter and quicker than men at repetitive tasks, and more docile—

59

less easily bored. We could free men for original work much sooner, if we used women."

"Not in my lab, you won't," said Oiie. "Keep 'em in their place."

"Do you find any women capable of original intellectual work, Dr. Shevek?"

"Well, it was more that they found me. Mitis, in North-setting, was my teacher. Also Gvarab; you know of her, I think."

"Gvarab was a woman?" Pae said in genuine surprise, and laughed.

Oiie looked unconvinced and offended. "Can't tell from your names, of course," he said coldly. "You make a point, I suppose, of drawing no distinction between the sexes."

Shevek said mildly, "Odo was a woman."

"There you have it," Oiie said. He did not shrug, but he very nearly shrugged. Pae looked respectful, and nodded, just as he did when old Atro maundered.

Shevek saw that he had touched in these men an impersonal animosity that went very deep. Apparently they, like the tables on the ship, contained a woman, a suppressed, silenced, bestialized woman, a fury in a cage. He had no right to tease them. They knew no relation but possession. They were possessed.

"A beautiful, virtuous woman," Pae said, "is an inspiration to us—the most precious thing on earth."

Shevek felt extremely uncomfortable. He got up and went over to the windows. "Your world is very beautiful," he said. "I wish I could see more. While I must stay inside, will you give me books?"

"Of course, sir! What sort?"

"History, pictures, stories, anything. Maybe they should be books for children. You see, I know very little. We learn about Urras, but mostly about Odo's times. Before that was eight and one half thousand years! And then since the Settlement of Anarres is a century and a half; since the last ship brought the last Settlers—ignorance. We ignore you; you ignore us. You are our history. We are perhaps your future. I want to learn, not to ignore. It is the reason I came. We must know each other. We are not primitive men. Our morality is no longer tribal, it cannot be. Such ignorance is a wrong, from which wrong will arise. So I come to learn."

60

He spoke very earnestly. Pae assented with enthusiasm. "Exactly, sir! We are all in complete agreement with your aims!"

Oiie looked at him from those black, opaque, oval eyes, and said, "Then you come, essentially, as an emissary of your society?"

Shevek returned to sit on the marble seat by the hearth, which he already felt as his seat, his territory. He wanted a territory. He felt the need for caution. But he felt more strongly the need that had brought him across the dry abyss from the other world, the need for communication, the wish to unbuild walls.

"I come," he said carefully, "as a syndic of the Syndicate of Initiative, the group that talks with Urras on the radio these last two years. But I am not, you know, an ambassador from any authority, any institution. I hope you did not ask me as that."

"No," Oiie said. "We asked you—Shevek the physicist. With the approval of our government and the Council of World Governments, of course. But you are here as the private guest of Ieu Eun University."

"Good."

"But we haven't been sure whether or not you came with the approval of—" He hesitated.

Shevek grinned. "Of my government?"

"We know that nominally there's no government on Anarres. However, obviously there's administration. And we gather that the group that sent you, your Syndicate, is a kind of faction; perhaps a revolutionary faction."

"Everybody on Anarres is a revolutionary, Oiie. . . . The network of administration and management is called PDC, Production and Distribution Coordination. They are a coordinating system for all syndicates, federatives, and individuals who do productive work. They do not govern persons; they administer production. They have no authority either to support me or to prevent me. They can only tell us the public opinion of us—where we stand in the social conscience. That's what you want to know? Well, my friends and I are mostly disapproved of. Most people on Anarres don't want to learn about Urras. They fear it and want nothing to do with the propertarians. I am sorry if I am rude! It is the same here, with some people, is it

61

not? The contempt, the fear, the tribalism. Well, so I came to begin to change that."

"Entirely on your own initiative," said Oiie.

"It is the only initiative I acknowledge," Shevek said, smiling, in dead earnest.

He spent the next couple of days talking with the scientists who came to see him, reading the books Pae brought him, and sometimes simply standing at the double-arched windows to gaze at the coming of summer to the great valley, and to listen for the brief, sweet conversations out there in the open air. Birds: he knew the singers' name now, and what they looked like from pictures in the books, but still when he heard the song or caught the flash of wings from tree to tree, he stood in wonder like a child.

He had expected to feel so strange, here on Urras, so lost, alien, and confused—and he felt nothing of the kind. Or course there were endless things he did not understand. He only glimpsed, now, how many things: this whole incredibly complex society with all its nations, classes, castes, cults, customs, and its magnificent, appalling, and interminable history. And each individual he met was a puzzle, full of surprises. But they were not the gross, cold egoists he had expected them to be: they were as complex and various as their culture, as their landscape; and they were intelligent; and they were kind. They treated him like a brother, they did all they could to make him feel not lost, not alien, but at home. And he did feel at home. He could not help it. The whole world, the softness of the air, the fall of sunlight across the hills, the very pull of the heavier gravity on his body, asserted to him that this was home indeed, his race's world; and all its beauty was his birthright.

The silence, the utter silence of Anarres: he thought of it at night. No birds sang there. There were no voices there but human voices. Silence, and the barren lands.

On the third day old Atro brought him a pile of newspapers. Pae, who was Shevek's very frequent companion, said nothing to Atro, but when the old man left he told Shevek, "Awful trash, those papers, sir. Amusing, but don't believe anything you read in them."

Shevek took up the topmost paper. It was badly

printed on coarse paper—the first crudely made artifact he had handled on Urras. In fact it looked like the PDC bulletins and regional reports that served as newspapers on Anarres, but its style was very different from those smudgy, practical, factual publications. It was full of exclamation points and pictures. There was a picture of Shevek in front of the spaceship, with Pae holding his arm and scowling. FIRST MAN FROM THE MOON! said the huge print over the picture. Fascinated, Shevek read on.

His first step on Earth! Urras' first visitor from the Anarres Settlement in 170 years, Dr. Shevek, was photographed yesterday at his arrival on the regular Moon freighter run at Peier Space Port. The distinguished scientist, winner of the Seo Oen Prize for service to all nations through science, has accepted a professorship at Ieu Eun University, an honor never before accorded to an off-worlder. Asked about his feelings on first viewing Urras, the tall, distinguished physicist replied, "It is a great honor to be invited to your beautiful planet. I hope that a new era of all-Cetian friendship is now beginning, when the Twin Planets will move forward together in brotherhood."

"But I never said anything!" Shevek protested to Pae.

"Of course not. We didn't let that lot get near you. That doesn't cramp a birdseed journalist's imagination! They'll report you as saying what they want you to say, no matter what you do say, or don't."

Shevek chewed his lip. "Well," he said at last, "if I had said anything, it would have been like that. But what is 'all-Cetian'?"

"The Terrans call us 'Cetians.' From their word for our sun, I believe. The popular press has picked it up lately, there's a sort of fad for the word."

"Then 'all-Cetian' means Urras and Anarres together?"

"I suppose so," Pae said with marked lack of interest.

Shevek went on reading the papers. He read that he was a towering giant of a man, that he was unshaven and possessed a 'mane,' whatever that was, of greying hair, that he was thirty-seven, forty-three and fifty-six; that he had written a great work of physics called (the spelling

63

depended on the paper) *Principals of Simultaneity* or *Principles of Simiultany,* that he was a goodwill ambassador from the Odonian government, that he was a vegetarian, and that, like all Anarresti, he did not drink. At this he broke down and laughed till his ribs hurt. "By damn, they do have imagination! Do they think we live on water vapor, like the rockmoss?"

"They mean you don't drink alcoholic liquors," said Pae, also laughing. "The one thing everybody knows about Odonians, I suppose, is that you don't drink alcohol. Is it true, by the way?"

"Some people distill alcohol from fermented holum root, for drinking. They say it gives the unconscious free play, like brainwave training. Most people prefer that, it's very easy and doesn't cause a disease. Is that common here?"

"Drinking is. I don't know about this disease. What's it called?"

"Alcoholism, I think."

"Oh, I see. . . . But what do working people do on Anarres for a bit of jollity, to escape the woes of the world together for a night?"

Shevek looked blank. "Well, we . . . I don't know. Perhaps our woes are inescapable?"

"Quaint," Pae said, and smiled disarmingly.

Shevek pursued his reading. One of the journals was in a language he did not know, and one in a different alphabet altogether. The one was from Thu, Pae explained, and the other from Benbili, a nation in the western hemisphere. The paper from Thu was well printed and sober in format; Pae explained that it was a government publication. "Here in A-Io, you see, educated people get their news from the telefax, and radio and television, and the weekly reviews. These papers are read by the lower classes almost exclusively—written by semiliterates for semiliterates, as you can see. We have complete freedom of the press in A-Io, which inevitably means we get a lot of trash. The Thuvian paper is much better written but it reports only those facts which the Thuvian Central Presidium wants reported. Censorship is absolute, in Thu. The state is all, and all for the state. Hardly the place for an Odonian, eh, sir?"

"And this paper?"

"I really have no idea. Benbili's a backward sort of country. Always having revolutions."

"A group of people in Benbili sent us a message on the Syndicate wave length, not long before I left Abbenay. They called themselves Odonians. Are there any such groups here, in A-Io?"

"Not that I ever heard of, Dr. Shevek."

The wall. Shevek knew the wall, by now, when he came up against it. The wall was this young man's charm, courtesy, indifference.

"I think you are afraid of me, Pae," he said, abruptly and genially.

"Afraid of you, sir?"

"Because I am, by my existence, disproof of the necessity of the state. But what is to fear? I will not hurt you, Saio Pae, you know. I am personally quite harmless. . . . Listen, I am not a doctor. We do not use titles. I am called Shevek."

"I know, I'm sorry, sir. In our terms, you see, it seems disrespectful. It just doesn't seem right." He apologized winningly, expecting forgiveness.

"Can you not recognize me as an equal?" Shevek asked, watching him without either forgiveness or anger.

Pae was for once nonplused. "But really, sir, you are, you know, a very important man—"

"There is no reason why you should change your habits for me," Shevek said. "It does not matter. I thought you might be glad to be free of the unnecessary, that's all."

Three days of confinement indoors left Shevek charged with surplus energy, and when he was released he wore out his escorts in his first eagerness to see everything at once. They took him over the University, which was a city in itself, sixteen thousand students and faculty. With its dormitories, refectories, theaters, meeting rooms, and so on, it was not very different from an Odonian community, except that it was very old, was exclusively male, was incredibly luxurious, and was not organized federatively but hierarchically, from the top down. All the same, Shevek thought, it *felt* like a community. He had to remind himself of the differences.

He was driven out into the country in hired cars, splendid machines of bizarre elegance. There were not many of them on the roads: the hire was expensive, and few people owned a car privately, because they were heavily taxed. All such luxuries which if freely allowed to the public would tend to drain irreplaceable natural resources or to foul the environment with waste products were strictly controlled by regulation and taxation. His guides dwelt on this with some pride. A-Io had led the world for centuries, they said, in ecological control and the husbanding of natural resources. The excesses of the Ninth Millennium were ancient history, their only lasting effect being the shortage of certain metals, which fortunately could be imported from the Moon.

Traveling by car or train, he saw villages, farms, towns; fortresses from the feudal days; the ruined towers of Ae, ancient capital of an empire, forty-four hundred years old. He saw the farmlands, lakes, and hills of Avan Province, the heartland of A-Io, and on the northern skyline the peaks of the Meitei Range, white, gigantic. The beauty of the land and the well-being of its people remained a perpetual marvel to him. The guides were right: the Urrasti knew how to use their world. He had been taught as a child that Urras was a festering mass of inequity, iniquity, and waste. But all the people he met, and all the people he saw, in the smallest country village, were well dressed, well fed, and, contrary to his expectations, industrious. They did not stand about sullenly waiting to be ordered to do things. Just like Anarresti, they were simply busy getting things done. It puzzled him. He had assumed that if you removed a human being's natural incentive to work—his initiative, his spontaneous creative energy—and replaced it with external motivation and coercion, he would become a lazy and careless worker. But no careless workers kept those lovely farmlands, or made the superb cars and comfortable trains. The lure and compulsion of *profit* was evidently a much more effective replacement of the natural initiative than he had been led to believe.

He would have liked to talk to some of those sturdy, self-respecting-looking people he saw in the small towns, to ask them for instance if they considered themselves to be poor; for if these were the poor, he had to revise his understanding of the word. But there never seemed to be time, with all his guides wanted him to see.

66

The other big cities of A-Io were too distant to be reached in a day's tour, but he was taken to Nio Esseia, fifty kilometers from the University, frequently. A whole series of receptions in his honor was held there. He did not enjoy these much, they were not at all his idea of a party. Everyone was very polite and talked a great deal, but not about anything interesting; and they smiled so much they looked anxious. But their clothes were gorgeous, indeed they seemed to put all the lightheartedness their manner lacked into the clothes, and their food, and all the different things they drank, and the lavish furnishings and ornaments of the rooms in the palaces where the receptions were held.

He was shown the sights of Nio Esseia: a city of five million—a quarter the population of his whole planet. They took him to Capitol Square and showed him the high bronze doors of the Directorate, the seat of the Government of A-Io; he was permitted to witness a debate in the Senate and a committee meeting of the Directors. They took him to the Zoo, the National Museum, the Museum of Science and Industry. They took him to a school, where charming children in blue and white uniforms sang the national anthem of A-Io for him. They took him through an electronic parts factory, a fully automated steel mill, and a nuclear fusion plant, so that he could see how efficiently a propertarian economy ran its manufacturing and power supply. They took him through a new housing development put up by the government so that he could see how the state looked after its people. They took him on a boat tour down the Sua Estuary, crowded with shipping from all over the planet, to the sea. They took him to the High Courts of Law, and he spent a whole day listening to civil and criminal cases being tried, an experience that left him bewildered and appalled; but they insisted that he should see what there was to be seen, and be taken wherever he wanted to go. When he asked, with some diffidence, if he might see the place where Odo was buried, they whisked him straight to the old cemetery in the Trans-Sua district. They even allowed newsmen from the disreputable papers to photograph him standing there in the shade of the great old willows, looking at the plain, well-kept tombstone:

*To be whole is to be part;
true voyage is return.*

He was taken to Rodarred, the seat of the Council of
World Governments, to address the plenary council of
that body. He had hoped to meet or at least see aliens
there, the ambassadors from Terra or from Hain, but the
schedule of events was too tightly planned to permit this.
He had worked hard on his speech, a plea for free communication and mutual recognition between the New
World and the Old. It was received with a ten-minute
standing ovation. The respectable weeklies commented on
it with approval, calling it a "disinterested moral gesture of
human brotherhood by a great scientist," but they did not
quote from it, not did the popular papers. In fact, despite
the ovation, Shevek had the curious feeling that nobody
had heard it.

He was given many privileges and entrees: to the Light
Research Laboratories, the National Archives, the Nuclear
Technology Laboratories, the National Library in Nio,
the Accelerator in Meafed, the Space Research Foundation in Drio. Though everything he saw on Urras made
him want to see more, still several weeks of the tourist life
was enough: it was all so fascinating, startling, and marvelous that at last it became quite overwhelming. He
wanted to settle down at the University and work and
think it all over for a while. But for a last day's sight-
seeing he asked to be shown around the Space Research
Foundation. Pae looked very pleased when he made this
request.

Much that he had seen recently was awesome to him
because it was so old, centuries old, even millennia. The
Foundation, on the contrary, was new: built within the
last ten years, in the lavish, elegant style of the times. The
architecture was dramatic. Great masses of color were
used. Heights and distances were exaggerated. The
laboratories were spacious and airy, the attached factories
and machine shops were housed behind splendid Neo-
Saetan porticos of arches and columns. The hangars were
huge multicolored domes, translucent and fantastic. The
men who worked there were, in contrast, very quiet and

68

solid. They took Shevek away from his usual escorts and showed him through the whole Foundation, including every stage of the experimental interstellar propulsion system they were working on, from the computers and the drawing boards to a half-finished ship, enormous and surreal in the orange, violet, and yellow light within the vast geodesic hangar.

"You have so much," Shevek said to the engineer who had taken charge of him, a man named Oegeo. "You have so much to work with, and you work with it so well. This is magnificent—the coordination, the cooperation, the greatness of the enterprise."

"Couldn't swing anything on this scale where you come from, eh?" the engineer said, grinning.

"Spaceships? Our space fleet is the ships the Settlers came in from Urras—built here on Urras—nearly two centuries ago. To build just a ship to carry grain across the sea, a barge, it takes a year's planning, a big effort of our economy."

Oegeo nodded. "Well, we've got the goods, all right. But you know, you're the man who can tell us when to scrap this whole job—throw it all away."

"Throw it away? What do you mean?"

"Faster than light travel," Oegeo said. "Transilience. The old physics says it isn't possible. The Terrans say it isn't possible. But the Hainish, who after all invented the drive we use now, say that it is possible, only they don't know how to do it, because they're just learning temporal physics from us. Evidently if it's in anybody's pocket, anybody in the known worlds, Dr. Shevek, it's in yours."

Shevek looked at him with a distancing stare, his light eyes hard and clear. "I am a theoretician, Oegeo. Not a designer."

"If you provide the theory, the unification of Sequency and Simultaneity in a general field theory of time, then we'll design the ships. And arrive on Terra, or Hain, or the next galaxy, in the instant we leave Urras! This tub," and he looked down the hangar at the looming framework of the half-built ship swimming in shafts of violet and orange light, "will be as outdated as an oxcart."

"You dream as you build, superbly," Shevek said, still withdrawn and stern. There was much more that Oegeo and the others wanted to show him and discuss with him, but before long he said, with a simplicity that precluded any ironic intention, "I think you had better take me back to the keepers."

They did so; they bade farewell with mutual warmth. Shevek got into the car, and then got out again. "I was forgetting," he said, "is there time to see one other thing in Drio?"

"There isn't anything else in Drio," Pae said, polite as ever and trying hard to hide his annoyance over Shevek's five-hour escapade among the engineers.

"I should like to see the fort."

"What fort, sir?"

"An old castle, from the times of the kings. It was used later as a prison."

"Anything like that would have been torn down. The Foundation rebuilt the town entirely."

When they were in the car and the chauffeur was closing the doors, Chifoilisk (another probable source of Pae's ill humor) asked, "What did you want to see another castle for, Shevek? Should have thought you'd had enough old ruins to hold you for a while."

"The Fort in Drio was where Odo spent nine years," Shevek replied. His face was set, as it had been since he talked with Oegeo. "After the Insurrection of 747. She wrote the *Prison Letters* there, and the *Analogy*."

"Afraid it's been pulled down," Pae said sympathetically. "Drio was a moribund sort of town, and the Foundation just wiped out and started fresh."

Shevek nodded. But as the car followed a riverside highway toward the turnoff to Ieu Eun it passed a bluff on the curve of the river Seisse, and up on the bluff there was a building, heavy, ruinous, implacable, with broken towers of black stone. Nothing could have been less like the gorgeous lighthearted buildings of the Space Research Foundation, the showy domes, the bright factories, the tidy lawns and paths. Nothing could have made them look so much like bits of colored paper.

"That, I believe, is the Fort," Chifoilisk remarked with his usual satisfaction at placing the tactless remark where it was least wanted.

"Gone all to ruins," Pae said. "Must be empty."

"Want to stop and have a look at it, Shevek?" Chifoilisk asked, ready to tap on the chauffeur's screen.

"No," Shevek said.

He had seen what he wanted to see. There was still a Fort in Drio. He did not need to enter it and seek down ruined halls for the cell in which Odo had spent nine years. He knew what a prison cell was like.

He looked up, his face still set and cold, at the ponderous dark walls that now loomed almost above the car. I have been here for a long time, the fort said, and I am still here.

When he was back in his rooms, after dinner in the Senior Faculty Refectory, he sat down alone by the unlighted fire. It was summer in A-Io, getting on towards the longest day of the year, and though it was past eight it was not yet dark. The sky outside the arched windows still showed a tinge of the daylight color of the sky, a pure tender blue. The air was mild, fragrant of cut grass and wet earth. There was a light in the chapel, across the grove, and a faint undertone of music on that lightly stirring air. Not the birds singing, but a human music. Shevek listened. Somebody was practicing the Numerical Harmonies on the chapel harmonium. They were as familiar to Shevek as to any Urrasti. Odo had not tried to renew the basic relationships of music, when she renewed the relationships of men. She had always respected the necessary. The Settlers of Anarres had left the laws of man behind them, but had brought the laws of harmony along.

The large, calm room was shadowy and silent, darkening. Shevek looked around it, the perfect double arches of the windows, the faintly gleaming edges of the parquet floor, the strong, dim curve of the stone chimney, the paneled walls, admirable in their proportion. It was a beautiful and humane room. It was a very old room. This Senior Faculty House, they told him, had been built in the year 540, four hundred years ago, two hundred and thirty years before the Settlement of Anarres. Generations of scholars had lived, worked, talked, thought, slept, died in this room before Odo was ever born. The Numerical Harmonies had drifted over the lawn, through the dark leaves of the grove, for centuries. I have been here for a long time, the room said to Shevek, and I am still here. What are you doing here?

He had no answer. He had no right to all the grace and

71

bounty of this world, earned and maintained by the work, the devotion, the faithfulness of its people. Paradise is for those who make Paradise. He did not belong. He was a frontiersman, one of a breed who had denied their past, their history. The settlers of Anarres had turned their backs on the Old World and its past, opted for the future only. But as surely as the future becomes the past, the past becomes the future. To deny is not to achieve. The Odonians who left Urras had been wrong, wrong in their desperate courage, to deny their history, to forgo the possibility of return. The explorer who will not come back or send back his ships to tell his tale is not an explorer, only an adventurer; and his sons are born in exile.

He had come to love Urras, but what good was his yearning love? He was not part of it. Nor was he part of the world of his birth.

The loneliness, the certainty of isolation, that he had felt in his first hour aboard the *Mindful*, rose up in him and asserted itself as his true condition, ignored, suppressed, but absolute.

He was alone, here, because he came from a self-exiled society. He had always been alone on his own world because he had exiled himself from his society. The Settlers had taken one step away. He had taken two. He stood by himself, because he had taken the metaphysical risk.

And he had been fool enough to think that he might serve to bring together two worlds to which he did not belong.

The blue of the night sky outside the windows drew his eyes. Over the vague darkness of foliage and the tower of the chapel, above the dark line of the hills, which at night always seemed smaller and more remote, a light was growing, a large, soft radiance. Moonrise, he thought, with a grateful sense of familiarity. There is no break in the wholeness of time. He had seen the Moon rise when he was a little child, from the window of the domicile in Wide Plains, with Palat; over the hills of his boyhood; over the dry plains of the Dust; over the roofs of Abbenay, with Takver watching it beside him.

But it had not been this Moon.

The shadows moved about him, but he sat unmoving as Anarres rose above the alien hills, at her full, mottled dun and bluish-white, lambent. The light of his world filled his empty hands.

Chapter 4

The westering sun shining in on his face woke Shevek as the dirigible, clearing the last high pass of the Ne Theras, turned due south. He had slept most of the day, the third of the long journey. The night of the farewell party was half a world behind him. He yawned and rubbed his eyes and shook his head, trying to shake the deep rumble of the dirigible engine out of his ears, and then came wide awake, realizing that the journey was nearly over, that they must be coming close to Abbenay. He pressed his face to the dusty window, and sure enough, down there between two low rusty ridges was a great walled field, the Port. He gazed eagerly, trying to see if there was a spaceship on the pad. Despicable as Urras was, still it was another world; he wanted to see a ship from another world, a voyager across the dry and terrible abyss, a thing made by alien hands. But there was no ship in the Port.

The freighters from Urras came in only eight times a year, and stayed just long enough to load and unload. They were not welcome visitors. Indeed they were, to some Anarresti, a perpetually renewed humiliation.

They brought fossil oils and petroleum products, certain delicate machine parts and electronic components that

Anarresti manufacturing was not geared to supply, and often a new strain of fruit tree or grain for testing. They took back to Urras a full load of mercury, copper, aluminum, uranium, tin, and gold. It was, for them, a very good bargain. The division of their cargoes eight times a year was the most prestigious function of the Urrasti Council of World Governments and the major event of the Urrasti world stock market. In fact, the Free World of Anarres was a mining colony of Urras.

The fact galled. Every generation, every year, in the PDC debates in Abbenay, fierce protests were made: "Why do we continue these profiteering business transactions with warmaking propertarians?" And cooler heads always gave the same answer: "It would cost the Urrasti more to dig the ores themselves; therefore they don't invade us. But if we broke the trade agreement, they would use force." It is hard, however, for people who have never paid money for anything to understand the psychology of cost, the argument of the marketplace. Seven generations of peace had not brought trust.

Therefore the work-posting called Defense never had to call for volunteers. Most Defense work was so boring that it was not called work in Pravic, which used the same word for work and play, but *kleggich,* drudgery. Defense workers manned the twelve old interplanetary ships, keeping them repaired and in orbit as a guard network; maintained radar and radio-telescopic scans in lonesome places; did dull duty at the Port. And yet they always had a waiting list. However pragmatic the morality a young Anarresti absorbed, yet life overflowed in him, demanding altruism, self-sacrifice, scope for the absolute gesture. Loneliness, watchfulness, danger, spaceships: they offered the lure of romance. It was pure romance that kept Shevek flattening his nose against the window until the vacant Port had dropped away behind the dirigible, and that left him disappointed because he had not seen a grubby ore freighter on the pad.

He yawned again, and stretched, and then looked out, ahead, to see what was to be seen. The dirigible was clearing the last low ridge of the Ne Theras. Before it, stretching out southward from the mountains' arms, brilliant in the afternoon sunlight, lay a great sloping bay of green.

He looked at it with wonder, as his ancestors, six thousand years ago, had looked at it.

In the third Millennium on Urras the astronomer-priests of Serdonou and Dhun had watched the seasons change the tawny brightness of the Otherworld, and had given mystical names to the plains and ranges and sun-reflecting seas. One region that grew green before all others in the lunar new year they called Ans Hos, the Garden of Mind: the Eden of Anarres.

In later millennia telescopes had proved them to be quite correct. Ans Hos was indeed the most favored spot on Anarres; and the first manned ship to the Moon had come down there in the green place between the mountains and the sea.

But the Eden of Anarres proved to be dry, cold, and windy, and the rest of the planet was worse. Life there had not evolved higher than fish and flowerless plants. The air was thin, like the air of Urras at a very high altitude. The sun burned, the wind froze, the dust choked.

For two hundred years after the first landing Anarres was explored, mapped, investigated, but not colonized. Why move to a howling desert when there was plenty of room in the gracious valleys of Urras?

But it was mined. The self-plundering eras of the Ninth and early Tenth Millennia had left the lodes of Urras empty; and as rocketry was perfected, it became cheaper to mine the Moon than to extract needed metals from low-grade ores or sea water. In the Urrasti year IX-738 a settlement was founded at the foot of the Ne Thera Mountains, where mercury was mined, in the old Ans Hos. They called the place Anarres Town. It was not a town, there were no women. Men signed on for two or three years' duty as miners or technicians, then went home to the real world.

The Moon and its mines were under the jurisdiction of the Council of World Governments, but around in the Moon's eastern hemisphere the nation of Thu had a little secret: a rocket base and a settlement of goldminers, with their wives and children. They really lived on the Moon, but nobody knew it except their government. It was the collapse of that government in the year 771 that led to the proposal, in the Council of World Governments, of giving the Moon to the International Society of

Odonians—buying them off with a world, before they fatally undermined the authority of law and national sovereignty on Urras. Anarres Town was evacuated, and from the midst of the turmoil in Thu a couple of hasty final rockets were sent to pick up the goldminers. Not all of them chose to return. Some of them liked the howling desert.

For over twenty years the twelve ships granted to the Odonian Settlers by the Council of World Governments went back and forth between the worlds, until the million souls who chose the new life had all been brought across the dry abyss. Then the port was closed to immigration and left open only to the freight ships of the Trade Agreement. By then Anarres Town held a hundred thousand people, and had been renamed Abbenay, which meant, in the new language of the new society, Mind.

Decentralization had been an essential element in Odo's plans for the society she did not live to see founded. She had no intention of trying to de-urbanize civilization. Though she suggested that the natural limit to the size of a community lay in its dependence on its own immediate region for essential food and power, she intended that all communities be connected by communication and transportation networks, so that goods and ideas could get where they were wanted, and the administration of things might work with speed and ease, and no community should be cut off from change and interchange. But the network was not to be run from the top down. There was to be no controlling center, no capital, no establishment for the self-perpetuating machinery of bureaucracy and the dominance drive of individuals seeking to become captains, bosses, chiefs of state.

Her plans, however, had been based on the generous ground of Urras. On arid Anarres, the communities had to scatter widely in search of resources, and few of them could be self-supporting, no matter how they cut back their notions of what is needed for support. They cut back very hard indeed, but to a minimum beneath which they would not go; they would not regress to pre-urban, pre-technological tribalism. They knew that their anarchism was the product of a very high civilization, of a complex diversified culture, of a stable economy and a highly industrialized technology that could maintain high production and rapid transportation of goods. However vast the distances separating settlements, they held to the ideal of complex organicism. They built the roads first, the houses second. The special resources and products of each region were interchanged continually with those of others, in an intricate process of balance: that balance of diversity which is the characteristic of life, of natural and social ecology.

But, as they said in the analogic mode, you can't have a nervous system without at least a ganglion, and preferably a brain. There had to be a center. The computers that coordinated the administration of things, the division of labor, and the distribution of goods, and the central federatives of most of the work syndicates, were in Abbenay, right from the start. And from the start the Settlers were aware that that unavoidable centralization was a lasting threat, to be countered by lasting vigilance.

> O child Anarchia, infinite promise
> infinite carefulness
> I listen, listen in the night
> by the cradle deep as the night
> is it well with the child

Pio Atean, who took the Pravic name Tober, wrote that in the fourteenth year of the Settlement. The Odonians' first efforts to make their new language, their new world, into poetry, were stiff, ungainly, moving.

Abbenay, the mind and center of Anarres, was there, now, ahead of the dirigible, on the great green plain.

That brilliant, deep green of the fields was unmistakable: a color not native to Anarres. Only here and on the warm shores of the Keran Sea did the Old World grains flourish. Elsewhere the staple grain crops were ground-holum and pale mene-grass.

When Shevek was nine his afternoon schoolwork for several months had been caring for the ornamental plants in Wide Plains community—delicate exotics, that had to be fed and sunned like babies. He had assisted an old man in the peaceful and exacting task, had liked him and liked the plants, and the dirt, and the work. When he saw the color of the Plain of Abbenay he remembered the old man, and the smell of fish-oil manure, and the color of the first leafbuds on small bare branches, that clear vigorous green.

He saw in the distance among the vivid fields a long smudge of white, which broke into cubes, like spilt salt, as the dirigible came over.

A cluster of dazzling flashes at the east edge of the city made him wink and see dark spots for a moment: the big parabolic mirrors that provided solar heat for Abbenay's refineries.

The dirigible came down at a cargo depot at the south end of town, and Shevek set off into the streets of the biggest city in the world.

They were wide, clean streets. They were shadowless, for Abbenay lay less than thirty degrees north of the equator, and all the buildings were low, except the strong, spare towers of the wind turbines. The sun shone white in a hard, dark, blue-violet sky. The air was clear and clean, without smoke or moisture. There was a vividness to things, a hardness of edge and corner, a clarity. Everything stood out separate, itself.

The elements that made up Abbenay were the same as in any other Odonian community, repeated many times: workshops, factories, domiciles, dormitories, learning centers, meeting halls, distributories, depots, refectories. The bigger buildings were most often grouped around open squares, giving the city a basic cellular texture: it was one subcommunity or neighborhood after another. Heavy industry and food-processing plants tended to cluster on the city's outskirts, and the cellular pattern was repeated in that related industries often stood side by side on a certain square or street. The first such that Shevek walked through was a series of squares, the textile district, full of holum-fiber processing plants, spinning and weaving mills, dye factories, and cloth and clothing distributories; the center of each square was planted with a little forest of poles strung from top to bottom with banners and pennants of all the colors of the dyer's art, proudly proclaiming the local industry. Most of the city's buildings were pretty much alike, plain, soundly built of stone or cast foamstone. Some of them looked very large to Shevek's eyes, but they were almost all of one storey only, because of the frequency of earthquake. For the same reason windows were small, and of a tough silicon plastic that did not shatter. They were small, but there were a lot of them, for there was no artificial lighting provided from an hour before sunrise to an hour after sunset. No heat was furnished when the outside temperature went above 55 degrees Fahrenheit. It was not that Abbenay was short of power, not with her wind turbines and the earth temperature-differential generators used for heating; but the principle of organic economy was too essential to the functioning of the society not to affect ethics and aesthetics profoundly. "Excess is excrement," Odo wrote in the *Analogy*. "Excrement retained in the body is a poison."

Abbenay was poisonless: a bare city, bright, the colors light and hard, the air pure. It was quiet. You could see it all, laid out as plain as spilt salt.

Nothing was hidden.

The squares, the austere streets, the low buildings, the unwalled workyards, were charged with vitality and activity. As Shevek walked he was constantly aware of other people walking, working, talking, faces passing, voices calling, gossiping, singing, people alive, people doing things, people afoot. Workshops and factories fronted on squares or on their open yards, and their doors were open. He passed a glassworks, the workman dipping up a great molten blob as casually as a cook serves soup. Next to it was a busy yard where foamstone was cast for construction. The gang foreman, a big woman in a smock white with dust, was supervising the pouring of a cast with a loud and splendid flow of language. After that came a small wire factory, a district laundry, a luthier's where musical instruments were made and repaired, the district small-goods distributory, a theater, a tile works. The activity going on in each place was fascinating, and mostly out in full view. Children were around, some involved in the work with the adults, some underfoot making mudpies, some busy with games in the street, one sitting perched up on the roof of the learning center with her nose deep in a book. The wiremaker had decorated the shopfront with patterns of vines worked in painted wire, cheerful and ornate. The blast of steam and conversation from the wide-open doors of the laundry was overwhelming. No doors were locked, few shut. There were no disguises and no advertisements. It was all there, all

the work, all the life of the city, open to the eye and to
the hand. And every now and then down Depot Street
a thing came careering by clanging a bell, a vehicle
crammed full of people and with people festooned on
stanchions all over the outside, old women cursing
heartily as it failed to slow down at their stop so they
could scramble off, a little boy on a homemade tricycle
pursuing it madly, electric sparks showering blue from
the overhead wires at crossings: as if that quiet intense
vitality of the streets built up every now and then to dis-
charge point, and leapt the gap with a crash and a blue
crackle and the smell of ozone. These were the Abbenay
omnibuses, and as they passed one felt like cheering.

Depot Street ended in a large airy place where five
other streets rayed in to a triangular park of grass and
trees. Most parks on Anarres were playgrounds of dirt
or sand, with a stand of shrub and tree holums. This one
was different. Shevek crossed the trafficless pavement and
entered the park, drawn to it because he had seen it often
in pictures, and because he wanted to see alien trees,
Urrasti trees, from close up, to experience the greenness
of those multitudinous leaves. The sun was setting, the
sky was wide and clear, darkening to purple at the zenith,
the dark of space showing through the thin atmosphere.
He entered under the trees, alert, wary. Were they not
wasteful, those crowding leaves? The tree holum got along
very efficiently with spines and needles, and no excess of
those. Wasn't all this extravagant foliage mere excess,
excrement? Such trees couldn't thrive without a rich soil,
constant watering, much care. He disapproved of their
lavishness, their thriftlessness. He walked under them,
among them. The alien grass was soft underfoot. It was
like walking on living flesh. He shied back onto the path.
The dark limbs of the trees reached out over his head,
holding their many wide green hands above him. Awe
came into him. He knew himself blessed though he had
not asked for blessing.

Some way before him, down the darkening path, a person sat reading on a stone bench.

Shevek went forward slowly. He came to the bench
and stood looking at the figure who sat with head bowed
over the book in the green-gold dusk under the trees. It
was a woman of fifty or sixty, strangely dressed, her hair

81

pulled back in a knot. Her left hand on her chin nearly
hid the stern mouth, her right held the papers on her
knee. They were heavy, those papers; the cold hand on
them was heavy. The light was dying fast but she never
looked up. She went on reading the proof sheets of *The
Social Organism*.

Shevek looked at Odo for a while, and then he sat
down on the bench beside her.

He had no concept of status at all, and there was
plenty of room on the bench. He was moved by a pure
impulse of companionship.

He looked at the strong, sad profile, and at the hands,
an old woman's hands. He looked up into the shadowy
branches. For the first time in his life he comprehended
that Odo, whose face he had known since his infancy,
whose ideas were central and abiding in his mind and the
mind of everyone he knew, that Odo had never set foot
on Anarres: that she had lived, and died, and was
buried, in the shadow of green-leaved trees, in unimaginable cities, among people speaking unknown languages, on
another world. Odo was an alien: an exile.

The young man sat beside the statue in the twilight,
one almost as quiet as the other.

At last, realizing it was getting dark, he got up and
made off into the streets again, asking directions to the
Central Institute of the Sciences.

It was not far; he got there not long after the lights
went on. A registrar or vigilkeeper was in the little office
at the entrance, reading. He had to knock at the open
door to get her attention. "Shevek," he said. It was customary to start conversation with a stranger by offering
your name as a kind of handle for him to take hold of.
There were not many other handles to offer. There was
no rank, no terms of rank, no conventional respectful
forms of address.

"Kokvan," the woman responded. "Weren't you expecting to get in yesterday?"

"They've changed the cargo-dirigible schedule. Is there
an empty bed in one of the dorms?"

"Number 46 is empty. Across the courtyard, the building to the left. There's a note for you here from Sabul.
He says call on him in the morning at the physics office."

"Thanks!" said Shevek, and strode off across the broad

paved courtyard swinging his luggage—a winter coat and a spare pair of boots—in his hand. Lights were on in rooms all round the quadrangle. There was a murmur, a presence of people in the quietness. Something stirred in the clear, keen air of the city night, a sense of drama, of promise.

Dinner hour was not over, and he made a quick detour by the Institute refectory to see if there was some spare food for a drop-in. He found that his name had already been put on the regular list, and he found the food excellent. There was even a dessert, stewed preserved fruit. Shevek loved sweets, and as he was one of the last diners and there was plenty of fruit left over, he took a second dish. He ate alone at a small table. At larger tables nearby groups of young people were talking over their empty plates; he overheard discussions on the behavior of argon at very low temperatures, the behavior of a chemistry teacher at a colloquium, the putative curvatures of time. A couple of people glanced at him; they did not come speak to him, as people in a small community would speak to a stranger; their glance was not unfriendly, perhaps a little challenging.

He found Room 46 in a long corridor of shut doors in the domicile. Evidently they were all singles, and he wondered why the registrar had sent him there. Since he was two years old he had always lived in dormitories, rooms of four to ten beds. He knocked at the door of 46. Silence. He opened the door. The room was a small single, empty, dimly illuminated by the light in the corridor. He lighted the lamp. Two chairs, a desk, a well-used slide rule, a few books, and, folded neatly on the bed platform, a hand-woven orange blanket. Somebody else lived here, the registrar had made a mistake. He shut the door. He opened it again to turn off the lamp. On the desk under the lamp was a note, scribbled on a torn-off scrap of paper: "Shevek, Physics off. morning. 2–4–1–154. Sabul."

He put his coat down on a chair, his boots on the floor. He stood awhile and read the titles of the books, standard references in physics and mathematics, green-bound, the Circle of Life stamped on the covers. He hung his coat in the closet and put his boots away. He drew the curtain of the closet carefully. He crossed the room to the door:

four paces. He stood there hesitant a minute longer, and then, for the first time in his life, he closed the door of his own room.

Sabul was a small, stocky, slovenly man of forty. His facial hair was darker and coarser than common, and thickened to a regular beard on his chin. He wore a heavy winter overtunic, and from the look of it had worn it since last winter; the ends of the sleeves were black with grime. His manner was abrupt and grudging. He spoke in scraps, as he scribbled notes on scraps. He growled. "You've got to learn Iotic," he growled at Shevek.

"Learn Iotic?"

"I said learn Iotic."

"What for?"

"So you can read Urrasti physics! Atro, To, Baisk, those men. Nobody's translated it into Pravic, nobody's likely to. Six people, maybe, on Anarres are capable of understanding it. In any language."

"How can I learn Iotic?"

"Grammar and a dictionary!"

Shevek stood his ground. "Where do I find them?"

"Here," Sabul growled. He rummaged among the untidy shelves of small green-bound books. His movements were brusque and irritable. He located two thick, unbound volumes on a bottom shelf and slapped them down on the desk. "Tell me when you're competent to read Atro in Iotic. Nothing I can do with you till then."

"What kind of mathematics do these Urrasti use?"

"Nothing you can't handle."

"Is anybody working here in chronotopology?"

"Yes, Turet. You can consult him. You don't need his lecture course."

"I planned to attend Gvarab's lectures."

"What for?"

"Her work in frequency and cycle—"

Sabul sat down and got up again. He was unbearably restless, restless yet rigid, a woodrasp of a man. "Don't waste time. You're far beyond the old woman in Sequency theory, and the other ideas she spouts are trash."

"I'm interested in Simultaneity principles."

"Simultaneity! What kind of profiteering crap is Mitis

84

feeding you up there?" The physicist glared, the veins on his temples bulging under the coarse, short hair.

"I organized a joint-work course in it myself."

"Grow up. Grow up. Time to grow up. You're here now. We're working on physics here, not religion. Drop the mysticism and grow up. How soon can you learn Iotic?"

"It took me several years to learn Pravic," Shevek said. His mild irony passed Sabul by completely.

"I did it in ten decades. Well enough to read To's *Introduction*. Oh, hell, you need a text to work on. Might as well be that. Here. Wait." He hunted through an overflowing drawer and finally achieved a book, a queer-looking book, bound in blue, without the Circle of Life on the cover. The title was stamped in gold letters and seemed to say *Poilea Afio-ite*, which didn't make any sense, and the shapes of some of the letters were unfamiliar. Shevek stared at it, took it from Sabul, but did not open it. He was holding it, the thing he had wanted to see, the alien artifact, the message from another world.

He remembered the book Palat had shown him, the book of numbers.

"Come back when you can read that," Sabul growled.

Shevek turned to go. Sabul raised his growl: "Keep those books with you! They're not for general consumption."

The young man paused, turned back, and said after a moment in his calm, rather diffident voice, "I don't understand."

"Don't let anybody else read them!"

Shevek made no response.

Sabul got up again and came close to him. "Listen. You're now a member of the Central Institute of Sciences, a Physics syndic, working with me, Sabul. You follow that? Privilege is responsibility. Correct?"

"I'm to acquire knowledge which I'm not to share," Shevek said after a brief pause, stating the sentence as if it were a proposition in logic.

"If you found a pack of explosive caps in the street would you 'share' them with every kid that went by? Those books are explosives. Now do you follow me?"

"Yes."

"All right." Sabul turned away, scowling with what appeared to be an endemic, not a specific rage. Shevek left, carrying the dynamite carefully, with revulsion and devouring curiosity.

He set to work to learn Iotic. He worked alone in Room 46, because of Sabul's warning, and because it came only too naturally to him to work alone.

Since he was very young he had known that in certain ways he was unlike anyone else he knew. For a child the consciousness of such difference is very painful, since, having done nothing yet and being incapable of doing anything, he cannot justify it. The reliable and affectionate presence of adults who are also, in their own way, different, is the only reassurance such a child can have; and Shevek had not had it. His father had indeed been utterly reliable and affectionate. Whatever Shevek was and whatever he did, Palat approved and was loyal. But Palat had not had this curse of difference. He was like the others, like all the others to whom community came so easy. He loved Shevek, but he could not show him what freedom is, that recognition of each person's solitude which alone transcends it.

Shevek was therefore used to an inward isolation, buffered by all the daily casual contacts and exchanges of communal life and by the companionship of a few friends. Here in Abbenay he had no friends, and because he was not thrown into the dormitory situation he made none. He was too conscious, at twenty, of the peculiarities of his mind and character to be outgoing; he was withdrawn and aloof; and his fellow students, sensing that the aloofness was real, did not often try to approach him.

The privacy of his room soon became dear to him. He savored his total independence. He left the room only for breakfast and dinner at the refectory and a quick daily hike through the city streets to appease his muscles, which had always been used to exercise; then back to Room 46 and the grammar of Iotic. Once every decad or two he was called on for "tenth-day" rotational community labor, but the people he worked with were strangers, not close acquaintances as they would have been in a small community, so that these days of manual work made no psychological interruption to his isolation, or to his progress in Iotic.

The grammar itself, being complex, illogical, and patterned, gave him pleasure. His learning went fast once he had built up the basic vocabulary, for he knew what he was reading; he knew the field and the terms, and whenever he got stuck either his own intuition or a mathematical equation would show him where he had got to. They were not always places he had been before. To's *Introduction to Temporal Physics* was no beginner's handbook. By the time he had worked his way to the middle of the book Shevek was no longer reading Iotic, he was reading physics; and he understood why Sabul had had him read the Urrasti physicists before he did anything else. They were far ahead of anything that had been done on Anarres for twenty or thirty years. The most brilliant insights of Sabul's own works on Sequency were in fact translations from the Iotic, unacknowledged.

He plunged on through the other books Sabul doled out to him, the major works of contemporary Urrasti physics. His life grew even more hermitic. He was not active in the student syndicate, and did not attend the meetings of any other syndicates or federatives except the lethargic Physics Federation. The meetings of such groups, the vehicles of both social action and sociability, were the framework of life in any small community, but here in the city they seemed much less important. One was not necessary to them; there were always others ready to run things, and doing it well enough. Except for tenth-day duties and the usual janitorial assignments in his domicile and the laboratories, Shevek's time was entirely his own. He often omitted exercise and occasionally meals. However, he never missed the one course he was attending, Gvarab's lecture group on Frequency and Cycle.

Gvarab was old enough that she often wandered and maundered. Attendance at her lectures was small and uneven. She soon picked out the thin boy with big ears as her one constant auditor. She began to lecture for him. The light, steady, intelligent eyes met hers, steadied her, woke her, she flashed to brilliance, regained the vision lost. She soared, and the other students in the room looked up confused or startled, even scared if they had the wits to be scared. Gvarab saw a much larger universe than most people were capable of seeing, and it made them blink. The light-eyed boy watched her steadily. In his face she saw her joy. What she offered, what she had offered for a whole lifetime, what no one had ever shared with her, he took, he shared. He was her brother, across the gulf of fifty years, and her redemption.

When they met in the physics offices or the refectory sometimes they fell straight to talking physics, but at other times Gvarab's energy was insufficient for that, and then they found little to say, for the old woman was as shy as the young man. "You don't eat enough," she would tell him. He would smile and his ears would get red. Neither knew what else to say.

After he had been a half year at the Institute, Shevek gave Sabul a three-page thesis entitled "A Critique of Atro's Infinite Sequency Hypothesis." Sabul returned it to him after a decad, growling, "Translate it into Iotic."

"I wrote it mostly in Iotic to start with," Shevek said, "since I was using Atro's terminology. I'll copy out the original. What for?"

"What for? So that damned profiteer Atro can read it! There's a ship in on the fifth of next decad."

"A ship?"

"A freighter from Urras!"

Thus Shevek discovered that not only petroleum and mercury went back and forth between the sundered worlds, and not only books, such as the books he had been reading, but also letters. Letters! Letters to propertarians, to subjects of governments founded on the inequity of power, to individuals who were inevitably exploited by and exploiters of others, because they had consented to be elements in the State-Machine. Did such people actually exchange ideas with free people in a nonaggressive, voluntary manner? Could they really admit equality and participate in intellectual solidarity, or were they merely trying to dominate, to assert their power, to possess? The idea of actually exchanging letters with a propertarian alarmed him, but it would be interesting to find out . . .

So many such discoveries had been forced on him during his first half year in Abbenay that he had to realize that he had been—and possibly still was?—very naïve: not an easy admission for an intelligent young man to make.

The first, and still the least acceptable, of these discoveries was that he was supposed to learn Iotic but keep his knowledge to himself: a situation so new to him and morally so confusing that he had not yet worked it out. Evidently he did not exactly harm anybody by not sharing his knowledge with them. On the other hand what conceivable harm could it do them to know that he knew Iotic, and that they could learn it too? Surely freedom lay rather in openness than in secrecy, and freedom is always worth the risk. He could not see what the risk was, anyway. It occurred to him once that Sabul wanted to keep the new Urrasti physics *private*—to own it, as a property, a source of power over his colleagues on Anarres. But this idea was so counter to Shevek's habits of thinking that it had great difficulty getting itself clear in his mind, and when it did he suppressed it at once, with contempt, as a genuinely disgusting thought.

Then there was the private room, another moral thorn. As a child, if you slept alone in a single it meant you had bothered the others in the dormitory until they wouldn't tolerate you; you had egoized. Solitude equated with disgrace. In adult terms, the principal referent for single rooms was a sexual one. Every domicile had a number of singles, and a couple that wanted to copulate used one of these free singles for a night, or a decad, or as long as they liked. A couple undertaking partnership took a double room; in a small town where no double was available, they often built one on to the end of a domicile, and long, low, straggling buildings might thus be created room by room, called "partners' truck trains." Aside from sexual pairing there was no reason for not sleeping in a dormitory. You could choose a small one or a large one, and if you didn't like your roommates, you could move to another dormitory. Everybody had the workshop, laboratory, studio, barn or office that he needed for his work; one could be as private or as public as one chose in the baths; sexual privacy was freely available and socially expected; and beyond that privacy was not functional. It was excess, waste. The economy of Anarres would not support the building, maintenance, heating, lighting of individual houses and apartments. A person whose nature was genuinely unsociable had to get away from society and look after himself. He was completely free to do so. He could build himself a house wherever he liked (though if it spoiled a good view or a fertile bit of land he might find himself under heavy pressure from his neighbors to move elsewhere). There were a good many solitaries and hermits on the fringes of the older Anarresti communities, pretending that they were not members of a social species. But for those who accepted the privilege and obligation of human solidarity, privacy was a value only where it served a function.

Shevek's first reaction to being put in a private room, then, was half disapproval and half shame. Why had they stuck him in here? He soon found out why. It was the right kind of place for his kind of work. If ideas arrived at midnight, he could turn on the light and write them down; if they came at dawn, they weren't jostled out of his head by the conversation and commotion of four or five roommates getting up; if they didn't come at all and he had to spend whole days sitting at his desk staring out the window, there was nobody behind his back to wonder why he was slacking. Privacy, in fact, was almost as desirable for physics as it was for sex. But all the same, was it necessary?

There was always a dessert at the Institute refectory at dinner. Shevek enjoyed it very much, and when there were extras he took them. And his conscience, his organic-societal conscience, got indigestion. Didn't everybody at every refectory, from Abbenay to Uttermost, get the same, share and share alike? He had always been told so and had always found it so. Of course there were local variations: regional specialties, shortages, surpluses, make-shifts in situations such as Project Camps, poor cooks, good cooks, in fact an endless variety within the unchanging framework. But no cook was so talented that he could make a dessert without the makings. Most refectories served dessert once or twice a decad. Here it was served nightly. Why? Were the members of the Central Institute of the Sciences better than other people?

Shevek did not ask these questions of anyone else. The social conscience, the opinion of others, was the most powerful moral force motivating the behavior of most Anarresti, but it was a little less powerful in him than in most of them. So many of his problems were of a kind other people did not understand that he had got used to working them out for himself, in silence. So he did with these problems, which were much harder for him, in some ways, than those of temporal physics. He asked no one's opinion. He stopped taking dessert at the refectory.

He did not, however, move to a dormitory. He weighed the moral discomfort against the practical advantage, and found the latter heavier. He worked better in the private room. The job was worth doing and he was doing it well. It was centrally functional to his society. The responsibility justified the privilege.

So he worked.

He lost weight; he walked light on the earth. Lack of physical labor, lack of variety of occupation, lack of social and sexual intercourse, none of these appeared to him as lacks, but as freedom. He was the free man: he could do what he wanted to do when he wanted to do it for as long as he wanted to do it. And he did. He worked. He work/played.

He was sketching out notes for a series of hypotheses which led to a coherent theory of Simultaneity. But that began to seem a petty goal; there was a much greater one, a unified theory of Time, to be reached, if he could just get to it. He felt that he was in a locked room in the middle of a great open country: it was all around him, if he could find the way out, the way clear. The intuition became an obsession. During that autumn and winter he got more and more out of the habit of sleeping. A couple of hours at night and a couple more sometime during the day were enough for him, and such naps were not the kind of profound sleep he had always had before, but almost a waking on another level, they were so full of dreams. He dreamed vividly, and the dreams were part of his work. He saw time turn back upon itself, a river flowing upward to the spring. He held the contemporaneity of two moments in his left and right hands; as he moved them apart he smiled to see the moments separate like dividing soap bubbles. He got up and scribbled down, without really waking, the mathematical formula that had been eluding him for days. He saw space shrink in upon him like the walls of a collapsing sphere driving in and in towards a central void, closing, closing, and he woke with a scream for help locked in his throat, struggling in silence to escape from the knowledge of his own eternal emptiness.

On a cold afternoon late in winter he stopped in at the

physics office on his way home from the library to see if there were any letters for him in the pickup box. He had no reason to expect any, since he had never written any of his friends at Northsetting Regional; but he hadn't been feeling very well for a couple of days, he had disproved some of his own most beautiful hypotheses and brought himself after half a year's hard work right around to where he had started from, the phasic model was simply too vague to be useful, his throat felt sore, he wished there was a letter from somebody he knew, or maybe somebody in the physics office to say hello to, at least. But nobody was there except Sabul.

"Look here, Shevek."

He looked at the book the older man held out: a thin book, bound in green, the Circle of Life on the cover. He took it and looked at the title page: "A Critique of Atro's Infinite Sequence Hypothesis." It was his essay, Atro's acknowledgement and defense, and his reply. It had all been translated or retranslated into Pravic, and printed by the PDC presses in Abbenay. There were two authors' names: Sabul, Shevek.

Sabul craned his neck over the copy Shevek held, and gloated. His growl became throaty and chuckling. "We've finished Atro. Finished him, the damned profiteer! Now let them try to talk about 'puerile imprecision'!" Sabul had nursed ten years' resentment against the *Physics Review* of Ieu Eun University, which had referred to his theoretical work as "crippled by provincialism and the puerile imprecision with which Odonian dogma infects every area of thought." "They'll see who's provincial now!" he said, grinning. In nearly a year's acquaintance Shevek could not recall having seen him smile.

Shevek sat down across the room, clearing a pile of papers off a bench to do so; the physics office was of course communal, but Sabul kept this back room of the two littered with materials he was using, so that there never seemed to be quite room for anyone else. Shevek looked down at the book he still held, then out the window. He felt, and looked, rather ill. He also looked tense; but with Sabul he had never been shy or awkward, as he often was with people whom he would have liked to know. "I didn't know you were translating it," he said.

"Translated it, edited it. Polished some of the rougher spots, filled in transitions you'd left out, and so forth. Couple of decads' work. You should be proud of it, your ideas to a large extent form the groundwork of the finished book."

It consisted entirely Shevek's and Atro's ideas.

"Yes," Shevek said. He looked down at his hands. Presently he said, "I'd like to publish the paper I wrote this quarter on Reversibility. It ought to go to Atro. It would interest him. He's still hung up on causation."

"Publish it? Where?"

"In Iotic, I meant—on Urras. Send it to Atro, like this last one, and he'll put it in one of the journals there."

"You can't give them a work to publish that hasn't been printed here."

"But that's what we did with this one. All this, except my rebuttal, came out in the *Ieu Eun Review*—before this came out here."

"I couldn't prevent that, but why do you think I hurried this into print? You don't think everybody in PDC approves of our trading ideas with Urras like this, do you? Defense insists that every word that leaves here on those freighters be passed by a PDC-approved expert. And on top of that, do you think all the provincial physicists who don't get in on this pipeline to Urras don't begrudge our using it? Think they aren't envious? There are people lying in wait, lying in wait for us to make a false step. If we're ever caught doing it, we'll lose that mail slot on the Urrasti freighters. You see the picture now?"

"How did the Institute get that mail slot in the first place?"

"Pegvur's election to the PDC, ten years ago." Pegvur had been a physicist of moderate distinction. "I've trod damned carefully to keep it, ever since. See?"

Shevek nodded.

"In any case, Atro doesn't want to read that stuff of yours. I looked that paper over and gave it back to you decads ago. When are you going to stop wasting time on these reactionary theories Gvarab clings to? Can't you see she's wasted her whole life on 'em? If you keep at it, you're going to make a fool of yourself. Which, of course, is your inalienable right. But you're not going to make a fool of *me*."

93

"What if I submit the paper for publication here, in Pravic, then?"

"Waste of time."

Shevek absorbed this with a slight nod. He got up, lanky and angular, and stood a moment, remote among his thoughts. The winter light lay harsh on his hair, which he now wore pulled back in a queue, and his still face. He came to the desk and took a copy off the little stack of new books. "I'd like to send one of these to Mitis," he said.

"Take all you want. Listen. If you think you know what you're doing better than I do, then submit that paper to the Press. You don't need permission! This isn't some kind of hierarchy, you know! I can't stop you. All I can do is give you my advice."

"You're the Press Syndicate's consultant on manuscripts in physics," Shevek said. "I thought I'd save time for everyone by asking you now."

His gentleness was uncompromising; because he would not compete for dominance, he was indomitable.

"Save time, what do you mean?" Sabul growled, but Sabul was also an Odonian: he writhed as if physically tormented by his own hypocrisy, turned away from Shevek, turned back to him, and said spitefully, his voice thick with anger, "Go ahead! Submit the damned thing! I'll declare myself incompetent to give counsel on it. I'll tell them to consult Gvarab. She's the Simultaneity expert, not I. The mystical gagaist! The universe as a giant harp-string, oscillating in and out of existence! What note does it play, by the way? Passages from the Numerical Harmonies, I suppose? The fact is that I am incompetent— in other words, unwilling—to counsel PDC or the Press on intellectual excrement!"

"The work I've done for you," Shevek said, "is part of the work I've done following Gvarab's ideas in Simultaneity. If you want one, you'll have to stand the other. Grain grows best in shit, as we say in Northsetting."

He stood a moment, and getting no verbal reply from Sabul, said goodbye and left.

He knew he had won a battle, and easily, without apparent violence. But violence had been done.

As Mitis had predicted, he was "Sabul's man." Sabul had ceased to be a functioning physicist years ago; his high reputation was built on expropriations from other minds. Shevek was to do the thinking, and Sabul would take the credit.

Obviously an ethically intolerable situation, which Shevek would denounce and relinquish. Only he would not. He needed Sabul. He wanted to publish what he wrote and to send it to the men who could understand it, the Urrasti physicists; he needed their ideas, their criticism, their collaboration.

So they had bargained, he and Sabul, bargained like profiteers. It had not been a battle, but a sale. You give me this and I'll give you that. Refuse me and I'll refuse you. Sold? Sold! Shevek's career, like the existence of his society, depended on the continuance of a fundamental, unadmitted profit contract. Not a relationship of mutual aid and solidarity, but an exploitative relationship; not organic, but mechanical. Can true function arise from basic dysfunction?

But all I want to do is get the job done, Shevek pleaded in his mind, as he walked across the mall towards the domicile quadrangle in the grey, windy afternoon. It's my duty, it's my joy, it's the purpose of my whole life. The man I have to work with is competitive, a dominance-seeker, a profiteer, but I can't change that; if I want to work, have to work with him.

He thought about Mitis and her warning. He thought about the Northsetting Institute and the party the night before he left. It seemed very long ago now, and so childishly peaceful and secure that he could have wept in nostalgia. As he passed under the porch of the Life Sciences Building a girl passing looked sidelong at him, and he thought that she looked like that girl—what was her name?—the one with short hair, who had eaten so many fried cakes the night of the party. He stopped and turned, but the girl was gone around the corner. Anyhow she had had long hair. Gone, gone, everything gone. He came out from the shelter of the porch into the wind. There was a fine rain on the wind, sparse. Rain was sparse when it fell at all. This was a dry world. Dry, pale, inimical. "Inimical!" Shevek said out loud in Iotic. He had never heard the language spoken; it sounded very strange. The rain stung his face like thrown gravel. It was an inimical rain. His sore throat had been joined by a terrific headache, of which he had only just become aware. He got to Room 46 and lay down on the bed platform, which seemed to be much farther down than usual. He shook, and could not stop shaking. He pulled the orange blanket up around him and huddled up, trying to sleep, but he could not stop shaking, because he was under constant atomic bombardment from all sides, increasing as the temperature increased.

He had never been ill, and never known any physical discomfort worse than tiredness. Having no idea what a high fever was like, he thought, during the lucid intervals of that long night, that he was going insane. Fear of madness drove him to seek help when day came. He was too frightened of himself to ask help from his neighbors on the corridor: he had heard himself raving in the night. He dragged himself to the local clinic, eight blocks away, the cold streets bright with sunrise spinning solemnly about him. At the clinic they diagnosed his insanity as a light pneumonia and told him to go to bed in Ward Two. He protested. The aide accused him of egoizing and explained that if he went home a physician would have to go to the trouble of calling on him there and arranging private care for him. He went to bed in Ward Two. All the other people in the ward were old. An aide came and offered him a glass of water and a pill. "What is it?" Shevek asked suspiciously. His teeth were chattering again.

"Antipyretic."

"What's that?"

"Bring down the fever."

"I don't need it."

The aide shrugged. "All right," she said, and went on.

Most young Anarresti felt that it was shameful to be ill: a result of their society's very successful prophylaxy, and also perhaps a confusion arising from the analogic use of the words "healthy" and "sick." They felt illness to be a crime, if an involuntary one. To yield to the criminal impulse, to pander to it by taking pain relievers, was immoral. They fought shy of pills and shots. As middle age and old age came on, most of them changed their view. The pain got worse than the shame. The aide gave the old men in Ward Two their medicine, and they joked with her. Shevek watched with dull incomprehension.

Later on there was a doctor with an injection needle.

"I don't want it," Shevek said. "Stop egoizing," the doctor said. "Roll over." Shevek obeyed.

Later on there was a woman who held a cup of water for him, but he shook so much that the water was spilt, wetting the blanket. "Let me alone," he said. "Who are you?" She told him, but he did not understand. He told her to go away, he felt very well. Then he explained to her why the cyclic hypothesis, though unproductive in itself, was essential to his approach to a possible theory of Simultaneity, a cornerstone. He spoke partly in his own language and partly in Iotic, and wrote the formulas and equations on a slate with a piece of chalk so that she and the rest of the group would understand, as he was afraid they would misunderstand about the cornerstone. She touched his face and tied his hair back for him. Her hands were cool. He had never felt anything pleasanter in all his life than the touch of her hands. He reached out for her hand. She was not there, she had gone.

A long time later, he was awake. He could breathe. He was perfectly well. Everything was all right. He felt disinclined to move. To move would disturb the perfect, stable moment, the balance of the world. The winter light along the ceiling was beautiful beyond expression. He lay and watched it. The old men down the ward were laughing together, old husky cackling laughs, a beautiful sound. The woman came in and sat down by his cot. He looked at her and smiled.

"How do you feel?"

"Newborn. Who are you?"

She also smiled. "The mother."

"Rebirth. But I'm supposed to get a new body, not the same old one."

"What on earth are you talking about?"

"Nothing on earth. On Urras. Rebirth is part of their religion."

"You're still lightheaded." She touched his forehead. "No fever." Her voice in saying those two words touched and struck something very deep in Shevek's being, a dark place, a place walled in, where it reverberated back and back in the darkness. He looked at the woman and said with terror, "You are Rulag."

"I told you I was. Several times!"

She maintained an expression of unconcern, even of

97

humor. There was no question of Shevek's maintaining anything. He had no strength to move, but he shrank away from her in unconcealed fear, as if she were not his mother, but his death. If she noticed this weak movement, she gave no sign.

She was a handsome woman, dark, with fine and well-proportioned features showing no lines of age, though she must be over forty. Everything about her person was harmonious and controlled. Her voice was low, pleasant in timbre. "I didn't know you were here in Abbenay," she said, "or where you were—or even whether you were. I was in the Press depot looking through new publications, picking things up for the Engineering library, and I saw a book by Sabul and Shevek. Sabul I knew, of course. But who's Shevek? Why does it sound so familiar? I didn't arrive at it for a minute or more. Strange, isn't it? But it didn't seem reasonable. The Shevek I knew would be only twenty, not likely to be co-authoring treatises in metacosmology with Sabul. But any other Shevek would have to be even younger than twenty! . . . So I came to see. A boy in the domicile said you were here. . . . This is a shockingly understaffed clinic. I don't understand why the syndics don't request some more postings from the Medical Federation, or else cut down the number of admissions; some of these aides and doctors are working eight hours a day! Of course, there are people in the medical arts who actually want that: the self-sacrifice impulse. Unfortunately it doesn't lead to meximum efficiency. . . . It was strange to find you. I would never have known you. . . . Are you and Palat in touch? How is he?"

"He's dead."

"Ah." There was no pretense of shock or grief in Rulag's voice, only a kind of dreary accustomedness, a bleak note. Shevek was moved by it, enabled to see her, for a moment, as a person.

"How long ago did he die?"

"Eight years."

"He couldn't have been more than thirty-five."

"There was an earthquake in Wide Plains. We'd been living there about five years, he was construction engineer for the community. The quake damaged the learning center. He was with the others trying to get out some of the children who were trapped inside. There was a second quake and the whole thing went down. There were thirty-two people killed."

"Were you there?"

"I'd gone to start training at the Regional Institute about ten days before the quake."

She mused, her face smooth and still. "Poor Palat. Somehow it's like him—to have died with others, a statistic, one of thirty-two. . . ."

"The statistics would have been higher if he hadn't gone into the building," Shevek said.

She looked at him then. Her gaze did not show what emotions she felt or did not feel. What she said might be spontaneous or deliberate, there was no way to tell. "You were fond of Palat."

He did not answer.

"You don't look like him. In fact you look like me, except in coloring. I thought you'd look like Palat. I assumed it. It's strange how one's imagination makes these assumptions. He stayed with you, then?"

Shevek nodded.

"He was lucky." She did not sigh, but a suppressed sigh was in her voice.

"So was I."

There was a pause. She smiled faintly. "Yes. I could have kept in touch with you. Do you hold it against me, my not having done so?"

"Hold it against you? I never knew you."

"You did. Palat and I kept you with us in the domicile, even after you were weaned. We both wanted to. Those first years are when the individual contact is essential; the psychologists have proved it conclusively. Full socialization can be developed only from that affectional beginning. . . . I was willing to continue the partnership. I tried to have Palat posted here to Abbenay. There never was an opening in his line of work, and he wouldn't come without a posting. He had a stubborn streak. . . . At first he wrote sometimes to tell me how you were, then he stopped writing."

"It doesn't matter," the young man said. His face, thin from illness, was covered with very fine drops of sweat, making his cheeks and forehead look silvery, as if oiled.

There was silence again, and Rulag said in her controlled, pleasant voice, "Well, yes; it mattered, and it still matters. But Palat was the one to stay with you and see you through your integrative years. He was supportive, he was parental, as I am not. The work comes first, with me. It has always come first. Still, I'm glad you're here now, Shevek. Perhaps I can be of some use to you, now. I know Abbenay is a forbidding place at first. One feels lost, isolated, lacking the simple solidarity the little towns have. I know interesting people, whom you might like to meet. And people who might be useful to you. I know Sabul; I have some notion of what you may have come up against, with him, and with the whole Institute. They play dominance games there. It takes some experience to know how to outplay them. In any case, I'm glad you're here. It gives me a pleasure I never looked for—a kind of joy. . . . I read your book. It is yours, isn't it? Why else would Sabul be co-publishing with a twenty-year-old student? The subject's beyond me, I'm only an engineer. I confess to being proud of you. That's strange, isn't it? Unreasonable. Propertarian, even. As if you were something that belonged to me! But as one gets older one needs certain reassurances that aren't, always, entirely reasonable. In order to go on at all."

He saw her loneliness. He saw her pain, and resented it. It threatened him. It threatened his father's loyalty, that clear constant love in which his life had taken root. What right had she, who had left Palat in need, to come in her need to Palat's son? He had nothing, nothing to give her, or anyone. "It might have been better," he said, "if you'd gone on thinking of me as a statistic too."

"Ah," she said, the soft, habitual, desolate response. She looked away from him.

The old men down at the end of the ward were admiring her, nudging each other.

"I suppose," she said, "that I was trying to make a claim on you. But I thought in terms of your making a claim on me. If you wanted to."

He said nothing.

"We aren't, except biologically, mother and son, of course." She had regained her faint smile. "You don't remember me, and the baby I remember isn't this man of twenty. All that is time past, irrelevant. But we are brother and sister, here and now. Which is what really matters, isn't it?"

"I don't know."

She sat without speaking for a minute, then stood up. "You need to rest. You were quite ill the first time I came. They say you'll be quite all right now. I don't suppose I'll be back."

He did not speak. She said, "Goodbye, Shevek," and turned from him as she spoke. He had either a glimpse or a nightmare imagination of her face changing drastically as she spoke, breaking down, going all to pieces. It must have been imagination. She walked out of the ward with the graceful measured gait of a handsome woman, and he saw her stop and speak, smiling, to the aide out in the hall.

He gave way to the fear that had come with her, the sense of the breaking of promises, the incoherence of time. He broke. He began to cry, trying to hide his face in the shelter of his arms, for he could not find the strength to turn over. One of the old men, the sick old men, came and sat on the side of the cot and patted his shoulder. "It's all right, brother. It'll be all right, little brother," he muttered. Shevek heard him and felt his touch, but took no comfort in it. Even from the brother there is no comfort in the bad hour, in the dark at the foot of the wall.

Chapter 5

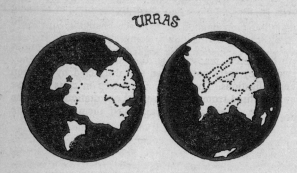

Shevek ended his career as a tourist with relief. The new term was opening at Ieu Eun; now he could settle down to live, and work, in Paradise, instead of merely looking at it from outside.

He took on two seminars and an open lecture course. No teaching was requested of him, but he had asked if he could teach, and the administrators had arranged the seminars. The open class was neither his idea nor theirs. A delegation of students came and asked him to give it. He consented at once. This was how courses were organized in Anarresti learning centers: by student demand, or on the teacher's initiative, or by students and teachers together. When he found that the administrators were upset, he laughed. "Do they expect students not to be anarchists?" he said. "What else can the young be? When you are on the bottom, you must organize from the bottom up!" He had no intention of being administered out of the course—he had fought this kind of battle before—and because he communicated his firmness to the students, they held firm. To avoid unpleasant publicity the Rectors of the University gave in, and Shevek began his course to a first-day audience of two thousand. Attendance soon dropped. He stuck to physics, never going off into the personal or the political, and it was physics on a pretty advanced level. But several hundred students continued to come. Some came out of mere curiosity, to see the man from the Moon; others were drawn by Shevek's personality, by the glimpses of the man and the libertarian which they could catch from his words even when they could not follow his mathematics. And a surprising number of them were capable of following both the philosophy and the mathematics.

They were superbly trained, these students. Their minds were fine, keen, ready. When they weren't working, they rested. They were not blunted and distracted by a dozen other obligations. They never fell asleep in class because they were tired from having worked on rotational duty the day before. Their society maintained them in complete freedom from want, distraction, and cares.

What they were free to do, however, was another question. It appeared to Shevek that their freedom from obligation was in exact proportion to their lack of freedom of initiative.

He was appalled by the examination system, when it was explained to him; he could not imagine a greater deterrent to the natural wish to learn than this pattern of cramming in information and disgorging it at demand. At first he refused to give any tests or grades, but this upset the University administrators so badly that, not wishing to be discourteous to his hosts, he gave in. He asked his students to write a paper on any problem in physics that interested them, and told them that he would give them all the highest mark, so that the bureaucrats would have something to write on their forms and lists. To his surprise a good many students came to him to complain. They wanted him to set the problems, to ask the right questions; they did not want to think about questions, but to write down the answers they had learned. And some of them objected strongly to his giving everyone the same mark. How could the diligent students be distinguished from the dull ones? What was the good in working hard? If no competitive distinctions were to be made, one might as well do nothing.

"Well, of course," Shevek said, troubled. "If you do not want to do the work, you should not do it."

They went away unappeased, but polite. They were

103

pleasant boys, with frank and civil manners. Shevek's readings in Urrasti history led him to decide that they were, in fact, though the word was seldom used these days, aristocrats. In feudal times the aristocracy had sent their sons to university, conferring superiority on the institution. Nowadays it was the other way round: the university conferred superiority on the man. They told Shevek with pride that the competition for scholarships to Ieu Eun was stiffer every year, proving the essential democracy of the institution. He said, "You put another lock on the door and call it democracy." He liked his polite, intelligent students, but he felt no great warmth towards any of them. They were planning careers as academic or industrial scientists, and what they learned from him was to them a means to that end, success in their careers. They either had, or denied the importance of, anything else he might have offered them.

He found himself, therefore, with no duties at all beyond the preparation of his three classes; the rest of his time was all his own. He had not been in a situation like this since his early twenties, his first years at the Institute in Abbenay. Since those years his social and personal life had got more and more complicated and demanding. He had been not only a physicist but also a partner, a father, an Odonian, and finally a social reformer. As such, he had not been sheltered, and had expected no shelter, from whatever cares and responsibilities came to him. He had not been free from anything: only free to do anything. Here, it was the other way around. Like all the students and professors, he had nothing to do but his intellectual work, literally nothing. The beds were made for them, the rooms were swept for them, the routine of the college was managed for them, the way was made plain for them. And no wives, no families. No women at all. Students at the University were not permitted to marry. Married professors usually lived during the five class days of the seven-day week in bachelor quarters on campus, going home only on weekends. Nothing distracted. Complete leisure to work; all materials at hand; intellectual stimulation, argument, conversation whenever wanted; no pressures. Paradise indeed! But he seemed unable to get to work.

There was something lacking—in him, he thought, not in the place. He was not up to it. He was not strong enough to take what was so generously offered. He felt himself dry and arid, like a desert plant, in this beautiful oasis. Life on Anarres had sealed him, closed off his soul; the waters of life welled all around him, and yet he could not drink.

He forced himself to work, but even there he found no certainty. He seemed to have lost the flair which, in his own estimation of himself, he counted as his main advantage over most other physicists, the sense for where the really important problem lay, the clue that led inward to the center. Here, he seemed to have no sense of direction. He worked at the Light Research Laboratories, read a great deal, and wrote three papers that summer and autumn: a productive half year, by normal standards. But he knew that in fact he had done nothing real.

Indeed the longer he lived on Urras, the less real it became to him. It seemed to be slipping out of his grasp—all that vital, magnificent, inexhaustible world which he had seen from the windows of his room, his first day on the world. It slipped out of his awkward, foreign hands, eluded him, and when he looked again he was holding something quite different, something he had not wanted at all, a kind of waste paper, wrappings, rubbish.

He got money for the papers he wrote. He already had in an account in the National Bank the 10,000 International Monetary Units of the Seo Oen award, and a grant of 5,000 from the Ioti Government. That sum was now augmented by his salary as a professor and the money paid him by the University Press for the three monographs. At first all this seemed funny to him; then it made him uneasy. He must not dismiss as ridiculous what was, after all, of tremendous importance here. He tried to read an elementary economics text; it bored him past endurance, it was like listening to somebody interminably recounting a long and stupid dream. He could not force himself to understand how banks functioned and so forth, because all the operations of capitalism were as meaningless to him as the rites of a primitive religion, as barbaric, as elaborate, and as unnecessary. In a human sacrifice to deity there might be at least a mistaken and terrible beauty; in the rites of the moneychangers, where greed, laziness, and envy were assumed to move all men's acts, even the terrible became banal. Shevek looked at this monstrous pettiness with contempt, and without interest. He did not admit, he could not admit, that in fact it frightened him.

Saio Pae had taken him "shopping" during his second week in A-Io. Though he did not consider cutting his hair—his hair, after all, was part of him—he wanted an Urrasti-style suit of clothes and pair of shoes. He had no desire to look any more foreign than he could help looking. The simplicity of his old suit made it positively ostentatious, and his soft, crude desert boots appeared very odd indeed among the Iotis' fanciful footgear. So at his request Pae had taken him to Saemtenevia Prospect, the elegant retail street of Nio Esseia, to be fitted by a tailor and a shoemaker.

The whole experience had been so bewildering to him that he put it out of mind as soon as possible, but he had dreams about it for months afterwards, nightmares. Saemtenevia Prospect was two miles long, and it was a solid mass of people, traffic, and things: things to buy, things for sale. Coats, dresses, gowns, robes, trousers, breeches, shirts, blouses, hats, shoes, stockings, scarves, shawls, vests, capes, umbrellas, clothes to wear while sleeping, while swimming, while playing games, while at an afternoon party, while at an evening party, while at a party in the country, while traveling, while at the theater, while riding horses, gardening, receiving guests, boating, dining, hunting—all different, all in hundreds of different cuts, styles, colors, textures, materials. Perfumes, clocks, lamps, statues, cosmetics, candles, pictures, cameras, games, vases, sofas, kettles, puzzles, pillows, dolls, colanders, hassocks, jewels, carpets, toothpicks, calendars, a baby's teething rattle of platinum with a handle of rock crystal, an electrical machine to sharpen pencils, a wristwatch with diamond numerals; figurines and souvenirs and kickshaws and mementos and gewgaws and bric-a-brac, everything either useless to begin with or ornamented so as to disguise its use; acres of luxuries, acres of excrement. In the first block Shevek had stopped to look at a shaggy, spotted coat, the central display in a glittering window of clothes and jewelry. "The coat costs 8,400 units?" he asked in disbelief, for he had recently read in a newspaper that a "living wage" was about 2,000 units a year. "Oh, yes, that's real fur, quite rare now that the animals are protected," Pae had said. "Pretty thing, isn't it? Women love furs." And they went on. After one more block Shevek had felt utterly exhausted. He could not look any more. He wanted to hide his eyes.

And the strangest thing about the nightmare street was that none of the millions of things for sale were made there. They were only sold there. Where were the workshops, the factories, where were the farmers, the craftsmen, the miners, the weavers, the chemists, the carvers, the dyers, the designers, the machinists, where were the hands, the people who made? Out of sight, somewhere else. Behind walls. All the people in all the shops were either buyers or sellers. They had no relation to the things but that of possession.

He found that once they had his measure he could order anything else he might need by telephone, and he determined never to go back to the nightmare street.

The suit of clothes and the shoes were delivered in a week. He put them on and stood before the full-length mirror in his bedroom. The fitted grey coat-gown, white shirt, black breeches, and stockings and polished shoes were becoming to his long, thin figure and narrow feet. He touched the surface of one shoe gingerly. It was made of the same stuff that covered the chairs in the other room, the material that felt like skin; he had asked someone recently what it was, and had been told that it *was* skin—animal hide, leather, they called it. He scowled at the touch, straightened up, and turned away from the mirror, but not before he had been forced to see that, thus clothed, his resemblance to his mother Rulag was stronger than ever.

There was a long break between terms in midautumn. Most students went home for the holiday. Shevek went mountain-hiking in the Meiteis for a few days with a group of students and researchers from the Light Research Laboratory, then returned to claim some hours on the big computer, which was kept very busy during term. But, sick of work that got nowhere, he did not work hard. He slept more than usual, walked, read, and told himself that the trouble was he had simply been in too much of a hurry; you couldn't get hold of a whole new world in a few months. The lawns and groves of the University were beautiful and disheveled, gold leaves flaring and blowing on the rainy wind under a soft grey sky. Shevek looked up the works of the great Ioti poets and read them; he understood them now when they spoke of flowers, and birds flying, and the colors of forests in autumn. That understanding came as a great pleasure to him. It was pleasant to return at dusk to his room, whose calm beauty of proportion never failed to satisfy him. He was used to that grace and comfort now, it had become familiar to him. So had the faces at Evening Commons, the colleagues, some liked more and some less but all, by now, familiar. So had the food, in all its variety and quantity, which at first had staggered him. The men who waited tables knew his wants and served him as he would have served himself. He still did not eat meat; he had tried it, out of politeness and to prove to himself that he had no irrational prejudices, but his stomach had its reasons which reason does not know, and rebelled. After a couple of near disasters he had given up the attempt and remained a vegetarian, though a hearty one. He enjoyed dinner very much. He had gained three or four kilos since coming to Urras; he looked very well now, sunburnt from his mountain expedition, rested by the holiday. He was striking figure as he got up from table in the great dining hall, with its beamed ceiling far overhead in shadow, and its paneled, portrait-hung walls, and its tables bright with candle flames and porcelain and silver. He greeted someone at another table and moved on, with an expression of peaceable detachment. From across the room Chifoilisk saw him, and followed him, catching up at the door.

"Have you got a few minutes to spare, Shevek?"

"Yes. My rooms?" He was accustomed to the constant use of the possessive pronoun by now, and spoke it without self-consciousness.

Chifoilisk seemed to hesitate. "What about the library? It's on your way, and I want to pick up a book there."

They set off across the quadrangle to the Library of the Noble Science—the old term of physics, which even on Anarres was preserved in certain usages—walking side by side in the pattering dark. Chifoilisk put up an umbrella. but Shevek walked in rain as the Ioti walked in sunshine, with enjoyment.

"You're getting soaked," Chifoilisk grumbled. "Got a bad chest, haven't you? Ought to take care."

"I'm very well," Shevek said, and smiled as he strode through the fresh, fine rain. "That doctor from the Government, you know, he gave me some treatments, inhalations. It works; I don't cough. I asked the doctor to describe the process and the drugs, on the radio to the Syndicate of Initiative in Abbenay. He did so. He was glad to do so. It is simple enough; it may relieve much suffering from the dust cough. Why, why not earlier? Why do we not work together, Chifoilisk?"

The Thuvian gave a little sardonic grunt. They came into the reading room of the library. Aisles of old books, under delicate double arches of marble, stood in dim serenity; the lamps on the long reading tables were plain spheres of alabaster. No one else was there, but an attendant hastened in behind them to light the fire laid on the marble hearth and to make sure they wanted nothing before he withdrew again. Chifoilisk stood before the hearth, watching the kindling catch. His brows bristled over his small eyes; his coarse, swarthy, intellectual face looked older than usual.

"I want to be disagreeable, Shevek," he said in his hoarse voice. He added, "Nothing unusual in that, I suppose"—a humility Shevek had not looked for in him.

"What's the matter?"

"I want to know whether you know what you're doing here."

After a pause Shevek said, "I think I do."

"You are aware, then, that you've been bought?"

"Bought?"

"Call it co-opted, if you like. Listen. No matter how intelligent a man is, he can't see what he doesn't know how to see. How can you understand your situation, here, in a capitalist economy, a plutocratic-oligarchic State? How can you see it, coming from your little commune of starving idealists up there in the sky?"

"Chifoilisk, there aren't many idealists left on Anarres, I assure you. The Settlers were idealists, yes, to leave this world for our deserts. But that was seven generations ago! Our society is practical. Maybe too practical, too much concerned with survival only. What is idealistic about social cooperation, mutual aid, when it is the only means of staying alive?"

"I can't argue the values of Odonianism with you. Not

that I haven't wanted to! I do know something about it, you know. We're a lot closer to it, in my country, than these people are. We're products of the same great revolutionary movement of the eighth century—we're socialists, like you."

"But you are archists. The State of Thu is even more centralized than the State of A-Io. One power structure controls all, the government, administration, police, army, education, laws, trades, manufactures. And you have the money economy."

"A money economy based on the principle that each worker is paid as he deserves, for the value of his labor—not by capitalists whom he's forced to serve, but by the state of which he's a member!"

"Does he establish the value of his own labor?"

"Why don't you come to Thu and see how real socialism functions?"

"I know how real socialism functions," Shevek said. "I could tell you, but would your government let me explain it, in Thu?"

Chifoilisk kicked a log that had not yet caught. His expression as he stared down into the fire was bitter, the lines between the nose and the corners of his lips cut deep. He did not answer Shevek's question. He said at last, "I'm not going to try to play games with you. It's no good; anyhow I won't do it. What I have to ask you is this: would you be willing to come to Thu?"

"Not now, Chifoilisk."

"But what can you accomplish—here?"

"My work. And also, here I am near the seat of the Council of World Governments—"

"The CWG? They've been in A-Io's pocket for thirty years. Don't look to them to save you!"

A pause. "Am I in danger, then?"

"You didn't realize even that?"

Another pause.

"Against whom do you warn me?" Shevek asked.

"Against Pae, in the first place."

"Oh, yes, Pae." Shevek leaned his hands against the ornate, gold-inlaid mantelpiece. "Pae is a pretty good physicist. And very obliging. But I don't trust him."

"Why not?"

"Well . . . he evades."

110

"Yes. An acute psychological judgment. But Pae isn't dangerous to you because he's personally slippery, Shevek. He's dangerous to you because he is a loyal, ambitious agent of the Ioti Government. He reports on you, and on me, regularly to the Department of National Security—the secret police. I don't underestimate you, God knows, but don't you see, your habit of approaching, everybody as a person, an individual, won't do here, it won't work. You have got to understand the powers behind the individuals."

While Chifoilisk spoke, Shevek's relaxed posture had stiffened; he now stood straight, like Chifoilisk, looking down at the fire. He said, "How do you know that about Pae?"

"By the same means I know that your room contains a concealed microphone, just as mine does. Because it's my business to know it."

"Are you also an agent of your government?"

Chifoilisk's face closed down; then he turned suddenly to Shevek, speaking softly and with hatred. "Yes," he said, "of course I am. If I weren't I wouldn't be here. Everyone knows that. My government sends abroad only men whom it can trust. And they can trust me! Because I haven't been bought, like all these damned rich Ioti professors. I believe in my government, in my country. I have faith in them." He forced his words out in a kind of torment. "You've got to look around you, Shevek! You're a child among thieves. They're good to you, they give you a nice room, lectures, students, money, tours of castles, tours of model factories, visits to pretty villages. All the best. All lovely, fine! But why? Why do they bring you here from the Moon, praise you, print your books, keep you so safe and snug in the lecture rooms and laboratories and libraries? Do you think they do it out of scientific disinterest, out of brotherly love? This is a profit economy, Shevek!"

"I know. I came to bargain with it."

"Bargain—what? For what?"

Shevek's face had taken on the cold, grave look it had worn when he left the Fort in Drio. "You know what I want, Chifoilisk. I want my people to come out of exile. I came here because I don't think you want that, in Thu. You are afraid of us, there. You fear we might bring

111

back the revolution, the old one, the real one, the revolution for justice which you began and then stopped halfway. Here in A-Io they fear me less because they have forgotten the revolution. They don't believe in it any more. They think if people can possess enough things they will be content to live in prison. But I will not believe that. I want the walls down. I want solidarity, human solidarity. I want free exchange between Urras and Anarres. I worked for it as I could on Anarres, now I work for it as I can on Urras. There, I acted. Here, I bargain."

"With what?"

"Oh, you know, Chifoilisk," Shevek said in a low voice, with diffidence. "You know what it is they want from me."

"Yes, I know, but I didn't know you did," the Thuvian said, also speaking low; his harsh voice became a harsher murmur, all breath and fricatives. "You've got it, then—the General Temporal Theory?"

Shevek looked at him, perhaps with a touch of irony.

Chifoilisk insisted: "Does it exist in writing?"

Shevek continued to look at him for a minute, and then answered directly, "No."

"Good!"

"Why?"

"Because if it did, they'd have it."

"What do you mean?"

"Just that. Listen, wasn't it Odo who said that where there's property there's theft?"

" 'To make a thief, make an owner; to create crime, create laws.' *The Social Organism*."

"All right. Where there are papers in locked rooms, there are people with keys to the rooms!"

Shevek winced. "Yes," he said presently, "this is very disagreeable."

"To you. Not to me. I haven't your individualistic moral scruples, you know. I knew you didn't have the Theory down in writing. If I'd thought you had, I would have made every effort to get it from you, by persuasion, by theft, by force if I thought we could abduct you without bringing on a war with A-Io. Anything, so that I could get it away from these fat Ioti capitalists and into the hands of the Central Presidium of my country. Because the highest cause I can ever serve is the strength and welfare of my country."

112

"You are lying," Shevek said peaceably. "I think you are a patriot, yes. But you set above patriotism your respect for the truth, scientific truth, and perhaps also your loyalty to individual persons. You would not betray me."

"I would if I could," Chifoilisk said savagely. He started to go on, stopped, and finally said with angry resignation, "Think as you please. I can't open your eyes for you. But remember, we want you. If you finally see what's going on here, then come to Thu. You picked the wrong people to try to make brothers of! And if—I have no business saying this. But it doesn't matter. If you won't come to us in Thu, at least don't give your Theory to the Ioti. Don't give the usurers anything! Get out. Go home. Give your own people what you have to give!"

"They don't want it," Shevek said, expressionless. "Do you think I did not try?"

Four or five days later Shevek, asking after Chifoilisk, was informed that he had gone back to Thu.

"To stay? He didn't tell me he was leaving."

"A Thuvian never knows when he's going to get an order from his Presidium," Pae said, for of course it was Pae who told Shevek. "He just knows that when it comes he'd better hop. And not stop for any leavetakings on the way. Poor old Chif! I wonder what he did wrong?"

Shevek went once or twice a week to see Atro in the pleasant little house on the edge of the campus where he lived with a couple of servants, as old as himself, to look after him. At nearly eighty he was, as he put it himself, a monument to a first-class physicist. Though he had not seen his life work go unrecognized as Gvarab had, through sheer age he had attained something of her disinterestedness. His interest in Shevek, at least, appeared to be entirely personal—a comradeship. He had been the first Sequency physicist to be converted to Shevek's approach to the understanding of time. He had fought, with Shevek's weapons, for Shevek's theories, against the whole establishment of scientific respectability, and the battle had gone on for several years before the publication of the uncut *Principles of Simultaneity* and the promptly ensuing victory of the Simultaneists. That battle had been the high point of Atro's life. He would not have fought for less than the truth, but it was the fighting he had loved, better than the truth.

Atro could trace his genealogy back for eleven hundred years, through generals, princes, great landowners. The family still owned an estate of seven thousand acres and fourteen villages in Sie Province, the most rural region of A-Io. He had provincial turns of speech, archaisms to which he clung with pride. Wealth impressed him not at all, and he referred to the entire government of his country as "demagogues and crawling politicians." His respect was not to be bought. Yet he gave it, freely, to any fool with what he called "the right name." In some ways he was totally incomprehensible to Shevek—an enigma: the aristocrat. And yet his genuine contempt for both money and power made Shevek feel closer to him than to anyone else he had met on Urras.

Once, as they sat together on the glassed-in porch where he raised all kinds of rare and out-of-season flowers, he chanced to use the phrase, "we Cetians." Shevek caught him up on it: " 'Cetians'—isn't that a birdseed word?" "Birdseed" was slang for the popular press, the newspapers, broadcasts, and fiction manufactured for the urban working people.

"Birdseed!" Atro repeated. "My dear fellow, where the devil do you pick up these vulgarisms? I mean by 'Cetians' precisely what the daily-paper writers and their lip-moving readers understand by the term. Urras and Anarres!"

"I was surprised that you used a foreign word—a non-Cetian word, in fact."

"Definition by exclusion," the old man parried gleefully. "A hundred years ago we didn't need the word. 'Mankind' would do. But sixty-some years ago that changed. I was seventeen, it was a nice sunny day in early summer, I remember it quite vividly. I was exercising my horse, and my elder sister called out the window, 'They're talking to somebody from Outer Space on the radio!' My poor dear mother thought we were all doomed; foreign devils, you know. But it was only the Hainish, quacking about peace and brotherhood. Well, nowadays 'mankind' is a bit over-inclusive. What defines brotherhood but nonbrotherhood? Definition by exclusion, my dear! You and I are kinsmen. Your people were probably herding goats in the moun-

114

tains while mine were oppressing serfs in Sie, a few centuries ago; but we're members of the same family. To know it, one only has to meet—to hear of—an alien. A being from another solar system. A man, so-called, who has nothing in common with us except the practical arrangement of two legs, two arms, and a head with some kind of brain in it!"

"But haven't the Hainish proved that we are—"

"All of alien origin, offspring of Hainish interstellar colonists, half a million years ago, or a million, or two or three million, yes, I know. Proved! By the Primal Number, Shevek, you sound like a first-year seminarian! How can you speak seriously of historical proof, over such a span of time? Those Hainish toss millennia about like handballs, but it's all juggling. Proof, indeed! The religion of my fathers informs me, with equal authority, that I'm a descendant of Pinra Od, whom God exiled from the Garden because he had the audacity to count his fingers and toes, add them up to twenty, and thus let Time loose upon the universe. I prefer that story to the aliens', if I must choose!"

Shevek laughed; Atro's humors gave him pleasure. But the old man was serious. He tapped Shevek on the arm, and, twitching his eyebrows and munching with his lips as he did when he was moved, said, "I hope you feel the same, my dear. I earnestly hope it. There's a great deal that's admirable, I'm sure, in your society, but it doesn't teach you to discriminate—which is after all the best thing civilization teaches. I don't want those damned aliens getting at you through your notions about brotherhood and mutualism and all that. They'll spout you whole rivers of 'common humanity' and 'leagues of all the worlds' and so on, and I'd hate to see you swallow it. The law of existence is struggle—competition—elimination of the weak —a ruthless war for survival. And I want to see the best survive. The kind of humanity I know. The Cetians. You and I: Urras and Anarres. We're ahead of them now, all those Hainish and Terrans and whatever else they call themselves, and we've got to stay ahead of them. They brought us the interstellar drive, but we're making better interstellar ships now than they are. When you come to release your theory, I earnestly hope you'll think of your duty to your own people, your own kind. Of what loyalty

115

means, and to whom it's due." The easy tears of old age had sprung into Atro's half-blind eyes. Shevek put his hand on the old man's arm, reassuring, but he said nothing.

"They'll get it, of course. Eventually. And they ought to. Scientific truth will out, you can't hide the sun under a stone. But before they get it, I want them to pay for it! I want us to take our rightful place. I want respect: and that's what you can win us. Transilience—if we've mastered transilience, their interstellar drive won't amount to a hill of beans. It's not money I want, you know. I want the superiority of Cetian science recognized, the superiority of the Cetian mind. If there has to be an interstellar civilization, then by God I don't want my people to be low-caste members of it! We should come in like noblemen, with a great gift in our hands—that's how it should be. Well, well, I get hot about it sometimes. By the way, how's it going, your book?"

"I've been working on Skask's gravitational hypothesis. I have a feeling he's wrong in using partial differential equations only."

"But your last paper was on gravity. When are you going to get to the real thing?"

"You know that the means are the end, to us Odonians," Shevek said lightly. "Besides, I can't very well present a theory of time that omits gravity, can I?"

"You mean you're giving it to us in bits and dribbles?" Atro asked, suspiciously. "That hadn't occurred to me. I'd better look over that last paper. Some of it didn't make much sense to me. My eyes get so tired these days. I think that damnable magnifier-projector-thingy I have to use for reading has something wrong with it. It doesn't seem to project the words clearly any more."

Shevek looked at the old man with compunction and affection, but he did not tell him any more about the state of his theory.

Invitations to receptions, dedications, openings, and so forth were delivered to Shevek daily. He went to some, because he had come to Urras on a mission and must try to fulfill it: he must urge the idea of brotherhood, he must represent, in his own person, the solidarity of the Two

Worlds. He spoke, and people listened to him and said, "How true."

He wondered why the government did not stop him from speaking. Chifoilisk must have exaggerated, for his own purposes, the extent of the control and censorship they could exert. He talked pure anarchism, and they did not stop him. But did they need to stop him? It seemed that he talked to the same people every time: well dressed, well fed, well mannered, smiling. Were they the only kind of people on Urras? "It is pain that brings men together," Shevek said standing up before them, and they nodded and said, "How true."

He began to hate them and, realizing that, abruptly ceased accepting their invitations.

But to do so was to accept failure and to increase his isolation. He wasn't doing what he had come here to do. It was not that they cut him off, he told himself; it was that—as always—he had cut himself off from them. He was lonely, stiflingly lonely, among all the people he saw every day. The trouble was that he was not *in touch*. He felt that he had not touched anything, anyone, on Urras in all these months.

In the Senior Commons at table one night he said, "You know, I don't know how you live, here. I see the private houses, from the outside. But from the inside I know only your not-private life—meeting rooms, refectories, laboratories. . . ."

The next day Oiie rather stiffly asked Shevek if he would come to dinner and stay overnight, the next weekend, at Oiie's home.

It was in Amoeno, a village a few miles from Ieu Eun, and it was by Urrasti standards a modest middle-class house, older than most, perhaps. It had been built about three hundred years ago, of stone, with wood-paneled rooms. The characteristic Ioti double arch was used in window frames and doorways. A relative absence of furniture pleased Shevek's eye at once: the rooms looked austere, spacious, with their expanses of deeply polished floor. He had always felt uneasy amidst the extravagant decorations and conveniences of the public buildings in which the receptions, dedications, and so forth were held. The Urrasti had taste, but it seemed often to be in conflict with an impulse toward display—conspicuous ex-

117

pense. The natural, aesthetic origin of the desire to own things was concealed and perverted by economic and competitive compulsions, which in turn told on the quality of the things: all they achieved was a kind of mechanical lavishness. Here, instead, was grace, achieved through restraint.

A serving man took their coats at the door. Oiie's wife came up to greet Shevek from the basement kitchen, where she had been instructing the cook.

As they talked before dinner, Shevek found himself speaking to her almost exclusively, with a friendliness, a wish to make her like him, that surprised himself. But it was so good to be talking with a woman again! No wonder he had felt his existence to be cut off, artificial, among men, always men, lacking the tension and attraction of the sexual difference. And Sewa Oiie was attractive. Looking at the delicate lines of her nape and temples he lost his objections to the Urrasti fashion of shaving women's heads. She was reticent, rather timid; he tried to make her feel at ease with him, and was very pleased when he seemed to be succeeding.

They went in to dinner and were joined at the table by two children. Sewa Oiie apologized: "One simply can't find a decent nursemaid in this part of the country any more," she said. Shevek assented, without knowing what a nursemaid was. He was watching the little boys, with the same relief, the same delight. He had scarcely seen a child since he left Anarres.

They were very clean, sedate children, speaking when spoken to, dressed in blue velvet coats and breeches. They eyed Shevek with awe, as a creature from Outer Space. The nine-year-old was severe with the seven-year-old, muttering at him not to stare, pinching him savagely when he disobeyed. The little one pinched back and tried to kick him under the table. The Principle of Superiority did not seem to be well established in his mind yet.

Oiie was a changed man at home. The secretive look left his face, and he did not drawl when he spoke. His family treated him with respect, but there was mutuality in the respect. Shevek had heard a good deal of Oiie's views on women, and was surprised to see that he treated his wife with courtesy, even delicacy. "This is chivalry," Shevek thought, having recently learned the word, but he soon decided it was something better than that. Oiie was fond of his wife and trusted her. He behaved to her and to his children very much as an Anarresti might. In fact, at home, he suddenly appeared as a simple, brotherly kind of man, a free man.

It seemed to Shevek a very small range of freedom, a very narrow family, but he felt so much at ease, so much freer himself, that he was disinclined to criticize.

In a pause after conversation, the younger boy said in his small, clear voice, "Mr. Shevek doesn't have very good manners."

"Why not?" Shevek asked before Oiie's wife could reprove the child. "What did I do?"

"You didn't say thank you."

"For what?"

"When I passed you the dish of pickles."

"Ini! Be quiet!"

Sadik! Don't egoize! The tone was precisely the same.

"I thought you were sharing them with me. Were they a gift? We say thank you only for gifts, in my country. We share other things without talking about it, you see. Would you like the pickles back again?"

"No, I don't like them," the child said, looking up with dark, very clear eyes into Shevek's face.

"That makes it particularly easy to share them," Shevek said. The older boy was writhing with the suppressed desire to pinch Ini, but Ini laughed, showing his little white teeth. After a while in another pause he said in a low voice, leaning towards Shevek, "Would you like to see my otter?"

"Yes."

"He's in the back garden. Mother put him out because she thought he might bother you. Some grownups don't like animals."

"I like to see them. We have no animals in my country."

"You don't?" said the older boy, staring. "Father! Mr. Shevek says they don't have any animals!"

Ini also stared. "But what do you have?"

"Other people. Fish. Worms. And holum trees."

"What are holum trees?"

The conversation went on for half an hour. It was the first time Shevek had been asked, on Urras, to describe

119

Anarres. The children asked the questions, but the parents listened with interest. Shevek kept out of the ethical mode with some scrupulousness; he was not there to propagandize his host's children. He simply told them what the Dust was like, what Abbenay looked like, what kind of clothes one wore, what people did when they wanted new clothes, what children did in school. This last became propaganda, despite his intentions. Ini and Aevi were entranced by his description of a curriculum that included farming, carpentry, sewage reclamation, printing, plumbing, roadmending, playwriting, and all the other occupations of the adult community, and by his admission that nobody was ever punished for anything.

"Though sometimes," he said, "they make you go away by yourself for a while."

"But what," Oiie said abruptly, as if the question, long kept back, burst from him under pressure, "what keeps people in order? Why don't they rob and murder each other?"

"Nobody owns anything to rob. If you want things you take them from the depository. As for violence, well, I don't know, Oiie; would you murder me, ordinarily? And if you felt like it, would a law against it stop you? Coercion is the least efficient means of obtaining order."

"All right, but how do you get people to do the dirty work?"

"What dirty work?" asked Oiie's wife, not following.

"Garbage collecting, grave digging," Oiie said; Shevek added, "Mercury mining," and nearly said, "Shit processing," but recollected the Ioti taboo on scatological words. He had reflected, quite early in his stay on Urras, that the Urrasti lived among mountains of excrement, but never mentioned shit.

"Well, we all do them. But nobody has to do them for very long, unless he likes the work. One day in each decad the community management committee or the block committee or whoever needs you can ask you to join in such work; they make rotating lists. Then the disagreeable work postings, or dangerous ones like the mercury mines and mills, normally they're for one half year only."

"But then the whole personnel must consist of people just learning the job."

"Yes. It's not efficient, but what else is to be done? You

can't tell a man to work on a job that will cripple him or kill him in a few years. Why should he do that?"

"He can refuse the order?"

"It's not an order, Oiie. He goes to Divlab—the Division of Labor office—and says, I want to do such and such, what have you got? And they tell him where there are jobs."

"But then why do people do the dirty work at all? Why do they even accept the one-day-in-ten jobs?"

"Because they are done together. . . . And other reasons. You know, life on Anarres isn't rich, as it is here. In the little communities there isn't very much entertainment, and there is a lot of work to be done. So, if you work at a mechanical loom mostly, every tenthday it's pleasant to go outside and lay a pipe or plow a field, with a different group of people. . . . And then there is challenge. Here you think that the incentive to work is finances, need for money or desire for profit, but where there's no money the real motives are clearer, maybe. People like to do things. They like to do them well. People take the dangerous, hard jobs because they take pride in doing them, they can—egoize, we call it—show off?—to the weaker ones. Hey, look, little boys, see how strong I am! You know? A person likes to do what he is good at doing. . . . But really, it is the question of ends and means. After all, work is done for the work's sake. It is the lasting pleasure of life. The private conscience knows that. And also the social conscience, the opinion of one's neighbors. There is no other reward, on Anarres, no other law. One's own pleasure, and the respect of one's fellows. That is all. When that is so, then you see the opinion of the neighbors becomes a very mighty force."

"No one ever defies it?"

"Perhaps not often enough," Shevek said.

"Does everybody work so hard, then?" Oiie's wife asked. "What happens to a man who just won't cooperate?"

"Well, he moves on. The others get tired of him, you know. They make fun of him, or they get rough with him, beat him up; in a small community they might agree to take his name off the meals listing, so he has to cook and eat all by himself; that is humiliating. So he moves on, and stays in another place for a while, and then maybe moves on again. Some do it all their lives. *Nuchnibi,* they're called. I am a sort of nuchnib. I am here evading my own work posting. I moved farther than most." Shevek spoke tranquilly; if there was bitterness in his voice it was not discernible to the children, nor explicable to the adults. But a little silence followed on his words.

"I don't know who does the dirty work here," he said. "I never see it being done. It's strange. Who does it? Why do they do it? Are they paid more?"

"For dangerous work, sometimes. For merely menial tasks, no. Less."

"Why do they do them, then?"

"Because low pay is better than no pay," Oiie said, and the bitterness in his voice was quite clear. His wife began speaking nervously to change the subject, but he went on, "My grandfather was a janitor. Scrubbed floors and changed dirty sheets in a hotel for fifty years. Ten hours a day, six days a week. He did it so that he and his family could eat." Oiie stopped abruptly, and glanced at Shevek with his old secretive, distrustful look, and then, almost with defiance, at his wife. She did not meet his eyes. She smiled and said in a nervous, childish voice, "Demaere's father was a very successful man. He owned four companies when he died." Her smile was that of a person in pain, and her dark, slender hands were pressed tightly one over the other.

"I don't suppose you have successful men on Anarres," Oiie said with heavy sarcasm. Then the cook entered to change the plates, and he stopped speaking at once. The child Ini, as if knowing that the serious talk would not resume while the servant was there, said, "Mother, may Mr. Shevek see my otter when dinner's over?"

When they returned to the sitting room Ini was allowed to bring in his pet: a half-grown land otter, a common animal on Urras. They had been domesticated, Oiie explained, since prehistoric times, first for use as fish retrievers, then as pets. The creature had short legs, an arched and supple back, glossy dark-brown fur. It was the first uncaged animal Shevek had seen close up, and it was more fearless of him than he was of it. The white, sharp teeth were impressive. He put his hand out cautiously to stroke it, as Ini insisted he do. The otter sat up on its haunches and looked at him. Its eyes were dark, shot with gold, intelligent, curious, innocent. *"Ammar,"* Shevek whispered, caught by that gaze across the gulf of being—"brother."

The otter grunted, dropped to all fours, and examined Shevek's shoes with interest.

"He likes you," Ini said.

"I like him," Shevek replied, a little sadly. Whenever he saw an animal, the flight of birds, the splendor of autumn trees, that sadness came into him and gave delight a cutting edge. He did not think consciously of Takver at such moments, he did not think of her absence. Rather it was as if she were there though he was not thinking about her. It was as if the beauty and strangeness of the beasts and plants of Urras had been charged with a message for him by Takver, who would never see them, whose ancestors for seven generations had never touched an animal's warm fur or seen the flash of wings in the shade of trees.

He spent the night in a bedroom under the eaves. It was cold, which was welcome after the perpetual overheating of rooms at the University, and quite plain: the bedstead, bookcases, a chest, a chair, and a painted wooden table. It was like home, he thought, ignoring the height of the bedstead and the softness of the mattress, the fine woollen blankets and silk sheets, the knickknacks of ivory on the chest, the leather bindings of the books, and the fact that the room, and everything in it, and the house it was in, and the land the house stood on, was private property, the property of Demaere Oiie, though he hadn't built it, and didn't scrub its floors. Shevek put aside such tiresome discriminations. It was a nice room and not really so different from a single in a domicile.

Sleeping in that room, he dreamed of Takver. He dreamed that she was with him in the bed, that her arms were about him, her body against his body . . . but what room, what room were they in? Where were they? They were on the Moon together, it was cold, and they were walking along together. It was a flat place, the Moon, all covered with bluish-white snow, though the snow was thin and easily kicked aside to show the luminous white ground. It was dead, a dead place. "It isn't really like this," he told Takver, knowing she was frightened. They were walking towards something, a distant line of something that looked flimsy and shiny like plastic, a remote, hardly visible barrier across the white plain of snow. In his heart Shevek was afraid to approach it, but he told Takver, "We'll be there soon." She did not answer him.

Chapter 6

When Shevek was sent home after a decad in hospital, his neighbor in Room 45 came in to see him. He was a mathematician, very tall and thin. He had an uncorrected walleye, so that you never could be sure whether he was looking at you and/or you were looking at him. He and Shevek had coexisted amicably, side by side in the Institute domicile, for a year, without ever saying a full sentence to each other.

Desar now came in and stared at or beside Shevek. "Anything?" he said.

"I'm doing fine, thanks."

"What about bring dinner commons."

"With yours?" Shevek said, influenced by Desar's telegraphic style.

"All right."

Desar brought two dinners on a tray over from the Institute refectory, and they ate together in Shevek's room. He did the same morning and night for three days till Shevek felt up to going out again. It was hard to see why Desar did this. He was not friendly, and the expectations of brotherhood seemed to mean little to him. One reason he held aloof from people was to hide his dishonesty; he was either appallingly lazy or frankly propertarian, for

125

Room 45 was full of stuff that he had no right or reason to keep—dishes from commons, books from libraries, a set of woodcarving tools from a craft-supply depot, a microscope from some laboratory, eight different blankets, a closet stuffed with clothes, some of which plainly did not fit Desar and never had, others of which appeared to be things he had worn when he was eight or ten. It looked as if he went to depositories and warehouses and picked things up by the armload whether he needed them or not. "What do you keep all this junk for?" Shevek asked when he was first admitted to the room. Desar stared between him. "Just builds up," he said vaguely.

Desar's chosen field in mathematics was so esoteric that nobody in the Institute or the Math Federation could really check on his progress. That was precisely why he had chosen it. He assumed that Shevek's motivation was the same. "Hell," he said, "work? Good post here. Sequency. Simultaneity, shit." At some moments Shevek liked Desar, and at others detested him, for the same qualities. He stuck to him, however, deliberately, as part of his resolution to change his life.

His illness had made him realize that if he tried to go on alone he would break down altogether. He saw this in moral terms, and judged himself ruthlessly. He had been keeping himself for himself, against the ethical imperative of brotherhood. Shevek at twenty-one was not a prig, exactly, because his morality was passionate and drastic; but it was still fitted to a rigid mold, the simplistic Odonianism taught to children by mediocre adults, an internalized preaching.

He had been doing wrong. He must do right. He did so.

He forbade himself physics five nights in ten. He volunteered for committee work in the Institute domicile management. He attended meetings of the Physics Federation and the Syndicate of Members of the Institute. He enrolled with a group who were practicing biofeedback exercises and brain-wave training. At the refectory he forced himself to sit down at the large tables, instead of at a small one with a book in front of him.

It was surprising: people seemed to have been waiting for him. They included him, welcomed him, invited him as bedfellow and companion. They took him about with them, and within three decads he learned more about Abbenay than he had in a year. He went with groups of cheerful young people to athletic fields, craft centers, swimming pools, festivals, museums, theaters, concerts.

The concerts: they were a revelation, a shock of joy.

He had never gone to a concert here in Abbenay, partly because he thought of music as something you do rather than something you hear. As a child he had always sung, or played one instrument or another, in local choirs and ensembles; he had enjoyed it very much, but had not had much talent. And that was all he knew of music.

Learning centers taught all the skills that prepare for the practice of art: training in singing, metrics, dance, the use of brush, chisel, knife, lathe, and so on. It was all pragmatic: the children learned to see, speak, hear, move, handle. No distinction was drawn between the arts and the crafts; art was not considered as having a place in life, but as being a basic technique of life, like speech. Thus architecture had developed, early and freely, a consistent style, pure and plain, subtle in proportion. Painting and sculpture served largely as elements of architecture and town planning. As for the arts of words, poetry and storytelling tended to be ephemeral, to be linked with song and dancing; only the theater stood wholly alone, and only the theater was ever called "the Art"—a thing complete in itself. There were many regional and traveling troupes of actors and dancers, repertory companies, very often with playwright attached. They performed tragedies, semi-improvised comedies, mimes. They were as welcome as rain in the lonely desert towns, they were the glory of the year wherever they came. Rising out of and embodying the isolation and community of the Anarresti spirit, the drama had attained extraordinary power and brilliance.

Shevek, however, was not very sensitive to the drama. He liked the verbal splendor, but the whole idea of acting was uncongenial to him. It was not until this second year in Abbenay that he discovered, at last, his Art: the art that is made out of time. Somebody took him along to a concert at the Syndicate of Music. He went back the next night. He went to every concert, with his new acquaintances if possible, without if need be. The music was a more urgent need, a deeper satisfaction, than the companionship.

His efforts to break out of his essential seclusion were, in fact, a failure, and he knew it. He made no close friend. He copulated with a number of girls, but copulation was not the joy it ought to be. It was a mere relief of need, like evacuating, and he felt ashamed of it afterward because it involved another person as object. Masturbation was preferable, the suitable course for a man like himself. Solitude was his fate; he was trapped in his heredity. She had said it: "The work comes first." Rulag had said it calmly, stating fact, powerless to change it, to break out of her cold cell. So it was with him. His heart yearned towards them, the kindly young souls who called him brother, but he could not reach them, nor they him. He was born to be alone, a damned cold intellectual, an egoist.

The work came first, but it went nowhere. Like sex, it ought to have been a pleasure, and it wasn't. He kept grinding over the same problems, getting not a step nearer the solution of To's Temporal Paradox, let alone the Theory of Simultaneity, which last year he had thought was almost in his grasp. That self-assurance now seemed incredible to him. Had he really thought himself capable, at age twenty, of evolving a theory that would change the foundations of cosmological physics? He had been out of his mind for a good while before the fever, evidently. He enrolled in two work groups in philosophical mathematics, convincing himself that he needed them and refusing to admit that he could have directed either course as well as the instructors. He avoided Sabul as much as he could.

In his first burst of new resolutions he had made a point of getting to know Gvarab better. She responded as well as she could, but the winter had been hard on her; she was ill, and deaf, and old. She started a spring course and then gave it up. She was erratic, hardly recognizing Shevek one time, and the next dragging him off to her domicile for a whole evening's talk. He had got somewhat beyond Gvarab's ideas, and he found these long talks hard. Either he had to let Gvarab bore him for hours, repeating what he already knew or had partly disproved, or he had to hurt and confuse her by trying to set her straight. It was beyond the patience or tact of anyone his age, and he ended up evading Gvarab when he could, always with a bad conscience.

There was nobody else to talk shop with. Nobody at the Institute knew enough about pure temporal physics to keep up with him. He would have liked to teach it, but he had not yet been given a teaching posting or a classroom at the Institute; the faculty-student Syndicate of Members turned down his request for one. They did not want a quarrel with Sabul.

As the year went on he took to spending a good deal of his time writing letters to Atro and other physicists and mathematicians on Urras. Few of these letters were sent. Some he wrote and then simply tore up. He discovered that the mathematician Loai An, to whom he had written a six-page discourse on temporal reversibility, had been dead for twenty years; he had neglected to read the biographical preface to An's *Geometries of Time*. Other letters, which he undertook to get carried by the freight ships from Urras, were stopped by the managers of the Port of Abbenay. The Port was under direct control of PDC, since its operation involved the coordination of many syndicates, and some of the coordinators had to know Iotic. These Port managers, with their special knowledge and important position, tended to acquire the bureaucratic mentality: they said "no" automatically. They mistrusted the letters to mathematicians, which looked like code, and which nobody could assure them weren't code. Letters to physicists were passed if Sabul, their consultant, approved them. He would not approve those that dealt with subjects outside his own brand of Sequency physics. "Not within my competence," he would growl, pushing the letter aside. Shevek would send it on to the Port managers anyhow, and it would come back marked "Not approved for export."

He brought this matter up at the Physics Federation, which Sabul seldom bothered to attend. Nobody there attached importance to the issue of free communication with the ideological enemy. Some of them lectured Shevek for working in a field so arcane that there was, by his own admission, nobody else on his own world competent in it. "But it's only new," he said, which got him nowhere."

"If it's new, share it with us, not with the propertarians!"

"I've tried to offier a course every quarter for a year now. You always say there isn't enough demand for it. Are you afraid of it because it's new?"

That won him no friends. He left them in anger.

He went on writing letters to Urras, even when he mailed none of them at all. The fact of writing for someone who might understand—who might have understood—made it possible for him to write, to think. Otherwise it was not possible.

The decads went by, and the quarters. Two or three times a year the reward came: a letter from Atro or another physicist in A-Io or Thu, a long letter, close-written, close-argued, all theory from salutation to signature, all intense abstruse meta-mathematical-ethico-cosmological temporal physics, written in a language he could not speak by men he did not know, fiercely trying to combat and destroy his theories, enemies of his homeland, rivals, strangers, brothers.

For days after getting a letter he was irascible and joyful, worked day and night, foamed out ideas like a fountain. Then slowly, with desperate spurts and struggles, he came back to earth, to dry ground, ran dry.

He was finishing his third year at the Institute when Gvarab died. He asked to speak at her memorial service, which was held, as the custom was, in the place where the dead person had worked: in this case one of the lecture rooms in the Physics laboratory building. He was the only speaker. No students attended; Gvarab had not taught for two years. A few elderly members of the Institute came, and Gvarab's middle-aged son, an agricultural chemist from Northeast, was there. Shevek stood where the old woman had used to stand to lecture. He told these people, in a voice hoarsened by his now customary winter chest cold, that Gvarab had laid the foundations of the science of time, and was the greatest cosmologist who had ever worked at the Institute. "We in physics have our Odo now," he said. "We have her, and we did not honor her." Afterwards an old woman thanked him, with tears in her eyes. "We always took tenthdays together, her and me, janitoring in our block, we used to have such good times talking," she said, wincing in the icy wind as they came out of the building. The agricultural chemist muttered civilites and hurried off to catch a ride back to Northeast. In a rage of grief, impatience, and futility, Shevek struck off walking at random through the city.

Three years here, and he had accomplished what? A

book, appropriated by Sabul; five or six unpublished papers; and a funeral oration for a wasted life.

Nothing he did was understood. To put it more honestly, nothing he did was meaningful. He was fulfilling no necessary function, personal or social. In fact—it was not an uncommon phenomenon in his field—he had burnt out at twenty. He would achieve nothing further. He had come up against the wall for good.

He stopped in front of the Music Syndicate auditorium to read the programs for the decad. There was no concert tonight. He turned away from the poster and came face to face with Bedap.

Bedap, always defensive and rather nearsighted, gave no sign of recognition. Shevek caught his arm.

"Shevek! By damn, it's you!" They hugged each other, kissed, broke apart, hugged again. Shevek was overwhelmed by love. Why? He had not even much liked Bedap that last year at the Regional Institute. They had never written, these three years. Their friendship was a boyhood one, past. Yet love was there: flamed up as from shaken coal.

They walked, talked, neither noticing where they went. They waved their arms and interrupted each other. The wide streets of Abbenay were quiet in the winter night. At each crossing the dim streetlight made a pool of silver, across which dry snow flurried like shoals of tiny fish, chasing their shadows. The wind came bitter cold behind the snow. Numbed lips and chattering teeth began to interfere with conversation. They caught the ten o'clock omnibus, the last, to the Institute; Bedap's domicile was out on the east edge of the city, a long pull in the cold.

He looked at Room 46 with ironic wonder. "Shev, you live like a rotten Urrasti profiteer."

"Come on, it's not that bad. Show me anything excremental!" The room in fact contained just about what it had when Shevek first entered it. Bedap pointed: "That blanket."

"That was here when I came. Somebody handmade it, and left it when they moved. Is a blanket excessive on a night like this?"

"It's definitely an excremental color," Bedap said. "As a functions analyst I must point out that there is no need for orange. Orange serves no vital function in the social organism at either the cellular or the organic level, and certainly not at the holorganismic or most centrally ethical level; in which case tolerance is a less good choice then excretion. Dye it dirty green, brother! What's all this stuff?"

"Notes."

"In code?" Bedap asked, looking through a notebook with the coolness Shevek remembered was characteristic of him. He had even less sense of privacy—or private ownership—than most Anarresti. Bedap had never had a favorite pencil that he carried around with him, or an old shirt he had got fond of and hated to dump in the recycle bin, and if given a present he tried to keep it out of regard for the giver's feelings, but always lost it. He was conscious of this trait and said it showed he was less primitive than most people, an early example of the Promised Man, the true and native Odonian. But he did have a sense of privacy. It began at the skull, his own or another's, and from there on in it was complete. He never pried. He said now, "Remember those fool letters we used to write in code when you were on the afforestation project?"

"That isn't code, it's Iotic."

"You've learned Iotic? Why do you write in it?"

"Because nobody on this planet can understand what I'm saying. Or wants to. The only one who did died three days ago."

"Sabul's dead?"

"No. Gvarab. Sabul isn't dead. Fat chance!"

"What's the trouble?"

"The trouble with Sabul? Half envy, the other half incompetence."

"I thought his book on causality was supposed to be first-rate. You said so."

"I thought so, till I read the sources. They're all Urrasti ideas. Not new ones, either. He hasn't had a thought of his own for twenty years. Or a bath."

"How are your thoughts?" asked Bedap, putting a hand on the notebooks and looking at Shevek under his brows. Bedap had small, rather squinting eyes, a strong face, a thickset body. He bit his fingernails, and in years of doing so had reduced them to mere strips across his thick, sensitive fingertips.

"No good," said Shevek, sitting down on the bed platform. "I'm in the wrong field."

Bedap grinned. "You?"

"I think at the end of this quarter I'll ask for reposting."

"To what?"

"I don't care. Teaching, engineering. I've got to get out of physics."

Bedap sat down in the desk chair, bit a fingernail, and said, "That sounds odd."

"I've recognized my limitations."

"I didn't know you had any. In physics, I mean. You had all sorts of limitations and defects. But not in physics. I'm no temporalist, I know. But you don't have to be able to swim to know a fish, you don't have to shine to recognize a star. . . ."

Shevek looked at his friend and said, blurted out, what he had never been able to say clearly to himself: "I've thought of suicide. A good deal. This year. It seems the best way."

"It's hardly the way to come out on the other side of suffering."

Shevek smiled stiffly. "You remember that?"

"Vividly. It was a very important conversation to me. And to Takver and Tirin, I think."

"Was it?" Shevek stood up. There was only four steps' pacing room, but he could not hold still. "It was important to me then," he said, standing at the window. "But I've changed, here. There's something wrong here. I don't know what it is."

"I do," Bedap said. "The wall. You've come up against the wall."

Shevek turned with a frightened look. "The wall?"

"In your case, the wall seems to be Sabul, and his supporters in the science syndicates and the PDC. As for me, I've been in Abbenay four decads. Forty days. Long enough to see that in forty years here I'll accomplish nothing, nothing at all, of what I want to do, the improvement of science instruction in the learning centers. Unless things are changed. Or unless I join the enemies."

"Enemies?"

"The little men. Sabul's friends! The people in power."

"What are you talking about, Dap? We have no power structure."

"No? What makes Sabul so strong?"

"Not a power structure, a government. This isn't Urras, after all!"

"No. We have no government, no laws, all right. But as far as I can see, *ideas* never were controlled by laws and governments, even on Urras. If they had been, how would Odo have worked out hers? How would Odonianism have become a world movement? The archists tried to stamp it out by force, and failed. You can't crush ideas by suppressing them. You can only crush them by ignoring them. By refusing to think, refusing to change. And that's precisely what our society is doing! Sabul uses you where he can, and where he can't, he prevents you from publishing, from teaching, even from working. Right? In other words, he has power over you. Where does he get it from? Not from vested authority, there isn't any. Not from intellectual excellence, he hasn't any. He gets it from the innate cowardice of the average human mind. Public opinion! That's the power structure he's part of, and knows how to use. The unadmitted, inadmissible government that rules the Odonian society by stifling the individual mind."

Shevek leaned his hands on the window sill, looking through the dim reflections on the pane into the darkness outside. He said at last, "Crazy talk, Dap."

"No, brother, I'm sane. What drives people crazy is trying to live outside reality. Reality is terrible. It can kill you. Given time, it certainly will kill you. The reality is pain—you said that! But it's the lies, the evasions of reality, that drive you crazy. It's the lies that make you want to kill yourself."

Shevek turned around to face him. "But you can't seriously talk of a government, here!"

"Tomar's *Definitions:* 'Government: The legal use of power to maintain and extend power.' Replace 'legal' with 'customary,' and you've got Sabul, and the Syndicate of Instruction, and the PDC."

"The PDC!"

"The PDC is, by now, basically an archistic bureaucracy."

After a moment Shevek laughed, not quite naturally, and said, "Well, come on, Dap, this is amusing, but it's a bit diseased, isn't it?"

"Shev, did you ever think that what the analogic mode

134

calls 'disease,' social disaffection, discontent, alienation, that this might analogically also be called pain—what you meant when you talked about pain, suffering? And that, like pain, it serves a function in the organism?"

"No!" Shevek said, violently. "I was talking in personal, in spiritual terms."

"But you spoke of physical suffering, of a man dying of burns. And I speak of spiritual suffering! Of people seeing their talent, their work, their lives wasted. Of good minds submitting to stupid ones. Of strength and courage strangled by envy, greed for power, fear of change. Change is freedom, change is life—is anything more basic to Odonian thought than that? But nothing changes any more! Our society is sick. You know it. You're suffering its sickness. Its suicidal sickness!"

"That's enough, Dap. Drop it."

Bedap said no more. He began to bite his thumbnail, methodically and thoughtfully.

Shevek sat down again on the bed platform and put his head in his hands. There was a long silence. The snow had ceased. A dry, dark wind pushed at the windowpane. The room was cold; neither of the young men had taken off his coat.

"Look, brother," Shevek said at last. "It's not our society that frustrates individual creativity. It's the poverty of Anarres. This planet wasn't meant to support civilization. If we let one another down, if we don't give up our personal desires to the common good, nothing, nothing on this barren world can save us. Human solidarity is our only resource."

"Solidarity, yes! Even on Urras, where food falls out of the trees, even there Odo said that human solidarity is our one hope. But we've betrayed that hope. We've let cooperation become obedience. On Urras they have government by the minority. Here we have government by the majority. But it is government! The social conscience isn't a living thing any more, but a machine, a power machine, controlled by bureaucrats!"

"You or I could volunteer and be lottery-posted to PDC within a few decads. Would that turn us into bureaucrats, bosses?"

"It's not the individuals posted to PDC, Shev. Most of them are like us. All too much like us. Well-meaning, naïve. And it's not just PDC. It's anywhere on Anarres. Learning centers, institutes, mines, mills, fisheries, canneries, agricultural development and research stations, factories, one-product communities—anywhere that function demands expertise and a stable institution. But that stability gives scope to the authoritarian impulse. In the early years of the Settlement we were aware of that, on the lookout for it. People discriminated very carefully then between administering things and governing people. They did it so well that we forgot that the will to dominance is as central in human beings as the impulse to mutual aid is, and has to be trained in each individual, in each new generation. Nobody's born an Odonian any more than he's born civilized! But we've forgotten that. We don't educate for freedom. Education, the most important activity of the social organism, has become rigid, moralistic, authoritarian. Kids learn to parrot Odo's words as if they were *laws*—the ultimate blasphemy!"

Shevek hesitated. He had experienced too much of the kind of teaching Bedap was talking about, as a child, and even here at the Institute, to be able to deny Bedap's accusation.

Bedap seized his advantage relentlessly. "It's always easier not to think for oneself. Find a nice safe hierarchy and settle in. Don't make changes, don't risk disapproval, don't upset your syndics. It's always easiest to let yourself be governed."

"But it's not government, Dap! The experts and the old hands are going to manage any crew or syndicate; they know the work best. The work has to get done, after all! As for PDC, yes, it might become a hierarchy, a power structure, if it weren't organized to prevent exactly that. Look how it's set up! Volunteers, selected by lot; a year of training; then four years as a Listing; then out. Nobody could gain power, in the archist sense, in a system like that, with only four years to do it in."

"Some stay on longer than four years."

"Advisers? They don't keep the vote."

"Votes aren't important. There are people behind the scenes—"

"Come on! That's sheer paranoia! Behind the scenes—how? What scenes? Anybody can attend any PDC meeting, and if he's an interested syndic, he can debate and vote! Are you trying to pretend that we have *politicians* here?" Shevek was furious with Bedap; his prominent ears were scarlet, his voice had got loud. It was late, not a light showing across the quadrangle. Desar, in Room 45, knocked on the wall for quiet.

"I'm saying what you know," Bedap replied in a much lowered voice. "That it's people like Sabul who really run PDC, and run it year after year."

"If you know that," Shevek accused in a harsh whisper, "then why haven't you made it public? Why haven't you called a criticism session in your syndicate, if you have facts? If your ideas won't stand public examination, I don't want them as midnight whispers."

Bedap's eyes had got very small, like steel beads. "Brother," he said, "you are self-righteous. You always were. Look outside your own damned pure conscience for once! I come to you and whisper because I know I can trust you, damn you! Who else can I talk to? Do I want to end up like Tirin?"

"Like Tirin?" Shevek was startled into raising his voice. Bedap hushed him with a gesture towards the wall. "What's wrong with Tirin? Where is he?"

"In the Asylum on Segvina Island."

"In the Asylum?"

Bedap hunched his knees up to his chin and wrapped his arms around them, as he sat sideways on the chair. He spoke quietly now, with reluctance.

"Tirin wrote a play and put it on, the year after you left. It was funny—crazy—you know his kind of thing." Bedap ran a hand through his rough, sandy hair, loosening it from its queue. "It could seem anti-Odonian, if you were stupid. A lot of people are stupid. There was a fuss. He got reprimanded. Public reprimand. I never saw one before. Everybody comes to your syndicate meeting and tells you off. It used to be how they cut a bossy gang foreman or manager down to size. Now they only use it to tell an individual to stop thinking for himself. It was bad. Tirin couldn't take it. I think it really drove him a bit out of his mind. He felt everybody was against him, after that. He started talking too much—bitter talk. Not irrational, but always critical, always bitter. And he'd talk to anybody that way. Well, he finished at the Institute, qualified as a math instructor, and asked for a posting. He got one.

137

To a road repair crew in Southsetting. He protested it as an error, but the Divlab computers repeated it. So he went."

"Tir never worked outdoors the whole time I knew him," Shevek interrupted. "Since he was ten. He always wangled desk jobs. Divlab was being fair."

Bedap paid no attention. "I don't really know what happened down there. He wrote me several times, and each time he'd been reposted. Always to physical labor, in little outpost communities. He wrote that he was quitting his posting and coming back to Northsetting to see me. He didn't come. He stopped writing. I traced him through the Abbenay Labor Files, finally. They sent me a copy of his card, and the last entry was just, 'Therapy. Segvina Island.' Therapy! Did Tirin murder somebody? Did he rape somebody? What do you get sent to the Asylum for, beside that?"

"You don't get sent to the Asylum at all. You request posting to it."

"Don't feed me that crap," Bedap said with sudden rage. "He never asked to be sent there! They drove him crazy and then sent him there. It's Tirin I'm talking about, Tirin, do you remember him?"

"I knew him before you did. What do you think the Asylum is—a prison? It's a refuge. If there are murderers and chronic work-quitters there, it's because they asked to go there, where they're not under pressure, and safe from retribution. But who are these people you keep talking about—'they'? 'They' drove him crazy, and so on. Are you trying to say that the whole social system is evil, that in fact 'they,' Tirin's persecutors, your enemies, 'they,' are us—the social organism?"

"If you can dismiss Tirin from your conscience as a work-quitter, I don't think I have anything else to say to you," Bedap replied, sitting hunched up on the chair. There was such plain and simple grief in his voice that Shevek's righteous wrath was stopped short.

Neither spoke for a while.

"I'd better go home," Bedap said, unfolding stiffly and standing up.

"It's an hour's walk from here. Don't be stupid."

"Well, I thought . . . since . . ."

"Don't be stupid."

138

"All right. Where's the shittery?"

"Left, third door."

When he came back Bedap proposed to sleep on the floor, but as there was no rug and only one warm blanket, this idea was, as Shevek monotonously remarked, stupid. They were both glum and cross; sore, as if they had fist-fought but not fought all their anger out. Shevek unrolled the bedding and they lay down. At the turning out of the lamp a silvery darkness came into the room, the half darkness of a city night when there is snow on the ground and light reflects faintly upward from the earth. It was cold. Each felt the warmth of the other's body as very welcome.

"I take it back about the blanket."

"Listen, Dap. I didn't mean to—"

"Oh, let's talk about it in the morning."

"Right."

They moved closer together. Shevek turned over onto his face and fell asleep within two minutes. Bedap struggled to hold on to consciousness, slipped into the warmth, deeper, into the defenselessness, the trustfulness of sleep, and slept. In the night one of them cried out aloud, dreaming. The other one reached his arm out sleepily, muttering reassurance, and the blind warm weight of his touch outweighed all fear.

They met again the next evening and discussed whether or not they should pair for a while, as they had when they were adolescent. It had to be discussed, because Shevek was pretty definitely heterosexual and Bedap pretty definitely homosexual; the pleasure of it would be mostly for Bedap. Shevek was perfectly willing, however, to reconfirm the old friendship; and when he saw that the sexual element of it meant a great deal to Bedap, was, to him, a true consummation, then he took the lead, and with considerable tenderness and obstinacy made sure that Bedap spent the night with him again. They took a free single in a domicile downtown, and both lived there for about a decad; then they separated again, Bedap to his dormitory and Shevek to Room 46. There was no strong sexual desire on either side to make the connection last. They had simply reasserted trust.

Yet Shevek sometimes wondered, as he went on seeing

Bedap almost daily, what it was he liked and trusted in his friend. He found Bedap's present opinions detestable and his insistence on talking about them tiresome. They argued fiercely almost every time they met. They caused each other a good deal of pain. Leaving Bedap, Shevek frequently accused himself of merely clinging to an outgrown loyalty, and swore angrily not to see Bedap again.

But the fact was that he liked Bedap more as a man than he ever had as a boy. Inept, insistent, dogmatic, destructive: Bedap could be all that; but he had attained a freedom of mind that Shevek craved, though he hated its expression. He had changed Shevek's life, and Shevek knew it, knew that he was going on at last, and that it was Bedap who had enabled him to go on. He fought Bedap every step of the way, but he kept coming, to argue, to do hurt and get hurt, to find—under anger, denial, and rejection—what he sought. He did not know what he sought. But he knew where to look for it.

It was, consciously, as unhappy a time for him as the year that had preceded it. He was still getting no further with his work; in fact he had abandoned temporal physics altogether and backtracked into humble lab work, setting up various experiments in the radiation laboratory with a deft, silent technician as partner, studying subatomic velocities. It was a well-trodden field, and his belated entry into it was taken by his colleagues as an admission that he had finally stopped trying to be original. The Syndicate of Members of the Institute gave him a course to teach, mathematical physics for entering students. He got no sense of triumph from finally having been given a course, for it was just that: he had been given it, been permitted it. He got little comfort from anything. That the walls of his hard puritanical conscience were widening out immensely was anything but a comfort. He felt cold and lost. But he had nowhere to retreat to, no shelter, so he kept coming farther out into the cold, getting farther lost.

Bedap had made many friends, an erratic and disaffected lot, and some of them took a liking to the shy man. He felt no closer to them than to the more conventional people he knew at the Institute, but he found their independence of mind more interesting. They preserved autonomy of conscience even at the cost of becoming eccentric. Some of them were intellectual nuchnibi who had not worked on a regular posting for years. Shevek disapproved of them severely, when he was not with them.

One of them was a composer named Salas. Salas and Shevek wanted to learn from each other. Salas had little math, but as long as Shevek could explain physics in the analogic or experiential modes, he was an eager and intelligent listener. In the same way Shevek would listen to anything Salas could tell him about musical theory, and anything Salas would play him on tape or on his instrument, the portative. But some of what Salas told him he found extremely troubling. Salas had taken a posting to a canal-digging crew on the Plains of the Temae, east of Abbenay. He came into the city on his three days off each decad, and stayed with one girl or another. Shevek assumed that he had taken the posting because he wanted a bit of outdoor work for a change; but then he found that Salas had never had a posting in music, or in anything but unskilled labor.

"What's your listing at Divlab?" he asked, puzzled.

"General labor pool."

"But you're skilled! You put in six or eight years at the Music Syndicate conservatory, didn't you? Why don't they post you to music teaching?"

"They did. I refused. I won't be ready to teach for another ten years. I'm a composer, remember, not a performer."

"But there must be postings for composers."

"Where?"

"In the Music Syndicate, I suppose."

"But the Music syndics don't like my compositions. And nobody much else does, yet. I can't be a syndicate all by myself, can I?"

Salas was a bony little man, already bald on the upper face and cranium; he wore what was left of his hair short, in a silky beige fringe around the back of his neck and chin. His smile was sweet, wrinkling his expressive face. "You see, I don't write the way I was trained to write at the conservatory. I write dysfunctional music." He smiled more sweetly than ever. "They want chorales. I hate chorales. They want wide-harmony pieces like Sessur wrote. I hate Sessur's music. I'm writing a piece of chamber music. Thought I might call it *The Simultaneity*

Principle. Five instruments each playing an independent cyclic theme; no melodic causality; the forward process entirely in the relationship of the parts. It makes a lovely harmony. But they don't hear it. They won't hear it. They can't!"

Shevek brooded a while. "If you called it *The Joys of Solidarity*," he said, "would they hear it?"

"By damn!" said Bedap, who was listening in. "That's the first cynical thing you ever said in your life, Shev. Welcome to the work crew!"

Salas laughed. "They'd give it a hearing, but they'd turn it down for taping or regional performance. It's not in the Organic Style."

"No wonder I never heard any professional music while I lived in Northsetting. But how can they justify this kind of censorship? You write music! Music is a cooperative art, organic by definition, social. It may be the noblest form of social behavior we're capable of. It's certainly one of the noblest jobs an individual can undertake. And by its nature, by the nature of any art, it's a sharing. The artist shares, it's the essence of his act. No matter what your syndics say, how can Divlab justify not giving you a posting in your own field?"

"They don't want to share it," Salas said gleefully. "It scares 'em."

Bedap spoke more gravely: "They can justify it because music isn't useful. Canal digging is important, you know; music's mere decoration. The circle has come right back around to the most vile kind of profiteering utilitarianism. The complexity, the vitality, the freedom of invention and initiative that was the center of the Odonian ideal, we've thrown it all away. We've gone right back to barbarism. If it's new, run away from it; if you can't eat it, throw it away!"

Shevek thought of his own work and had nothing to say. Yet he could not join in Bedap's criticism. Bedap had forced him to realize that he was, in fact, a revolutionary; but he felt profoundly that he was such *by virtue of* his upbringing and education as an Odonian and an Anarresti. He could not rebel against his society, because his society, properly conceived, was a revolution, a permanent one, an ongoing process. To reassert its validity and strength, he thought, one need only act, without fear of punishment and without hope of reward: act from the center of one's soul.

Bedap and some of his friends were taking off a decad together, going on a hiking tour in the Ne Theras. He had persuaded Shevek to come. Shevek liked the prospect of ten days in the mountains, but not the prospect of ten days of Bedap's opinions. Bedap's conversation was all too much like a Criticism Session, the communal activity he had always liked least, when everybody stood up and complained about defects in the functioning of the community and, usually, defects in the characters of the neighbors. The nearer the vacation came the less he looked forward to it. But he stuck a notebook in his pocket, so he could get away and pretend to be working, and went.

They met behind the Eastern Points trucking depot early in the morning, three women and three men. Shevek did not know any of the women, and Bedap introduced him to only two of them. As they set off on the road toward the mountains he fell in beside the third one. "Shevek," he said.

She said, "I know."

He realized that he must have met her somewhere before and should know her name. His ears got red.

"Are you being funny?" Bedap asked, moving in on the left. "Takver was at Northsetting Institute with us. She's been living in Abbenay for two years. Haven't you two seen each other here till now?"

"I've seen him a couple of times," the girl said, and laughed at him. She had the laugh of a person who likes to eat well, a big, childish gape. She was tall and rather thin, with round arms and broad hips. She was not very pretty; her face was swarthy, intelligent, and cheerful. In her eyes there was a darkness, not the opacity of bright dark eyes but a quality of depth, almost like deep, black, fine ash, very soft. Shevek, meeting her eyes, knew that he had committed an unforgivable fault in forgetting her and, in the instant of knowing it, knew also that he had been forgiven. That he was in luck. That his luck had changed.

They started up into the mountains.

In the cold evening of the fourth day of their excursion he and Takver sat on the bare steep slope above a gorge. Forty meters below them a mountain torrent rattled down the ravine among spraywet rocks. There was little running

143

water on Anarres; the water table was low in most places, rivers were short. Only in the mountains were there quick-running streams. The sound of water shouting and clattering and singing was new to them.

They had been scrambling up and down such gorges all day in the high country and were leg-weary. The rest of their party were in the Wayshelter, a stone lodge built by and for vacationers, and well kept up; the Ne Theras Federative was the most active of the volunteer groups that managed and protected the rather limited "scenic" areas of Anarres. A firewarden who lived there in summer was helping Bedap and the others put together a dinner from the well-stocked pantries. Takver and Shevek had gone out, in that order, separately, without announcing their destination or, in fact, knowing it.

He found her on the steep slope, sitting among the delicate bushes of moonthorn that grew like knots of lace over the mountainsides, its stiff, fragile branches silvery in the twilight. In a gap between eastern peaks a colorless luminosity of the sky heralded moonrise. The stream was noisy in the silence of the high, bare hills. There was no wind, no cloud. The air above the mountains was like amethyst, hard, clear, profound.

They had been sitting there some while without speaking.

"I've never been drawn to a woman in my life as I have been to you. Ever since we started this hike." Shevek's tone was cold, almost resentful.

"I didn't mean to spoil your vacation," she said, with her large childish laugh, too loud for the twilight.

"It doesn't spoil it!"

"That's good. I thought you meant it distracted you."

"Distracted! It's like an earthquake."

"Thank you."

"It's not you," he said harshly. "It's me."

"That's what you think," she said.

There was a longish pause.

"If you want to copulate," she said, "why haven't you asked me?"

"Because I'm not sure that's what I do want."

"Neither am I." Her smile was gone. "Listen," she said. Her voice was soft, and had not much timbre; it had the same furry quality as her eyes. "I ought to tell you." But

144

what she ought to tell him remained unsaid for quite a while. He looked at her at last with such pleading apprehension that she hastened to speak, and said in a rush, "Well, all I mean is, I don't want to copulate with you now. Or anybody."

"You've sworn off sex?"

"No!" she said with indignation, but no explanation.

"I might as well have," he said, flinging a pebble down into the stream. "Or else I'm impotent. It's been half a year, and that was just with Dap. Nearly a year, actually. It kept getting more unsatisfying each time, till I quit trying. It wasn't worth it. Not worth the trouble. And yet I—I remember—I know what it *ought* to be."

"Well, that's it," said Takver. "I used to have an awful lot of fun copulating, until I was eighteen or nineteen. It was exciting, and interesting, and pleasure. But then . . . I don't know. Like you said, it got unsatisfying. I didn't want pleasure. Not just pleasure. I mean."

"You want kids?"

"Yes, when the time comes."

He pitched another rock down into the stream, which was fading into the shadows of the ravine leaving only its noise behind, a ceaseless harmony composed of disharmonies.

"I want to get a job done," he said.

"Does being celibate help?"

"There's a connection. But I don't know what it is, it's not causal. About the time sex began to go sour on me, so did the work. Increasingly. Three years without getting anywhere. Sterility. Sterility on all sides. As far as the eye can see the infertile desert lies in the pitiless glare of the merciless sun, a lifeless, trackless, feckless, fuckless, waste strewn with the bones of luckless wayfarers. . . ."

Takver did not laugh; she gave a whimper of laughter, as though it hurt. He tried to make out her face clearly. Behind her dark head the sky was hard and clear.

"What's wrong with pleasure, Takver? Why don't you want it?"

"Nothing's wrong with it. And I do want it. Only I don't need it. And if I take what I don't need, I'll never get to what I do need."

"What is it you need?"

She looked down at the ground, scratching the surface

145

of a rock outcrop with her fingernail. She said nothing. She leaned forward to pick a sprig of moonthorn, but did not take it, merely touched it, felt the furred stem and fragile leaf. Shevek saw in the tension of her movements that she was trying with all her strength to contain or restrain a storm of emotion, so that she could speak. When she did, it was in a low voice and a little roughly. "I need the bond," she said. "The real one. Body and mind and all the years of life. Nothing else. Nothing less."

She glanced up at him with defiance, it might have been hatred.

Joy was rising mysteriously in him, like the sound and smell of the running water rising through the darkness. He had a feeling of unlimitedness, of clarity, total clarity, as if he had been set free. Behind Takver's head the sky was brightening with moonrise; the far peaks floated clear and silver. "Yes, that's it," he said, without self-consciousness, without any sense of talking to someone else; he said what came into his head, meditatively. "I never saw it."

There was a little resentment still in Takver's voice. "You never had to see it."

"Why not?"

"I suppose because you never saw the possibility of it."

"What do you mean, the possibility?"

"The person!"

He considered this. They sat about a meter apart, hugging their knees because it was getting cold. Breath came to the throat like ice water. They could see each other's breath, faint vapor in the steadily growing moonlight.

"The night I saw it," Takver said, "was the night before you left Northsetting Institute. There was a party, you remember. Some of us sat and talked all night. But that was four years ago. And you didn't even know my name." The rancor was gone from her voice; she seemed to want to excuse him.

"You saw in me, then, what I've seen in you this last four days?"

"I don't know. I can't tell. It wasn't just sexual. I'd noticed you before, that way. This was different; I *saw* you. But I don't know what you see now. And I didn't really know what I saw then. I didn't know you well at all. Only, when you spoke, I seemed to see clear into you, into the center. But you might have been quite different from what

146

I thought you were. That wouldn't be your fault, after all," she added. "It's just that I knew what I saw in you was what I needed. Not just wanted!"

"And you've been in Abbenay for two years, and didn't—"

"Didn't what? It was all on my side, in my head, you didn't even know my name. One person can't make a bond, after all!"

"And you were afraid that if you came to me I might not want the bond."

"Not afraid. I knew you were a person who . . . wouldn't be forced. . . . Well, yes, I was afraid. I was afraid of you. Not of making a mistake. I knew it wasn't a mistake. But you were—yourself. You aren't like most people, you know. I was afraid of you because I knew you were my equal!" Her tone as she ended was fierce, but in a moment she said very gently, with kindness, "It doesn't really matter, you know, Shevek."

It was the first time he had heard her say his name. He turned to her and said stammering, almost choking, "Doesn't matter? First you show me—you show me what matters, what really matters, what I've needed all my life —and then you say it doesn't matter!"

They were face to face now, but they had not touched. "Is it what you need, then?"

"Yes. The bond. The chance."

"Now—for life?"

"Now and for life."

Life, said the stream of quick water down on the rocks in the cold dark.

When Shevek and Takver came down from the mountains, they moved into a double room. None was free in the blocks near the Institute, but Takver knew of one not far away in an old domicile in the north end of town. In order to get the room they went to the block housing manager—Abbenay was divided into about two hundred local administrative regions, called blocks—a lens grinder who worked at home and kept her three young children at home with her. She therefore kept the housing files in a shelf on top of a closet so the children wouldn't get at them. She checked that the room was registered as vacant;

147

Shevek and Takver registered it as occupied by signing their names.

The move was not complicated, either. Shevek brought a box of papers, his winter boots, and the orange blanket. Takver had to make three trips. One was to the district clothing depository to get them both a new suit, an act which she felt obscurely but strongly was essential to beginning their partnership. Then she went to her old dormitory, once for her clothes and papers, and again, with Shevek, to bring a number of curious objects: complex concentric shapes made of wire, which moved and changed slowly and inwardly when suspended from the ceiling. She had made these with scrap wire and tools from the craft-supply depot, and called them Occupations of Uninhabited Space. One of the room's two chairs was decrepit, so they took it by a repair shop, where they picked up a sound one. They were then furnished. The new room had a high ceiling, which made it airy and gave plenty of space for the Occupations. The domicile was built on one of Abbenay's low hills, and the room had a corner window that caught the afternoon sunlight and gave a view of the city, the streets and squares, the roofs, the green of parks, the plains beyond.

Intimacy after long solitude, the abruptness of joy, tried both Shevek's stability and Takver's. In the first few decads he had wild swings of elation and anxiety; she had fits of temper. Both were oversensitive and inexperienced. The strain did not last, as they became experts in each other. Their sexual hunger persisted as passionate delight, their desire for communion was daily renewed because it was daily fulfilled.

It was now clear to Shevek, and he would have thought it folly to think otherwise, that his wretched years in this city had all been part of his present great happiness, because they had led up to it, prepared him for it. Everything that had happened to him was part of what was happening to him now. Takver saw no such obscure concatenations of effect/cause/effect, but then she was not a temporal physicist. She saw time naïvely as a road laid out. You walked ahead, and you got somewhere. If you were lucky, you got somewhere worth getting to.

But when Shevek took her metaphor and recast it in his terms, explaining that, unless the past and the future were

148

made part of the present by memory and intention, there was, in human terms, no road, nowhere to go, she nodded before he was half done. "Exactly," she said. "That's what I was doing these last four years. It isn't *all* luck. Just partly."

She was twenty-three, a half year younger than Shevek. She had grown up in a farming community, Round Valley, in Northeast. It was an isolated place, and before Takver had come to the Institute in Northsetting she had worked harder than most young Anarresti. There had been scarcely enough people in Round Valley to do the jobs that had to be done, but they were not a large enough community, or productive enough in the general economy, to get high priority from the Divlab computers. They had to look after themselves. Takver at eight had picked straw and rocks out of holum grain at the mill for three hours a day after three hours of school. Little of her practical training as a child had been towards personal enrichment: it had been part of the community's effort to survive. At harvest and planting seasons everyone over ten and under sixty had worked in the fields, all day. At fifteen she had been in charge of coordinating the work schedules on the four hundred farm plots worked by the community of Round Valley, and had assisted the planning dietician in the town refectory. There was nothing unusual in all this, and Takver thought little of it, but it had of course formed certain elements in her character and opinions. Shevek was glad he had done his share of kleggich, for Takver was contemptuous of people who evaded physical labor. "Look at Tinan," she would say, "whining and howling because he got a draft posting for four decads to a root-holum harvest. He's so delicate you'd think he was a fish egg! Has he ever touched dirt?" Takver was not particularly charitable, and she had a hot temper.

She had studied biology at Northsetting Regional Institute, with sufficient distinction that she had decided to come to the Central Institute for further study. After a year she had been asked to join in a new syndicate that was setting up a laboratory to study techniques of increasing and improving the edible fish stocks in the three oceans of Anarres. When people asked her what she did she said, "I'm a fish geneticist." She liked the work; it combined two things she valued: accurate, factual research

149

and a specific goal of increase or betterment. Without such work she would not have been satisfied. But it by no means sufficed her. Most of what went on in Takver's mind and spirit had little to do with fish genetics.

Her concern with landscapes and living creatures was passionate. This concern, feebly called "love of nature," seemed to Shevek to be something much broader than love. There are souls, he thought, whose umbilicus has never been cut. They never got weaned from the universe. They do not understand death as an enemy; they look forward to rotting and turning into humus. It was strange to see Takver take a leaf into her hand, or even a rock. She became an extension of it, it of her.

She showed Shevek the sea-water tanks at the research laboratory, fifty or more species of fish, large and small, drab and gaudy, elegant and grotesque. He was fascinated and a little awed.

The three oceans of Anarres were as full of animal life as the land was empty of it. The seas had not been connected for several million years, so their life forms had followed insular courses of evolution. Their variety was bewildering. It had never occurred to Shevek that life could proliferate so wildly, so exuberantly, that indeed exuberance was perhaps the essential quality of life.

On land, the plants got on well enough, in their sparse and spiny fashion, but those animals that had tried airbreathing had mostly given up the project as the planet's climate entered a millennial era of dust and dryness. Bacteria survived, many of them lithophagous, and a few hundred species of worm and crustacean.

Man fitted himself with care and risk into this narrow ecology. If he fished, but not too greedily, and if he cultivated, using mainly organic wastes for fertilizer, he could fit in. But he could not fit anybody else in. There was no grass for herbivores. There were no herbivores for carnivores. There were no insects to fecundate flowering plants; the imported fruit trees were all hand-fertilized. No animals were introduced from Urras to imperil the delicate balance of life, only the settlers came, and so well scrubbed internally and externally that they brought a minimum of their personal fauna and flora with them. Not even the flea had made it to Anarres.

"I like marine biology," Takver said to Shevek in front

of the fish tanks, "because it's so complex, a real web. This fish eats that fish eats small fry eat ciliates eat bacteria and round you go. On land, there's only three phyla, all nonchordates—if you don't count man. It's a queer situation, biologically speaking. We Anarresti are unnaturally isolated. On the Old World there are eighteen phyla of land animal; there are classes, like the insects, that have so many species they've never been able to count them, and some of those species have populations of billions. Think of it: everywhere you looked animals, other creatures, sharing the earth and air with you. You'd feel so much more a *part*." Her gaze followed the curve of a small blue fish's flight through the dim tank. Shevek, intent, followed the fish's track and her thought's track. He wandered among the tanks for a long time, and often came back with her to the laboratory and the aquaria, submitting his physicist's arrogance to those small strange lives, to the existence of beings to whom the present is eternal, beings that do not explain themselves and need not ever justify their ways to man.

Most Anarresti worked five to seven hours a day, with two to four days off each decad. Details of regularity, punctuality, which days off, and so on were worked out between the individual and his work crew or gang or syndicate or coordinating federative, on whichever level cooperation and efficiency could best be achieved. Takver ran her own research projects, but the work and the fish had their own imperative demands; she spent from two to ten hours a day at the laboratory, no days off. Shevek had two teaching posts now, an advanced math course in a learning center and another at the Institute. Both courses were in the morning, and he got back to the room by noon. Usually Takver was not back yet. The building was quite silent. The sunlight had not yet worked round to the double window that looked south and west over the city and the plains; the room was cool and shadowed. The delicate concentric mobiles hanging at different levels overhead moved with the introverted precision, silence, mystery of the organs of the body or the processes of the reasoning mind. Shevek would sit down at the table under the windows and begin to work, reading or making notes or calculating. Gradually the sunlight entered, shifted across the papers on the table, across his hands on the papers, and filled the room with radiance. And he worked. The false starts and futilities of the past years proved themselves to be groundwork, foundations, laid in the dark but well laid. On these, methodically and carefully but with a deftness and certainty that seemed nothing of his own but a knowledge working through him, using him as its vehicle, he built up the beautiful steadfast structure of the Principles of Simultaneity.

Takver, like any man or woman who undertakes companionship of the creator spirit, did not always have an easy time of it. Although her existence was necessary to Shevek her actual presence could be a distraction. She didn't like to get home too early, because he often quit working when she got home, and she felt this to be wrong. Later on, when they were middle-aged and stodgy, he could ignore her, but at twenty-four he couldn't. Therefore she arranged her tasks in the laboratory so that she did not get home till midafternoon. This was not a perfect arrangement either, for he needed looking after. On days when he had no classes, when she came in he might have been sitting at the table for six or eight hours straight. When he got up he would lurch with fatigue, his hands would shake, and he was scarcely coherent. The usage the creator spirit gives its vessels is rough, it wears them out, discards them, gets a new model. For Takver there were no replacements, and when she saw how hard Shevek was used she protested. She would have cried out as Odo's husband, Asieo, did once, "For God's sake, girl, can't you serve Truth *a little at a time?*"—except that she was the girl, and was unacquainted with God.

They would talk, go out for a walk or to the baths, then to dinner at the Institute commons. After dinner there were meetings, or a concert, or they saw their friends, Bedap and Salas and their circle, Desar and others from the Institute, Takver's colleagues and friends. But the meetings and the friends were peripheral to them. Neither social nor sociable participation was necessary to them; their partnership was enough, and they could not hide the fact. It did not seem to offend the others. Rather the reverse. Bedap, Salas, Desar, and the rest came to them as thirsty people come to a fountain. The others were peripheral to them: but they were central to the others. They did nothing much; they were not more benevolent than other people or more brilliant talkers; and yet their friends loved them, depended on them, and kept bringing them presents—the small offerings that circulated among these people who possessed nothing and everything: a handknit scarf, a bit of granite studded with crimson garnets, a vase hand-thrown at the Potters' Federation workshop, a poem about love, a set of carved wooden buttons, a spiral shell from the Sorruba Sea. They gave the present to Takver, saying, "Here, Shev might like this for a paperweight," or to Shevek, saying, "Here, Tak might like this color." In giving they sought to share in what Shevek and Takver shared, and to celebrate, and to praise.

It was a long summer, warm and bright, the summer of the 160th year of the Settlement of Anarres. Plentiful rains in the spring had greened the Plains of Abbenay and laid the dust so that the air was unusually clear; the sun was warm by day and at night the stars shone thick. When the Moon was in the sky one could make out the coastlines of its continents clearly, under the dazzling white whorls of its clouds.

"Why does it look so beautiful?" Takver said, lying beside Shevek under the orange blanket, the light out. Over them the Occupations of Uninhabited Space hung, dim; out the window the full Moon hung, brilliant. "When we know that it's a planet just like this one, only with a better climate and worse people—when we know they're all propertarians, and fight wars, and make laws, and eat while others starve, and anyhow are all getting older and having bad luck and getting rheumatic knees and corns on their toes just like people here . . . when we know all that, why does it still look so happy—as if life there must be so happy? I can't look at that radiance and imagine a horrid little man with greasy sleeves and an atrophied mind like Sabul living on it; I just can't."

Their naked arms and breasts were moonlit. The fine, faint down on Takver's face made a blurring aureole over her features; her hair and the shadows were black. Shevek touched her silver arm with his silver hand, marveling at the warmth of the touch in that cool light.

"If you can see a thing whole," he said, "it seems that it's always beautiful. Planets, lives. . . . But close up, a world's all dirt and rocks. And day to day, life's a hard job, you get tired, you lose the pattern. You need distance, interval. The way to see how beautiful the earth is, is to see it as the moon. The way to see how beautiful life is, is from the vantage point of death."

"That's all right for Urras. Let it stay off there and be the moon—I don't want it! But I'm not going to stand up on a gravestone and look down on life and say, 'O lovely!' I want to see it whole right in the middle of it, here, now. I don't give a hoot for eternity."

"It's nothing to do with eternity," said Shevek, grinning, a thin shaggy man of silver and shadow. "All you have to do to see life whole is to see it as mortal. I'll die, you'll die; how could we love each other otherwise? The sun's going to burn out, what else keeps it shining?"

"Ah! your talk, your damned philosophy!"

"Talk? It's not talk. It's not reason. It's hand's touch. I touch the wholeness, I hold it. Which is moonlight, which is Takver? How shall I fear death? When I hold it, when I hold in my hands the light—"

"Don't be propertarian," Takver muttered.

"Dear heart, don't cry."

"I'm not crying. You are. Those are your tears."

"I'm cold. The moonlight's cold."

"Lie down."

A great shiver went through his body as she took him in her arms.

"I am afraid, Takver," he whispered.

"Brother, dear soul, hush."

They slept in each other's arms that night, many nights.

Chapter 7

URRAS

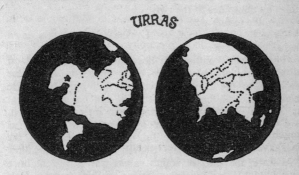

Shevek found a letter in a pocket of the new, fleece-lined coat he had ordered for winter from the shop in the nightmare street. He had no idea how the letter had got there. It certainly had not been in the mail delivered to him thrice daily, which consisted entirely of manuscripts and reprints from physicists all over Urras, invitations to receptions, and artless messages from schoolchildren. This was a flimsy piece of paper stuck down to itself without envelope; it bore no stamp or frank from any of the three competing mail companies.

He opened it, vaguely apprehensive, and read: "If you are an Anarchist why do you work with the power system betraying your World and the Odonian Hope or are you here to bring us that Hope. Suffering from injustice and repression we look to the Sister World the light of freedom in the dark night. Join with us your brothers!" There was no signature, no address.

It shook Shevek both morally and intellectually, jolted him, not with surprise but with a kind of panic. He knew they were here: but where? He had not met one, not seen one, he had not met a poor man yet. He had let a wall be built around him and had never noticed. He had accepted shelter, like a propertarian. He had been co-opted—just as Chifoilisk had said.

But he did not know how to break down the wall. And if he did, where could he go? The panic closed in on him tighter. To whom could he turn? He was surrounded on all sides by the smiles of the rich.

"I'd like to talk with you, Efor."

"Yes sir. Excuse me, sir, I make room set this down here."

The servant handled the heavy tray deftly, flicked off dish covers, poured out the bitter chocolate so it rose frothing to the cup's rim without spill or splatter. He clearly enjoyed the breakfast ritual and his adeptness at it, and as clearly wanted no unusual interruptions in it. He often spoke quite clear Iotic, but now as soon as Shevek said he wanted a talk Efor had slid into the staccato of the city dialect. Shevek had learned to follow it a little; the shift of sound values was consistent once you caught it, but the apocopations left him groping. Half the words were left out. It was like a code, he thought: as if the "Nioti," as they called themselves, did not want to be understood by outsiders.

The manservant stood awaiting Shevek's pleasure. He knew—he had learned Shevek's idiosyncrasies within the first week—that Shevek did not want him to hold a chair, or to wait on him while he ate. His erect attentive pose was enough to wither any hope of informality.

"Will you sit down, Efor?"

"If you please sir," the man replied. He moved a chair half an inch, but did not sit down in it.

"This is what I want to talk about. You know I don't like to give you orders."

"Try manage things like you want sir without troubling for orders."

"You do—I don't mean that. You know, in my country nobody gives any orders."

"So I hear sir."

"Well, I want to know you as my equal, my brother. You are the only one I know here who is not rich—not one of the owners. I want very much to talk with you, I want to know about your life—"

He stopped in despair, seeing the contempt on Efor's

lined face. He had made all the mistakes possible. Efor took him for a patronizing, prying fool.

He dropped his hands to the table in a gesture of hopelessness and said, "Oh, hell, I am sorry, Efor!" I cannot say what I mean. Please ignore it."

"Just as you say sir." Efor withdrew.

That was the end of that. The "unpropertied classes" remained as remote from him as when he had read about them in history at Northsetting Regional Institute.

Meanwhile, he had promised to spend a week with the Oiies, between winter and spring terms.

Oiie had invited him to dinner several times since his first visit, always rather stiffly, as if he were carrying out a duty of hospitality, or perhaps a governmental order. In his own house, however, though never wholly off his guard with Shevek, he was genuinely friendly. By the second visit his two sons had decided that Shevek was an old friend, and their confidence in Shevek's response obviously puzzled their father. It made him uneasy; he could not really approve of it; but he could not say it was unjustified. Shevek behaved to them like an old friend, like an elder brother. They admired him, and the younger, Ini, came to love him passionately, Shevek was kind, serious honest, and told very good stories about the Moon; but there was more to it than that. He represented something to the child that Ini could not describe. Even much later in his life, which was profoundly and obscurely influenced by that childhood fascination, Ini found no words for it, only words that held an echo of it: the word *voyager*, the word *exile*.

The only heavy snow of the winter fell that week. Shevek had never seen a snowfall of more than an inch or so. The extravagance, the sheer quantity, of the storm exhilarated him. He reveled in its excess. It was too white, too cold, silent, and indifferent to be called excremental by the sincerest Odonian; to see it as other than an innocent magnificence would be pettiness of soul. As soon as the sky cleared he went out in it with the boys, who appreciated it just as he did. They ran around in the big back garden of the Oiie house, threw snowballs, built tunnels, castles, and fortresses of snow.

Sewa Oiie stood with her sister-in-law Vea at the window, watching the children, the man, and the little

157

otter playing. The otter had made himself a snowslide down one wall of the snow castle and was excitedly tobogganing down it on his belly over and over again. The boys' cheeks were fiery. The man, his long, rough, dun-grey hair tied back with a piece of string and his ears red with cold, executed tunneling operations with energy. "Not here!—Dig *there!*—Where's the shovel?—Ice in my pocket!"—the boys' high voices rang out continually.

"There is our alien," Sewa said, smiling.

"The greatest physicist alive," said the sister-in-law. "How funny!"

When he came in, puffing and stamping off snow and exhaling that fresh, cold vigor and well-being which only people just in out of the snow possess, he was introduced to the sister-in-law. He put out his big, hard, cold hand and looked down at Vea with friendly eyes. "You are Demaere's sister?" he said. "Yes, you look like him." And this remark, which from anyone else would have struck Vea as insipid, pleased her immensely. "He is a man," she kept thinking that afternoon, "a real man. What is it about him?"

Vea Doem Oiie was her name, in the Ioti mode; her husband Doem was the head of a large industrial combine and traveled a good deal, spending half of each year abroad as a business representative of the government. This was explained to Shevek, while he watched her. In her, Demaere Oiie's slightness, pale coloring, and oval black eyes had been transmuted into beauty. Her breasts, shoulders, and arms were round, soft, and very white. Shevek sat beside her at the dinner table. He kept looking at her bare breasts, pushed upward by the stiff bodice. The notion of going thus half naked in freezing weather was extravagant, as extravagant as the snow, and the small breasts had also an innocent whiteness, like the snow. The curve of her neck went up smoothly into the curve of the proud, shaven, delicate head.

She really is quite attractive, Shevek informed himself. She's like the beds here: soft. Affected, though. Why does she mince out her words like that?

He clung to her rather thin voice and mincing manner as to a raft on deep water, and never knew it, never knew he was drowning. She was going back to Nio Esseia on the train after dinner, she had merely come out for the day and he would never see her again.

Oiie had a cold, Sewa was busy with the children. "Shevek, do you think you might walk Vea to the station?"

"Good Lord, Demaere! Don't make the poor man protect me! You don't think there'll be wolves, do you? Will savage Mingrads come sweeping into town and abduct me to their harems? Will I be found on the stationmaster's doorstep tomorrow morning, a tear frozen in my eye and my tiny, rigid hands clasping a bunch of withered posies? Oh, I do rather like that!" Over Vea's rattling, tinkling talk her laugh broke like a wave, a dark, smooth, powerful wave that washed out everything and left the sand empty. She did not laugh with herself but at herself, the body's dark laughter, wiping out words.

Shevek put on his coat in the hall and was waiting for her at the door.

They walked in silence for a half a block. Snow crunched and squeaked under their feet.

"You're really much too polite for . . ."

"For what?"

"For an anarchist," she said, in her thin and affectedly drawling voice (it was the same intonation Pae used, and Oiie when he was at the University). "I'm disappointed. I thought you'd be dangerous and uncouth."

"I am."

She glanced up at him sidelong. She wore a scarlet shawl tied over her head; her eyes looked black and bright against the vivid color and the whiteness of snow all around.

"But here you are tamely walking me to the station, Dr. Shevek."

"Shevek," he said mildly. "No 'doctor.' "

"Is that your whole name—first and last?"

He nodded, smiling. He felt well and vigorous, pleased by the bright air, the warmth of the well-made coat he wore, the prettiness of the woman beside him. No worries or heavy thoughts had hold on him today.

"Is it true that you get your names from a computer?"

"Yes."

"How dreary, to be named by a machine!"

"Why dreary?"

"It's so mechanical, so impersonal."

159

"But what is more personal than a name no other living person bears?"

"No one else? You're the only Shevek?"

"While I live. There were others, before me."

"Relatives, you mean?"

"We don't count relatives much; we are all relatives, you see. I don't know who they were, except for one, in the early years of the Settlement. She designed a kind of bearing they use in heavy machines, they still call it a 'shevek.'" He smiled again, more broadly. "There is a good immortality!"

Vea shook her head. "Good Lord!" she said. "How do you tell men from women?"

"Well, we have discovered methods. . . ."

After a moment her soft, heavy laugh broke out. She wiped her eyes, which watered in the cold air. "Yes, perhaps you are uncouth! . . . Did they all take made-up names, then, and learn a made-up language—everything new?"

"The Settlers of Anarres? Yes. They were romantic people, I suppose."

"And you're not?"

"No. We are very pragmatic."

"You can be both," she said.

He had not expected any subtlety of mind from her. "Yes, that's true," he said.

"What's more romantic than your coming here, all alone, without a coin in your pocket, to plead for your people?"

"And to be spoiled with luxuries while I am here."

"Luxuries? In university rooms? Good Lord! You poor dear! Haven't they taken you anywhere decent?"

"Many places, but all the same. I wish I could come to know Nio Esseia better. I have seen only the outside of the city—the wrapping of the package." He used the phrase because he had been fascinated from the start by the Urrasti habit of wrapping everything up in clean, fancy paper or plastic or cardboard or foil. Laundry, books, vegetables, clothes, medicines, everything came inside layers and layers of wrappings. Even packets of paper were wrapped in several layers of paper. Nothing was to touch anything else. He had begun to feel that he, too, had been carefully packaged.

"I know. They made you go to the Historical Museum, and take a tour of the Dobunnae Monument, and listen to a speech in the Senate!" He laughed, because that had been precisely the itinerary one day last summer. "I know! They're so stupid with foreigners. I shall see to it that you see the real Nio!"

"I should like that."

"I know all kinds of wonderful people. I collect people. Here you are trapped among all these stuffy professors and politicians. . . ." She rattled on. He took pleasure in her inconsequential talk just as he did in the sunshine and the snow.

They came to the little station of Amoeno. She had her return ticket; the train was due in any moment.

"Don't wait, you'll freeze."

He did not reply but just stood, bulky in the fleece-lined coat, looking amiably at her.

She looked down at the cuff of her coat and brushed a speck of snow off the embroidery.

"Have you a wife, Shevek?"

"No."

"No family at all?"

"Oh—yes. A partner; our children. Excuse me, I was thinking of something else. A 'wife,' you see. I think of that as something that exists only on Urras."

"What's a 'partner'?" She glanced up mischievously into his face.

"I think you would say a wife or husband."

"Why didn't she come with you?"

She did not want to; and the younger child is only one . . . no, two, now. Also—" He hesitated.

"Why didn't she want to come?"

"Well, there she has work to do, not here. If I had known how she would like so many things here, I would have asked her to come. But I did not. There is the question of safety, you see."

"Safety here?"

He hesitated again, and finally said, "Also when I go home."

"What will happen to you?" Vea asked, round-eyed. The train was pulling over the hill outside town.

"Oh, probably nothing. But there are some who consider me a traitor. Because I try to make friends with Urras,

161

you see. They might make trouble when I go home. I don't want that for her and the children. We had a little of it before I left. Enough."

"You'll be in actual danger, you mean?"

He bent toward her to hear, for the train was pulling into the station with a clatter of wheels and carriages. "I don't know," he said, smiling. "You know, our trains look very much like these? A good design need not change." He went with her to a first-class carriage. Since she did not open the door, he did. He put his head in after her, looking around the compartment. "Inside they are not alike, though! This is all private—for yourself?"

"Oh, yes. I detest second class. Men chewing maera-gum and spitting. Do people chew maera on Anarres? No, surely not. Oh, there are so many things I'd love to know about you and your country!"

"I love to tell about it, but nobody asks."

"Do let's meet again and talk about it, then! When you're next in Nio, will you call me? Promise."

"I promise," he said good-naturedly.

"Good! I know you don't break promises. I don't know anything about you yet, except that. I can *see* that. Goodbye, Shevek." She put her gloved hand on his for a moment as he held the door. The engine gave its two-note honk; he shut the door, and watched the train pull out. Vea's face a flicker of white and scarlet at the window.

He walked back to the Oiies' in a very cheerful frame of mind, and had a snowball battle with Ini until dark.

REVOLUTION IN BENBILI! DICTATOR FLEES!
REBEL LEADERS HOLD CAPITAL!
EMERGENCY SESSION IN CWG. POSSIBILITY
A-IO MAY INTERVENE.

The birdseed paper was excited into its hugest typeface. Spelling and grammar fell by the wayside; it read like Efor talking: "By last night rebels hold all west of Meskti and pushing army hard. . . ." It was the verbal mode of the Nioti, past and future rammed into one highly charged unstable present tense.

Shevek read the papers and looked up a description of Benbili in the CWG Encyclopedia. The nation was in form a parliamentary democracy, in fact a military dic-

162

tatorship, run by generals. It was a large country in the western hemisphere, mountains and arid savannahs, underpopulated, poor. "I should have gone to Benbili," Shevek thought, for the idea of it drew him; he imagined pale plains, the wind blowing. The news had stirred him strangely. He listened for bulletins on the radio, which he had seldom turned on after finding that its basic function was advertising things for sale. Its reports, and those of the official telefax in public rooms, were brief and dry: a queer contrast to the popular papers, which shouted Revolution! on every page.

General Havevert, the President, got away safe in his famous armored airplane, but some lesser generals were caught and emasculated, a punishment the Benbili traditionally preferred to execution. The retreating army burned the fields and towns of their people as they went. Guerrilla partisans harried the army. The revolutionaries in Mesktî, the capital, opened the jails, giving amnesty to all prisoners. Reading that, Shevek's heart leapt. There was hope, there was still hope. . . . He followed the news of the distant revolution with increasing intensity. On the fourth day, watching a telefax broadcast of debate in the Council of World Governments, he saw the Ioti ambassador to the CWG announce that A-Io, rising to the support of the democratic government of Benbili, was sending armed reinforcements to President-General Havevert.

The Benbili revolutionaries were mostly not even armed. The Ioti troops would come with guns, armored cars, airplanes, bombs. Shevek read the description of their equipment in the paper and felt sick at his stomach.

He felt sick and enraged, and there was nobody he could talk to. Pae was out of the question. Atro was an ardent militarist. Oiie was an ethical man, but his private insecurities, his anxieties as a property owner, made him cling to rigid notions of law and order. He could cope with his personal liking for Shevek only by refusing to admit that Shevek was an anarchist. The Odonian society called itself anarchistic, he said, but they were in fact mere primitive populists whose social order functioned without apparent government because there were so few of them and because they had no neighbor states. When their property was threatened by an aggressive rival, they would

163

either wake up to reality or be wiped out. The Benbili rebels were waking up to reality now: they were finding freedom is no good if you have no guns to back it up. He explained this to Shevek in the one discussion they had on the subject. It did not matter who governed, or thought they governed, the Benbilis: the politics of reality concerned the power struggle between A-Io and Thu.

"The politics of reality," Shevek repeated. He looked at Oiie and said, "That is a curious phrase for a physicist to use."

"Not at all. The politician and the physicist both deal with things as they are, with real forces, the basic laws of the world."

"You put your petty miserable 'laws' to protect wealth, your 'forces' of guns and bombs, in the same sentence with the law of entropy and the force of gravity? I had thought better of your mind, Demaere!"

Oiie shrank from that thunderbolt of contempt. He said no more, and Shevek said no more, but Oiie never forgot it. It lay imbedded in his mind thereafter as the most shameful moment of his life. For if Shevek the deluded and simple-minded utopist had silenced him so easily, that was shameful; but if Shevek the physicist and the man whom he could not help liking, admiring, so that he longed to deserve his respect, as if it were somehow a finer grade of respect than any currently available elsewhere—if this Shevek despised him, then the shame was intolerable, and he must hide it, lock it away the rest of his life in the darkest room of his soul.

The subject of the Benbili revolution had sharpened certain problems for Shevek also: particularly the problem of his own silence.

It was difficult for him to distrust the people he was with. He had been brought up in a culture that relied deliberately and constantly on human solidarity, mutual aid. Alienated as he was in some ways from that culture, and alien as he was to this one, still the lifelong habit remained: he assumed people would be helpful. He trusted them.

But Chifoilisk's warnings, which he had tried to dismiss, kept returning to him. His own perceptions and instincts reinforced them. Like it or not, he must learn distrust. He

164

must be silent; he must keep his property to himself, he must keep his bargaining power.

He said little, these days, and wrote down less. His desk was a moraine of insignificant papers; his few working notes were always right on his body, in one of his numerous Urrasti pockets. He never left his desk computer without clearing it.

He knew that he was very near achieving the General Temporal Theory that the Ioti wanted so badly for their spaceflight and their prestige. He knew also that he had not achieved it and might never do so. He had never admitted either fact clearly to anyone.

Before he left Anarres, he had thought the thing was in his grasp. He had the equations. Sabul knew he had them, and had offered him reconciliation, recognition, in return for the chance to print them and get in on the glory. He had refused Sabul, but it had not been a grand moral gesture. The moral gesture, after all, would have been to give them to his own press at the Syndicate of Initiative, and he hadn't done that either. He wasn't quite sure he was ready to publish. There was something not quite right, something that needed a little refining. As he had been working ten years on the theory, it wouldn't hurt to take a little longer, to get it polished perfectly smooth.

The little something not quite right kept looking wronger. A little flaw in the reasoning. A big flaw. A crack right through the foundations. . . . The night before he left Anarres he had burned every paper he had on the General Theory. He had come to Urras with nothing. For half a year he had, in their terms, been bluffing them.

Or had he been bluffing himself?

It was quite possible that a general theory of temporality was an illusory goal. It was also possible that, though Sequency and Simultaneity might someday be unified in a general theory, he was not the man to do the job. He had been trying for ten years and had not done it. Mathematicians and physicists, athletes of intellect, do their great work young. It was more than possible—probable—that he was burnt out, finished.

He was perfectly aware that he had had the same low moods and intimations of failure in the periods just before his moments of highest creativity. He found himself trying to encourage himself with that fact, and was furious at his own naïveté. To interpret temporal order as causal order was a pretty stupid thing for a chronosophist to do. Was he senile already? He had better simply get to work on the small but practical task of refining the concept of interval. It might be useful to someone else.

But even in that, even in talking with other physicists about it, he felt that he was holding something back. And they knew he was.

He was sick of holding back, sick of not talking, not talking about the revolution, not talking about physics, not talking about anything.

He crossed the campus on his way to a lecture. The birds were singing in the newly leafed trees. He had not heard them sing all winter, but now they were at it, pouring it out, the sweet tunes. *Ree-dee,* they sang, *tee-dee. This is my propertee-tee, this is my territoree-ree-ree, it belongs to mee, mee.*

Shevek stood still for a minute under the trees, listening.

Then he turned off the path, crossed the campus in a different direction, towards the station, and caught a morning train to Nio Esseia. There had to be a door open somewhere on this damned planet!

He thought, as he sat in the train, of trying to get out of A-Io: of going to Benbili, maybe. But he did not take the thought seriously. He would have to ride on a ship or airplane, he would be traced and stopped. The only place where he could get out of sight of his benevolent and protective hosts was in their own big city, under their noses.

It was not an escape. Even if he did get out of the country, he would still be locked in, locked in Urras. You couldn't call that escape, whatever the archists, with their mystique of national boundaries, might call it. But he suddenly felt cheerful, as he had not for days, when he thought that his benevolent and protective hosts might think, for a moment, that he had escaped.

It was the first really warm day of spring. The fields were green, and flashed with water. On the pasture lands each stock beast was accompanied by her young. The infant sheep were particularly charming, bouncing like white elastic balls, their tails going round and round. In a pen by himself the herd sire, ram or bull or stallion, heavy-necked, stood potent as a thundercloud, charged with generation. Gulls swept over brimming ponds, white over blue, and white clouds brightened the pale blue sky. The branches of orchard trees were tipped with red, and a few blossoms were open, rose and white. Watching from the train window Shevek found his restless and rebellious mood ready to defy even the day's beauty. It was an unjust beauty. What had the Urrasti done to deserve it? Why was it given to them, so lavishly, so graciously, and so little, so very little, to his own people?

I'm thinking like an Urrasti, he said to himself. Like a damned propertarian. As if deserving meant anything. As if one could earn beauty, or life! He tried to think of nothing at all, to let himself be borne forward and to watch the sunlight in the gentle sky and the little sheep bouncing in the fields of spring.

Nio Esseia, a city of five million souls, lifted its delicate glittering towers across the green marshes of the Estuary as if it were built of mist and sunlight. As the train swung in smoothly on a long viaduct the city rose up taller, brighter, solider, until suddenly it enclosed the train entirely in the roaring darkness of an underground approach, twenty tracks together, and then released it and its passengers into the enormous, brilliant spaces of the Central Station, under the central dome of ivory and azure, said to be the largest dome ever raised on any world by the hand of man.

Shevek wandered across acres of polished marble under that immense ethereal vault, and came at last to the long array of doors through which crowds of people came and went constantly, all purposeful, all separate. They all looked, to him, anxious. He had often seen that anxiety before in the faces of Urrasti, and wondered about it. Was it because, no matter how much money they had, they always had to worry about making more, lest they die poor? Was it guilt, because no matter how little money they had, there was always somebody who had less? Whatever the cause, it gave all the faces a certain sameness, and he felt very much alone among them. In escaping his guides and guards he had not considered what it might be like to be on one's own in a society where men did not trust one another, where the basic moral assumption was not mutual aid, but mutual aggression. He was a little frightened.

He had vaguely imagined wandering about the city and

getting into conversation with people, members of the unpropertied class, if there still was such a thing, or the working classes, as they called them. But all these people hurried along, on business, wanting no idle talk, no waste of their valuable time. Their hurry infected him. He must go somewhere, he thought, as he came out into the sunlight and the crowded magnificence of Moie Street. Where? The National Library? The Zoo? But he did not want to sightsee.

Irresolute, he stopped in front of a shop near the station that sold newspapers and trinkets. The headline of the paper said THU SENDS TROOPS TO AID BENBILI REBELS, but he did not react to it. He looked at the color photographs in the rack, instead of the newspaper. It occurred to him that he had no mementos of Urras. When one traveled one ought to bring back a souvenir. He liked the photographs, scenes of A-Io: the mountains he had climbed, the skyscrapers of Nio, the university chapel (almost the view out his window), a farm girl in pretty provincial dress, the towers of Rodarred, and the one that had first caught his eye, a baby sheep in a flowered meadow, kicking its legs and, apparently, laughing. Little Pilun would like that sheep. He selected one of each card and took them to the counter. "And five's fifty and the lamb makes it sixty; and a map, right you are, sir, one forty. Nice day, spring's here at last, isn't it, sir? Nothing smaller than that, sir?" Shevek had produced a twenty-unit bank note. He fumbled out the change he had received when he bought his ticket, and, with a little study of the denominations of the bills and coins, got together one unit forty. "That's right, sir. Thank you and have a pleasant day!"

Did the money buy the politeness, as well as the postcards and the map? How polite would the shopkeeper have been if he had come in as an Anarresti came in to a goods depository: to take what he wanted, nod to the registrar, and walk out?

No use, no use thinking this way. When in the Land of Property think like a propertarian. Dress like one, eat like one, act like one, be one.

There were no parks in downtown Nio, the land was far too valuable to waste on amenity. He kept getting deeper into the same great, glittering streets that he had

168

been taken through many times. He came to Saemtenevia Street and crossed it hurriedly, not wanting a repetition of the daylight nightmare. Now he was in the commercial district. Banks, office buildings, government buildings. Was all Nio Esseia this? Huge shining boxes of stone and glass, immense, ornate, enormous packages, empty, empty.

Passing a ground-floor window marked Art Gallery, he turned in, thinking to escape the moral claustrophobia of the streets and find the beauty of Urras again in a museum. But all the pictures in the museum had price tickets attached to their frames. He stared at a skillfully painted nude. Her ticket read 4,000 IMU. "That's a Fei Feite," said a dark man appearing noiselessly at his elbow. "We had five a week ago. Biggest thing on the art market before long. A Feite is a sure investment, sir."

"Four thousand units is the money it costs to keep two families alive for a year in this city," Shevek said.

The man inspected him and said drawling, "Yes, well, you see, sir, that happens to be a work of art."

"Art? A man makes art because he has to. Why was that made?"

"You're an artist, I take it," the man said, now with open insolence.

"No, I am a man who knows shit when he sees it!" The dealer shrank back. When he was out of Shevek's reach, he began to say something about the police. Shevek grimaced and strode out of the shop. Halfway down the block he stopped. He couldn't go on this way.

But where could he go?

To someone . . . to someone, another person. A human being. Someone who would give help, not sell it. Who? Where?

He thought of Oiie's children, the little boys who liked him, and for some time could think of no one else. Then an image rose in his mind, distant, small, and clear: Oiie's sister. What was her name? Promise you'll call, she had said, and since then she had twice written him invitations to dinner parties, in a bold childish hand, on thick, sweet-scented paper. He had ignored them, among all the invitations from strangers. Now he remembered them.

He remembered at the same time the other message, the one that had appeared inexplicably in his coat pocket: *Join with us your brothers.* But he could not find any brothers, on Urras.

He went into the nearest shop. It was a sweetshop, all golden scrolls and pink plaster, with rows of glass cases full of boxes and tins and baskets of candies and confections, pink, brown, cream, gold. He asked the woman behind the cases if she would help him find a telephone number. He was now subdued, after his fit of bad temper in the art dealer's, and so humbly ignorant and foreign that the woman was won over. She not only helped him look up the name in the ponderous directory of telephone numbers, but placed the call for him on the shop phone.

"Hello?"

He said, "Shevek." Then he stopped. The telephone to him was a vehicle of urgent needs, notifications of deaths, births, and earthquakes. He had no idea what to say.

"Who? Shevek? Is it really? How dear of you to call! I don't mind waking up at all if it's you."

"You were sleeping?"

"Sound asleep, and I'm still in bed. It's lovely and warm. Where on earth are you?"

"On Kae Sekae Street, I think."

"Whatever for? Come on out. What time is it? Good Lord, nearly noon. I know, I'll meet you halfway. By the boat pool in the Old Palace gardens. Can you find it? Listen, you must stay, I'm having an absolutely paradisial party tonight." She rattled on awhile; he agreed to all she said. As he came out past the counter the shopwoman smiled at him. "Better take her a box of sweets, hadn't you, sir?"

He stopped. "Should I?"

"Never does any harm, sir."

There was something impudent and genial in her voice. The air of the shop was sweet and warm, as if all the perfumes of spring were crowded into it. Shevek stood there amidst the cases of pretty little luxuries, tall, heavy, dreamy, like the heavy animals in their pens, the rams and bulls stupefied by the yearning warmth of spring.

"I'll make you up just the thing," the woman said, and she filled a little metal box, exquisitely enameled, with miniature leaves of chocolate and roses of spun sugar. She wrapped the tin in tissue paper, put the packet in a silvered cardboard box, wrapped the box in heavy rose-colored paper, and tied it with green velvet ribbon. In all her deft movements a humorous and sympathetic complicity could be sensed, and when she handed Shevek the completed package, and he took it with muttered thanks and turned to go, there was no sharpness in her voice as she reminded him, "That's ten sixty, sir." She might even have let him go, pitying him, as women will pity strength; but he came back obediently and counted out the money.

He found his way by subway train to the gardens of the Old Palace, and to the boat pool, where charmingly dressed children sailed toy ships, marvelous little craft with silken cordage and brasswork like jewelry. He saw Vea across the broad, bright circle of the water and went around the pool to her, aware of the sunlight, and the spring wind, and the dark trees of the park putting forth their early, pale-green leaves.

They ate lunch at a restaurant in the park, on a terrace covered with a high glass dome. In the sunlight inside the dome the trees were in full leaf, willows, hanging over a pool where fat white birds paddled, watching the diners with indolent greed, awaiting scraps. Vea did not take charge of the ordering, making it clear that Shevek was in charge of her, but skillful waiters advised him so smoothly that he thought he had managed it all himself; and fortunately he had plenty of money in his pocket. The food was extraordinary. He had never tasted such subtleties of flavor. Used to two meals a day, he usually skipped the lunch the Urrasti ate, but today he ate right through it, while Vea delicately picked and pecked. He had to stop at last, and she laughed at his rueful look.

"I ate too much."

"A little walk might help."

It was a very little walk: a slow ten-minute stroll over the grass, and then Vea collapsed gracefully in the shade of a high bank of shrubs, all bright with golden flowers. He sat down by her. A phrase Takver used came into his mind as he looked at Vea's slender feet, decorated with little white shoes on very high heels. "A body profiteer," Takver called women who used their sexuality as a weapon in a power struggle with men. To look at her, Vea was the body profiteer to end them all. Shoes, clothes, cosmetics, jewels, gestures, everything about her asserted provocation. She was so elaborately and ostentatiously a female body that she seemed scarcely to be a human being. She incarnated all the sexuality the Ioti repressed into their dreams, their novels and poetry, their endless paintings of female nudes, their music, their architecture with its curves and domes, their candies, their baths, their mattresses. She was the woman in the table.

Her head, entirely shaven, had been dusted with a talc containing tiny flecks of mica dust, so that a faint glitter obscured the nakedness of the contours. She wore a filmy shawl or stole, under which the forms and texture of her bare arms showed softened and sheltered. Her breasts were covered: Ioti women did not go outside with naked breasts, reserving their nudity for its owners. Her wrists were laden with gold bracelets, and in the hollow of her throat a single jewel shone blue against the soft skin.

"How does that stay there?"

"What?" Since she could not see the jewel herself she could pretend to be unaware of it, obliging him to point, perhaps to bring his hand up over her breasts to touch the jewel. Shevek smiled, and touched it. "It is glued on?"

"Oh, that. No, I've got a tiny little magnet set in there, and it's got a tiny little bit of metal on the back, or is it the other way round? Anyhow, we stick together."

"You have a magnet under your skin?" Shevek inquired with unsophisticated distaste.

Vea smiled and removed the sapphire so he could see that there was nothing but the tiniest silver dimple of a scar. "You do disapprove of me so totally—it's refreshing. I feel that whatever I say or do, I can't possibly lower myself in your opinion, because I've already reached bottom!"

"That is not so," he protested. He knew she was playing, but knew few of the rules of the game.

"No, no; I know moral horror when I see it. Like this." She put on a dismal scowl; they both laughed. "Am I so different from Anarresti women, really?"

"Oh, yes, really."

"Are they all terribly strong, with muscles? Do they wear boots, and have big flat feet, and sensible clothing, and shave once a month?"

"They don't shave at all."

"Never? Not anywhere? Oh, Lord! Let's talk about something else."

"About you." He leaned on the grassy bank, near enough to Vea that he was surrounded by the natural and artificial perfumes of her body. "I want to know, is an Urrasti woman content to be always inferior?"

"Inferior to whom?"

"To men."

"Oh—that! What makes you think I am?"

"It seems that everything your society does is done by men. The industry, arts, management, government, decisions. And all your life you bear the father's name and the husband's name. The men go to school and you don't go to school; they are all the teachers, and judges, and police, and government, aren't they? Why do you let them control everything? Why don't you do what you like?"

"But we do. Women do exactly as they like. And they don't have to get their hands dirty, or wear brass helmets, or stand about shouting in the Directorate, to do it."

"But what is it that you do?"

"Why, run the men, of course! And you know, it's perfectly safe to tell them that, because they never believe it. They say, 'Haw haw, funny little woman!' and pat your head and stalk off with their medals jangling, perfectly self-content."

"And you too are self-content?"

"Indeed I am."

"I don't believe it."

"Because it doesn't fit your principles. Men always have theories, and things always have to fit them."

"No, not because of theories, because I can see that you are not content. That you are restless, unsatisfied, dangerous."

"Dangerous!" Vea laughed radiantly. "What an utterly marvelous compliment! Why am I dangerous, Shevek?"

"Why, because you know that in the eyes of men you are a thing, a thing owned, bought, sold. And so you think only of tricking the owners, of getting revenge—"

She put her small hand deliberately on his mouth. "Hush," she said. "I know you don't intend to be vulgar. I forgive you. But that's quite enough."

He scowled savagely at the hypocrisy, and at the realization that he might really have hurt her. He could still feel the brief touch of her hand on his lips. "I am sorry!" he said.

"No, no. How can you understand, coming from the Moon? And you're only a man, anyway. . . . I'll tell you something, though. If you took one of your 'sisters' up there on the Moon, and gave her a chance to take off her boots, and have an oil bath and a depilation, and put on a pair of pretty sandals, and a belly jewel, and perfume, she'd love it. And you'd love it too! Oh, you would! But you won't, you poor things with your theories. All brothers and sisters and no fun!"

"You are right," Shevek said. "No fun. Never. All day long on Anarres we dig lead in the bowels of the mines, and when night comes, after our meal of three holum grains cooked in one spoonful of brackish water, we antiphonally recite the Sayings of Odo, until it is time to go to bed. Which we all do separately, and wearing boots."

His fluency in Iotic was not sufficient to permit him the word flight this might have been in his own language, one of his sudden fantasies which only Takver and Sadik had heard often enough to get used to; but, lame as it was, it startled Vea. Her dark laugh broke out, heavy and spontaneous. "Good Lord, you're funny, too! Is there anything you aren't?"

"A salesman," he said.

She studied him, smiling. There was something professional, actress-like, in her pose. People do not usually gaze at one another intently at very close range, unless they are mothers with infants, or doctors with patients, or lovers.

He sat up. "I want to walk more," he said.

She reached up her hand for him to take and help her rise. The gesture was indolent and inviting, but she said with an uncertain tenderness in her voice, "You really are like a brother. . . . Take my hand. I'll let you go again!"

They wandered along the paths of the great garden. They went into the palace, preserved as a museum of the ancient times of royalty, as Vea said she loved to look at the jewelry there. Portraits of arrogant lords and princes stared at them from the brocade-covered walls and the carven chimneypieces. The rooms were full of silver, gold, crystal, rare woods, tapestries, and jewels. Guards stood behind the velvet ropes. The guards' black and scarlet uniforms consorted well with the splendors, the hangings

174

of spun gold, the counterpanes of woven feathers, but their faces did not match; they were bored faces, tired, tired of standing all day among strangers doing a useless task. Shevek and Vea came to a glass case in which lay the cloak of Queen Teaea, made of the tanned skins of rebels flayed alive, which that terrible and defiant woman had worn when she went among her plague-stricken people to pray God to end the pestilence, fourteen hundred years ago. "It looks awfully like goatskin to me," Vea said, examining the discolored, time-tattered rag in the glass case. She glanced up at Shevek. "Are you all right?"

"I think I would like to go outside this place."

Once outside in the garden his face became less white, but he looked back at the palace walls with hatred. "Why do you people cling to your shame?" he said.

"But it's all just history. Things like that couldn't happen now!"

She took him to a matinee at the theater, a comedy about young married people and their mothers-in-law, full of jokes about copulation which never mentioned copulation. Shevek attempted to laugh when Vea did. After that they went to a downtown restaurant, a place of incredible opulence. The dinner cost a hundred units. Shevek ate very little of it, having eaten at noon, but he gave in to Vea's urging and drank two or three glasses of wine, which was pleasanter than he had expected it to be, and seemed to have no deleterious effect on his thinking. He had not enough money to pay for the dinner, but Vea made no offer to share the cost, merely suggesting that he write a check, which he did. They then took a hired car to Vea's apartment; she also let him pay the driver. Could it be, he wondered, that Vea was actually a prostitute, that mysterious entity? But prostitutes as Odo wrote of them were poor women, and surely Vea was not poor; "her" party, she had told him, was being got ready by "her" cook, "her" maid, and "her" caterer. Moreover men at the University spoke of prostitutes contemptuously as dirty creatures, while Vea, despite her continual allurements, displayed such sensitivity to open talk about anything sexual that Shevek watched his language with her as he might have done, at home, with a shy child of ten. All together, he did not know what exactly Vea was.

Vea's rooms were large and luxurious, with glittering

175

views of the lights of Nio, and furnished entirely in white, even the carpeting. But Shevek was getting callous to luxury, and besides was extremely sleepy. The guests were not due to arrive for an hour. While Vea was changing her clothes, he fell asleep in a huge white armchair in the living room. The maid rattling something on the table woke him in time to see Vea come back in, dressed now in Ioti formal evening wear for women, a full-length pleated skirt draped from the hips, leaving the whole torso naked. In her navel a little jewel glittered, just as in the pictures he had seen with Tirin and Bedap a quarter-century ago at the Northsetting Regional Institute of Science, just so. . . . Half awake and wholly roused, he stared at her.

She gazed back at him, smiling a little.

She sat down on a low, cushioned stool near him, so she could look up into his face. She arranged her white skirt over her ankles, and said, "Now, tell me how it really is between men and women on Anarres."

It was unbelievable. The maid and the caterer's man were both in the room; she knew he had a partner, and he knew she did; and not a word about copulating had passed between them. Yet her dress, movements, tone—what were they but the most open invitation?

"Between a man and a woman there is what they want there to be between them," he said, rather roughly. "Each, and both."

"Then it's true, you really have no morality?" she asked, as if shocked but delighted.

"I don't know what you mean. To hurt a person there is the same as to hurt a person here."

"You mean you have all the same old rules? You see, I believe that morality is just another superstition, like religion. It's got to be thrown out."

"But my society," he said, completely puzzled, "is an attempt to *reach* it. To throw out the moralizing, yes—the rules, the laws, the punishments—so that men can see good and evil and choose between them."

"So you threw out all the do's and don'ts. But you know, I think you Odonians missed the whole point. You threw out the priests and judges and divorce laws and all that, but you kept the real trouble behind them. You just stuck it inside, into your consciences. But it's still there.

176

You're just as much slaves as ever! You aren't really free."

"How do you know?"

"I read an article in a magazine about Odonianism," she said. "And we've been together all day. I don't know you, but I know some things about you. I know that you've got a—a Queen Teaea inside you, right inside that hairy head of yours. And she orders you around just like the old tyrant did her serfs. She says, 'Do this!' and you do, and 'Don't!' and you don't."

"That is where she belongs," he said, smiling. "Inside my head."

"No. Better to have her in a palace. Then you could rebel gainst her. You would have! Your great-great-grandfather did; at least he ran off to the Moon to get away. But he took Queen Teaea with him, and you've still got her!"

"Maybe. But she has learned, on Anarres, that if she tells me to hurt another person, I hurt myself."

"The same old hypocrisy. Life is a fight, and the strongest wins. All civilization does is hide the blood and cover up the hate with pretty words!"

"Your civilization, perhaps. Ours hides nothing. It is all plain. Queen Teaea wears her own skin, there. We follow one law, only one, the law of human evolution."

"The law of evolution is that the strongest survives!"

"Yes, and the strongest, in the existence of any social species, are those who are most social. In human terms, most ethical. You see, we have neither prey nor enemy, on Anarres. We have only one another. There is no strength to be gained from hurting one another. Only weakness."

"I don't care about hurting and not hurting. I don't care about other people, and nobody else does, either. They pretend to. I don't want to pretend. I want to be free!"

"But Vea," he began, with tenderness, for the plea for freedom moved him very much, but the doorbell rang. Vea stood up, smoothed her skirt, and advanced smiling to welcome her guests.

During the next hour thirty or forty people came. At first Shevek felt cross, dissatisfied, and bored. It was just another of the parties where everybody stood about with glasses in their hands smiling and talking loudly. But presently it became more entertaining. Discussions and arguments got going, people sat down to talk, it began to be like a party at home. Delicate little pastries and bits of meat and fish were passed around, glasses were constantly refilled by the attentive waiter. Shevek accepted a drink. He had watched Urrasti guzzling alcohol for months now, and none of them had seemed to fall ill from it. The stuff tasted like medicine, but somebody explained that it was mostly carbonated water, which he liked. He was thirsty, so he drank it right off.

A couple of men were determined to talk physics with him. One of them was well mannered, and Shevek managed to evade him for a while, for he found it hard to talk physics with nonphysicists. The other was overbearing, and no escape was possible from him; but irritation, Shevek found, made it much easier to talk. The man knew everything, apparently because he had a lot of money. "As I see it," he informed Shevek, "your Simultaneity Theory simply denies the most obvious fact about time, the fact that time passes."

"Well, in physics one is careful about what one calls 'facts.' It is different from business," Shevek said very mildly and agreeably, but there was something in his mildness that made Vea, chatting with another group nearby, turn around to listen. "Within the strict terms of Simultaneity Theory, succession is not considered as a physically objective phenomenon, but as a subjective one."

"Now stop trying to scare Dearri, and tell us what that means in baby talk," Vea said. Her acuteness made Shevek grin.

"Well, we think that time 'passes,' flows past us, but what if it is we who move forward, from past to future, always discovering the new? It would be a little like reading a book, you see. The book is all there, all at once, between its covers. But if you want to read the story and understand it, you must begin with the first page, and go forward, always in order. So the universe would be a very great book, and we would be very small readers."

"But the *fact* is," said Dearri, "that we experience the universe as a succession, a flow. In which case, what's the use of this theory of how on some higher plane it may be all eternally coexistent? Fun for you theorists, maybe, but it has no practical application, no relevance to real life.

Unless it means we can build a time machine!" he added with a kind of hard, false joviality.

"But we don't experience the universe only successively," Shevek said. "Do you never dream, Mr. Dearri?" He was proud of himself for having, for once, remembered to call someone 'Mr.'

"What's that got to do with it?"

"It is only in consciousness, it seems, that we experience time at all. A little baby has no time; he can't distance himself from the past and understand how it relates to his present, or plan how his present might relate to his future. He does not know time passes; he does not understand death. The unconscious mind of the adult is like that still. In a dream there is no time, and succession is all changed about, and cause and effect are all mixed together. In myth and legend there is no time. What past is it the tale means when it says 'Once upon a time'? And so, when the mystic makes the reconnection of his reason and his unconscious, he sees all becoming as one being, and understands the eternal return."

"Yes, the mystics," the shyer man said, eagerly. "Tebores, in the Eighth Millennium. He wrote, *The unconscious mind is coextensive with the universe.*"

"But we're not babies," Dearri cut in, "we're rational men. Is your Simultaneity some kind of mystical regressivism?"

There was a pause, while Shevek helped himself to a pastry which he did not want, and ate it. He had lost his temper once today and made a fool of himself. Once was enough.

"Maybe you could see it," he said, "as an effort to strike a balance. You see, Sequency explains beautifully our sense of linear time, and the evidence of evolution. It includes creation, and mortality. But there it stops. It deals with all that changes, but it cannot explain why things also endure. It speaks only of the arrow of time—never of the circle of time."

"The circle?" asked the politer inquisitor, with such evident yearning to understand that Shevek quite forgot Dearri, and plunged in with enthusiasm, gesturing with hands and arms as if trying to show his listener, materially, the arrows, the cycles, the oscillations he spoke of. "Time goes in cycles, as well as in a line. A planet revolving: you

179

see? One cycle, one orbit around the sun, is a year, isn't it? And two orbits, two years, and so on. One can count the orbits endlessly—an observer can. Indeed such a system is how we count time. It constitutes the time-teller, the *clock*. But within the system, the cycle, where is time? Where is beginning or end? Infinite repetition is an atemporal process. It must be compared, referred to some other cyclic or noncyclic process, to be seen as temporal. Well, this is very queer and interesting, you see. The atoms, you know, have a cyclic motion. The stable compounds are made of constituents that have a regular, periodic motion relative to one another. In fact, it is the tiny time-reversible cycles of the atom that give matter enough permanence that evolution is possible. The little timelessnesses added together make up time. And then on the big scale, the cosmos: well, you know we think that the whole universe is a cyclic process, an oscillation of expansion and contraction, without any before or after. Only *within* each of the great cycles, where we live, only there is there linear time, evolution, change. So then time has two aspects. There is the arrow, the running river, without which there is no change, no progress, or direction, or creation. And there is the circle or the cycle, without which there is chaos, meaningless succession of instants, a world without clocks or seasons or promises."

"You can't assert two contradictory statements about the same thing," said Dearri, with the calmness of superior knowledge. "In other words, one of these "aspects' is real, the other's simply an illusion."

"Many physicists have said that," Shevek assented.

"But what do you say?" asked the one who wanted to know.

"Well, I think it's an easy way out of the difficulty. . . . Can one dismiss either being, or becoming, as an illusion? Becoming without being is meaningless. Being without becoming is a big bore. . . . If the mind is able to perceive time in both these ways, then a true chronosophy should provide a field in which the relation of the two aspects or processes of time could be understood."

"But what's the good of this sort of 'understanding,' " Dearri said, "if it doesn't result in practical, technological applications? Just word juggling, isn't it."

"You ask questions like a true profiteer," Shevek said,

180

and not a soul there knew he had insulted Dearri with the most contemptuous word in his vocabulary; indeed Dearri nodded a bit, accepting the compliment with satisfaction. Vea, however, sensed a tension, and burst in, "I don't really understand a word you say, you know, but it seems to me that if I *did* understand what you said about the book—that everything really all exists *now*—then couldn't we foretell the future? If it's already there?"

"No, no," the shyer man said, not at all shyly. "It's not there like a couch or a house. Time isn't space. You can't walk around in it!" Vea nodded brightly, as if quite relieved to be put in her place. Seeming to gain courage from his dismissal of the woman from the realms of higher thought, the shy man turned to Dearri and said, "It seems to me the application of temporal physics is in ethics. Would you agree to that, Dr. Shevek?"

"Ethics? Well, I don't know. I do mostly mathematics, you know. You cannot make equations of ethical behavior."

"Why not?" said Dearri.

Shevek ignored him. "But it's true, chronosophy does involve ethics. Because our sense of time involves our ability to separate cause and effect, means and end. The baby, again, the animal, they don't see the difference between what they do now and what will happen because of it. They can't make a pulley, or a promise. We can. Seeing the difference between *now* and *not now*, we can make the connection. And there morality enters in. Responsibility. To say that a good end will follow from a bad means is just like saying that if I pull a rope on this pulley it will lift the weight on that one. To break a promise is to deny the reality of the past; therefore it is to deny the hope of a real future. If time and reason are functions of each other, if we are creatures of time, then we had better know it, and try to make the best of it. To act responsibly."

"But look here," said Dearri, with ineffable satisfaction in his own keenness, "you just said that in your Simultaneity system there *is* no past and future, only a sort of eternal present. So how can you be responsible for the book that's already written? All you can do is read it. There's no choice, no freedom of action left."

"That is the dilemma of determinism. You are quite

181

right, it is implicit in Simultanist thinking. But Sequency thinking also has its dilemma. It is like this, to make a foolish little picture—you are throwing a rock at a tree, and if you are a Simultanist the rock has already hit the tree, and if you are a Sequentist it never can. So which do you choose? Maybe you prefer to throw rocks without thinking about it, no choice. I prefer to make things difficult, and choose both."

"How—how do you reconcile them?" the shy man asked earnestly.

Shevek nearly laughed in despair. "I don't know. I have been working a long time on it! After all, the rock does hit the tree. Neither pure sequency nor pure unity will explain it. We don't want purity, but complexity, the relationship of cause and effect, means and end. Our model of the cosmos must be as inexhaustible as the cosmos. A complexity that includes not only duration but creation, not only being but becoming, not only geometry but ethics. It is not the answer we are after, but only how to ask the question. . . ."

"All very well, but what industry needs is answers," said Dearri.

Shevek turned slowly, looked down at him, and said nothing at all.

There was a heavy silence, into which Vea leapt, graceful and inconsequential, returning to her theme of foreseeing the future. Others were drawn in by this topic, and they all began telling their experiences with fortune-tellers and clairvoyants.

Shevek resolved to say nothing more, no matter what he was asked. He was thirstier than ever; he let the waiter refill his glass, and drank the pleasant, fizzy stuff. He looked around the room, trying to dissipate his anger and tension in watching other people. But they were also behaving very emotionally, for Ioti—shouting, laughing loudly, interrupting each other. One pair was indulging in sexual foreplay in a corner. Shevek looked away, disgusted. Did they egoize even in sex? To caress and copulate in front of unpaired people was as vulgar as to eat in front of hungry people. He returned his attention to the group around him. They were off prediction, now, and onto politics. They were all disputing about the war, about what Thu would do next, what A-Io would do next, what the CWG would do next.

"Why do you talk only in abstractions?" he inquired suddenly, wondering as he spoke why he was speaking, when he had resolved not to. "It is not names of countries, it is people killing each other. Why do the soldiers go? Why does a man go kill strangers?"

"But that's what soldiers are *for*," said a little fair woman with an opal in her navel. Several men began to explain the principle of national sovereignty to Shevek. Vea interrupted, "But let him talk. How would you solve the mess, Shevek?"

"Solution's in plain sight."

"Where?"

"Anarres!"

"But what you people do on the Moon doesn't solve our problems here."

"Man's problem is all the same. Survival. Species, group, individual."

"National self-defense—" somebody shouted.

They argued, he argued. He knew what he wanted to say, and knew it must convince everyone because it was clear and true, but somehow he could not get it said properly. Everybody shouted. The little fair woman patted the broad arm of the chair she was sitting in, and he sat down on it. Her shaven, silken head came peering up under his arm. "Hello, Moon Man!" she said. Vea had joined another group for a time, but now was back near him. Her face was flushed and her eyes looked large and liquid. He thought he saw Pae across the room, but there were so many faces that they blurred together. Things happened in fits and starts, with blanks in between, as if he were being allowed to witness the operation of the Cyclic Cosmos of old Gvarab's hypothesis from behind the scenes. "The principle of legal authority must be upheld, or we'll degenerate into mere anarchy!" thundered a fat, frowning man. Shevek said, "Yes, yes, degenerate! We have enjoyed it for one hundred and fifty years now." The little fair woman's toes, in silver sandals, peeped out from under her skirt, which was sewn all over with hundreds and hundreds of tiny pearls. Vea said, "But tell us about Anarres—what's it *really* like? Is it so wonderful there really?"

He was sitting on the arm of the chair, and Vea was curled up on the hassock at his knees, erect and supple, her soft breasts staring at him with their blind eyes, her face smiling, complacent, flushed.

Something dark turned over in Shevek's mind, darkening everything. His mouth was dry. He finished the glassful the waiter had just poured him. "I don't know," he said; his tongue felt half paralyzed. "No. It is not wonderful. It is an ugly world. Not like this one. Anarres is all dust and dry hills. All meager, all dry. And the people aren't beautiful. They have big hands and feet, like me and the waiter there. But not big bellies. They get very dirty, and take baths together, nobody here does that. The towns are very small and dull, they are dreary. No palaces. Life is dull, and hard work. You can't always have what you want, or even what you need, because there isn't enough. You Urrasti have enough. Enough air, enough rain, grass, oceans, food, music, buildings, factories, machines, books, clothes, history. You are rich, you own. We are poor, we lack. You have, we do not have. Everything is beautiful, here. Only not the faces. On Anarres nothing is beautiful, nothing but the faces. The other faces, the men and women. We have nothing but that, nothing but each other. Here you see the jewels, there you see the eyes. And in the eyes you see the splendor, the splendor of the human spirit. Because our men and women are free—possessing nothing, they are free. And you the possessors are possessed. You are all in jail. Each alone, solitary, with a heap of what he owns. You live in prison, die in prison. It is all I can see in your eyes—the wall, the wall!"

They were all looking at him.

He heard the loudness of his voice still ringing in the silence, felt his ears burning. The darkness, the blankness, turned over once more in his mind. "I feel dizzy," he said, and stood up.

Vea was at his arm. "Come along this way," she said, laughing a little and breathless. He followed her as she threaded her way through the people. He now felt his face was very pale, and the dizziness did not pass; he hoped she was taking him to the washroom, or to a window where he could breathe fresh air. But the room they came into was large and dimly lit by reflection. A high, white bed bulked against the wall; a looking-glass covered half another wall. There was a close, sweet fragrance of draperies, linens, the perfume Vea used.

"You are too much," Vea said, bringing herself directly before him and looking up into his face, in the dimness, with that breathless laugh. "Really too much—you are impossible—magnificent!" She put her hands on his shoulders. "Oh, the looks on their faces! I've got to kiss you for that!" And she lifted herself on tiptoe, presenting him her mouth, and her white throat, and her naked breasts.

He took hold of her and kissed her mouth, forcing her head backward, and then her throat and breasts. She yielded at first as if she had no bones, then she writhed a little, laughing and pushing weakly at him, and began to talk. "Oh, no, no, now behave," she said. "Now, come on, we do have to go back to the party. No, Shevek, now calm down, this won't do at all!" He paid no attention. He pulled her with him toward the bed, and she came, though she kept talking. He fumbled with one hand at the complicated clothes he was wearing and managed to get his trousers unfastened. Then there was Vea's clothing, the lowslung but tight-fitted skirt band, which he could not loosen. "Now, stop," she said. "No, now listen, Shevek, it won't do, not now. I haven't taken a contraceptive, if I got stuffed I'd be in a pretty mess, my husband's coming back in two weeks! No, let me be," but he could not let her be; his face was pressed against her soft, sweaty, scented flesh. "Listen, don't mess up my clothes, people will notice, for heaven's sake. Wait—just wait, we can arrange it, we can fix up a place to meet, I do have to be careful of my reputation, I can't trust the maid, just wait, not now—Not now! Not now!" Frightened at last by his blind urgency, his force, she pushed at him as hard as she could, her hands against his chest. He took a step backward, confused by her sudden high tone of fear and her struggle; but he could not stop, her resistance excited him further. He gripped her to him, and his semen spurted out against the white silk of her dress.

"Let me go! Let me go!" she was repeating in the same high whisper. He let her go. He stood dazed. He fumbled at his trousers, trying to close them. "I am— sorry—I thought you wanted—"

"For God's sake!" Vea said, looking down at her

185

skirt in the dim light, twitching the pleats away from her. "Really! Now I'll have to change my dress."

Shevek stood, his mouth open, breathing with difficulty, his hands hanging; then all at once he turned and blundered out of the dim room. Back in the bright room of the party he stumbled through the crowded people, tripped over a leg, found his way blocked by bodies, clothes, jewels, breasts, eyes, candle flames, furniture. He ran up against a table. On it lay a silver platter on which tiny pastries stuffed with meat, cream, and herbs were arranged in concentric circles like a huge pale flower. Shevek gasped for breath, doubled up, and vomited all over the platter.

"I'll take him home," Pae said.

"Do, for heaven's sake," said Vea. "Were you looking for him, Saio?"

"Oh, a bit. Fortunately Demaere called you."

"You are certainly welcome to him."

"He won't be any trouble. Passed out in the hall. May I use your phone before I go?"

"Give my love to the Chief," Vea said archly.

Oiie had come to his sister's flat with Pae, and left with him. They sat in the middle seat of the big Government limousine that Pae always had on call, the same one that had brought Shevek from the space port last summer. He now lay as they had dumped him on the back seat.

"Was he with your sister all day, Demaere?"

"Since noon, apparently."

"Thank God!"

"Why are you so worried about his getting into the slums? Any Odonian's already convinced we're a lot of oppressed wage slaves, what's the difference if he sees a bit of corroboration?"

"I don't care what he sees. We don't want *him seen*. Have you been reading the birdseed papers? Or the broadsheets that were circulating last week in Old Town, about the 'Forerunner'? The myth—the one who comes before the millennium—'a stranger, an outcast, an exile, bearing in empty hands the time to come.' They quoted that. The rabble are in one of their damned apocalyptic moods. Looking for a figurehead. A catalyst. Talking about a general strike. They'll never learn. They need a lesson all the

186

same. Damned rebellious cattle, send them to fight Thu, it's the only good we'll ever get from them."

Neither man spoke again during the ride.

The night watchman of the Senior Faculty House helped them get Shevek up to his room. They loaded him onto the bed. He began to snore at once.

Oiie stayed to take off Shevek's shoes and put a blanket over him. The drunken man's breath was foul; Oiie stepped away from the bed, the fear and the love he felt for Shevek rising up in him, each strangling the other. He scowled, and muttered, "Dirty fool." He snapped the light off and returned to the other room. Pae was standing at the desk going through Shevek's papers.

"Leave off," Oiie said, his expression of disgust deepening. "Come on. It's two in the morning. I'm tired."

"What has the bastard been doing, Demaere? Still nothing here, absolutely nothing. Is he a complete fraud? Have we been taken in by a damned naïve peasant from Utopia? Where's his theory? Where's our instantaneous spaceflight? Where's our advantage over the Hainish? Nine, ten months we've been feeding the bastard, for nothing!" Nevertheless he pocketed one of the papers before he followed Oiie to the door.

Chapter 8

ANARRES

They were out on the athletic fields of Abbenay's North Park, six of them, in the long gold and heat and dust of the evening. They were all pleasantly replete, for dinner had gone on most of the afternoon, a street festival and feast with cooking over open fires. It was the midsummer holiday, Insurrection Day, commemorating the first great uprising in Nio Esseia in the Urrasti year 740, nearly two hundred years ago. Cooks and refectory workers were honored as the guests of the rest of the community on that day, because a syndicate of cooks and waiters had begun the strike that led to the insurrection. There were many such traditions and festivals on Anarres, some instituted by the Settlers and others, like the harvest homes and the Feast of the Solstice, that had risen spontaneously out of the rhythms of life on the planet and the need of those who work together to celebrate together.

They were talking, all rather desultorily except for Takver. She had danced for hours, eaten quantities of fried bread and pickles, and was feeling very lively. "Why did Kvigot get posted to the Keran Sea fisheries, where he'll have to start all over again, while Turib takes on his research program here?" she was saying. Her research syndicate had been assimilated into a project managed directly by PDC, and she had become a strong partisan of some of Bedap's ideas. "Because Kvigot is a good biologist who doesn't agree with Simas's fuddy-duddy theories, and Turib is a nothing who scrubs Simas's back in the baths. See who takes over directing the program when Simas retires. She will, Turib will, I'll bet you!"

"What does that expression mean?" asked somebody who felt indisposed for social criticism.

Bedap, who had been putting on weight at the waist and was serious about exercise, was trotting earnestly around the playing field. The others were sitting on a dusty bank under trees, getting their exercise verbally.

"It's an Iotic verb," Shevek said. "A game the Urrasti play with probabilities. The one who guesses right gets the other one's property." He had long ago ceased to observe Sabul's ban on mentioning his Iotic studies.

"How did one of their words get into Pravic?"

"The Settlers," said another. "They had to learn Pravic as adults; they must have thought in the old languages for a long time. I read somewhere that the word *damn* isn't in the Pravic Dictionary—it's Iotic too. Farigv didn't provide any swearwords when he invented the language, or if he did his computers didn't understand the necessity."

"What's *hell*, then?" Takver asked. "I used to think it meant the shit depot in the town where I grew up. 'Go to hell!' The worst place to go."

Desar, the mathematician, who had now taken a permanent posting to the Institute staff, and who still hung around Shevek, though he seldom spoke to Takver, said in his cryptographic style, "Means Urras."

"On Urras, it means the place you go to when you're damned."

"That's a posting to Southwest in summer," said Terrus, an ecologist, an old friend of Takver's.

"It's in the religious mode, in Iotic."

"I know you have to read Iotic, Shev, but do you have to read religion?"

"Some of the old Urrasti physics is all in the religious mode. Concepts like that come up. 'Hell' means the place of absolute evil."

"The manure depot in Round Valley," Takver said. "I thought so."

Bedap came pumping up, dust-whitened, sweat-
189

streaked. He sat down heavily beside Shevek and panted.

"Say something in Iotic," asked Richat, a student of Shevek's. "What does it sound like?"

"You know: Hell! Damn!"

"But stop swearing at me," said the girl, giggling, "and say a whole sentence."

Shevek good-naturedly said a sentence in Iotic. "I don't really know how it's pronounced," he added, "I just guess."

"What did it mean?"

"If the passage of time is a feature of human consciousness, past and future are functions of the mind. From a pre-Sequentist, Keremcho."

"How weird to think of people speaking and you couldn't understand them!"

"They can't even understand each other. They speak hundreds of different languages, all the crazy archists on the Moon. . . ."

"Water, water," said Bedap, still panting.

"There is no water," said Terrus. "It hasn't rained for eighteen decads. A hundred and eighty-three days to be precise. Longest drought in Abbenay for forty years."

"If it goes on, we'll have to recycle urine, the way they did in the Year 20. Glass of piss, Shev?"

"Don't joke," said Terrus. "That's the thread we walk on. Will it rain enough? The leaf crops in Southrising are a dead loss already. No rain there for thirty decads."

They all looked up into the hazy, golden sky. The serrated leaves of the trees under which they sat, tall exotics from the Old World, drooped on their branches, dusty, curled by the dryness.

"Never be another Great Drought," Desar said, "Modern desalinization plants. Prevent."

"They might help alleviate it," Terrus said.

Winter that year came early, cold, and dry in the Northern Hemisphere. Frozen dust on the wind in the low, wide streets of Abbenay. Water to the baths strictly rationed: thirst and hunger outranked cleanliness. Food and clothing for the twenty million people of Anarres came from the holum plants, leaf, seed, fiber, root. There was some stockpile of textiles in the warehouses and depots, but there had never been much reserve of food. Water went to the land, to keep the plants alive. The sky over the city was cloudless and would have been clear, but it was yellowed with dust windborne from drier lands to the south and west. Sometimes when the wind blew down from the north, from the Ne Theras, the yellow haze cleared and left a brilliant, empty sky, dark blue hardening to purple at the zenith.

Takver was pregnant. Mostly she was sleepy and benign. "I am a fish," she said, "a fish in water. I am inside the baby inside me." But at times she was overtaxed by her work, or left hungry by the slightly decreased meals at commons. Pregnant women, like children and old people, could get a light extra meal daily, lunch at eleven, but she often missed this because of the exacting schedule of her work. She could miss a meal, but the fish in her laboratory tanks could not. Friends often brought by something saved out from their dinner or left over at their commons, a filled bun or a piece of fruit. She ate all gratefully but continued to crave sweets, and sweets were in short supply. When she was tired she was anxious and easily upset, and her temper flared at a word.

Late in the autumn Shevek completed the manuscript of the *Principles of Simultaneity*. He gave it to Sabul for approval for the press. Sabul kept it for a decad, two decads, three decads, and said nothing about it. Shevek asked him about it. He replied that he had not yet got around to reading it, he was too busy. Shevek waited. It was midwinter. The dry wind blew day after day; the ground was frozen. Everything seemed to have come to a halt, an uneasy halt, waiting for rain, for birth.

The room was dark. The lights had just come on in the city; they looked weak under the high, dark-grey sky. Takver came in, lit the lamp, crouched down in her overcoat by the heat grating. "Oh it's cold! Awful. My feet feel like I've been walking on glaciers, I nearly cried on the way home they hurt so. Rotten profiteering boots! Why can't we make a decent pair of boots? What are you sitting in the dark for?"

"I don't know."

"Did you go to commons? I got a bite at Surplus on the way home. I had to stay, the kukuri eggs were hatching and we had to get the fry out of the tanks before the adults ate them. Did you eat?"

"No."

"Don't be sulky. Please don't be sulky tonight. If one more thing goes wrong, I'll cry. I'm sick of crying all the time. Damned stupid hormones! I wish I could have babies like the fish, lay the eggs and swim off and that's the end of it. Unless I swam back and ate them. . . . Don't sit and look like a statue like that. I just can't stand it." She was slightly in tears, as she crouched by the breath of heat from the grating, trying to unfasten her boots with stiff fingers.

Shevek said nothing.

"What *is* it? You can't just sit there!"

"Sabul called me in today. He won't recommend the *Principles* for publication, or export."

Takver stopped struggling with the bootlace and sat still. She looked at Shevek over her shoulder. At last she said, "What did he say exactly?"

"The critique he wrote is on the table."

She got up, shuffled over to the table wearing one boot, and read the paper, leaning over the table, her hands in her coat pockets.

" 'That Sequency Physics is the highroad of chronosophical thought in the Odonian Society has been a mutually agreed principle since the Settlement of Anarres. Egoistic divagation from this solidarity of principle can result only in sterile spinning of impractical hypotheses without social organic utility, or repetition of the superstitious-religious speculations of the irresponsible hired scientists of the Profit States of Urras. . . .' Oh, the profiteer! The petty-minded, envious little Odo-spouter! Will he send this critique to the Press?"

"He's done so."

She knelt to wrestle off her boots. She glanced up several times at Shevek, but she did not go to him or try to touch him, and for some while she did not say anything. When she spoke her voice was not loud and strained as before, but had its natural husky, furry quality. "What will you do, Shev?"

"There's nothing to do."

"We'll print the book. Form a printing syndicate, learn to set type, and do it."

"Paper's at minimum ration. No nonessential printing.
192

Only PDC publications, till the tree-holum plantations are safe."

"Then can you change the presentation somehow? Disguise what you say. Decorate it with Sequency trimmings. So that he'll accept it."

"You can't disguise black as white."

She did not ask if he could bypass Sabul or go over his head. Nobody on Anarres was supposed to be over anybody's head. There were no bypasses. If you could not work in solidarity with your syndics, you worked alone.

"What if . . ." She stopped. She got up and put her boots by the heater to dry. She took off her coat, hung it up, and put a heavy hand-loomed shawl over her shoulders. She sat down on the bed platform, grunting a little as she lowered herself the last few inches. She looked up at Shevek, who sat in profile between her and the windows.

"What if you offered to let him sign as co-author? Like the first paper you wrote."

"Sabul won't put his name to 'superstitious-religious speculations.' "

"Are you sure? Are you sure that isn't just what he wants? He knows what this is, what you've done. You've always said he's shrewd. He knows it'll put him and the whole Sequency school in the recycle bin. But if he could share with you, share the credit? All he is, is ego. If he could say that it was *his* book . . ."

Shevek said bitterly, "I'd as soon share you with him as that book."

"Don't look at it that way, Shev. It's the *book* that's important—the ideas. Listen. We want to keep this child to be born with us as a baby, we want to love it. But if for some reason it would die if we kept it, it could only live in a nursery, if we never could set eyes on it or know its name—if we had that choice, which would we choose? To keep the stillborn? Or to give life?"

"I don't know," he said. He put his head in his hands, rubbing his forehead painfully. "Yes, of course. Yes. But this—But I—"

"Brother, dear heart," Takver said. She clenched her hands together on her lap, but she did not reach out to him. "It doesn't matter what name is on the book. People will know. The truth is the book."

"I am that book," he said. Then he shut his eyes, and sat motionless. Takver went to him then, timidly, touching him as gently as if she touched a wound.

Early in the year 164 the first, incomplete, drastically edited version of the *Principles of Simultaneity* was printed in Abbenay, with Sabul and Shevek as joint authors. PDC was printing only essential records and directives, but Sabul had influence at the Press and in the Information division of PDC, and had persuaded them of the propaganda value of the book abroad. Urras, he said, was rejoicing over the drought and possible famine on Anarres; the last shipment of Ioti journals was full of gloating prophecies of the imminent collapse of the Odonian economy. What better denial, said Sabul, than the publication of a major work of pure thought, "a monument of science," he said in his revised critique, "soaring above material adversity to prove the unquenchable vitality of the Odonian Society and its triumph over archist propertarianism in every area of human thought."

So the work was printed; and fifteen of the three hundred copies went aboard the Ioti freighter *Mindful*. Shevek never opened a copy of the printed book. In the export packet, however, he put a copy of the original, complete manuscript, handwritten. A note on the cover asked that it be given to Dr. Atro of the College of the Noble Science of Ieu Eun University, with the compliments of the author. It was certain that Sabul, who gave final approval to the packet, would notice the addition. Whether he took the manuscript out or left it in, Shevek did not know. He might confiscate it out of spite; he might let it go, knowing that his emasculated abridgment would not have the desired effect on Urrasti physicists. He said nothing about the manuscript to Shevek. Shevek did not ask about it.

Shevek said very little to anyone, that spring. He took on a volunteer posting, construction work on a new water-recycling plant in South Abbenay, and was away at that work or teaching most of the day. He returned to his studies in subatomics, often spending evenings at the Institute's accelerator or the laboratories with the particle specialists. With Takver and their friends he was quiet, sober, gentle, and cold.

Takver got very big in the belly and walked like a

194

person carrying a large, heavy basket of laundry. She stayed at work at the fish labs till she had found and trained an adequate replacement for herself, then she came home and began labor, more than a decad past her time. Shevek arrived home in midafternoon. "You might go fetch the midwife," Takver said. "Tell her the contractions are four or five minutes apart, but they're not speeding up much, so don't hurry very much."

He hurried, and when the midwife was out, he gave way to panic. Both the midwife and the block medic were out, and neither had left a note on the door saying where they could be found, as they usually did. Shevek's heart began pounding in his chest, and he saw things suddenly with a dreadful clarity. He saw that this absence of help was an evil omen. He had withdrawn from Takver since the winter, since the decision about the book. She had been increasingly quiet, passive, patient. He understood that passivity now: it was a preparation for her death. It was she who had withdrawn from him, and he had not tried to follow her. He had looked only at his own bitterness of heart, and never at her fear, or courage. He had let her alone because he wanted to be let alone, and so she had gone on, gone far, too far, would go on alone, forever.

He ran to the block clinic, arriving so out of breath and unsteady on his legs that they thought he was having a heart attack. He explained. They sent a message off to another midwife and told him to go home, the partner would be wanting company. He went home, and at every stride the panic in him grew, the terror, the certainty of loss.

But once there he could not kneel by Takver and ask her forgiveness, as he wanted desperately to do. Takver had no time for emotional scenes; she was busy. She had cleared the bed platform except for a clean sheet, and she was at work bearing a child. She did not howl or scream, as she was not in pain, but when each contraction came she managed it by muscle and breath control, and then let out a great *houff* of breath, like one who makes a terrific effort to lift a heavy weight. Shevek had never seen any work that so used all the strength of the body.

He could not look on such work without trying to help in it. He could serve as handhold and brace when she needed leverage. They found this arrangement very quickly

195

by trial and error, and kept to it after the midwife had come in. Takver gave birth afoot, squatting, her face against Shevek's thigh, her hands gripping his braced arms. "There you are," the midwife said quietly under the hard, engine-like pounding of Takver's breathing, and she took the slimy but recognizably human creature that had appeared. A gush of blood followed, and an amorphous mass of something not human, not alive. The terror he had forgotten came back into Shevek redoubled. It was death he saw. Takver had let go his arms and was huddled down quite limp at his feet. He bent over her, stiff with horror and grief.

"That's it," said the midwife, "help her move aside so I can clean this up."

"I want to wash," Takver said feebly.

"Here, help her wash up. Those are sterile cloths—there."

"Waw, waw, waw," said another voice.

The room seemed to be full of people.

"Now then," the midwife said. "Here, get that baby back with her, at the breast, to help shut off the bloodflow. I want to get this placenta to the freezer in the clinic. I'll be ten minutes."

"Where is—Where is the—"

"In the crib!" said the midwife, leaving. Shevek located the very small bed, which had been standing ready in the corner for four decads, and the infant in it. Somehow in this extreme rush of events the midwife had found time to clean the infant and even put a gown on it, so that it was not so fishlike and slippery as when he had seen it first. The afternoon had got dark, with the same peculiar rapidity and lack of time lapse. The lamp was on. Shevek picked up the baby to take it to Takver. Its face was incredibly small, with large, fragile-looking, closed eyelids. "Give it here," Takver was saying. "Oh, do hurry up, please give it to me."

He brought it across the room and very cautiously lowered it onto Takver's stomach. "Ah!" she said softly, a call of pure triumph.

"What is it?" she asked after a while, sleepily.

Shevek was sitting beside her on the edge of the bed platform. He carefully investigated, somewhat taken aback by the length of gown as contrasted with the extreme shortness of limb. "Girl."

The midwife came back, went around putting things to rights. "You did a first-rate job," she remarked, to both of them. They assented mildly. "I'll look in in the morning," she said leaving. The baby and Takver were already asleep. Shevek put his head down near Takver's. He was accustomed to the pleasant musky smell of her skin. This had changed; it had become a perfume, heavy and faint, heavy with sleep. Very gently he put one arm over her as she lay on her side with the baby against her breast. In the room heavy with life he slept.

An Odonian undertook monogamy just as he might undertake a joint enterprise in production, a ballet or a soap works. Partnership was a voluntarily constituted federation like any other. So long as it worked, it worked, and if it didn't work it stopped being. It was not an institution but a function. It had no sanction but that of private conscience.

This was fully in accord with Odonian social theory. The validity of the promise, even promise of indefinite term, was deep in the grain of Odo's thinking; though it might seem that her insistence on freedom to change would invalidate the idea of promise or vow, in fact the freedom made the promise meaningful. A promise is a direction taken, a self-limitation of choice. As Odo pointed out, if no direction is taken, if one goes nowhere, no change will occur. One's freedom to choose and to change will be unused, exactly as if one were in jail, a jail of one's own building, a maze in which no one way is better than any other. So Odo came to see the promise, the pledge, the idea of fidelity, as essential in the complexity of freedom.

Many people felt that this idea of fidelity was misapplied to sexual life. Odo's femininity swayed her, they said, towards a refusal of real sexual freedom; here, if nowhere else, Odo did not write for men. As many women as men made this criticism, so it would appear that it was not masculinity that Odo failed to understand, but a whole type of section of humanity, people to whom experiment is the soul of sexual pleasure.

Though she may not have understood them, and probably considered them propertarian aberrations from the norm—the human species being, if not a pair-bonding species, yet a time-binding one—still she provided better for the promiscuous than for those who tried long-term partnership. No law, no limit, no penalty, no punishment, no disapproval applied to any sexual practice of any kind, except the rape of a child or woman, for which the rapist's neighbors were likely to provide summary revenge if he did not get promptly into the gentler hands of a therapy center. But molestation was extremely rare in a society where complete fulfillment was the norm from puberty on, and the only social limit imposed on sexual activity was the mild one of pressure in favor of privacy, a kind of modesty imposed by the communality of life.

On the other hand, those who undertook to form and keep a partnership, whether homosexual or heterosexual, met with problems unknown to those content with sex wherever they found it. They must face not only jealousy and possessiveness and the other diseases of passion for which monogamous union provides such a fine medium of growth, but also the external pressures of social organization. A couple that undertook partnership did so knowing that they might be separated at any time by the exigencies of labor distribution.

Divlab, the administration of the division of labor, tried to keep couples together, and to reunite them as soon as possible on request; but it could not always be done, especially in urgent levies, nor did anyone expect Divlab to remake whole lists and reprogram computers trying to do it. To survive, to make a go of life, an Anarresti knew he had to be ready to go where he was needed and do the work that needed doing. He grew up knowing labor distribution as a major factor of life, an immediate, permanent social necessity; whereas conjugality was a personal matter, a choice that could be made only within the larger choice.

But when a direction is chosen freely and followed whole-heartedly, it may seem that all things further the going. So the possibility and actuality of separation often served to strengthen the loyalty of partners. To maintain genuine spontaneous fidelity in a society that had no legal or moral sanctions against infidelity, and to maintain it during voluntarily accepted separations that could come at any time and might last years, was something of a challenge. But the human being likes to be challenged, seeks freedom in adversity.

In the year 164 many people who had never sought it got a taste of that kind of freedom, and liked it, liked the sense of test and danger. The drought that began in the summer of 163 met no relief in winter. By the summer of 164 there was hardship, and the threat of disaster if the drought went on.

Rationing was strict; labor drafts were imperative. The struggle to grow enough food and to get the food distributed became convulsive, desperate. Yet people were not desperate at all. Odo wrote: "A child free from the guilt of ownership and the burden of economic competition will grow up with the will to do what needs doing and the capacity for joy in doing it. It is useless work that darkens the heart. The delight of the nursing mother, of the scholar, of the successful hunter, of the good cook, of the skillful maker, of anyone doing needed work and doing it well—this durable joy is perhaps the deepest source of human affection and of sociality as a whole." There was an undercurrent of joy, in that sense, in Abbenay that summer. There was a lightheartedness at work however hard the work, a readiness to drop all care as soon as what could be done had been done. The old tag of "solidarity" had come alive again. There is exhilaration in finding that the bond is stronger, after all, than all that tries the bond.

Early in the summer PDC put up posters suggesting that people shorten their working day by an hour or so, since the protein issue at commons was now insufficient for full normal expense of energy. The exuberant activity of the city streets had already been slowing down. People off work early loitered in the squares, played bowls in the dry parks, sat in workshop doorways and struck up conversation with passersby. The population of the city was visibly thinned, as several thousands had volunteered or been posted to emergency farm work. But mutual trust allayed depression or anxiety. "We'll see each other through," they said, serenely. And great impulses of vitality ran just under the surface. When the wells in the northern suburbs failed, temporary mains from other districts were laid by volunteers working in their free time, skilled and unskilled, adults and adolescents, and the job was done in thirty hours.

Late in summer Shevek was posted to an emergency farm draft to Red Springs community in Southrising. On the promise of some rain that had fallen in the equatorial storm season, they were trying to get a crop of grain holum planted and reaped before the drought returned.

He had been expecting an emergency posting, since his construction job was finished and he had listed himself as available in the general labor pool. All summer he had done nothing but teach his courses, read, go out on whatever volunteer calls came up in their block and in the city, and come home to Takver and the baby. Takver had gone back to her laboratory, mornings only, after five decads. As a nursing mother she was entitled to both protein and carbohydrate supplements at meals, and she always availed herself of both; their friends could not share extra food with her any more, there was no extra food. She was thin but flourishing, and the baby was small but solid.

Shevek got a great deal of pleasure from the baby. Having sole charge of her in the mornings (they left her in the nursery only while he taught or did volunteer work), he felt that sense of being necessary which is the burden and reward of parenthood. An alert, responsive baby, she gave Shevek the perfect audience for his suppressed verbal fantasies, what Takver called his crazy streak. He would sit the baby on his knees and address wild cosmological lectures to her, explaining how time was actually space turned inside out, the chronon being thus the everted viscera of the quantum, and distance one of the accidental properties of light. He gave extravagant and ever-changing nicknames to the baby, and recited ridiculous mnemonics at her: Time is a manacle, Time is tyrannical, Super-mechanical, Superorganical—POP!—and at the pop, the baby arose a short distance into the air, squeaking and waving her fat fists. Both received great satisfaction from these exercises. When he received his posting it was a wrench. He had hoped for something close to Abbenay, not clear around in Southrising. But along with the unpleasant necessity of leaving Takver and the baby for sixty days came the steady assurance of coming back to them. So long as he had that, he had no complaints.

The night before he left, Bedap came and ate at the

Institute refectory with them, and they came back together to the room. They sat talking in the hot night, the lamp unlit, the windows open. Bedap, who ate at a small commons where special arrangements were not a burden for the cooks to handle, had saved up his special-beverages ration for a decad and taken it all in the form of a liter bottle of fruit juice. He produced it with pride: a going-away party. They doled it around and savored it luxuriously, curling their tongues. "Do you remember," Takver said, "all the food, the night before you left Northsetting? I ate nine of those fried cakes."

"You wore your hair cut short then," Shevek said, startled by the recollection, which he had never before paired up to Takver. "That was you, wasn't it?"

"Who did you think it was?"

"By damn, what a kid you were then!"

"So were you, it's ten years now. I cut my hair so I'd look different and interesting. A lot of good it did!" She laughed her loud, cheerful laugh, quickly strangling it so as not to wake the baby, asleep in her crib behind the screen. Nothing, however, woke the baby once she had got to sleep. "I used to want so badly to be different. I wonder why?"

"There's a point, around age twenty," Bedap said, "when you have to choose whether to be like everybody else the rest of your life, or to make a virtue of your peculiarities."

"Or at least accept them with resignation," said Shevek.

"Shev is on a resignation binge," Takver said. "It's old age coming on. It must be terrible to be thirty."

"Don't worry, you won't be resigned at ninety," Bedap said, patting her back. "Are you even resigned to your child's name yet?"

The five- and six-letter names issued by the central registry computer, being unique to each living individual, took the place of the numbers which a computer-using society must otherwise attach to its members. An Anarresti needed no identification but his name. The name, therefore, was felt to be an important part of the self, though one no more chose it than one's nose or height. Takver disliked the name the baby had got, Sadik. "It still sounds like a mouthful of gravel," she said, "it doesn't *fit* her."

"I like it," Shevek said. "It sounds like a tall, slender girl with long black hair."

"But it is a short, fat girl with invisible hair," Bedap observed.

"Give her time, brother! Listen. I'm going to make a speech."

"Speech! Speech!"

"Shh—"

"Why shh? That baby would sleep through a cataclysm."

"Be quiet. I feel emotional." Shevek raised his cup of fruit juice. "I want to say—What I want to say is this. I'm glad Sadik was born now. In a hard year, in a hard time, when we need our brotherhood. I'm glad she was born now, and here. I'm glad she's one of us, an Odonian, our daughter and our sister. I'm glad she's sister to Bedap. That she's sister to Sabul, even to Sabul! I drink to this hope: that as long as she lives, Sadik will love her sisters and brothers as well, as joyfully, as I do now tonight. And that the rain will fall. . . ."

PDC, the principal users of radio, telephone, and mails, coordinated the means of long-distance communication, just as they did the means of long-distance travel and shipping. There being no "business" on Anarres, in the sense of promoting, advertising, investing, speculating, and so forth, the mail consisted mostly of correspondence among industrial and professional syndicates, their directives and newsletters plus those of the PDC, and a small volume of personal letters. Living in a society where anyone could move whenever and wherever he wanted, an Anarresti tended to look for his friends where he was, not where he had been. Telephones were seldom used within a community; communities weren't all that big. Even Abbenay kept up the close regional pattern in its "blocks," the semiautonomous neighborhoods in which you could get to anyone or anything you needed, on foot. Telephone calls thus were mostly long-distance, and were handled by the PDC: personal calls had to be arranged beforehand by mail, or were not conversations but simply messages left at the PDC center. Letters went unsealed, not by law, of course, but by convention. Personal communication at long distance is costly in materials and labor, and since the private and the public economy was the same, there was considerable feeling against unnecessary writing or calling. It was a trivial habit; it smacked of privatism, of egoizing. This was probably why the letters went unsealed: you had no right to ask people to carry a message that they couldn't read. A letter went on a PDC mail dirigible if you were lucky, and on a produce train if you weren't. Eventually it got to the mail depot in the town addressed, and there it lay, there being no postmen, until somebody told the addressee that he had a letter and he came to get it.

The individual, however, decided what was and what was not necessary. Shevek and Takver wrote each other regularly, about once a decad. He wrote:

The trip was not bad, three days, a passenger track truck clear through. This is a big levy—three thousand people, they say. The effects of the drought are much worse here. Not the shortages. The food in commons is the same ration as in Abbenay, only here you get boiled gara-greens at both meals every day because they have a local surplus. We too begin to feel we have had a surplus. But it is the climate here that makes misery. This is the Dust. The air is dry and the wind always blowing. There are brief rains, but within an hour after rain the ground loosens and the dusts begins to rise. It has rained less than half the annual average this season here. Everyone on the Project gets cracked lips, nosebleed, eye irritations, and coughs. Among the people who live in Red Springs there is a lot of the dust cough. Babies have a specially hard time, you see many with skin and eyes inflamed. I wonder if I would have noticed that half a year ago. One becomes keener with parenthood. The work is just work and everyone is comradely, but the dry wind wears. Last night I thought of the Ne Theras and in the night the sound of the wind was like the sound of the stream. I will not regret this separation. It has allowed me to see that I had begun to give less, as if I possessed you and you me and there was nothing more to be done. The real fact has nothing to do with ownership. What we do is assert the wholeness of Time. Tell me what Sadik does. I am teaching a class on the free days to some people who asked for it, one girl is a natural mathematician whom I shall recommend to the Institute. Your brother,

Takver wrote to him:

I am worried by a rather queer thing. The lectures for 3d Quarter were posted three days ago and I went to find out what schedule you would have at the Inst. but no class or room was listed for you. I thought they had left you off by mistake so went to the Members Synd. and they said yes they wanted you to give the Geom. class. So I went to the Inst. Coord. office that old woman with the nose and she knew nothing, no no I don't know anything, go to Central Posting! That is nonsense I said and went to Sabul. But he was not in the Phys. offices and I have not seen him yet though I have been back twice. With Sadik who wears a wonderful white hat Terrus knitted her out of unraveled yarn and looks tremendously fetching. I refuse to go hunt out Sabul in the room or worm-tunnel or wherever he lives. Maybe he is off doing volunteer work ha! ha! Perhaps you should telephone the Institute and find out what sort of mistake they have made? In fact I did go down and check at Divlab Central Posting but there wasn't any new listing for you. People there were all right but that old woman with the nose is inefficient and not helpful, and nobody takes an interest. Bedap is right we have let bureaucracy creep up on us. Please come back (with mathematical genius girl if necessary), separation is educational all right but your presence is the education I want. I am getting a half liter fruit juice plus calcium allotment a day because my milk was running short and S. yelled a lot. Good old doctors!! All, always, T.

Shevek never got this letter. He had left Southrising before it got to the mail depot in Red Springs.

It was about twenty-five hundred miles from Red Springs to Abbenay. An individual on the move would have simply hitchhiked, all transport vehicles being available as passenger vehicles for as many people as they would hold; but since four hundred and fifty people were being redistributed to their regular postings in Northwest, a train was provided for them. It was made up of passenger cars, or at least of cars being used at the moment for passengers. The least popular was the boxcar that had recently carried a shipment of smoked fish.

After a year of the drought the normal transport lines were insufficient, despite the fierce efforts of the transport workers to meet demands. They were the largest federative in the Odonian society: self-organized, of course, in regional syndicates coordinated by representatives who met and worked with the local and central PDC. The network maintained by the transport federative was effective in normal times and in limited emergencies; it was flexible, adaptable to circumstance, and the Syndics of Transport had great team and professional pride. They called their engines and dirigibles names like *Indomitable, Endurance, Eat-the-Wind;* they had mottoes—We Always Get There—Nothing Is Too Much!—But now, when whole regions of the planet were threatened with immediate famine if food was not brought in from other regions, and when large emergency drafts of workers must be shifted, the demands laid on transport were too much. There were not enough vehicles; there were not enough people to run them. Everything the federative had on wings or wheels was pressed into service, and apprentices, retired workers, volunteers, and emergency draftees were helping man the trucks, the trains, the ships, the ports, the yards.

The train Shevek was on went along in short rushes and long waits, since all provision trains took precedence over it. Then it stopped altogether for twenty hours. An overworked or underschooled dispatcher had made an error, and there had been a wreck up the line.

The little town where the train stopped had no extra food in its commons or warehouses. It was not a farm community, but a mill town, manufacturing concrete and foamstone, built on the fortunate congruence of lime deposits and a navigable river. There were truck gardens, but it was a town dependent upon transport for food. If the four hundred and fifty people on the train ate, the one hundred and sixty local people would not. Ideally, they would all share, all half-eat or half-starve together. If there had been fifty, or even a hundred, people on the train, the community probably would have spared them at least a baking of bread. But four hundred and fifty? If they gave that many anything, they would be wiped out for days. And would the next provisions train come, after those days? And how much grain would be on it? They gave nothing.

The travelers, having had nothing in the way of breakfast that day, thus fasted for sixty hours. They did not get a meal until the line had been cleared and their train had run on a hundred and fifty miles to a station with a refectory stocked for passengers.

It was Shevek's first experience of hunger. He had fasted sometimes when he was working because he did not want to be bothered with eating, but two full meals a day had always been available: constant as sunrise and sunset. He had never even thought what it might be like to have to go without them. Nobody in his society, nobody in the world, had to go without them.

While he got hungrier, while the train sat hour after hour on the siding between a scarred and dusty quarry and a shut-down mill, he had grim thoughts about the reality of hunger, and about the possible inadequacy of his society to come through a famine without losing the solidarity that was its strength. It was easy to share when there was enough, even barely enough, to go round. But when there was not enough? Then force entered in; might making right; power, and its tool, violence, and its most devoted ally, the averted eye.

The passengers' resentment of the townsfolk got bitter, but it was less ominous than the behavior of the townsfolk —the way they hid behind "their" walls with "their" property, and ignored the train, never looked at it. Shevek was not the only gloomy passenger; a long conversation meandered up and down beside the stopped cars, people dropping in and out of it, arguing and agreeing, all on the same general theme that his thoughts followed. A raid on the truck gardens was seriously proposed, and bitterly debated, and might have been carried out, if the train had not hooted at last for departure.

But when at last it crawled into the station down the line, and they got a meal—a half loaf of holum bread and a bowl of soup—their gloom gave place to elation. By the time you got to the bottom of the bowl you noticed that

206

the soup was pretty thin, but the first taste of it, the first taste had been wonderful, worth fasting for. They all agreed on that. They got back into the train laughing and joking together. They had seen each other through.

A truck-train convoy picked up the Abbenay passengers at Equator Hill and brought them the last five hundred miles. They came into the city late on a windy night of early autumn. It was getting on for midnight; the streets were empty. Wind flowed through them like a turbulent dry river. Over dim street lamps the stars flared with a bright shaken light. The dry storm of autumn and passion carried Shevek through the streets, half running, three miles to the northern quarter, alone in the dark city. He took the three steps of the porchway in one, ran down the hall, came to the door, opened it. The room was dark. Stars burned in the dark windows. "Takver!" he said, and heard the silence. Before he turned on the lamp, there in the dark, in the silence, all at once, he learned what separation was.

Nothing was gone. There was nothing to be gone. Only Sadik and Takver were gone. The Occupations of Uninhabited Space turned softly, gleaming a little, in the draft from the open door.

There was a letter on the table. Two letters. One from Takver. It was brief: she had received an emergency posting to the Comestible Algae Experimental Development Laboratories in Northeast, for an indeterminate period. She wrote:

I could not in conscience refuse now. I went and talked to them at Divlab and also read their project sent in to Ecology at PDC, and it is true they need me because I have worked exactly on this algae-ciliate-shrimp-kukuri cycle. I requested at Divlab that you be posted to Rolny but of course they won't act on that until you also request it, and if this is not possible because of work at the Inst. then you won't. After all if it goes on too long I will tell them get another geneticist, and come back! Sadik is very well and can say yite for light. It will not be very long. All, for life, your sister, Takver. Oh please come if you can.

The other note was scribbled on a tiny bit of paper: "Shevek: Physics off. on yr return. Sabul."

Shevek roamed around the room. The storm, the impetus that had hurled him through the streets, was still in him. It had come up against the wall. He could go no further, yet he must move. He looked in the closet. Nothing was in it but his winter coat and a shirt which Takver, who liked fine handwork, had embroidered for him; her few clothes were gone. The screen was folded back, showing the empty crib. The sleeping platform was not made up, but the orange blanket covered the rolled-up bedding neatly. Shevek came up against the table again, read Takver's letter again. His eyes filled with tears of anger. A rage of disappointment shook him, a wrath, a foreboding.

No one was to blame. That was the worst of it. Takver was needed, needed to work against hunger—hers, his, Sadik's hunger. Society was not against them. It was for them; with them; it was them.

But he had given up his book, and his love, and his child. How much can a man be asked to give up?

"Hell!" he said aloud. Pravic was not a good swearing language. It is hard to swear when sex is not dirty and blasphemy does not exist. "Oh, hell!" he repeated. He crumpled up Sabul's grubby little note vindictively, and then brought his hands down clenched against the edge of the table, twice, three times, in his passion seeking pain. But there was nothing. There was nothing to be done and nowhere to be gone. He was left at last with the bedding to unroll, with lying down alone and getting to sleep, with evil dreams and without comfort.

First thing in the morning, Bunub knocked. He met her at the door and did not stand aside to let her in. She was their neighbor down the hall, a woman of fifty, a machinist in the Air Vehicle Engine factory. Takver had always been entertained by her, but she infuriated Shevek. For one thing, she wanted their room. She had claimed it when it first came vacant, she said, but the enmity of the block housing registrar had prevented her getting it. Her room did not have the corner window, the object of her undying envy. It was a double, though, and she lived alone in it, which, given the housing shortage, was egoistic of her; but Shevek would never have wasted time on disapproving her if she had not forced him by making excuses. She explained, explained. She had a partner, a lifelong partner, "just like you two," simper. Only where was the partner? Somehow he was always spoken of in the past tense. Meanwhile the double room was pretty well justified by the succession of men that passed through Bunub's door, a different man every night, as if Bunub were a roaring girl of seventeen. Takver observed the procession with admiration. Bunub came and told her all about the men, and complained, complained. Her not having the corner room was only one among unnumbered grievances. She had a mind both insidious and invidious, which could find the bad in anything and take it straight to her bosom. The factory where she worked was a poisonous mass of incompetence, favoritism, and sabotage. Meetings of her syndicate were bedlams of unrighteous innuendo all directed at her. The entire social organism was dedicated to the persecution of Bunub. All this made Takver laugh, sometimes wildly, right in Bunub's face. "Oh, Bunub, you are so funny!" she would gasp and the woman, with greying hair and a thin mouth and down-cast eyes, would smile thinly, not offended, not at all, and continue her monstrous recitations. Shevek knew that Takver was right to laugh at her, but he could not do it.

"It's terrible," she said, slithering in past him and going straight to the table to read Takver's letter. She picked it up; Shevek plucked it out of her hand with a calm rapidity she had not prepared for. "Perfectly terrible. Not even a decad's notice. Just, 'Come here! Right now!' And they say we're free people, we're supposed to be free people. What a joke! Breaking up a happy partnership that way. That's why they did it, you know. They're against partnerships, you can see it all the time, they intentionally post partners apart. That's what happened with me and Labeks, exactly the same thing. We'll never get back together. Not with the whole of Divlab lined up against us. There's the little empty crib. Poor little thing! She never ceased crying these four decads, day and night. Kept me awake for hours. It's the shortages, of course; Takver just didn't have enough milk. And then to send a nursing mother off to a posting hundreds of miles away like that, imagine! I don't suppose you'll be able to join her there, where is it they sent her to?"

"Northeast. I want to get over to breakfast, Bunub. I'm hungry."

"Isn't it typical how they did it while you were away."

"Did what while I was away?"

"Sent her away—broke up the partnership." She was reading Sabul's note, which she had uncrumpled with care. "They know when to move in! I suppose you'll be leaving this room now, won't you? They won't let you keep a double. Takver talked about coming back soon, but I could see she was just trying to keep her spirits up. Freedom, we're supposed to be free, big joke! Pushed around from here to there—"

"Oh, by damn, Bunub, if Takver hadn't wanted the posting she'd have refused it. You know we're facing a famine."

"Well. I wondered if she hadn't been looking for a move. It often happens after a baby comes. I thought long ago you should have given that baby to a nursery. The amount it cried. Children come between partners. Tie them down. It's only natural, as you say, that she should have been looking for a change, and jumped at it when she got it."

"I did not say that. I'm going to breakfast." He strode out, quivering at five or six sensitive spots which Bunub had accurately wounded. The horror of the woman was that she voiced all his own most despicable fears. She now stayed behind in the room, probably to plan her move into it.

He had overslept, and got to commons just before they closed the doors. Ravenous still from the journey, he took a double helping of both porridge and bread. The boy behind the serving tables looked at him frowning. These days nobody took double helpings. Shevek stared frowning back and said nothing. He had gone eighty-odd hours now on two bowls of soup and one kilo of bread, and he had a right to make up for what he had missed, but he was damned if he would explain. Existence is its own justification, need is right. He was an Odonian, he left guilt to profiteers.

He sat down by himself, but Desar joined him immediately, smiling, staring at or beside him with disconcerting wall eyes. "Been gone while," Desar said.

"Farm draft. Six decads. How have things been here?"

"Lean."

"They'll get leaner," Shevek said, but without real conviction, for he was eating, and the porridge tasted exceedingly good. Frustration, anxiety, famine! said his forebrain, seat of intellect; but his hindbrain, squatting in unrepentant savagery back in the deep skull's darkness, said Food now! Food now! Good, good!

"Seen Sabul?"

"No. I got in late last night." He glanced up at Desar and said with attempted indifference, "Takver got a famine posting; she had to leave four days ago."

Desar nodded with genuine indifference. "Heard that. You hear about Institute reorganizing?"

"No. What's up?"

The mathematician spread out his long, slender hands on the table and looked down at them. He was always tongue-tied and telegraphic; in fact, he stammered; but whether it was a verbal or a moral stammer Shevek had never decided. As he had always liked Desar without knowing why, so there were moments when he disliked Desar intensely, again without knowing why. This was one of the moments. There was a slyness in the expression of Desar's mouth, his downcast eyes, like Bunub's downcast eyes.

"Shakedown. Cutting back to functional staff. Shipeg's out." Shipeg was a notoriously stupid mathematician who had always managed, by assiduous flattery of students, to get himself one student-requisitioned course each term. "Sent him off. Some regional institute."

"He'd do less harm hoeing ground-holum," Shevek said. Now that he was fed, it appeared to him that the drought might after all be of service to the social organism. The priorities were becoming clear again. Weaknesses, soft spots, sick spots would be scoured out, sluggish organs restored to full function, the fat would be trimmed off the body politic.

"Put in word for you, Institute meeting," Desar said, looking up but not meeting, because he could not meet, Shevek's eyes. As he spoke, though Shevek did not yet understand what he meant, he knew that Desar was lying. He knew it positively. Desar had not put in a word for him, but a word against him.

The reason for his moments of detesting Desar was clear to him now: a recognition, heretofore unadmitted, of the element of pure malice in Desar's personality. That Desar also loved him and was trying to gain power over him was equally clear, and, to Shevek, equally detestable. The devious ways of possessiveness, the labyrinths of love/hate, were meaningless to him. Arrogant, intolerant, he walked right through their walls. He did not speak again to the mathematician, but finished his breakfast and went off across the quadrangle, through the bright morning of early autumn, to the physics office.

He went to the back room which everybody called "Sabul's office," the room where they had first met, where Sabul had given him the grammar and dictionary of Iotic. Sabul looked up warily across the desk, looked down again, busy with papers, the hardworking, abstracted scientist; then allowed awareness of Shevek's presence to seep into his overloaded brain; then became, for him, effusive. He looked thin and aged, and when he got up he stooped more than he had used to do, a placating kind of stoop. "Bad times," he said. "Eh? Bad times!"

"They'll get worse," Shevek said lightly. "How's everything here?"

"Bad, bad." Sabul shook his grizzled head. "This is a bad time for pure science, for the intellectual."

"Is there ever a good one?"

Sabul produced an unnatural chuckle.

"Did anything come in for us on the summer shipments from Urras?" Shevek inquired, clearing off sitting room on the bench. He sat down and crossed his legs. His light skin had tanned and the fine down that covered his face had bleached to silver while he worked in the fields in Southrising. He looked spare, and sound, and young, compared to Sabul. Both men were aware of the contrast.

"Nothing of interest."

"No reviews of the *Principles*?"

"No." Sabul's tone was surly, more like himself.

"No letters?"

"No."

"That's odd."

"What's odd about it? What did you expect, a lectureship at Ieu Eun University? The Seo Oen Prize?"

"I expected reviews and replies. There's been time." He said this as Sabul said, "Hardly been time for reviews yet."

There was a pause.

212

"You'll have to realize, Shevek, that a mere conviction of rightness isn't self-justifying. You worked hard on the book, I know. I worked hard editing it, too, trying to make clear that it wasn't just an irresponsible attack on Sequency theory, but had positive aspects. But if other physicists don't see value in your work, then you've got to begin looking at the values you hold and seeing where the discrepancy lies. If it means nothing to other people, what's the good of it? What's its function?"

"I'm a physicist, not a functions analyst," Shevek said amiably.

"Every Odonian has to be a functions analyst. You're thirty, aren't you? By that age a man should know not only his cellular function but his organic function—what his optimum role in the social organism is. You haven't had to think about that, perhaps, as much as most people—"

"No. Since I was ten or twelve I've known what kind of work I had to do."

"What a boy thinks he likes to do isn't always what his society needs from him."

"I'm thirty, as you say. Rather an old boy."

"You've reached that age in an unusually sheltered, protected environment. First the Northsetting Regional Institute—"

"And a forest project, and farm projects, and practical training, and block committees, and volunteer work since the drought; the usual amount of necessary kleggich. I like doing it, in fact. But I do physics too. What are you getting at?"

As Sabul did not answer but merely glared under his heavy, oily brows, Shevek added, "You might as well say it plainly, because you're not going to arrive at it by way of my social conscience."

"Do you consider the work you've done here functional?"

"Yes. 'The more that is organized, the more central the organism: centrality here implying the field of real function.' Tomar's *Definitions*. Since temporal physics attempts to organize everything comprehensible to the human mind, it is by definition a centrally functional activity."

"It doesn't get bread into people's mouths."

"I just spent six decades helping to do that. When I'm

213

called again, I'll go again. Meanwhile I stick by my trade. If there's physics to be done, I claim the right to do it."

"What you have to face is the fact that at this point there is no physics to be done. Not the kind you do. We've got to gear to practicality." Sabul shifted in his chair. He looked sullen and uneasy. "We've had to release five people for reposting. I'm sorry to say that you're one of them. There it is."

"Just where I thought it was," Shevek said, though in fact he had not till that moment realized that Sabul was kicking him out of the Institute. As soon as he heard it, however, it seemed familiar news; and he would not give Sabul the satisfaction of seeing him shaken.

"What worked against you was a combination of things. The abstruse, irrelevant nature of the research you've done these last several years. Plus a certain feeling, not necessarily justified, but existing among many student and teaching members of the Institute, that both your teaching and your behavior reflect a certain disaffection, a degree of privatism, of nonaltruism. This was spoken of in meeting. I spoke for you, of course. But I'm only one syndic among many."

"Since when was altruism an Odonian virtue?" Shevek said. "Well, never mind. I see what you mean." He stood up. He could not keep seated any longer, but otherwise had himself in control, and spoke perfectly naturally. "I take it you didn't recommend me for a teaching post elsewhere."

"What would have been the use?" said Sabul, almost melodious in self-exculpation. "No one's taking on new teachers. Teachers and students are working side by side at famine-prevention jobs all over the planet. Of course, this crisis won't last. In a year or so we'll be looking back on it, proud of the sacrifices we made and the work we did, standing by each other, share and share alike. But right now . . ."

Shevek stood erect, relaxed, gazing out the small, scratched window at the blank sky. There was a mighty desire in him to tell Sabul, finally, to go to hell. But it was a different and profounder impulse that found words. "Actually," he said, "you're probably right." With that he nodded to Sabul and left.

He caught an omnibus downtown. He was still in a

214

hurry, driven. He was following a pattern and wanted to come to the end of it, come to rest. He went to the Division of Labor Central Posting offices to request a posting to the community to which Takver had gone.

Divlab, with its computers and its huge task of coordination, occupied a whole square; its buildings were handsome, imposing by Anarresti standards, with fine, plain lines. Inside, Central Posting was high-ceilinged and barn-like, very full of people and activity, the walls covered with posting notices and directions as to which desk or department to go to for this business or that. As Shevek waited in one of the lines he listened to the people in front of him, a boy of sixteen and a man in his sixties. The boy was volunteering for a famine-prevention posting. He was full of noble feelings, spilling over with brotherhood, adventurousness, hope. He was delighted to be going off on his own, leaving his childhood behind. He talked a great deal, like a child, in a voice not yet used to its deeper tones. Freedom, freedom! rang in his excited talk, in every word; and the old man's voice grumbled and rumbled through it, teasing but not threatening, mocking but not cautioning. Freedom, the ability to go somewhere and do something, freedom was what the old man praised and cherished in the young one, even while he mocked his self-importance. Shevek listened to them with pleasure. They broke the morning's series of grotesques.

As soon as Shevek explained where he wanted to go, the clerk got a worried look, and went off for an atlas, which she opened on the counter between them. "Now look," she said. She was an ugly little woman with buck teeth; her hands on the colored pages of the atlas were deft and soft. "That's Rolny, see, the peninsula sticking down into the North Temaenian. It's just a huge sandpit. There's nothing on it at all but the marine laboratories away out there at the end, see? Then the coast's all swamp and salt marsh till you get clear round here to Harmony —a thousand kilometers. And west of it is the Coast Barrens. The nearest you could get to Rolny would be some town in the mountains. But they're not asking for emergency postings there; they're pretty self-sufficing. Of course, you could go there anyhow," she added in a slightly different tone.

"It's too far from Rolny," he said, looking at the map,

noticing in the mountains of Northeast the little isolated town where Takver had grown up. Round Valley. "Don't they need a janitor at the marine lab? A statistician? Somebody to feed the fish?"

"I'll check."

The human/computer network of files in Divlab was set up with admirable efficiency. It did not take the clerk five minutes to get the desired information sorted out from the enormous, continual input and outgo of information concerning every job being done, every position wanted, every workman needed, and the priorities of each in the general economy of the world-wide society. "They just filled an emergency draft—that's the partner, isn't it? They got everybody they wanted, four technicians and an experienced seiner. Staff complete."

Shevek leaned his elbows on the counter and bowed his head, scratching it, a gesture of confusion and defeat masked by self-consciousness. "Well," he said, "I don't know what to do."

"Look, brother, how long is the partner's posting?"

"Indefinite."

"But it's a famine-prevention job, isn't it? It's not going to go on like this forever. It can't! It'll rain, this winter."

He looked up into his sister's earnest, sympathetic, harried face. He smiled a little, for he could not leave her effort to give hope without response.

"You'll get back together. Meanwhile—"

"Yes. Meanwhile," he said.

She awaited his decision.

It was his to make; and the options were endless. He could stay in Abbenay and organize classes in physics if he could find volunteer students. He could go to Rolny Peninsula and live with Takver though without any place in the research station. He could live anywhere and do nothing but get up twice a day and go to the nearest commons to be fed. He could do what he pleased.

The identity of the words "work" and "play" in Pravic had, of course, a strong ethical significance. Odo had seen the danger of a rigid moralism arising from the use of the word "work" in her analogic system: the cells must work together, the optimum working of the organism, the work done by each element, and so forth. Cooperation and function, essential concepts of the *Analogy*, both im-

216

plied work. The proof of an experiment, twenty test tubes in a laboratory or twenty million people on the Moon, is simply, does it work? Odo had seen the moral trap. "The saint is never busy," she had said, perhaps wistfully.

But the choices of the social being are never made alone.

"Well," Shevek said, "I just came back from a famine-prevention posting. Anything else like that need doing?"

The clerk gave him an elder-sisterly look, incredulous but forgiving. "There's about seven hundred Urgent calls posted around the room," she said. "Which one would you like?"

"Any of them need math?"

"They're mostly farming and skilled labor. Do you have any engineering training?"

"Not much."

"Well, there's work-coordinating. That certainly takes a head for figures. How about this one?"

"All right."

"That's down in Southwest, in the Dust, you know."

"I've been in the Dust before. Besides, as you say, someday it will rain. . . ."

She nodded, smiling, and typed onto his Divlab record: *FROM Abbenay, NW Cent Inst Sci, TO Elbow, SW, wk co, phosphate mill #1: EMERG PSTG: 5–1–3–165— indefinite.*

Chapter 9

URRAS

Shevek was awakened by the bells in the chapel tower pealing the Prime Harmony for morning religious service. Each note was like a blow on the back of his head. He was so sick and shaky he could not even sit up for a long time. He finally managed to shuffle into the bathroom and take a long cold bath, which relieved the headache; but his whole body continued to feel strange to him—to feel, somehow, vile. As he began to be able to think again, fragments and moments of the night before came into his mind, vivid, senseless little scenes from the party at Vea's. He tried not to think about them, and then could think of nothing else. Everything, everything became vile. He sat down at his desk, and sat there staring, motionless, perfectly miserable, for half an hour.

He had been embarrassed often enough, and had felt himself a fool. As a young man he had suffered from the sense that others thought him strange, unlike them; in later years he had felt, having deliberately invited, the anger and contempt of many of his fellows on Anarres. But he had never really accepted their judgment. He had never been ashamed.

He did not know that this paralyzing humiliation was a chemical sequel to getting drunk, like the headache. Nor would the knowledge have made much difference to him. Shame—the sense of vileness and of self-estrangement—was a revelation. He saw with a new clarity, a hideous clarity; and saw far past those incoherent memories of the end of the evening at Vea's. It was not only poor Vea who had betrayed him. It was not only the alcohol that he had tried to vomit up; it was all the bread he had eaten on Urras.

He leaned his elbows on the desk and put his head in his hands, pressing in on the temples, the cramped position of pain; and he looked at his life in the light of shame.

On Anarres he had chosen, in defiance of the expectations of his society, to do the work he was individually called to do. To do it was to rebel: to risk the self for the sake of society.

Here on Urras, that act of rebellion was a luxury, a self-indulgence. To be a physicist in A-Io was to serve not society, not mankind, not the truth, but the State.

On his first night in this room he had asked them, challenging and curious, "What are you going to do with me?" He knew now what they had done with him. Chifoilisk had told him the simple fact. They owned him. He had thought to bargain with them, a very naïve anarchist's notion. The individual cannot bargain with the State. The State recognizes no coinage but power: and it issues the coins itself.

He saw now—in detail, item by item from the beginning—that he had made a mistake in coming to Urras; his first big mistake, and one that was likely to last him the rest of his life. Once he had seen it, once he had rehearsed all the evidences of it that he had suppressed and denied for months—and it took him a long time, sitting there motionless at his desk—until he had arrived at the ludicrous and abominable last scene with Vea, and had lived through that again too, and felt his face go hot until his ears sang: then he was done with it. Even in this postalcoholic vale of tears, he felt no guilt. That was all done, now, and what must be thought about was, what must he do now? Having locked himself in jail, how might he act as a free man?

He would not do physics for the politicians. That was clear, now.

If he stopped working, would they let him go home?

At this, he drew a long breath and raised his head, looking with unseeing eyes at the sunlit green landscape out the window. It was the first time he had let himself think of going home as a genuine possibility. The thought threatened to break down the gates and flood him with urgent yearning. To speak Pravic, to speak to friends, to see Takver, Pilun, Sadik, to touch the dust of Anarres. . . .

They would not let him go. He had not paid his way. Nor could he let himself go: give up and run.

As he sat at the desk in the bright morning sunlight he brought his hands down against the edge of the desk deliberately and sharply, twice, three times; his face was calm and appeared thoughtful.

"Where do I go?" he said aloud.

A knock on the door. Efor came in with a breakfast tray and the morning papers. "Come in at six usual but catching up your sleep," he observed, setting out the tray with admirable deftness.

"I got drunk last night," Shevek said.

"Beautiful while it lasts," said Efor. "That be all, sir? Very well," and he exited with the same deftness, bowing on the way to Pae, who entered as he left.

"Didn't mean to barge in on your breakfast! On my way back from chapel, just thought I'd look in."

"Sit down. Have some chocolate." Shevek was unable to eat unless Pae made some pretense at least of eating with him. Pae took a honey roll and crumbled it about on a plate. Shevek still felt rather shaky but very hungry now, and attacked his breakfast with energy. Pae seemed to find it harder than usual to start conversation.

"You're still getting this trash?" he asked at last in an amused tone, touching the folded newspapers Efor had set on the table.

"Efor brings them."

"Does he?"

"I asked him to," Shevek said, glancing at Pae, a split-second reconnoitering glance. "They broaden my comprehension of your country. I take an interest in your lower classes. Most Anarresti came from the lower classes."

"Yes, of course," the younger man said, looking respectful and nodding. He ate a small bite of honey roll. "I think I'd like a drop of that chocolate after all," he said, and rang the bell on the tray. Efor appeared at the door. "Another cup," Pae said without turning. "Well, sir, we'd looked forward to taking you about again, now the weather's turning fine, and showing you more of the country. Even a visit abroad, perhaps. But this damned war has put an end to all such plans, I'm afraid."

Shevek looked at the headline of the topmost paper: IO, THU CLASH NEAR BENBILI CAPITAL.

"There's later news than that on the telefax," Pae said. "We've liberated the capital. General Havevert will be reinstalled."

"Then the war is over?"

"Not while Thu still holds the two eastern provinces."

"I see. So your army and Thu's army will fight in Benbili. But not here?"

"No, no. It would be utter folly for them to invade us, or us them. We've outgrown the kind of barbarism that used to bring war into the heart of the high civilizations! The balance of power is kept by this kind of police action. However, we are officially at war. So all the tiresome old restrictions will come into effect, I'm afraid."

"Restrictions?"

"Classification of research done in the College of Noble Science, for one thing. Nothing to it, really, just a government rubber stamp. And sometimes a delay getting a paper published, when the higher-ups think it must be dangerous because they don't understand it! . . . And travel's a bit limited, especially for you and the other non-nationals here, I'm afraid. So long as the state of war lasts, you're not actually supposed to leave the campus, I believe, without clearance from the Chancellor. But pay no attention to that. I can get you out of here whenever you like without going through all the rigmarole."

"You hold the keys," Shevek said, with an ingenuous smile.

"Oh, I'm an absolute specialist in it. I love getting around rules and outwitting the authorities. Perhaps I'm a natural anarchist, eh? Where the devil is that old fool I sent for a cup?"

"He must go down to the kitchens to get one."

"Needn't take half the day about it. Well, I won't wait. Don't want to take up what's left of your morning. By the way, did you see the latest *Bulletin of the Space Research*

221

Foundation? They print Reumere's plans for the ansible."

"What is the ansible?"

"It's what he's calling an instantaneous communication device. He says if the temporalists—that's you, of course —will just work out the time-inertia equations, the engineers—that's him—will be able to build the damned thing, test it, and thus incidentally prove the validity of the theory, within months or weeks."

"Engineers are themselves proof of the existence of causal reversibility. You see Reumere has his effect built before I have provided the cause." He smiled again, rather less ingenuously. When Pae had shut the door behind himself, Shevek suddenly stood up. "You filthy profiteering liar!" he said in Pravic, white with rage, his hands clenched to keep them from picking something up and throwing it after Pae.

Efor came in carrying a cup and saucer on a tray. He stopped short, looking apprehensive.

"It's all right, Efor. He didn't—He didn't want the cup. You can take it all now."

"Very good, sir."

"Listen. I should like no visitors, for a while. Can you keep them out?"

"Easy sir. Anybody special?"

"Yes, him. Anybody. Say I am working."

"He'll be glad to hear that, sir," Efor said, his wrinkles melting with malice for an instant; then with respectful familiarity, "Nobody you don't want get past me," and finally with formal propriety, "Thank you, sir, and good morning."

Food, and adrenalin, had dispelled Shevek's paralysis. He walked up and down the room, irritable and restless. He wanted to act. He had spent nearly a year now doing nothing, except being a fool. It was time he did something.

Well, what had he come here to do?

To do physics. To assert, by his talent, the rights of any citizen in any society: the right to work, to be maintained while working, and to share the product with all who wanted it. The rights of an Odonian and of a human being.

His benevolent and protective hosts let him work, and maintained him while working, all right. The problem came on the third limb. But he himself had not got there yet. He had not done his job. He couldn't share what he didn't have.

He went back to the desk, sat down, and took a couple of scraps of heavily scribbled paper out of the least accessible and least useful pocket of his tight-fitting, stylish trousers. He spread these scraps out with his fingers and looked at them. It occurred to him that he was getting to be like Sabul, writing very small, in abbreviations, on shreds of paper. He knew now why Sabul did it: he was possessive and secretive. A psychopathy on Anarres was rational behavior on Urras.

Again Shevek sat quite motionless, his head bowed, studying the two little bits of paper on which he had noted down certain essential points of the General Temporal Theory, so far as it went.

For the next three days he sat at the desk and looked at the two bits of paper.

At times he got up and walked around the room, or wrote something down, or employed the desk computer, or asked Efor to bring him something to eat, or lay down and fell asleep. Then he went back to the desk and sat there.

On the evening of the third day he was sitting, for a change, on the marble seat by the hearth. He had sat down there on the first night he entered this room, this gracious prison cell, and generally sat there when he had visitors. He had no visitors at the moment, but he was thinking about Saio Pae.

Like all power seekers, Pae was amazingly shortsighted. There was a trivial, abortive quality to his mind; it lacked depth, affect, imagination. It was, in fact, a primitive instrument. Yet its potentiality had been real, and though deformed had not been lost. Pae was a very clever physicist. Or, more exactly, he was very clever about physics. He had not done anything original, but his opportunism, his sense for where advantage lay, led him time after time to the most promising field. He had the flair for *where to set to work,* just as Shevek did, and Shevek respected it in him as in himself, for it is a singularly important attribute in a scientist. It was Pae who had given Shevek the book translated from the Terran, the symposium on the theories of Relativity, the ideas of which had come to occupy his mind more and more of late. Was it possible that

223

after all he had come to Urras simply to meet Saio Pae, his enemy? That he had come seeking him, knowing that he might receive from his enemy what he could not receive from his brothers and friends, what no Anarresti could give him: knowledge of the foreign, of the alien: news. . . .

He forgot Pae. He thought about the book. He could not state clearly to himself what, exactly, he had found so stimulating about it. Most of the physics in it was, after all, outdated; the methods were cumbersome, and the alien attitude sometimes quite disagreeable. The Terrans had been intellectual imperialists, jealous wall builders. Even Ainsetain, the originator of the theory, had felt compelled to give warning that his physics embraced no mode but the physical and should not be taken as implying the metaphysical, the philosophical, or the ethical. Which, of course, was superficially true; and yet he had used *number*, the bridge between the rational and the perceived, between psyche and matter, "Number the Indisputable," as the ancient founders of the Noble Science had called it. To employ mathematics in this sense was to employ the mode that preceded and led to all other modes. Ainsetain had known that; with endearing caution he had admitted that he believed his physics did, indeed, describe reality.

Strangeness and familiarity: in every movement of the Terran's thought Shevek caught this combination, was constantly intrigued. And sympathetic: for Ainsetain, too, had been after a unifying field theory. Having explained the force of gravity as a function of the geometry of spacetime, he had sought to extend the synthesis to include electromagnetic forces. He had not succeeded. Even during his lifetime, and for many decades after his death, the physicists of his own world had turned away from his effort and its failure, pursuing the magnificent incoherences of quantum theory with its high technological yields, at last concentrating on the technological mode so exclusively as to arrive at a dead end, a catastrophic failure of imagination. Yet their original intuition had been sound: at the point where they had been, progress had lain in the indeterminacy which old Ainsetain had refused to accept. And his refusal had been equally correct—in the long run. Only he had lacked the tools to prove it—the Saeba variables and the theories of infinite velocity and complex cause. His unified field existed, in Cetian physics, but it existed on terms which he might not have been willing to accept; for the velocity of light as a limiting factor had been essential to his great theories. Both his Theories of Relativity were as beautiful, as valid, and as useful as ever after these centuries, and yet both depended upon a hypothesis that could not be proved true and that could be and had been proved, in certain circumstances, false.

But was not a theory of which *all* the elements were provably true a simple tautology? In the region of the unprovable, or even the disprovable, lay the only chance for breaking out of the circle and going ahead.

In which case, did the unprovability of the hypothesis of real coexistence—the problem which Shevek had been pounding his head against desperately for these last three days, and indeed these last ten years—really matter?

He had been groping and grabbing after certainty, as if it were something he could possess. He had been demanding a security, a guarantee, which is not granted, and which, if granted, would become a prison. By simply assuming the validity of real coexistence he was left free to use the lovely geometries of relativity; and then it would be possible to go ahead. The next step was perfectly clear. The coexistence of succession could be handled by a Saeban transformation series; thus approached, successivity and presence offered no antithesis at all. The fundamental unity of the Sequency and Simultaneity points of view became plain; the concept of interval served to connect the static and the dynamic aspect of the universe. How could he have stared at reality for ten years and not seen it? There would be no trouble at all in going on. Indeed he had already gone on. He was there. He saw all that was to come in this first, seemingly casual glimpse of the method, given him by his understanding of a failure in the distant past. The wall was down. The vision was both clear and whole. What he saw was simple, simpler than anything else. It was simplicity: and contained in it all complexity, all promise. It was revelation. It was the way clear, the way home, the light.

The spirit in him was like a child running out into the sunlight. There was no end, no end. . . .

And yet in his utter ease and happiness he shook with fear; his hands trembled, and his eyes filled up with tears, as if he had been looking into the sun. After all, the flesh is not transparent. And it is strange, exceedingly strange, to know that one's life has been fulfilled.

Yet he kept looking, and going farther, with that same childish joy, until all at once he could not go any farther; he came back, and looking around through his tears saw that the room was dark and the high windows were full of stars.

The moment was gone; he saw it going. He did not try to hold on to it. He knew he was part of it, not it of him. He was in its keeping.

After a while he got up shakily and lighted the lamp. He wandered around the room a little, touching things, the binding of a book, the shade of a lamp, glad to be back among these familiar objects, back in his own world—for at this instant the difference between this planet and that one, between Urras and Anarres, was no more significant to him than the difference between two grains of sand on the shore of the sea. There were no more abysses, no more walls. There was no more exile. He had seen the foundations of the universe, and they were solid.

He went into the bedroom, walking slowly and a little unsteadily, and dropped onto the bed without undressing. He lay there with his arms behind his head, occasionally foreseeing and planning one detail or another of the work that had to be done, absorbed in a solemn and delightful thankfulness, which merged gradually into serene reverie, and then into sleep.

He slept for ten hours. He woke up thinking of the equations that would express the concept of interval. He went to the desk and set to work on them. He had a class that afternoon, and met it; he took his dinner at the Senior Faculty commons and talked with his colleagues there about the weather, and the war, and whatever else they brought up. If they noticed any change in him he did not know it, for he was not really aware of them at all. He came back to his room and worked.

The Urrasti counted twenty hours in the day. For eight days he spent twelve to sixteen hours daily at his desk, or roaming about his room, his light eyes turned often to the windows, outside which shone the warm spring sunlight, or the stars and the tawny, waning Moon.

Coming in with the breakfast tray, Efor found him lying half-dressed on the bed, his eyes shut, talking in a foreign language. He roused him. Shevek woke with a convulsive start, got up and staggered into the other room, to the desk, which was perfectly empty; he stared at the computer, which had been cleared, and then stood there like a man who has been hit on the head and does not know it yet. Efor succeeded in getting him to lie down again and said, "Fever there, sir. Call the doctor?"

"No!"

"Sure, sir?"

"No! Don't let anybody in here. Say I am ill, Efor."

"Then they'll fetch the doctor sure. Can say you're still working, sir. They like that."

"Lock the door when you go out," Shevek said. His nontransparent body had let him down; he was weak with exhaustion, and therefore fretful and panicky. He was afraid of Pae, of Oiie, of a police search party. Everything he had heard, read, half-understood about the Urrasti police, the secret police, came vivid and terrible into his memory, as when a man admitting his illness to himself recalls every word he ever read about cancer. He stared up at Efor in feverish distress.

"You can trust me," the man said in his subdued, wry, quick way. He brought Shevek a glass of water and went out, and the lock of the outer door clicked behind him.

He looked after Shevek during the next two days, with a tact that owed little to his training as a servant.

"You should have been a doctor, Efor," Shevek said, when his weakness had become a merely bodily, not unpleasant lassitude.

"What my old sow say. She never wants nobody nurse her beside me when she get the pip. She say, 'You got the touch.' I guess I do."

"Did you ever work with the sick?"

"No sir. Don't want to mix up with hospitals. Black day the day I got to die in one of them pest-holes."

"The hospitals? What's wrong with them?"

"Nothing, sir, not them you be took to if you was worse," Efor said with gentleness.

"What kind did you mean, then?"

"Our kind. Dirty. Like a trashman's ass-hole," Efor said, without violence, descriptively. "Old. Kid die in one.

There's holes in the floor, big holes, the beams show through, see? I say, 'How come?' See, rats come up the holes, right in the beds. They say, 'Old building, been a hospital six hundred years.' Stablishment of the Divine Harmony for the Poor, its name. An ass-hole what it is."

"It was your child that died in the hospital?"

"Yes, sir, my daughter Laia."

"What did she die of?"

"Valve in her heart. They say. She don't grow much. Two years old when she die."

"You have other children?"

"Not living. Three born. Hard on the old sow. But now she say, 'Oh, well, don't have to be heartbreaking over 'em, just as well after all!' Is there anything else I can do for you, sir?" The sudden switch to upper-class syntax jolted Shevek; he said impatiently, "Yes! Go on talking."

Because he had spoken spontaneously, or because he was unwell and should be humored, this time Efor did not stiffen up. "Think of going for army medic, one time," he said, "but they get me first. Draft. Say, 'Orderly, you be orderly.' So I do. Good training, orderly. Come out of the army straight into gentlemen's service."

"You could have been trained as a medic, in the army?" The conversation went on. It was difficult for Shevek to follow, both in language and in substance. He was being told about things he had no experience of at all. He had never seen a rat, or an army barracks, or an insane asylum, or a poorhouse, or a pawnshop, or an execution, or a thief, or a tenement, or a rent collector, or a man who wanted to work and could not find work to do, or a dead baby in a ditch. All these things occurred in Efor's reminiscences as commonplaces or as commonplace horrors. Shevek had to exercise his imagination and summon every scrap of knowledge he had about Urras to understand them at all. And yet they were familiar to him in a way that nothing he had yet seen here was, and he did understand.

This was the Urras he had learned about in school on Anarres. This was the world from which his ancestors had fled, preferring hunger and the desert and endless exile. This was the world that had formed Odo's mind and had jailed her eight times for speaking it. This was the human

228

suffering in which the ideals of his society were rooted, the ground from which they sprang.

It was not "the real Urras." The dignity and beauty of the room he and Efor were in was as real as the squalor to which Efor was native. To him a thinking man's job was not to deny one reality at the expense of the other, but to include and to connect. It was not an easy job.

"Look tired again, sir," Efor said. "Better rest."

"No, I'm not tired."

Efor observed him a moment. When Efor functioned as a servant his lined, clean-shaven face was quite expressionless; during the last hour Shevek had seen it go through extraordinary changes of harshness, humor, cynicism, and pain. At the moment its expression was sympathetic yet detached.

"Different from all that where you come from," Efor said.

"Very different."

"Nobody ever out of work, there."

There was a faint edge of irony, or question, in his voice.

"No."

"And nobody hungry?"

"Nobody goes hungry while another eats."

"Ah."

"But we have been hungry. We have starved. There was a famine, you know, eight years ago. I knew a woman then who killed her baby, because she had no milk, and there was nothing else, nothing else to give it. It is not all . . . all milk and honey on Anarres, Efor."

"I don't doubt it, sir," Efor said with one of his curious returns to polite diction. Then he said with a grimace, drawing his lips back from his teeth, "All the same there's none of *them* there!"

"Them?"

"You know, Mr. Shevek. What you said once. The owners."

The next evening Atro called by. Pae must have been on the watch, for a few minutes after Efor admitted the old man, he came strolling in, and inquired with charming sympathy after Shevek's indisposition. "You've been working much too hard these last couple of weeks, sir," he said, "you mustn't wear yourself out like this." He did not sit down, but took his leave very soon, the soul of civility. Atro went on talking about the war in Benbili, which was becoming, as he put it, "a large-scale operation."

"Do the people in this country approve of this war?" Shevek asked, interrupting a discourse on strategy. He had been puzzled by the absence of moral judgment in the birdseed papers on this subject. They had given up their ranting excitement; their wording was often exactly the same as that of the telefax bulletins issued by the government.

"Approve? You don't think we'd lie down and let the damned Thuvians walk all over us? Our status as a world power is at stake!"

"But I meant the people, not the government. The . . . the people who must fight."

"What's it to them? They're used to mass conscriptions. It's what they're for, my dear fellow! To fight for their country. And let me tell you, there's no better soldier on earth than the Ioti man of the ranks, once he's broken in to taking orders. In peacetime he may spout sentimental pacifism, but the grit's there, underneath. The common soldier has always been our greatest resource as a nation. It's how we became the leader we are."

"By climbing up on a pile of dead children?" Shevek said, but anger or, perhaps, an unadmitted reluctance to hurt the old man's feelings, kept his voice muffled, and Atro did not hear him.

"No," Atro went on, "you'll find the soul of the people true as steel, when the country's threatened. A few rabble-rousers in Nio and the mill towns make a big noise between wars, but it's grand to see how the people close ranks when the flag's in danger. You're unwilling to believe that, I know. The trouble with Odonianism, you know, my dear fellow, is that it's womanish. It simply doesn't include the virile side of life. 'Blood and steel, battle's brightness,' as the old poet says. It doesn't understand courage—love of the flag."

Shevek was silent for a minute; then he said, gently, "That may be true, in part. At least, we have no flags."

When Atro had gone, Efor came in to take out the dinner tray. Shevek stopped him. He came up close to him, saying, "Excuse me, Efor," and put a slip of paper down on the tray. On it he had written, "Is there a microphone in this room?"

The servant bent his head and read it, slowly, and then looked up at Shevek, a long look at short range. Then his eyes glanced for a second at the chimney of the fireplace.

"Bedroom?" Shevek inquired by the same means.

Efor shook his head, put the tray down, and followed Shevek into the bedroom. He shut the door behind him with the noiselessness of a good servant.

"Spotted that one first day, dusting," he said with a grin that deepened the lines on his face into harsh ridges.

"Not in here?"

Efor shrugged. "Never spotted it. Could run the water in there, sir, like they do in the spy stories."

They proceeded on into the magnificent gold and ivory temple of the shitstool. Efor turned on the taps and then looked around the walls. "No," he said. "Don't think so. And spy eye I could spot. Get onto them when I work for a man in Nio once. Can't miss 'em once you get onto 'em."

Shevek took another piece of paper out of his pocket and showed it to Efor. "Do you know where this came from?"

It was the note he had found in his coat, "Join with us your brothers."

After a pause—he read slowly, moving his closed lips —Efor said, "I don't know where it come from."

Shevek was disappointed. It had occurred to him that Efor himself was in an excellent position to slip something into his "master's" pocket.

"Know who it come from. In a manner."

"Who? How can I get to them?"

Another pause. "Dangerous business, Mr. Shevek." He turned away and increased the rush of water from the taps.

"I don't want to involve you. If you can just tell me— tell me where to go. What I should ask for. Even one name."

A still longer pause. Efor's face looked pinched and hard. "I don't—" he said, and stopped. Then he said, abruptly, and very low, "Look, Mr. Shevek, God knows they want you, we need you, but look, you don't know

231

what it's like. How you going to hide? A man like you? Looking like you look? This a trap here, but it's a trap anywhere. You can run but you can't hide. I don't know what to tell you. Give you names, sure. Ask any Nioti, he tell you where to go. We had about enough. We got to have some air to breathe. But you get caught, shot, how do I feel? I work for you eight months, I come to like you. To admire you. They approach me all the time. I say, 'No. Let him be. A good man and he got no part of our troubles. Let him go back where he come from where the people are free. Let somebody go free from this God damned prison we living in!' "

"I can't go back. Not yet. I want to meet these people."

Efor stood silent. Perhaps it was his life's habit as a servant, as one who obeys, that made him nod at last and say, whispering, "Tuio Maedda, he who you want. In Joking Lane, in Old Town. The grocery."

"Pae says I am forbidden to leave the campus. They can stop me if they see me take the train."

"Taxi, maybe," Efor said. "I call you one, you go down by the stairs. I know Kae Oimon on the stand. He got sense. But I don't know."

"All right. Right now. Pae was just here, he saw me, he thinks I'm staying in because I'm ill. What time is it?"

"Half past seven."

"If I go now, I have the night to find where I should go. Call the taxi, Efor."

"I'll pack you a bag, sir—"

"A bag of what?"

"You'll need clothes—"

"I'm wearing clothes! Go on."

"You can't just go with nothing," Efor protested. This made him more anxious and uneasy than anything else. "You got money?"

"Oh—yes. I should take that."

Shevek was on the move already; Efor scratched his head, looked grim and dour, but went off to the hall phone to call the taxi. He returned to find Shevek waiting outside the hall door with his coat on. "Go downstairs," Efor said, grudgingly. "Kae be at the back door, five minutes. Tell him go out by Grove Road, no checkpoint there like at the main gate. Don't go by the gate, they stop you there sure."

"Will you be blamed for this, Efor?"

They were both whispering.

"I don't know you gone. Morning, I say you don't get up yet. Sleeping. Keep 'em off a while."

Shevek took him by the shoulders, embraced him, shook his hand. "Thank you, Efor!"

"Good luck," the man said, bewildered. Shevek was already gone.

Shevek's costly day with Vea had taken most of his ready cash, and the taxi ride in to Nio took ten units more. He got out at a major subway station and by using his map worked his way by subway into Old Town, a section of the city he had never seen. Joking Lane was not on the map, so he got off the train at the central stop for Old Town. When he came up from the spacious marble station into the street he stopped in confusion. This did not look like Nio Esseia.

A fine, foggy rain was falling, and it was quite dark; there were no street lights. The lampposts were there, but the lights were not turned on, or were broken. Yellow gleams slitted from around shuttered windows here and there. Down the street, light streamed from an open doorway, around which a group of men were lounging, talking loud. The pavement, greasy with rain, was littered with scraps of paper and refuse. The shopfronts, as well as he could make them out, were low, and were all covered up with heavy metal or wooden shutters, except for one which had been gutted by fire and stood black and blank, shards of glass still sticking in the frames of the broken windows. People went by, silent hasty shadows.

An old woman was coming up the stairs behind him, and he turned to her to ask his way. In the light of the yellow globe that marked the subway entrance he saw her face clearly: white and lined, with the dead, hostile stare of weariness. Big glass earrings bobbed on her cheeks. She climbed the stairs laboriously, hunched over with fatigue or with arthritis or some deformity of the spine. But she was not old, as he had thought; she was not even thirty.

"Can you tell me where Joking Lane is," he asked her, stammering. She glanced at him with indifference, hurried her pace as she reached the top of the stairs, and went on without a word.

233

He set off at random down the street. The excitement of his sudden decision and flight from Ieu Eun had turned to apprehension, a sense of being driven, hunted. He avoided the group of men around the door, instinct warning him that the single stranger does not approach that kind of group. When he saw a man ahead of him walking alone, he caught up and repeated his question. The man said, "I don't know," and turned aside.

There was nothing to do but go on. He came to a better-lighted cross street, which wound off into the misty rain in both directions in a dim, grim garishness of lighted signs and advertisements. There were many wineshops and pawnshops, some of them still open. A good many people were in the street, jostling past, going in and out of the wineshops. There was a man lying down, lying in the gutter, his coat bunched up over his head, lying in the rain, asleep, sick, dead. Shevek stared at him with horror, and at the others who walked past without looking.

As he stood there paralyzed, somebody stopped by him and looked up into his face, a short, unshaven, wry-necked fellow of fifty or sixty, with red-rimmed eyes and a toothless mouth opened in a laugh. He stood and laughed witlessly at the big, terrified man, pointing a shaky hand at him. "Where you get all that hair, eh, eh, that hair, where you get all that hair," he mumbled.

"Can—can you tell me how to get to Joking Lane?"

"Sure, joking, I'm joking, no joke I'm broke. Hey you got a little blue for a drink on a cold night? Sure you got a little blue."

He came closer. Shevek drew away, seeing the open hand but not understanding.

"Come on, take a joke mister, one little blue," the man mumbled without threat or pleading, mechanically, his mouth still open in the meaningless grin, his hand held out.

Shevek understood. He groped in his pocket, found the last of his money, thrust it into the beggar's hand, and then, cold with a fear that was not fear for himself, pushed past the man, who was mumbling and trying to catch at his coat, and made for the nearest open door. It was under a sign that read "Pawn and Used Goods Best Values." Inside, among the racks of worn-out coats, shoes, shawls, battered instruments, broken lamps, odd dishes, canisters, spoons, beads, wrecks and fragments, every piece of rubbish marked with its price, he stood trying to collect himself.

"Looking for something?"

He put his question once more.

The shopkeeper, a dark man as tall as Shevek but stooped and very thin, looked him over. "What you want to get there for?"

"I'm looking for a person who lives there."

"Where you from?"

"I need to get to this street, Joking Lane. Is it far from here?"

"Where you from, mister?"

"I am from Anarres, from the Moon," Shevek said angrily. "I have to get to Joking Lane, now, tonight."

"You're him? The scientist fellow? What the hell you doing here?"

"Getting away from the police! Do you want to tell them I'm here, or will you help me?"

"God damn," the man said. "God damn. Look—" He hesitated, was about to say something, about to say something else, said, "You just go on," and in the same breath though apparently with a complete change of mind, said, "All right. I'm closing. Take you there. Hold on. God damn!"

He rummaged in the back of the shop, switched off the light, came outside with Shevek, pulled down metal shutters and locked them, padlocked the door, and set off at a sharp pace, saying, "Come on!"

They walked twenty or thirty blocks, getting deeper into the maze of crooked streets and alleys in the heart of Old Town. The misty rain fell softly in the unevenly lit darkness, bringing out smells of decay, of wet stone and metal. They turned down an unlit, unsigned alley between high old tenements, the ground floors of which were mostly shops. Shevek's guide stopped and knocked on the shuttered window of one: V. Maedda, Fancy Groceries. After a good while the door was opened. The pawnbroker conferred with a person inside, then gestured to Shevek, and they both entered. A girl had let them in. "Tuio's in back, come on," she said, looking up into Shevek's face in the weak light from a back hallway. "Are you him?" Her

235

voice was faint and urgent; she smiled strangely. "Are you really him?"

Tuio Maedda was a dark man in his forties, with a strained, intellectual face. He shut a book in which he had been writing and got quickly to his feet as they entered. He greeted the pawnbroker by name, but never took his eyes off Shevek.

"He come to my shop asking the way here, Tuio. He say he the, you know, the one from Anarres."

"You are, aren't you?" Maedda said slowly. "Shevek. What are you doing here?" He stared at Shevek with alarmed, luminous eyes.

"Looking for help."

"Who sent you to me?"

"The first man I asked. I don't know who you are. I asked him where I could go, he said to come to you."

"Does anybody else know you're here?"

"They don't know I've gone. Tomorrow they will."

"Go get Remeivi," Maedda said to the girl. "Sit down, Dr. Shevek. You'd better tell me what's going on."

Shevek sat down on a wooden chair but did not unfasten his coat. He was so tired he was shaking. "I escaped," he said. "From the University, from the jail. I don't know where to go. Maybe it's all jails here. I came here because they talk about the lower classes, the working classes, and I thought, that sounds like my people. People who might help each other."

"What kind of help are you looking for?"

Shevek made an effort to pull himself together. He looked around the little, littered office, and at Maedda. "I have something they want," he said. "An idea. A scientific theory. I came here from Anarres because I thought that here I could do the work and publish it. I didn't understand that here an idea is a property of the State. I don't work for a State. I can't take the money and the things they give me. I want to get out. But I can't go home. So I came here. You don't want my science, and maybe you don't like your government either."

Maedda smiled. "No. I don't. But our government don't like me any better. You didn't pick the safest place to come, either for you or for us. . . . Don't worry. Tonight's tonight; we'll decide what to do."

Shevek took out the note he had found in his coat

236

pocket and handed it to Maedda. "This is what brought me. Is it from people you know?"

" 'Join with us your brothers. . . .' I don't know. Could be."

"Are you Odonians?"

"Partly. Syndicalists, libertarians. We work with the Thuvianists, the Socialist Workers Union, but we're anti-centralist. You arrived at a pretty hot moment, you know."

"The war?"

Maedda nodded. "A demonstration's been announced for three days from now. Against the draft, war taxes, the rise in food prices. There's four hundred thousand unemployed in Nio Esseia, and they jack up taxes and prices." He had been watching Shevek steadily all the time they talked; now, as if the examination was done, he looked away, leaning back in his chair. "This city's about ready for anything. A strike is what we need, a general strike, and massive demonstrations. Like the Ninth Month Strike that Odo led," he added with a dry, strained smile. "We could use an Odo now. But they've got no Moon to buy us off with this time. We make justice here, or nowhere." He looked back at Shevek, and presently said in a softer voice, "Do you know what your society has meant, here, to us, these last hundred and fifty years? Do you know that when people here want to wish each other luck they say, 'May you get reborn on Anarres!' To know that it exists, to know that there is a society without government, without police, without economic exploitation, that they can never say again that it's just a mirage, an idealist's dream! I wonder if you fully understand why they've kept you so well hidden out there at Ieu Eun, Dr. Shevek. Why you never were allowed to appear at any meeting open to the public. Why they'll be after you like dogs after a rabbit the moment they find you're gone. It's not just because they want this idea of yours. But because you are an idea. A dangerous one. The idea of anarchism, made flesh. Walking amongst us."

"Then you've got your Odo," the girl said in her quiet, urgent voice. She had re-entered as Maedda was speaking. "After all, Odo was only an idea. Dr. Shevek is the proof."

Maedda was silent for a minute. "An undemonstrable proof," he said.

"Why?"

"If people know he's here, the police will know it too."

"Let them come and try to take him," the girl said, and smiled.

"The demonstration is going to be absolutely nonviolent," Maedda said with sudden violence. "Even the SWU have accepted that!"

"I haven't accepted it, Tuio. I'm not going to let my face get knocked in or my brains blown out by the blackcoats. If they hurt me, I'll hurt back."

"Join them, if you like their methods. Justice is not achieved by force!"

"And power isn't achieved by passivity."

"We are not seeking power. We are seeking the end of power! What do you say?" Maedda appealed to Shevek. "The means are the end. Odo said it all her life. Only peace brings peace, only just acts bring justice! We cannot be divided on that on the eve of action!"

Shevek looked at him, at the girl, and at the pawnbroker who stood listening tensely near the door. He said in a tired, quiet voice, "If I would be of use, use me. Maybe I could publish a statement on this in one of your papers. I did not come to Urras to hide. If all the people know I am here, maybe the government would be afraid to arrest me in public? I don't know."

"That's it," Maedda said. "Of course." His dark eyes blazed with excitement. "Where the devil is Remeivi? Go call his sister, Siro, tell her to hunt him out and get him over here.—Write why you came here, write about Anarres, write why you won't sell yourself to the government, write what you like—we'll get it printed. Siro! Call Meisthe too.—We'll hide you, but by God we'll let ever man in A-Io know you're here, you're with us!" The words poured out of him, his hands jerked as he spoke, and he walked quickly back and forth across the room. "And then, after the demonstration, after the strike, we'll see. Maybe things will be different then! Maybe you won't have to hide!"

"Maybe all the prison doors will fly open," Shevek said. "Well, give me some paper, I'll write."

The girl Siro came up to him. Smiling, she stooped as if bowing to him, a little timorously, with decorum, and kissed him on the cheek; then she went out. The touch of her lips was cool, and he felt it on his cheek for a long time.

He spent one day in the attic of a tenement in Joking Lane, and two nights and a day in a basement under a used-furniture store, a strange dim place full of empty mirror frames and broken bedsteads. He wrote. They brought him what he had written, printed, within a few hours: at first in the newspaper *Modern Age,* and later, after the *Modern Age* presses had been closed down and the editors arrested, as handbills run on a clandestine press, along with plans and incitations for the demonstration and general strike. He did not read over what he had written. He did not listen closely to Maedda and the others, who described the enthusiasm with which the papers were read, the spreading acceptance of the plan for the strike, the effect his presence at the demonstration would make in the eyes of the world. When they left him alone, sometimes he took a small notebook from his shirt pocket and looked at the coded notes and equations of the General Temporal Theory. He looked at them and could not read them. He did not understand them. He put the notebook away again and sat with his head between his hands.

Anarres had no flag to wave, but among the placards proclaiming the general strike, and the blue and white banners of the Syndicalists and the Socialist Workers, there were many homemade signs showing the green Circle of Life, the old symbol of the Odonian Movement of two hundred years before. All the flags and signs shone bravely in the sunlight.

It was good to be outside, after the rooms with locked doors, the hiding places. It was good to be walking, swinging his arms, breathing the clear air of a spring morning. To be among so many people, so immense a crowd, thousands marching together, filling all the side streets as well as the broad thoroughfare down which they marched, was frightening, but it was exhilarating too. When they sang, both the exhilaration and the fear became a blind exaltation; he eyes filled with tears. It was deep, in the deep streets, softened by open air and by distances, indistinct, overwhelming, that lifting up of thousands of voices in one song. The singing of the front of the march, far away up the street, and of the endless crowds coming on behind, was put out of phase by the distance the sound must travel, so that the melody seemed always to be lagging and catching up with itself, like a canon, and all the parts of the song were being sung at one time, in the same moment, though each singer sang the tune as a line from beginning to end.

He did not know their songs, and only listened and was borne along on the music, until from up front there came sweeping back wave by wave down the great slow-moving river of people a tune he knew. He lifted his head and sang it with them, in his own language as he had learned it: the Hymn of the Insurrection. It had been sung in these streets, in this same street, two hundred years ago, by these people, his people.

> O eastern light, awaken
> Those who have slept!
> The darkness will be broken,
> The promise kept.

They fell silent in the ranks around Shevek to hear him, and he sang aloud, smiling, walking forward with them.

There might have been a hundred thousand human beings in Capitol Square, or twice that many. The individuals, like the particles of atomic physics, could not be counted, nor their positions ascertained, nor their behavior predicted. And yet, as a mass, that enormous mass did what it had been expected to do by the organizers of the strike: it gathered, marched in order, sang, filled Capitol Square and all the streets around, stood in its numberlessness restless yet patient in the bright noon listening to the speakers, whose single voices, erratically amplified, clapped and echoed off the sunlit façades of the Senate and the Directorate, rattled and hissed over the continuous, soft, vast murmur of the crowd itself.

There were more people standing here in the Square than lived in all Abbenay, Shevek thought, but the thought was meaningless, an attempt to quantify direct experience. He stood with Maedda and the others on the steps of the Directorate, in front of the columns and the tall bronze doors, and looked out over the tremulous, somber field of faces, and listened as they listened to the speakers: not hearing and understanding in the sense in which the individual rational mind perceives and understands, but rather as one looks at, listens to one's own thoughts, or as a thought perceives and understands the self. When he spoke, speaking was little different from listening. No conscious will of his own moved him, no self-consciousness was in him. The multiple echoes of his voice from distant loud-speakers and the stone fronts of the massive buildings, however, distracted him a little, making him hesitate at times and speak very slowly. But he never hesitated for words. He spoke their mind, their being, in their language, though he said no more than he had said out of his own isolation, out of the center of his own being, a long time ago.

"It is our suffering that brings us together. It is not love. Love does not obey the mind, and turns to hate when forced. The bond that binds us is beyond choice. We are brothers. We are brothers in what we share. In pain, which each of us must suffer alone, in hunger, in poverty, in hope, we know our brotherhood. We know it, because we have had to learn it. We know that there is no help for us but from one another, that no hand will save us if we do not reach out our hand. And the hand that you reach out is empty, as mine is. You have nothing. You possess nothing. You own nothing. You are free. All you have is what you are, and what you give.

"I am here because you see in me the promise, the promise that we made two hundred years ago in this city —the promise kept. We have kept it, on Anarres. We have nothing but our freedom. We have nothing to give you but your own freedom. We have no law but the single principle of mutual aid between individuals. We have no government but the single principle of free association. We have no states, no nations, no presidents, no premiers, no chiefs, no generals, no bosses, no bankers, no landlords, no wages, no charity, no police, no soldiers, no wars. Nor do we have much else. We are sharers, not owners. We are not prosperous. None of us is rich. None of us is powerful. If it is Anarres you want, if it is the future you seek, then I tell you that you must come to it with empty hands. You must come to it alone, and naked, as the child comes into the world, into his future, without any past, without any prop-

241

erty, wholly dependent on other people for his life. You cannot take what you have not given, and you must give yourself. You cannot buy the Revolution. You cannot make the Revolution. You can only be the Revolution. It is in your spirit, or it is nowhere."

As he finished speaking the clattering racket of police helicopters drawing near began to drown out his voice.

He stood back from the microphones and looked upward, squinting into the sun. As many of the crowd did so the movement of their heads and hands was like the passage of wind over a sunlit field of grain.

The noise of the rotating vanes of the machines in the huge stone box of Capitol Square was intolerable, a clacking and yapping like the voice of a monstrous robot. It drowned out the chatter of the machine guns fired from the helicopters. Even as the crowd noise rose up in tumult the clack of the helicopters was still audible through it, the mindless yell of weaponry, the meaningless word.

The helicopter fire centered on the people who stood on or nearest the steps of the Directorate. The columned portico of the building offered immediate refuge to those on the steps, and within moments it was jammed solid. The noise of the crowd, as people pressed in panic toward the eight streets that led out of Capitol Square, rose up into a wailing like a great wind. The helicopters were close overhead, but there was no telling whether they had ceased firing or were still firing; the dead and wounded in the crowd were too close pressed to fall.

The bronze-sheathed doors of the Directorate gave with a crash that no one heard. People pressed and trampled toward them to get to shelter, out from under the metal rain. They pushed by hundreds into the high halls of marble, some cowering down to hide in the first refuge they saw, others pushing on to find a way through the building and out the back, others staying to wreck what they could until the soldiers came. When they came, marching in their neat black coats up the steps among dead and dying men and women, they found on the high, grey, polished wall of the great foyer a word written at the height of a man's eyes, in broad smears of blood: DOWN

They shot the dead man who lay nearest the word, and later on when the Directorate was restored to order the

242

word was washed off the wall with water, soap, and rags, but it remained; it had been spoken; it had meaning.

He realized it was impossible to go any farther with his companion, who was getting weak, beginning to stumble. There was nowhere to go, except away from Capitol Square. There was nowhere to stop, either. The crowd had twice rallied in Mesee Boulevard, trying to present a front to the police, but the army's armored cars came behind the police and drove the people forward, towards Old Town. The blackcoats had not fired either time, though the noise of guns could be heard on other streets. The clacking helicopters cruised up and down above the streets; one could not get out from under them.

His companion was breathing in sobs, gulping for air as he struggled along. Shevek had been half-carrying him for several blocks, and they were now far behind the main mass of the crowd. There was no use trying to catch up. "Here, sit down here," he told the man, and helped him to sit down on the top step of a basement entry to some kind of warehouse, across the shuttered windows of which the word STRIKE was chalked in huge letters. He went down to the basement door and tried it; it was locked. All doors were locked. Property was private. He took a piece of paving stone that had come loose from a corner of the steps and smashed the hasp and padlock off the door, working neither furtively nor vindictively, but with the assurance of one unlocking his own front door. He looked in. The basement was full of crates and empty of people. He helped his companion down the steps, shut the door behind them, and said, "Sit here, lie down if you want. I'll see if there's water."

The place, evidently a chemical warehouse, had a row of washtubs as well as a hose system for fires. Shevek's companion had fainted by the time he got back to him. He took the opportunity to wash the man's hand with a trickle from the hose and to get a look at his wound. It was worse than he had thought. More then one bullet must have struck it, tearing two fingers off and mangling the palm and wrist. Shards of splintered bone stuck out like toothpicks. The man had been standing near Shevek and Maedda when the helicopters began firing and, hit, had lurched against Shevek, grabbing at him for support.

Shevek had kept an arm around him all through the escape through the Directorate; two could keep afoot better than one in the first wild press.

He did what he could to stop the bleeding with a tourniquet and to bandage, or at least cover, the destroyed hand, and he got the man to drink some water. He did not know his name; by his white armband he was a Socialist Worker; he looked to be about Shevek's age, forty, or a little older.

At the mills in Southwest Shevek had seen men hurt much worse than this in accidents and had learned that people may endure and survive incredibly much in the way of gross injury and pain. But there they had been looked after. There had been a surgeon to amputate, plasma to compensate blood loss, a bed to lie down in.

He sat down on the floor beside the man, who now lay semiconscious in shock, and looked around at the stacks of crates, the long dark alleys between them, the whitish gleam of daylight from the barred window slits along the front wall, the white streaks of saltpeter on the ceiling, the tracks of workmen's boots and dolly wheels on the dusty cement floor. One hour hundreds of thousands of people singing under the open sky; the next hour two men hiding in a basement.

"You are contemptible," Shevek said in Pravic to his companion. "You cannot keep doors open. You will never be free." He felt the man's forehead gently; it was cold and sweaty. He loosened the tourniquet for a while, then got up, crossed the murky basement to the door, and went up onto the street. The fleet of armored cars had passed. A very few stragglers of the demonstration went by, hurrying, their heads down, in enemy territory. Shevek tried to stop two; a third finally halted for him. "I need a doctor, there is a man hurt. Can you send a doctor back here?"

"Better get him out."

"Help me carry him."

The man hurried on. "They coming through here," he called back over his shoulder. "You better get out."

No one else came by, and presently Shevek saw a line of blackcoats far down the street. He went back down into the basement, shut the door, returned to the wounded man's side, sat down on the dusty floor. "Hell," he said.

After a while he took the little notebook out of his shirt pocket and began to study it.

In the afternoon, when he cautiously looked outside, he saw an armored car stationed across the street and two others slewed across the street at the crossing. That explained the shouts he had been hearing: it would be soldiers giving orders to each other.

Atro had once explained to him how this was managed, how the sergeants could give the privates orders, how the lieutenants could give the privates and the sergeants orders, how the captains . . . and so on and so on up to the generals, who could give everyone else orders and need take them from none, except the commander in chief. Shevek had listened with incredulous disgust. "You call that organization?" he had inquired. "You even call it discipline? But it is neither. It is a coercive mechanism of extraordinary inefficiency—a kind of seventh-millennium steam engine! With such a rigid and fragile structure what could be done that was worth doing?" This had given Atro a chance to argue the worth of warfare as the breeder of courage and manliness and the weeder-out of the unfit, but the very line of his argument had forced him to concede the effectiveness of guerillas, organized from below, self-disciplined. "But that only works when the people think they're fighting for something of their own—you know, their homes, or some notion or other," the old man had said. Shevek had dropped the argument. He now continued it, in the darkening basement among the stacked crates of unlabeled chemicals. He explained to Atro that he now understood why the army was organized as it was. It was indeed quite necessary. No rational form of organization would serve the purpose. He simply had not understood that the purpose was to enable men with machine guns to kill unarmed men and women easily and in great quantities when told to do so. Only he still could not see where courage, or manliness, or fitness entered in.

He occasionally spoke to his companion, too, as it got darker. The man was lying now with his eyes open, and he moaned a couple of times in a way that touched Shevek, a childish, patient sort of moan. He had made a gallant effort to keep up and keep going, all the time they were in the first panic of the crowd forcing into and through the Directorate, and running, and then walking towards Old Town; he had held the hurt hand under his coat, pressed against his side, and had done his best to keep going and not to hold Shevek back. The second time he moaned, Shevek took his good hand and whispered, "Don't, don't. Be quiet, brother," only because he could not bear to hear the man's pain and not be able to do anything for him. The man probably thought he meant he should be quiet lest he give them away to the police, for he nodded weakly and shut his lips together.

The two of them endured there three nights. During all that time there was sporadic fighting in the warehouse district, and the army blockade remained across that block of Mesee Boulevard. The fighting never came very close to it, and it was strongly manned, so the men in hiding had no chance to get out without surrendering themselves. Once when his companion was awake Shevek asked him, "If we went out to the police what would they do with us?"

The man smiled and whispered, "Shoot us."

As there had been scattered gunfire around, near and far, for hours, and an occasional solid explosion, and the clacking of the helicopters, his opinion seemed well founded. The reason for his smile was less clear.

He died of loss of blood that night, while they lay side by side for warmth on the mattress Shevek had made from packing-crate straw. He was already stiff when Shevek woke, and sat up, and listened to the silence in the great dark basement and outside on the street and in all the city, a silence of death.

Chapter 10

Rail lines in Southwest ran for the most part on embankments a meter or more above the plain. There was less dust drift on an elevated roadbed, and it gave travelers a good view of desolation.

Southwest was the only one of the eight Divisions of Anarres that lacked any major body of water. Marshes were formed by polar melt in summer in the far south; towards the equator there were only shallow alkaline lakes in vast salt pans. There were no mountains; every hundred kilometers or so a chain of hills ran north-south, barren, cracked, weathered into cliffs and pinnacles, They were streaked with violet and red, and on cliff faces the rockmoss, a plant that lived in any extreme of heat, cold, aridity, and wind, grew in bold verticals of grey-green, making a plaid with the striations of the sandstone. There was no other color in the landscape but dun, fading to whitish where salt pans lay half covered with sand. Rare thunderclouds moved over the plains, vivid white in the purplish sky. They cast no rain, only shadows. The embankment and the glittering rails ran straight behind the truck train to the end of sight and straight before it to the end of sight.

"Nothing you can do with Southwest," said the driver, "but get across it."

His companion did not answer, having fallen asleep. His head jiggled to the vibration of the engine. His hands, work-hard and blackened by frostbite, lay loose on his thighs; his face in relaxation was lined and sad. He had hitched the ride in Copper Mountain, and since there were no other passengers the driver had asked him to ride in the cab for company. He had gone to sleep at once. The driver glanced at him from time to time with disappointment but sympathy. He had seen so many worn-out people in the last years that it seemed the normal condition to him.

Late in the long afternoon the man woke up, and after staring out at the desert a while he asked, "You always do this run alone?"

"Last three, four years."

"Ever break down out here?"

"Couple of times. Plenty of rations and water in the locker. You hungry, by the way?"

"Not yet."

"They send down the breakdown rig from Lonesome within a day or so."

"That's the next settlement?"

"Right. Seventeen hundred kilometers from Sedep Mines to Lonesome. Longest run between towns on Anarres. I've been doing it for eleven years."

"Not tired of it?"

"No. Like to run a job by myself."

The passenger nodded agreement.

"And it's steady. I like routine; you can think. Fifteen days on the run, fifteen off with the partner in New Hope. Year in, year out; drought, famine, whatever. Nothing changes, it's always drought down here. I like the run. Get the water out, will you? Cooler's back underneath the locker."

They each had a long swig from the bottle. The water had a flat, alkaline taste, but was cool. "Ah, that's good!" the passenger said gratefully. He put the bottle away and, returning to his seat in the front of the cab, stretched, bracing his hands against the roof. "You're a partnered man, then," he said. There was a simplicity in the way

248

he said it that the driver liked, and he answered, "Eighteen years."

"Just starting."

"By damn, I agree with that! Now that's what some don't see. But the way I see it, if you copulate around enough in your teens, that's when you get the most out of it, and also you find out that it's all pretty much the same damn thing. And a good thing, too! But still, what's different isn't the copulating; it's the other person. And eighteen years is just a start, all right, when it comes to figuring out *that* difference. At least, if it's a woman you're trying to figure out. A woman won't let on to being so puzzled by a man, but maybe they bluff. . . . Anyhow, that's the pleasure of it. The puzzles and the bluffs and the rest of it. The variety. Variety doesn't come with just moving around. I was all over Anarres, young. Drove and loaded in every Division. Must have known a hundred girls in different towns. It got boring. I came back here, and I do this run every three decads year in year out through this same desert where you can't tell one sandhill from the next and it's all the same for three thousand kilos whichever way you look, and go home to the same partner—and I never been bored once. It isn't changing around from place to place that keeps you lively. It's getting time on your side. Working with it, not against it."

"That's it," said the passenger.

"Where's the partner?"

"In Northeast. Four years now."

"That's too long," the driver said. "You should have been posted together."

"Not where I was."

"Where's that?"

"Elbow, and then Grand Valley."

"I heard about Grand Valley." He now looked at the passenger with the respect due a survivor. He saw the dry look of the man's tanned skin, a kind of weathering to the bone, which he had seen in others who had come through the famine years in the Dust. "We shouldn't have tried to keep those mills running."

"Needed the phosphates."

"But they say, when the provisions train was stopped in Portal, they kept the mills going, and people died of

249

hunger on the job. Just went a little out of the way and lay down and died. Was it like that?"

The man nodded. He said nothing. The driver pressed no further, but said after a while, "I wondered what I'd do if my train ever got mobbed."

"It never did?"

"No. See, I don't carry foodstuffs; one truckload, at most, for Upper Sedep. This is an ores run. But if I got on a provisions run, and they stopped me, what would I do? Run 'em down and get the food to where it ought to go? But hell, you going to run down kids, old men? They're doing wrong but you going to *kill* em for it? I don't know!"

The straight shining rails ran under the wheels. Clouds in the west laid great shivering mirages on the plain, the shadows of dreams of lakes gone dry ten million years ago.

"A syndic, fellow I've known for years, he did just that, north of here, in '66. They tried to take a grain truck off his train. He backed the train, killed a couple of them before they cleared the track, they were like worms in rotten fish, thick, he said. He said, there's eight hundred people waiting for that grain truck, and how many of them might die if they don't get it? More than a couple, a lot more. So it looks like he was right. But by damn! I can't add up figures like that. I don't know if it's right to count people like you count numbers. But then, what do you do? Which ones do you kill?"

"The second year I was in Elbow, I was worklister, the mill syndicate cut rations. People doing six hours in the plant got full rations—just barely enough for that kind of work. People on half time got three-quarter rations. If they were sick or too weak to work, they got half. On half rations you couldn't get well. You couldn't get back to work. You might stay alive. I was supposed to put people on half rations, people that were already sick. I was working full time, eight, ten hours sometimes, desk work, so I got full rations: I earned them, I earned them by making lists of who should starve." The man's light eyes looked ahead into the dry light. "Like you said, I was to count people."

"You quit?"

"Yes, I quit. Went to Grand Valley. But somebody else

took over the lists at the mills in Elbow. There's always somebody willing to make lists."

"Now that's wrong," the driver said, scowling into the glare. He had a bald brown face and scalp, no hair left between cheeks and occiput, though he wasn't past his middle forties. It was a strong, hard, and innocent face. "That's dead wrong. They should have shut the mills down. You can't ask a man to do that. Aren't we Odonians? A man can lose his temper, all right. That's what the people who mobbed trains did. They were hungry, the kids were hungry, been hungry too long, there's food coming through and its not for you, you lose your temper and go for it. Same thing with the friend, those people were taking apart the train he was in charge of, he lost his temper and put it in reverse. He didn't count any noses. Not then! Later, maybe. Because he was sick when he saw what he'd done. But what they had you doing, saying this one lives and that one dies—that's not a job a person has a right to do, or ask anybody else to do."

"It's been a bad time, brother," the passenger said gently, watching the glaring plain where the shadows of water wavered and drifted with the wind.

The old cargo dirigible wallowed over the mountains and moored in at the airport on Kidney Mountain. Three passengers got off there. Just as the last of them touched ground, the ground picked itself up and bucked. "Earthquake," he remarked; he was a local coming home. "Damn, look at that dust! Someday we'll come down here and there won't be any mountain."

Two of the passengers chose to wait till the trucks were loaded and ride with them. Shevek chose to walk, since the local said that Chakar was only about six kilometers down the mountain.

The road went in a series of long curves with a short rise at the end of each. The rising slopes to the left of the road and the falling slopes to the right were thick with scrub holum; lines of tall tree holum, spaced just as if they had been planted, followed veins of ground water along the mountainsides. At the crest of a rise Shevek saw the clear gold of sunset above the dark and many-folded hills. There was no sign of mankind here except the road itself, going down into shadow. As he started down, the air grum-

251

bled a little and he felt a strangeness: no jolt, no tremor, but a displacement, a conviction that things were wrong. He completed the step he had been making, and the ground was there to meet his foot. He went on; the road stayed lying down. He had been in no danger, but he had never in any danger known himself so close to death. Death was in him, under him; the earth itself was uncertain, unreliable. The enduring, the reliable, is a promise made by the human mind. Shevek felt the cold, clean air in his mouth and lungs. He listened. Remote, a mountain torrent thundered somewhere down in the shadows.

He came in the late dusk to Chakar. The sky was dark violet over the black ridges. Street lamps flared bright and lonely. Housefronts looked sketchy in the artificial light, the wilderness dark behind them. There were many empty lots, many single houses: an old town, a frontier town, isolated, scattered. A woman passing directed Shevek to Domicile Eight: "That way, brother, past the hospital, the end of the street." The street ran into the dark under the mountainside and ended at the door of a low building. He entered and found a country-town domicile foyer that took him back to his childhood, to the places in Liberty, Drum Mountain, Wide Plains, where he and his father had lived: the dim light, the patched matting; a leaflet describing a local machinists training group, a notice of syndicate meetings, and a flyer for a performance of a play three decads ago, tacked to the announcement board; a framed amateur painting of Odo in prison over the common-room sofa; a homemade harmonium; a list of residents and a notice of hot-water hours at the town baths posted by the door.

Sherut, Takver, No. 3.

He knocked, watching the reflection of the hall light in the dark surface of the door, which did not hang quite true in its frame. A woman said, "Come in!" He opened the door.

The brighter light in the room was behind her. He could not see well enough for a moment to be sure it was Takver. She stood facing him. She reached out, as if to push him away or to take hold of him, an uncertain, unfinished gesture. He took her hand, and then they held each other, they came together and stood holding each other on the unreliable earth.

252

"Come in," Takver said, "oh come in, come in."

Shevek opened his eyes. Farther into the room, which still seemed very bright, he saw the serious, watchful face of a small child.

"Sadik, this is Shevek."

The child went to Takver, took hold of her leg, and burst into tears.

"But don't cry, why are you crying, little soul?"

"Why are you?" the child whispered.

"Because I'm happy! Only because I'm happy. Sit on my lap. But Shevek, Shevek! The letter from you only came yesterday. I was going to go by the telephone when I took Sadik home to sleep. You said you'd *call* tonight. Not *come* tonight! Oh, don't cry, Sadiki, look, I'm not any more, am I?"

"The man cried too."

"Of course I did."

Sadik looked at him with mistrustful curiosity. She was four years old. She had a round head, a round face, she was round, dark, furry, soft.

There was no furniture in the room but the two bed platforms. Takver had sat down on one with Sadik on her lap, Shevek sat down on the other and stretched out his legs. He wiped his eyes with the backs of his hands, and held the knuckles out to show Sadik. "See," he said, "they're wet. And the nose dribbles. Do you keep a handkerchief?"

"Yes. Don't you?"

"I did, but it got lost in a washhouse."

"You can share the handkerchief I use," Sadik said after a pause.

"He doesn't know where it is," said Takver.

Sadik got off her mother's lap and fetched a handkerchief from a drawer in the closet. She gave it to Takver, who passed it across to Shevek. "It's clean," Takver said, with her large smile. Sadik watched closely while Shevek wiped his nose.

"Was there an earthquake here a little while ago?" he asked.

"It shakes all the time, you really stop noticing," Takver said, but Sadik, delighted to dispense information, said in her high but husky voice, "Yes, there was a big one before dinner. When there's an earthquake the windows go gliggle

253

and the floor waves, and you ought to go into the doorway or outside."

Shevek looked at Takver; she returned the look. She had aged more than four years. She had never had very good teeth, and now had lost two, just back of the upper eye-teeth, so that the gaps showed when she smiled. Her skin no longer had the fine taut surface of youth, and her hair, pulled back neatly, was dull.

Shevek saw clearly that Takver had lost her young grace, and looked a plain, tired woman near the middle of her life. He saw this more clearly than anyone else could have seen it. He saw everything about Takver in a way that no one else could have seen it, from the standpoint of years of intimacy and years of longing. He saw her as she was.

Their eyes met.

"How—how's it been going here?" he asked, reddening all at once and obviously speaking at random. She felt the palpable wave, the outrush of his desire. She also flushed slightly, and smiled. She said in her husky voice, "Oh, same as when we talked on the phone."

"That was six decads ago!"

"Things go along pretty much the same here."

"It's very beautiful here—the hills." He saw in Takver's eyes the darkness of the mountain valleys. The acuteness of his sexual desire grew abruptly, so that he was dizzy for a moment, then he got over the crisis temporarily and tried to command his erection to subside. "Do you think you'll want to stay here?" he said.

"I don't care," she said, in her strange, dark, husky voice.

"Your nose is still dribbling," Sadik remarked, keenly, but without emotional bias.

"Be glad that's all," Shevek said. Takver said, "Hush, Sadik, don't egoize!" Both the adults laughed. Sadik continued to study Shevek.

"I do like the town, Shev. The people are nice—all characters. But the work isn't much. It's just lab work in the hospital. The shortage of technicians is just about over, I could leave soon without leaving them in the lurch. I'd like to go back to Abbenay, if you were thinking of that. Have you got a reposting?"

"Didn't ask for one and haven't checked. I've been on the road for a decad."

"What were you doing on the road?"

"Traveling on it, Sadik."

"He was coming from half across the world, from the south, from the deserts, to come to us," Takver said. The child smiled, settled herself more comfortably on her lap, and yawned.

"Have you eaten, Shev? Are you worn out? I must get this child to bed, we were just thinking of leaving when you knocked."

"She sleeps in the dormitory already?"

"Since the beginning of this quarter."

"I was four already," Sadik stated.

"You say, I am four already," said Takver, dumping her off gently in order to get her coat from the closet. Sadik stood up, in profile to Shevek; she was extremely conscious of him, and directed her remarks towards him. "But I *was* four, now I'm more than four."

"A temporalist, like the father!"

"You can't be four and more than four at the same time, can you?" the child asked, sensing approbation, and now speaking directly to Shevek.

"Oh, yes, easily. And you can be four and nearly five at the same time, too." Sitting on the low platform, he could hold his head on a level with the child's so that she did not have to look up at him. "But I'd forgotten that you were nearly five, you see. When I last saw you you were hardly more than nothing."

"Really?" Her tone was indubitably flirtatious.

"Yes. You were about so long." He held his hands not very far apart.

"Could I talk yet?"

"You said waa, and a few other things."

"Did I wake up everybody in the dom like Cheben's baby?" she inquired, with a broad, gleeful smile.

"Of course."

"When did I learn how to really talk?"

"At about one half year old," said Takver, "and you have never shut up since. Where's the hat. Sadikiki?"

"At school. I hate the hat I wear," she informed Shevek.

They walked the child through the windy streets to the

255

learning-center dormitory and took her into the lobby. It was a little, shabby place too, but brightened by children's paintings, several fine brass model engines, and a litter of toy houses and painted wooden people. Sadik kissed her mother good night, then turned to Shevek and put up her arms; he stooped to her; she kissed him matter-of-factly but firmly, and said, "Good night!" She went off with the night attendant, yawning. They heard her voice, the attendant's mild hushing.

"She's beautiful, Takver. Beautiful, intelligent, sturdy."

"She's spoiled, I'm afraid."

"No, no. You've done well, fantastically well—in such a time—"

"It hasn't been so bad here, not the way it was in the south," she said, looking up into his face as they left the dormitory. "Children were fed, here. Not very well, but enough. A community here can grow food. If nothing else there's the scrub holum. You can gather wild holum seeds and pound them for meal. Nobody starved here. But I did spoil Sadik. I nursed her till she was three, of course, why not when there was nothing good to wean her to! But they disapproved, at the research station at Rolny. They wanted me to put her in the nursery there full time. They said I was being propertarian about the child and not contributing full strength to the social effort in the crisis. They were right, really. But they were so righteous. None of them understood about being lonely. They were all groupers, no characters. It was the women who nagged me about nursing. Real body profiteers. I stuck it out there because the food was good—trying out the algaes to see if they were palatable, sometimes you got quite a lot over standard rations, even if it did taste like glue—until they could replace me with somebody who fitted in better. Then I went to Fresh Start for about ten decads. That was winter, two years ago, that long time the mail didn't get through, when things were so bad where you were. At Fresh Start I saw this posting listed, and came here. Sadik stayed with me in the dom till this autumn. I still miss her. The room's so silent."

"Isn't there a roommate?"

"Sherut, she's very nice, but she works night shift at the hospital. It was time Sadik went, it's good for her living with the other children. She was getting shy. She was very good about going there, very stoical. Little children are stoical. They cry over bumps, but they take the big things as they come, they don't whine like so many adults."

They walked along side by side. The autumn stars had come out, incredible in number and brilliance, twinkling and almost blinking because of the dust stirred up by the earthquake and the wind, so that the whole sky seemed to tremble, a shaking of diamond chips, a scintillation of sunlight on a black sea. Under that uneasy splendor the hills were dark and solid, the roofs hard-edged, the light of the street lamps mild.

"Four years ago," Shevek said. "It was four years ago that I came back to Abbenay, from that place in South-rising—what was it called?—Red Springs. It was a night like this, windy, the stars. I ran, I ran all the way from Plains Street to the domicile. And you weren't there, you'd gone. Four years!"

"The moment I left Abbenay I knew I'd been a fool to go. Famine or no famine. I should have refused the posting."

"It wouldn't have made much difference. Sabul was waiting to tell me I was through at the Institute."

"If I'd been there, you wouldn't have gone down to the Dust."

"Maybe not, but we mightn't have kept postings together. For a while it seemed as if nothing could hold together, didn't it? The towns in Southwest—there weren't any children left in them. There still aren't. They sent them north, into regions where there was local food, or a chance of it. And they stayed to keep the mines and mills going. It's a wonder we pulled through, all of us, isn't it? . . . But by damn, I will do my own work for a while now!"

She took his arm. He stopped short, as if her touch had electrocuted him on the spot. She shook him, smiling. "You didn't eat, did you?"

"No. Oh Takver, I have been sick for you, sick for you!"

They came together, holding on to each other fiercely, in the dark street between the lamps, under the stars. They broke apart as suddenly, and Shevek backed up against the nearest wall. "I'd better eat something," he said, and Takver said, "Yes, or you'll fall flat on your face! Come on." They went a block to the commons, the largest

257

building in Chakar. Regular dinner was over, but the cooks were eating, and provided the traveler a bowl of stew and all the bread he wanted. They all sat at the table nearest the kitchen. The other tables had already been cleaned and set for next morning. The big room was cavernous, the ceiling rising into shadow, the far end obscure except where a bowl or cup winked on a dark table, catching the light. The cooks and servers were a quiet crew, tired after the day's work; they ate fast, not talking much, not paying much attention to Takver and the stranger. One after another they finished and got up to take their dishes to the washers in the kitchen. One old woman said as she got up, "Don't hurry, ammari, they've got an hour's washing yet to do." She had a grim face and looked dour, not maternal, not benevolent; but she spoke with compassion, with the charity of equals. She could do nothing for them but say, "Don't hurry," and look at them for a moment with the look of brotherly love.

They could do no more for her, and little more for each other.

They went back to Domicile Eight, Room 3, and there their long desire was fulfilled. They did not even light the lamp; they both liked making love in darkness. The first time they both came as Shevek came into her, the second time they struggled and cried out in a rage of joy, prolonging their climax as if delaying the moment of death, the third time they were both half asleep, and circled about the center of infinite pleasure, about each other's being, like planets circling blindly, quietly, in the flood of sunlight, about the common center of gravity, swinging, circling endlessly.

Takver woke at dawn. She leaned on her elbow and looked across Shevek at the grey square of the window, and then at him. He lay on his back, breathing so quietly that his chest scarcely moved, his face thrown back a little, remote and stern in the thin light. We came, Takver thought, from a great distance to each other. We have always done so. Over great distances, over years, over abysses of chance. It is because he comes from so far away that nothing can separate us. Nothing, no distances, no years, can be greater than the distance that's already between us, the distance of our sex, the difference of our being, our minds; that gap, that abyss which we bridge

258

with a look, with a touch, with a word, the easiest thing in the world. Look how far away he is, asleep. Look how far away he is, he always is. But he comes back, he comes back, he comes back. . . .

Takver put in notice of departure at the hospital in Chakar, but stayed till they could replace her in the laboratory. She worked her eight-hour shift—in the third quarter of the year 168 many people were still on the long work shifts of emergency postings, for though the drought had broken in the winter of 167, the economy had by no means returned to normal yet. "Long post and short commons" was still the rule for people in skilled work, but the food was now adequate to the day's work, which had not been true a year ago and two years ago.

Shevek did not do much of anything for a while. He did not consider himself ill; after the four years of famine everyone was so used to the effects of hardship and malnutrition that they took them as the norm. He had the dust cough that was endemic in southern desert communities, a chronic irritation of the bronchia similar to silicosis and other miners' diseases, but this was also something one took for granted where he had been living. He simply enjoyed the fact that if he felt like doing nothing, there was nothing he had to do.

For a few days he and Sherut shared the room daytimes, both of them sleeping till late afternoon; then Sherut, a placid woman of forty, moved in with another woman who worked night shift, and Shevek and Takver had the room to themselves for the four decads they stayed on in Chakar. While Takver was at work he slept, or walked out in the fields or on the dry, bare hills above the town. He went by the learning center late in the afternoon and watched Sadik and the other children on the playgrounds, or got involved, as adults often did, in one of the children's projects—a group of mad seven-year-old carpenters, or a pair of sober twelve-year-old surveyors having trouble with triangulation. Then he walked with Sadik to the room; they met Takver as she got off work and went to the baths together and to commons. An hour or two after dinner he and Takver took the child back to her dormitory and returned to the room. The days were utterly peaceful, in the autumn sunlight, in the silence of the hills. It was to Shevek a time outside time, beside the flow, unreal, enduring, enchanted. He and Takver sometimes talked very late; other nights they went to bed not long after dark and slept nine hours, ten hours, in the profound, crystalline silence of the mountain night.

He had come with luggage: a tattered little fiberboard case, his name printed large on it in black ink; all Anarresti carried papers, keepsakes, the spare pair of boots, in the same kind of case when they traveled, orange fiberboard, well scratched and dented. His contained a new shirt he had picked up as he came through Abbenay, a couple of books and some papers, and a curious object, which as it lay in the case appeared to consist of a series of flat loops of wire and a few glass beads. He revealed this, with some mystery, to Sadik, his second evening there.

"It's a necklace," the child said with awe. People in the small towns wore a good deal of jewelry. In sophisticated Abbenay there was more sense of the tension between the principle of nonownership and the impulse to self-adornment, and there a ring or pin was the limit of good taste. But elsewhere the deep connection between the aesthetic and the acquisitive was simply not worried about; people bedecked themselves unabashedly. Most districts had a professional jeweler who did his work for love and fame, as well as the craft shops, where you could make to suit your own taste with the modest materials offered—copper, silver, beads, spinels, and the garnets and yellow diamonds of Southrising. Sadik had not seen many bright, delicate things, but she knew necklaces, and so identified it.

"No: look," her father said, and with solemnity and deftness raised the object by the thread that connected its several loops. Hanging from his hand it came alive, the loops turning freely, describing airy spheres one within the other, the glass beads catching the lamplight.

"Oh, beauty!" the child said. "What is it?"

"It hangs from the ceiling; is there a nail? The coat hook will do, till I can get a nail from Supplies. Do you know who made it, Sadik?"

"No— You did."

"She did. The mother. She did." He turned to Takver. "It's my favorite, the one that was over the desk. I gave the others to Bedap. I wasn't going to leave them there for old what's-her-name, Mother Envy down the corridor."

"Oh—Bunub! I hadn't thought of her in years!" Takver laughed shakily. She looked at the mobile as if she was afraid of it.

Sadik stood watching it as it turned silently seeking its balance. "I wish," she said at last, carefully, "that I could share it one night over the bed I sleep in in the dormitory."

"I'll make one for you, dear soul. For every night."

"Can you really make them, Takver?"

"Well, I used to. I think I could make you one." The tears were now plain in Takver's eyes. Shevek put his arms around her. They were both still on edge, overstrained. Sadik looked at them holding each other for a moment with a calm, observing eye, then returned to watching the Occupation of Uninhabited Space.

When they were alone, evenings, Sadik was often the subject of their talk. Takver was somewhat overabsorbed in the child, for want of other intimacies, and her strong common sense was obscured by maternal ambitions and anxieties. This was not natural to her; neither competitiveness nor protectiveness was a strong motive in Anarresti life. She was glad to talk her worries out and get rid of them, which Shevek's presence enabled her to do. The first nights, she did most of the talking, and he listened as he might have listened to music or to running water, without trying to reply. He had not talked very much, for four years now; he was out of the habit of conversation. She released him from that silence, as she had always done. Later, it was he who talked the most, though always dependent on her response.

"Do you remember Tirin?" he asked one night. It was cold; winter had arrived, and the room, the farthest from the domicile furnace, never got very warm, even with the register wide open. They had taken the bedding from both platforms and were well cocooned together on the platform nearer the register. Shevek was wearing a very old, much-washed shirt to keep his chest warm, as he liked to sit up in bed. Takver, wearing nothing, was under the blankets from the ears down. "What became of the orange blanket?" she said.

"What a propertarian! I left it."

"To Mother Envy? How sad. I'm not a propertarian. I'm just sentimental. It was the first blanket we slept under."

261

"No, it wasn't. We must have used a blanket up in the Ne Theras."

"If we did, I don't remember it." Takver laughed. "Who did you ask about?"

"Tirin."

"Don't remember."

"At Northsetting Regional. Dark boy, snub nose—"

"Oh, Tirin! Of course. I was thinking of Abbenay."

"I saw him, in Southwest."

"You saw Tirin? How was he?"

Shevek said nothing for a while, tracing out the weave of the blanket with one finger. "Remember what Bedap told us about him?"

"That he kept getting kleggich postings, and moving around, and finally went to Segvina Island, didn't he? And then Dap lost track of him."

"Did you see the play he put on, the one that made trouble for him?"

"At the Summer Festival, after you left? Oh yes. I don't remember it, that's so long ago now. It was silly. Witty—Tirin was witty. But silly. It was about an Urrasti, that's right. This Urrasti hides himself in a hydroponics tank on the Moon freighter, and breathes through a straw, and eats the plant roots. I told you it was silly! And so he gets himself smuggled onto Anarres. And then he runs around trying to buy things at depots, and trying to sell things to people, and saving gold nuggets till he's holding so many he can't move. So he has to sit where he is, and he builds a palace, and calls himself the Owner of Anarres. And there was an awfully funny scene where he and this woman want to copulate, and she's just wide open and ready, but he can't do it until he's given her his gold nuggets first, to pay her. And she didn't want them. That was funny, with her flopping down and waving her legs, and him launching himself onto her, and then he'd leap up like he'd been bitten, saying, 'I must not! It is not *moral!* It is not good *business!*' Poor Tirin! He was so funny, and so alive."

"He played the Urrasti?"

"Yes. He was marvelous."

"He showed me the play. Several times."

"Where did you meet him? In Grand Valley?"

"No, before, in Elbow. He was janitor for the mill."

262

"Had he chosen that?"

"I don't think Tir was able to choose at all, by then. . . . Bedap always thought that he was forced to go to Segvina, that he was bullied into asking for therapy. I don't know. When I saw him, several years after therapy, he was a destroyed person."

"You think they did something at Segvina—?"

"I don't know; I think the Asylum does try to offer shelter, a refuge. To judge from their syndical publications, they're at least altruistic. I doubt that they drove Tir over the edge."

"But what did break him, then? Just not finding a posting he wanted?"

"The play broke him."

"The play? The fuss those old turds made about it? Oh, but listen, to be driven crazy by that kind of moralistic scolding you'd have to be crazy already. All he had to do was ignore it!"

"Tir was crazy already. By our society's standards."

"What do you mean?"

"Well, I think Tir's a born artist. Not a craftsman—a creator. An inventor-destroyer, the kind who's got to turn everything upside down and inside out. A satirist, a man who praises through rage."

"Was the play that good?" Takver asked naïvely, coming out an inch or two from the blankets and studying Shevek's profile.

"No, I don't think so. It must have been funny on stage. He was only twenty when he wrote it, after all. He keeps writing it over. He's never written anything else."

"He keeps writing the same play?"

"He keeps writing the same play."

"Ugh," Takver said with pity and disgust.

"Every couple of decads he'd come and show it to me. And I'd read it or make a show of reading it and try to talk with him about it. He wanted desperately to talk about it, but he couldn't. He was too frightened."

"Of what? I don't understand."

"Of me. Of everybody. Of the social organism, the human race, the brotherhood that rejected him. When a man feels himself alone against all the rest, he might well be frightened."

"You mean, just because some people called his play immoral and said he shouldn't get a teaching posting, he decided everybody was against him? That's a bit silly!"

"But who was for him?"

"Dap was—all his friends."

"But he lost them. He got posted away."

"Why didn't he refuse the posting, then?"

"Listen, Takver. I thought the same thing, exactly. We always say that. You said it—you should have refused to go to Rolny. I said it as soon as I got to Elbow: I'm a free man, I didn't have to come here! . . . We always think it, and say it, but we don't do it. We keep our initiative tucked away safe in our mind, like a room where we can come and say, 'I don't have to do anything, I make my own choices, I'm free.' And then we leave the little room in our mind, and go where PDC posts us, and stay till we're reposted."

"Oh, Shev, that's not true. Only since the drought. Before that there wasn't half so much posting. People just worked up jobs where they wanted them, and joined a syndicate or formed one, and then registered with Divlab. Divlab mostly posted people who preferred to be in General Labor Pool. It's going to go back to that again, now."

"I don't know. It ought to, of course. But even before the famine it wasn't going in that direction, but away from it. Bedap was right: every emergency, every labor draft even, tends to leave behind it an increment of bureaucratic machinery within PDC, and a kind of rigidity: this is the way it was done, this is the way it is done, this is the way it *has* to be done. . . . There was a lot of that, before the drought. Five years of stringent control may have fixed the pattern permanently. Don't look so skeptical! Listen, you tell me, how many people do you know who refused to accept a posting—even before the famine?"

Takver considered the question. "Leaving out nuchnibi?"

"No, no. Nuchnibi are important."

"Well, several of Dap's friends—that nice composer, Salas, and some of the scruffy ones too. And real nuchnibi used to come through Round Valley when I was a kid. Only they cheated, I always thought. They told such lovely lies and stories, and told fortunes, everybody was glad to see them and keep them and feed them as long as they'd stay. But they never would stay long. But then people would just pick up and leave town, kids usually, some of them just hated farm work, and they'd just quit their posting and leave. People do that everywhere, all the time. They move on, looking for something better. You just don't *call* it refusing posting!"

"Why not?"

"What are you getting at?" Takver grumbled, retiring further under the blanket.

"Well, this. That we're ashamed to say we've refused a posting. That the social conscience completely dominates the individual conscience, instead of striking a balance with it. We don't cooperate—we *obey*. We fear being outcast, being called lazy, dysfunctional, egoizing. We fear our neighbor's opinion more than we respect our own freedom of choice. You don't believe me, Tak, but try, just try stepping over the line, just in imagination, and see how you feel. You realize then what Tirin is, and why he's a wreck, a lost soul. He is a criminal! We have created crime, just as the propertarians did. We force a man outside the sphere of our approval, and then condemn him for it. We've made laws, laws of conventional behavior, built walls all around ourselves, and we can't see them, because they're part of our thinking. Tir never did that. I knew him since we were ten years old. He never did it, he never could build walls. He was a natural rebel. He was a natural Odonian—a real one! He was a free man, and the rest of us, his brothers, drove him insane in punishment for his first free act."

"I don't think," Takver said, muffled in the bed, and defensively, "that Tir was a very strong person."

"No, he was extremely vulnerable."

There was a long silence.

"No wonder he haunts you," she said. "His play. Your book."

"But I'm luckier. A scientist can pretend that his work isn't himself, it's merely the impersonal truth. An artist can't hide behind the truth. He can't hide anywhere."

Takver watched him from the corner of her eye for some time, then turned over and sat up, pulling the blanket up around her shoulders. "Brr! It's cold. . . . I was wrong, wasn't I, about the book. About letting Sabul cut it up and put his name on it. It seemed right. It seemed like setting the work before the workman, pride before vanity, community before ego, all that. But it wasn't really that at all, was it? It was a capitulation. A surrender to Sabul's authoritarianism."

"I don't know. It did get the thing printed."

"The right end, but the wrong means! I thought about it for a long time, at Rolny, Shev. I'll tell you what was wrong. I was pregnant. Pregnant women have no ethics. Only the most primitive kind of sacrifice impulse. To hell with the book, and the partnership, and the truth, if they threaten the precious fetus! It's a racial preservation drive, but it can work right against community; it's biological, not social. A man can be grateful he never gets into the grip of it. But he'd better realize than a woman can, and watch out for it. I think that's why the old archisms used women as property. Why did the women let them? Because they were pregnant all the time—because they were already possessed, enslaved!"

"All right, maybe, but our society, here, is a true community wherever it truly embodies Odo's ideas. It was a woman who made the Promise! What are you doing— indulging guilt feelings? Wallowing?" The word he used was not "wallowing," there being no animals on Anarres to make wallows; it was a compound, meaning literally "coating continually and thickly with excrement." The flexibility and precision of Pravic lent itself to the creation of vivid metaphors quite unforeseen by its inventors.

"Well, no. It was lovely, having Sadik! But I *was* wrong about the book."

"We were both wrong. We always go wrong together. You don't really think you made up my mind for me?"

"In that case I think I did."

"No. The fact is, neither of us made up our mind. Neither of us chose. We let Sabul choose for us. Our own, internalized Sabul—convention, moralism, fear of social ostracism, fear of being different, fear of being free! Well, never again. I learn slowly, but I learn."

"What are you going to do?" asked Takver, a thrill of agreeable excitement in her voice.

"Go to Abbenay with you and start a syndicate, a printing syndicate. Print the *Principles*, uncut. And whatever else we like. Bedap's *Sketch of Open Education in Science*, that the PDC wouldn't circulate. And Tirin's play. I owe him that. He taught me what prisons are, and who

266

builds them. Those who build walls are their own prisoners. I'm going to go fulfill my proper function in the social organism. I'm going to go unbuild walls."

"It may get pretty drafty," Takver said, huddled in blankets. She leaned against him, and he put his arm around her shoulders. "I expect it will," he said.

Long after Takver had fallen asleep that night Shevek lay awake, his hands under his head, looking into darkness, hearing silence. He thought of his long trip out of the Dust, remembering the levels and mirages of the desert, the train driver with the bald, brown head and candid eyes, who had said that one must work with time and not against it.

Shevek had learned something about his own will these last four years. In its frustration he had learned its strength. No social or ethical imperative equaled it. Not even hunger could repress it. The less he had, the more absolute became his need to be.

He recognized that need, in Odonian terms, as his "cellular function," the analogic term for the individual's individuality, the work he can do best, therefore his best contribution to his society. A healthy society would let him exercise that optimum function freely, in the coordination of all such functions finding its adaptability and strength. That was a central idea of Odo's *Analogy*. That the Odonian society on Anarres had fallen short of the ideal did not, in his eyes, lessen his responsibility to it; just the contrary. With the myth of the State out of the way, the real mutuality and reciprocity of society and individual became clear. Sacrifice might be demanded of the individual, but never compromise: for though only the society could give security and stability, only the individual, the person, had the power of moral choice—the power of change, the essential function of life. The Odonian society was conceived as a permanent revolution, and revolution begins in the thinking mind.

All this Shevek had thought out, in these terms, for his conscience was a completely Odonian one.

He was therefore certain, by now, that his radical and unqualified will to create was, in Odonian terms, its own justification. His sense of primary responsibility towards his work did not cut him off from his fellows, from his society, as he had thought. It engaged him with them absolutely.

He also felt that a man who had this sense of responsibility about one thing was obliged to carry it through in all things. It was a mistake to see himself as its vehicle and nothing else, to sacrifice any other obligation to it.

That sacrificiality was what Takver had spoken of recognizing in herself when she was pregnant, and she had spoken with a degree of horror, of self-disgust, because she too was an Odonian, and the separation of means and ends was, to her too, false. For her as for him, there was no end. There was process: process was all. You could go in a promising direction or you could go wrong, but you did not set out with the expectation of ever stopping anywhere. All responsibilities, all commitments thus understood took on substance and duration.

So his mutual commitment with Takver, their relationship, had remained thoroughly alive during their four years' separation. They had both suffered from it, and suffered a good deal, but it had not occurred to either of them to escape the suffering by denying the commitment.

For after all, he thought now, lying in the warmth of Takver's sleep, it was joy they were both after—the completeness of being. If you evade suffering you also evade the chance of joy. Pleasure you may get, or pleasures, but you will not be fulfilled. You will not know what it is to come home.

Takver sighed softly in her sleep, as if agreeing with him, and turned over, pursuing some quiet dream.

Fulfillment, Shevek thought, is a function of time. The search for pleasure is circular, repetitive, atemporal. The variety seeking of the spectator, the thrill hunter, the sexually promiscuous, always ends in the same place. It has an end. It comes to the end and has to start over. It is not a journey and return, but a closed cycle, a locked room, a cell.

Outside the locked room is the landscape of time, in which the spirit may, with luck and courage, construct the fragile, makeshift, improbable roads and cities of fidelity: a landscape inhabitable by human beings.

It is not until an act occurs within the landscape of the past and the future that it is a human act. Loyalty, which asserts the continuity of past and future, binding time into a whole, is the root of human strength; there is no good to be done without it.

So, looking back on the last four years, Shevek saw them not as wasted, but as part of the edifice that he and Takver were building with their lives. The thing about working with time, instead of against it, he thought, is that it is not wasted. Even pain counts.

Chapter 11

URRAS

Rodarred, the old capital of Avan Province, was a pointed city: a forest of pines, and above the spires of the pines, an airier forest of towers. The streets were dark and narrow, mossy, often misty, under the trees. Only from the seven bridges across the river could one look up and see the tops of the towers. Some of them were hundreds of feet tall, others were mere shoots, like ordinary houses gone to seed. Some were of stone, others of porcelain, mosaic, sheets of colored glass, sheathings of copper, tin, or gold, ornate beyond belief, delicate, glittering. In these hallucinatory and charming streets the Urrasti Council of World Governments had had its seat for the three hundred years of its existence. Many embassies and consulates to the CWG and to A-Io also clustered in Rodarred, only an hour's ride from Nio Esseia and the national seat of government.

The Terran Embassy to the CWG was housed in the River Castle, which crouched between the Nio highway and the river, sending up only one squat, grudging tower with a square roof and lateral window slits like narrowed eyes. Its walls had withstood weapons and weathers for fourteen hundred years. Dark trees clustered near its landward side, and between them a drawbridge lay across a moat. The drawbridge was down, and its gates stood open. The moat, the river, the green grass, the black walls, the flag on top of the tower, all glimmered mistily as the sun broke through a river fog, and the bells in all the towers of Rodarred began their prolonged and insanely harmonious task of ringing seven o'clock.

A clerk at the very modern reception desk inside the castle was occupied with a tremendous yawn. "We aren't really open till eight o'clock," he said hollowly.

"I want to see the Ambassador."

"The Ambassador is at breakfast. You'll have to make an appointment." In saying this the clerk wiped his watery eyes and was able to see the visitor clearly for the first time. He stared, moved his jaw several times, and said, "Who are you? Where— What do you want?"

"I want to see the Ambassador."

"You just hold on," the clerk said in the purest Nioti accent, still staring, and put out his hand to a telephone.

A car had just drawn up between the drawbridge gate and the entrance of the Embassy, and several men were getting out of it, the metal fittings of their black coats glittering in the sunlight. Two other men had just entered the lobby from the main part of the building, talking together, strange-looking people, strangely clothed. Shevek hurried around the reception desk towards them, trying to run. "Help me!" he said.

They looked up startled. One drew back, frowning. The other one looked past Shevek at the uniformed group who were just entering the Embassy. "Right in here," he said with coolness, took Shevek's arm, and shut himself and Shevek into a little side office, with two steps and a gesture, as neat as a ballet dancer. "What's up? You're from Nio Esseia?"

"I want to see the Ambassador."

"Are you one of the strikers?"

"Shevek. My name is Shevek. From Anarres."

The alien eyes flashed, brilliant, intelligent, in the jet-black face. *Mai-god!* the Terran said under his breath, and then, in Iotic, "Are you asking asylum?"

"I don't know. I—"

"Come with me, Dr. Shevek. I'll get you somewhere you can sit down."

There were halls, stairs, the black man's hand on his arm.

People were trying to take his coat off. He struggled against them, afraid they were after the notebook in his shirt pocket. Somebody spoke authoritatively in a foreign language. Somebody else said to him, "It's all right. He's trying to find out if you're hurt. Your coat's bloody."

"Another man," Shevek said. "Another man's blood."

He managed to sit up, though his head swam. He was on a couch in a large, sunlit room; apparently he had fainted. A couple of men and a woman stood near him. He looked at them without understanding.

"You are in the Embassy of Terra, Dr. Shevek. You are on Terran soil here. You are perfectly safe. You can stay here as long as you want."

The woman's skin was yellow-brown, like ferrous earth, and hairless, except on the scalp; not shaven, but hairless. The features were strange and childlike, small mouth, low-bridged nose, eyes with long full lids, cheeks and chin rounded, fat-padded. The whole figure was rounded, supple, childlike.

"You are safe here," she repeated.

He tried to speak, but could not. One of the men pushed him gently on the chest, saying, "Lie down, lie down." He lay back, but he whispered, "I want to see the Ambassador."

"I'm the Ambassador. Keng is my name. We are glad you came to us. You are safe here. Please rest now, Dr. Shevek, and we'll talk later. There is no hurry." Her voice had an odd, singsong quality, but it was husky, like Takver's voice.

"Takver," he said, in his own language, "I don't know what to do."

She said, "Sleep," and he slept.

After two days' sleep and two days' meals, dressed again in his grey Ioti suit, which they had cleaned and pressed for him, he was shown into the Ambassador's private salon on the third floor of the tower.

The Ambassador neither bowed to him nor shook his hand, but joined her hands palm to palm before her breast and smiled. "I'm glad you feel better, Dr. Shevek. No, I should say simply Shevek, shouldn't I? Please sit down.

I'm sorry that I have to speak to you in Iotic, a foreign language to both of us. I don't know your language. I am told that it's a most interesting one, the only rationally invented language that has become the tongue of a great people."

He felt big, heavy, hairy, beside this suave alien. He sat down in one of the deep, soft chairs. Keng also sat down, but grimaced as she did so. "I have a bad back," she said, "from sitting in these comfortable chairs!" And Shevek realized then that she was not a woman of thirty or less, as he had thought, but was sixty or more; her smooth skin and childish physique had deceived him. "At home," she went on, "we mostly sit on cushions on the floor. But if I did that here I would have to look up even more at everyone. You Cetians are all so tall! . . . We have a little problem. That is, we really do not, but the government of A-Io does. Your people on Anarres, the ones who maintain radio communication with Urras, you know, have been asking very urgently to speak with you. And the Ioti Government is embarrassed." She smiled, a smile of pure amusement. "They don't know what to say."

She was calm. She was calm as a waterworn stone which, contemplated, calms. Shevek sat back in his chair and took a very considerable time to answer.

"Does the Ioti Government know that I'm here?"

"Well, not officially. We have said nothing, they have not asked. But we have several Ioti clerks and secretaries working here in the Embassy. So, of course, they know."

"Is it a danger to you—my being here?"

"Oh no. Our embassy is to the Council of World Governments, not to the nation of A-Io. You had a perfect right to come here, which the rest of the Council would force A-Io to admit. And as I told you, this castle is Terran soil." She smiled again; her smooth face folded into many little creases, and unfolded. "A delightful fantasy of diplomats! This castle eleven light-years from my Earth, this room in a tower in Rodarred, in A-Io, on the planet Urras of the sun Tau Ceti, is Terran soil."

"Then you can tell them I am here."

"Good. It will simplify matters. I wanted your consent."

"There was no . . . message for me, from Anarres?"

"I don't know. I didn't ask. I didn't think of it from your point of view. If you are worried about something, we might broadcast to Anarres. We know the wave length

273

your people there have been using, of course, but we haven't used it because we were not invited to. It seemed best not to press. But we can easily arrange a conversation for you."

"You have a transmitter?"

"We would relay through our ship—the Hainish ship that stays in orbit around Urras. Hain and Terra work together, you know. The Hainish Ambassador knows you're with us; he is the only person who has been officially informed. So the radio is at your service."

He thanked her, with the simplicity of one who does not look behind the offer for the offer's motive. She studied him for a moment, her eyes shrewd, direct, and quiet. "I heard your speech," she said.

He looked at her as from a distance. "Speech?"

"When you spoke at the great demonstration in Capitol Square. A week ago today. We always listen to the clandestine radio, the Socialist Workers' and the Libertarians' broadcasts. Of course, they were reporting the demonstration. I heard you speak. I was very moved. Then there was a noise, a strange noise, and one could hear the crowd beginning to shout. They did not explain. There was screaming. Then it died off the air suddenly. It was terrible, terrible to listen to. And you were there. How did you escape from that? How did you get out of the city? Old Town is still cordoned off; there are three regiments of the army in Nio; they round up strikers and suspects by the dozen and hundred every day. How did you get here?"

He smiled faintly. "In a taxi."

"Through all the checkpoints? And in that bloodstained coat? And everyone knows what you look like."

"I was under the back seat. The taxi was commandeered, is that the word? It was a risk some people took for me." He looked down at his hands, clasped on his lap. He sat perfectly quietly and spoke quietly, but there was an inner tension, a strain, visible in his eyes and in the lines around his mouth. He thought a while, and went on in the same detached way, "It was luck, at first. When I came out of hiding, I was lucky not to be arrested at once. But I got into Old Town. After that it was not just luck. They thought for me where I might go, they planned

274

how to get me there, they took the risks." He said a word in his own language, then translated it: "Solidarity. . . ."

"It is very strange," said the Ambassador from Terra. "I know almost nothing about your world, Shevek. I know only what the Urrasti tell us, since your people won't let us come there. I know, of course, that the planet is arid and bleak, and how the colony was founded, that it is an experiment in nonauthoritarian communism, that it has survived for a hundred and seventy years. I have read a little of Odo's writings—not very much. I thought that it was all rather unimportant to matters on Urras now, rather remote, an interesting experiment. But I was wrong, wasn't I? It is important. Perhaps Anarres is the key to Urras. . . . The revolutionists in Nio, they come from that same tradition. They weren't just striking for better wages or protesting the draft. They are not only socialists, they are anarchists; they were striking against power. You see, the size of the demonstration, the intensity of popular feeling, and the government's panic reaction, all seemed very hard to understand. Why so much commotion? The government here is not despotic. The rich are very rich indeed, but the poor are not so very poor. They are neither enslaved nor starving. Why aren't they satisfied with bread and speeches? Why are they supersensitive? . . . Now I begin to see why. But what is still inexplicable is that the government of A-Io, knowing this libertarian tradition was still alive, and knowing the discontent in the industrial cities, still brought you here. Like bringing the match to the powder mill!"

"I was not to be near the powder mill. I was to be kept from the populace, to live among scholars and the rich. Not to see the poor. Not to see anything ugly. I was to be wrapped up in cotton in a box in a wrapping in a carton in a plastic film, like everything here. There I was to be happy and do my work, the work I could not do on Anarres. And when it was done I was to give it to them, so they could threaten you with it."

"Threaten us, you mean, and Hain, and the other interspatial powers? Threaten us with what?"

"With the annihilation of space."

She was silent a while. "Is that what you do?" she said in her mild, amused voice.

"No. It is not what I do! In the first place, I am not an

275

inventor, an engineer. I am a theorist. What they want from me is a theory. A theory of the General Field in temporal physics. Do you know what that is?"

"Shevek, your Cetian physics, your Noble Science, is completely beyond my grasp. I am not trained in mathematics, in physics, in philosophy, and it seems to consist of all of those, and cosmology, and more besides. But I know what you mean when you say the Theory of Simultaneity, in the way I know what is meant by the Theory of Relativity; that is, I know that relativity theory led to certain great practical results; and so I gather that your temporal physics may make new technologies possible."

He nodded. "What they want," he said, "is the instantaneous transferral of matter across space. Transilience. Space travel, you see, without traversal of space or lapse of time. They may arrive at it yet; not from my equations, I think. But they can make the ansible, with my equations, if they want it. Men cannot leap the great gaps, but ideas can."

"What is an ansible, Shevek?"

"An idea." He smiled without much humor. "It will be a device that will permit communication without any time interval between two points in space. The device will not transmit messages, of course; simultaneity is identity. But to our perceptions, that simultaneity will function as a transmission, a sending. So we will be able to use it to talk between worlds, without the long waiting for the message to go and the reply to return that electromagnetic impulses require. It is really a very simple matter. Like a kind of telephone."

Keng laughed. "The simplicity of physicists! So I could pick up the—ansible?—and talk with my son in Delhi? And with my granddaughter, who was five when I left, and who lived eleven years while I was traveling from Terra to Urras in a nearly light-speed ship. And I could find out what's happening at home *now*, not eleven years ago. And decisions could be made, and agreements reached, and information shared. I could talk to diplomats on Chiffewar, you could talk to physicists on Hain, it wouldn't take ideas a generation to get from world to world. . . . Do you know, Shevek, I think your very simple matter might change the lives of all the billions of people in the nine Known Worlds?"

He nodded.

"It would make a league of worlds possible. A federation. We have been held apart by the years, the decades between leaving and arriving, between question and response. It's as if you had invented human speech! We can talk—at last we can talk together."

"And what will you say?"

His bitterness startled Keng. She looked at him and said nothing.

He leaned forward in his chair and rubbed his forehead painfully. "Look," he said, "I must explain to you why I have come to you, and why I came to this world also. I came for the idea. For the sake of the idea. To learn, to teach, to share in the idea. On Anarres, you see, we have cut ourselves off. We don't talk with other people, the rest of humanity. I could not finish my work there. And if I had been able to finish it, they did not want it, they saw no use in it. So I came here. Here is what I need—the talk, the sharing, an experiment in the Light Laboratory that proves something it wasn't meant to prove, a book of Relativity Theory from an alien world, the stimulus I need. And so I finished the work, at last. It is not written out yet, but I have the equations and the reasoning, it is done. But the ideas in my head aren't the only ones important to me. My society is also an idea. I was made by it. An idea of freedom, of change, of human solidarity, an important idea. And though I was very stupid I saw at last that by pursuing the one, the physics, I am betraying the other. I am letting the propertarians *buy the truth* from me."

"What else could you do, Shevek?"

"Is there no alternative to selling? Is there not such a thing as the gift?"

"Yes—"

"Do you not understand that I want to give this to you —and to Hain and the other worlds—and to the countries of Urras? But to you all! So that one of you cannot use it, as A-Io wants to do, to get power over the others, to get richer or to win more wars. So that you cannot use the truth for your private profit, but only for the common good."

"In the end, the truth usually insists upon serving only the common good," Keng said.

"In the end, yes, but I am not willing to wait for the end. I have one lifetime, and I will not spend it for greed and profiteering and lies. I will not serve *any* master."

Keng's calmness was a much more forced, willed affair than it had been at the beginning of their talk. The strength of Shevek's personality, unchecked by any self-consciousness or consideration of self-defense, was formidable. She was shaken by him, and looked at him with compassion and a certain awe.

"What is it like," she said, "what can it be like, the society that made you? I heard you speak of Anarres, in the Square, and I wept listening to you, but I didn't really believe you. Men always speak so of their homes, of the absent land. . . . But you are *not* like other men. There is a difference in you."

"The difference of the idea," he said. "It was for that idea that I came here, too. For Anarres. Since my people refuse to look outward, I thought I might make others look at us. I thought it would be better not to hold apart behind a wall, but to be a society among the others, a world among the others, giving and taking. But there I was wrong—I was absolutely wrong."

"Why so? Surely—"

"Because there is nothing, nothing on Urras that we Anarresti need! We left with empty hands, a hundred and seventy years ago, and we were right. We took nothing. Because there is nothing here but States and their weapons, the rich and their lies, and the poor and their misery. There is no way to act rightly, with a clear heart, on Urras. There is nothing you can do that profit does not enter into, and fear of loss, and the wish for power. You cannot say good morning without knowing which of you is 'superior' to the other, or trying to prove it. You cannot act like a brother to other people, you must manipulate them, or command them, or obey them, or trick them. You cannot touch another person, yet they will not leave you alone. There is no freedom. It is a box—Urras is a box, a package, with all the beautiful wrapping of blue sky and meadows and forests and great cities. And you open the box, and what is inside it? A black cellar full of dust, and a dead man. A man whose hand was shot off because he held it out to others. I have been in Hell at last. Desar was right; it is Urras; Hell is Urras."

For all his passion he spoke simply, with a kind of humility, and again the Ambassador from Terra watched him with a guarded yet sympathetic wonder, as if she had no idea how to take that simplicity.

"We are both aliens here, Shevek," she said at last. "I from much farther away in space and time. Yet I begin to think that I am much less alien to Urras than you are. . . . Let me tell you how this world seems to me. To me, and to all my fellow Terrans who have seen the planet, Urras is the kindliest, most various, most beautiful of all the inhabited worlds. It is the world that comes as close as any could to Paradise."

She looked at him calmly and keenly; he said nothing.

"I know it's full of evils, full of human injustice, greed, folly, waste. But it is also full of good, of beauty, vitality, achievement. It is what a world should be! It is *alive*, tremendously alive—alive, despite all its evils, with hope. Is that not true?"

He nodded.

"Now, you man from a world I cannot even imagine, you who see my Paradise as Hell, will you ask what *my* world must be like?"

He was silent, watching her, his light eyes steady.

"My world, my Earth, is a ruin. A planet spoiled by the human species. We multiplied and gobbled and fought until there was nothing left, and then we died. We controlled neither appetite nor violence; we did not adapt. We destroyed ourselves. But we destroyed the world first. There are no forests left on my Earth. The air is grey, the sky is grey, it is always hot. It is habitable, it is still habitable, but not as this world is. This is a living world, a harmony. Mine is a discord. You Odonians chose a desert; we Terrans made a desert. . . . We survive there, as you do. People are tough! There are nearly a half billion of us now. Once there were nine billion. You can see the old cities still everywhere. The bones and bricks go to dust, but the little pieces of plastic never do—they never adapt either. We failed as a species, as a social species. We are here now, dealing as equals with other human societies on other worlds, only because of the charity of the Hainish. They came; they brought us help. They built ships and gave them to us, so we could leave our ruined world. They treat us gently, charitably, as the strong man treats the

279

sick one. They are a very strange people, the Hainish; older than any of us; infinitely generous. They are altruists. They are moved by a guilt we don't even understand, despite all our crimes. They are moved in all they do, I think, by the past, their endless past. Well, we had saved what could be saved, and made a kind of life in the ruins, on Terra, in the only way it could be done: by total centralization. Total control over the use of every acre of land, every scrap of metal, every ounce of fuel. Total rationing, birth control, euthanasia, universal conscription into the labor force. The absolute regimentation of each life toward the goal of racial survival. We had achieved that much, when the Hainish came. They brought us . . . a little more hope. Not very much. We have outlived it. . . . We can only look at this splendid world, this vital society, this Urras, this Paradise, from the outside. We are capable only of admiring it, and maybe envying it a little. Not very much."

"Then Anarres, as you heard me speak of it—what would Anarres mean to you, Keng?"

"Nothing. Nothing, Shevek. We forfeited our chance for Anarres centuries ago, before it ever came into being."

Shevek got up and went over to the window, one of the long horizontal window slits of the tower. There was a niche in the wall below it, into which an archer would step up to look down and aim at assailants at the gate; if one did not take that step up one could see nothing from it but the sunwashed, slightly misty sky. Shevek stood below the window gazing out, the light filling his eyes.

"You don't understand what time is," he said. "You say the past is gone, the future is not real, there is no change, no hope. You think Anarres is a future that cannot be reached, as your past cannot be changed. So there is nothing but the present, this Urras, the rich, real, stable present, the moment now. And you think that is something which can be possessed! You envy it a little. You think it's something you would like to have. But it is not real, you know. It is not stable, not solid—nothing is. Things change, change. You cannot have anything. . . . And least of all can you have the present, unless you accept with it the past and the future. Not only the past but also the future, not only the future but also the past! Because they are real: only their reality makes the present real. You will not achieve or even understand Urras unless you accept the reality, the enduring reality, of Anarres. You are right, we are the key. But when you said that, you did not really believe it. You don't believe in Anarres. You don't believe in me, though I stand with you, in this room, in this moment. . . . My people were right, and I was wrong, in this: We cannot come to you. You will not let us. You do not believe in change, in chance, in evolution. You would destroy us rather than admit our reality, rather than admit that there is hope! We cannot come to you. We can only wait for you to come to us."

Keng sat with a startled and thoughtful, and perhaps slightly dazed, expression.

"I don't understand—I don't understand," she said at last. "You are like somebody from our own past, the old idealists, the visionaries of freedom; and yet I don't understand you, as if you were trying to tell me of future things; and yet, as you say, you are here, now! . . ." She had not lost her shrewdness. She said after a little while, "Then why is it that you came to me, Shevek?"

"Oh, to give you the idea. My theory, you know. To save it from becoming a property of the Ioti, an investment or a weapon. If you are willing, the simplest thing to do would be to broadcast the equations, to give them to physicists all over this world, and to the Hainish and the other worlds, as soon as possible. Would you be willing to do that?"

"More than willing."

"It will come to only a few pages. The proofs and some of the implications would take longer, but that can come later, and other people can work on them if I cannot."

"But what will you do then? Do you mean to go back to Nio? The city is quiet now, apparently; the insurrection seems to be defeated, at least for the time being; but I'm afraid the Ioti government regards you as an insurrectionary. There is Thu, of course—"

"No. I don't want to stay here. I am no altruist! If you would help me in this too, I might go home. Perhaps the Ioti would be willing to send me home, even. It would be consistent, I think: to make me disappear, to deny my existence. Of course, they might find it easier to do by killing me or putting me in jail for life. I don't want to die yet, and I don't want to die here in Hell at all. Where

281

does your soul go, when you die in Hell?" He laughed; he had regained all his gentleness of manner. But if you could send me home, I think they would be relieved. Dead anarchists make martyrs, you know, and keep living for centuries. But absent ones can be forgotten."

"I thought I knew what 'realism' was," Keng said. She smiled, but it was not an easy smile.

"How can you, if you don't know what hope is?"

"Don't judge us too hardly, Shevek."

"I don't judge you at all. I only ask your help, for which I have nothing to give in return."

"Nothing? You call your theory nothing?"

"Weigh it in the balance with the freedom of one single human spirit," he said, turning to her, "and which will weigh heavier? Can you tell? I cannot."

Chapter 12

ANARRES

"I want to introduce a project," said Bedap, "from the Syndicate of Initiative. You know that we've been in radio contact with Urras for about twenty decads—"

"Against the recommendation of this council, and the Defense Federative, and a majority vote of the List!"

"Yes," Bedap said, looking the speaker up and down, but not protesting the interruption. There were no rules of parliamentary procedure at meetings in PDC. Interruptions were sometimes more frequent than statements. The process, compared to a well-managed executive conference, was a slab of raw beef compared to a wiring diagram. Raw beef, however, functions better than a wiring diagram would, in its place—inside a living animal.

Bedap knew all his old opponents on the Import-Export Council; he had been coming and fighting them for three years now. This speaker was a new one, a young man, probably a new lottery posting to the PDC List. Bedap looked him over benevolently and went on, "Let's not refight old quarrels, shall we? I propose a new one. We've received an interesting message from a group on Urras. It came on the wave length our Ioti contacts use, but it didn't come at a scheduled time, and was a weak signal. It seems to have been sent from a country called Benbili, not from A-Io. The group called themselves 'The Odonian Society.' It appears that they're post-Settlement Odonians, existing in some fashion in the loopholes of law and government on Urras. Their message was to 'the brothers on Anarres.' You can read it in the Syndicate bulletin, it's interesting. They ask if they might be allowed to send people here."

"Send people here? Let Urrasti come here? Spies?"

"No, as settlers."

"They want the Settlement reopened, is that it, Bedap?"

"They say they're being hounded by their government, and are hoping for—"

"Reopen the Settlement! To any profiteer who calls himself an Odonian?"

To report an Anarresti managerial debate in full would be difficult; it went very fast, several people often speaking at once, nobody speaking at great length, a good deal of sarcasm, a great deal left unsaid; the tone emotional, often fiercely personal; an end was reached, yet there was no conclusion. It was like an argument among brothers, or among thoughts in an undecided mind.

"If we let these so-called Odonians come, how do they propose to get here?"

There spoke the opponent Bedap dreaded, the cool, intelligent woman named Rulag. She had been his cleverest enemy all year in the council. He glanced at Shevek, who was attending this council for the first time, to draw his attention to her. Somebody had told Bedap that Rulag was an engineer, and he had found in her the engineer's clarity and pragmatism of mind, plus the mechanist's hatred of complexity and irregularity. She opposed the Syndicate of Initiative on every issue, including that of its right to exist. Her arguments were good, and Bedap respected her. Sometimes when she spoke of the strength of Urras, and the danger of bargaining with the strong from a position of weakness, he believed her.

For there were times when Bedap wondered, privately, whether he and Shevek, when they got together in the winter of '68 and discussed the means by which a frustrated physicist might print his work and communicate it to physicists on Urras, had not set off an uncontrollable chain of events. When they had finally set up radio contact, the Urrasti had been more eager to talk, to exchange information, than they had expected; and when they had printed reports of those exchanges, the opposition on Anarres had been more virulent than they had expected. People on both worlds were paying more attention to them than was really comfortable. When the enemy enthusiastically embraces you, and the fellow countrymen bitterly reject you, it is hard not to wonder if you are, in fact, a traitor.

"I suppose they'd come on one of the freighters," he replied. "Like good Odonians, they'd hitchhike. If their government, or the Council of World Governments, let them. Would they let them? Would the archists do the anarchists a favor? That's what I'd like to find out. If we invited a small group, six or eight, of these people, what would happen at that end?"

"Laudable curiosity," Rulag said. "We'd know the danger better, all right, if we knew better how things really work on Urras. But the danger lies in the act of finding out." She stood up, signifying that she wanted to hold the floor for more than a sentence or two. Bedap winced, and glanced again at Shevek, who sat beside him. "Look out for this one," he muttered. Shevek made no response, but he was usually reserved and shy at meetings, no good at all unless he got moved deeply by something, in which case he was a surprisingly good speaker. He sat looking down at his hands. But as Rulag spoke, Bedap noticed that though she was addressing him, she kept glancing at Shevek.

"Your Syndicate of Initiative," she said, emphasizing the pronoun, "has proceeded with building a transmitter, with broadcasting to Urras and receiving from them, and with publishing the communications. You've done all this against the advice of the majority of the PDC, and increasing protests from the entire Brotherhood. There have been no reprisals against your equipment or yourselves yet, largely, I believe, because we Odonians have become unused to the very idea of anyone's adopting a course harmful to others and persisting in it against advice and protest. It's a rare event. In fact, you are the first of us who have behaved in the way that archist critics always predicted people would behave in a society without laws: with total irresponsibility towards the society's welfare. I don't propose to go again into the harm you've already done, and handing out of scientific information to a powerful enemy, the confession of our weakness that each of your broadcasts to Urras represents. But now, thinking that we've got used to all that, you're proposing something very much worse. What's the difference, you'll say, between talking to a few Urrasti on the shortwave and talking to a few of them here in Abbenay? What's the difference? What's the difference between a shut door and an open one? Let's open the door—that's what he's saying, you know, ammari. Let's open the door, let the Urrasti come! Six or eight pseudo-Odonians on the next freighter. Sixty or eighty Ioti profiteers on the one after, to look us over and see how we can be divided up as a property among the nations of Urras. And the next trip will be six or eight hundred armed ships of war: guns, soldiers, an occupying force. The end of Anarres, the end of the Promise. Our hope lies, it has lain for a hundred and seventy years, in the Terms of the Settlement: No Urrasti off the ships, except the Settlers, then, or ever. No mixing. No contact. To abandon that principle now is to say to the tyrants whom we defeated once, The experiment has failed, come re-enslave us!"

"Not at all," Bedap said promptly. "The message is clear: The experiment has succeeded, we're strong enough now to face you as equals."

The argument proceeded as before, a rapid hammering of issues. It did not last long. No vote was taken, as usual. Almost everyone present was strongly for sticking to the Terms of the Settlement, and as soon as this became clear Bedap said, "All right, I'll take that as settled. Nobody comes in on the *Kuieo Fort* or the *Mindful*. In the matter of bringing Urrasti to Anarres, the Syndicate's aims clearly must yield to the opinion of the society as a whole; we asked your advice, and we'll follow it. But there's another aspect of the same question. Shevek?"

"Well, there's the question," Shevek said, "Of sending an Anarresti to Urras."

There were exclamations and queries. Shevek did not raise his voice, which was not far above a mumble, but persisted. "It wouldn't harm or threaten anyone living on Anarres. And it appears that it's a matter of the individual's right; a kind of test of it, in fact. The Terms of the Settlement don't forbid it. To forbid it now would be an assumption of authority by the PDC, an abridgment of the right of the Odonian individual to initiate action harmless to others."

Rulag sat forward. She was smiling a little. "Anyone can leave Anarres," she said. Her light eyes glanced from Shevek to Bedap and back. "He can go whenever he likes, if the propertarians' freighters will take him. He can't come back."

"Who says he can't?" Bedap demanded.

"The Terms of the Closure of the Settlement. Nobody will be allowed off the freight ships farther than the boundary of the Port of Anarres."

"Well, now, that was surely meant to apply to Urrasti, not Anarresti," said an old adviser, Ferdaz, who liked to stick his oar in even when it steered the boat off the course he wanted.

"A person coming from Urras is an Urrasti," said Rulag.

"Legalisms, legalisms! What's all this quibbling?" said a calm, heavy woman named Trepil.

"Quibbling!" cried the new member, the young man. He had a Northrising accent and a deep, strong voice. "If you don't like quibbling, try this. If there are people here that don't like Anarres, let 'em go. I'll help. I'll carry 'em to the Port, I'll even kick 'em there! But if they try to come sneaking back, there's going to be some of us there to meet them. Some real Odonians. And they won't find us smiling and saying, "Welcome home, brothers.' They'll find their teeth knocked down their throats and their balls kicked up into their bellies. Do you understand that? Is it clear enough for you?"

"Clear, no; plain, yes. Plain as a fart," said Bedap. "Clarity is a function of thought. You should learn some Odonianism before you speak here."

"You're not worthy to say the name of Odo!" the young man shouted. "You're traitors, you and the whole Syndicate! There are people all over Anarres watching you. You think we don't know that Shevek's been asked to go to Urras, to go sell Anarresti science to the profiteers? You think we don't know that all you snivelers would love to go there and live rich and let the propertarians pat you on the back? You can go! Good riddance! But if you try coming back here, you'll meet with *justice!*"

He was on his feet and leaning across the table, shouting straight into Bedap's face. Bedap looked up at him and said, "You don't mean justice, you mean punishment. Do you think they're the same thing?"

"He means violence," Rulag said. "And if there is violence, you will have caused it. You and your Syndicate. And you will have deserved it."

A thin, small, middle-aged man beside Trepil began speaking, at first so softly, in a voice hoarsened by the dust cough, that few of them heard him. He was a visiting delegate from a Southwest miners' syndicate, not expected to speak on this matter. ". . . what men deserve," he was saying. "For we each of us deserve everything, every luxury that was ever piled in the tombs of the dead kings, and we each of us deserve nothing, not a mouthful of bread in hunger. Have we not eaten while another starved? Will you punish us for that? Will you reward us for the virtue of starving while others ate? No man earns punishment, no man earns reward. Free your mind of the idea of *deserving*, the idea of *earning*, and you will begin to be able to think." They were, of course, Odo's words from the *Prison Letters*, but spoken in the weak, hoarse voice they made a strange effect, as if the man were working them out word by word himself, as if they came from his own heart, slowly, with difficulty, as the water wells up slowly, slowly, from the desert sand.

Rulag listened, her head erect, her face set, like that of a person repressing pain. Across the table from her Shevek sat with his head bowed. The words left a silence after them, and he looked up and spoke into it.

"You see," he said, "what we're after is to remind ourselves that we didn't come to Anarres for safety, but for freedom. If we must all agree, all work together, we're no better than a machine. If an individual can't work in solidarity with his fellows, it's his duty to work alone. His duty and his right. We have been denying people that right. We've been saying, more and more often, you must work with the others, you must accept the rule of the majority. But any rule is tyranny. The duty of the individual is to accept *no* rule, to be the initiator of his own acts, to be responsible. Only if he does so will the society live, and change, and adapt, and survive. We are not subjects of a State founded upon law, but members of a society founded upon revolution. Revolution is our obligation: our hope of evolution. 'The Revolution is in the individual spirit, or it is nowhere. It is for all, or it is nothing. If it is seen as having any end, it will never truly begin.' We can't stop here. We must go on. We must take the risks."

Rulag replied, as quietly as he, but very coldly, "you have no right to involve us all in a risk that private motives compel you to take."

"No one who will not go as far as I'm willing to go has any right to stop me from going," Shevek answered. Their eyes met for a second; both looked down.

"The risk of a trip to Urras involves nobody but the person going," Bedap said. "It changes nothing in the Terms of the Settlement, and nothing in our relationship with Urras, except, perhaps, morally—to our advantage. But I don't think we're ready, any of us, to decide on it. I'll withdraw the topic for the present, if it's agreeable to the rest of you."

They assented, and he and Shevek left the meeting.

"I've got to go over to the Institute," Shevek said as they came out of the PDC building. "Sabul sent me one of his toenail clippings—first in years. What's on his mind, I wonder?"

"What's on that woman Rulag's mind, I wonder! She's got a personal grudge against you. Envy, I suppose. We won't put you two across a table again, or we'll get nowhere. Though that young fellow from Northrising was bad news, too. Majority rule and might makes right! Are we going to get our message across, Shev? Or are we only hardening the opposition to it?"

"We may really have to send somebody off to Urras—prove our right to by acts, if words won't do it."

"Maybe. So long as it isn't me! I'll talk myself purple about our right to leave Anarres, but if I had to do it, by damn, I'd slit my throat."

Shevek laughed. "I've got to go. I'll be home in an hour or so. Come eat with us tonight."

"I'll meet you at the room."

Shevek set off down the street with his long stride; Bedap stood hesitating in front of the PDC building. It was midafternoon, a windy, sunny, cold spring day. The streets of Abbenay were bright, scoured-looking, alive with light and people. Bedap felt both excited and let down. Everything, including his emotions, was promising yet unsatisfactory. He went off to the domicile in the Pekesh Block where Shevek and Takver now lived, and found, as he had hoped, Takver at home with the baby.

Takver had miscarried twice and then Pilun had come along, late and a little unexpected, but very welcome. She had been small at birth and now, getting on to two, was still small, with thin arms and legs. When Bedap held her he was always vaguely frightened of or repelled by the feeling of those arms, so fragile that he could have broken them simply with a twist of his hand. He was very fond of Pilun, fascinated by her cloudy grey eyes and won by her utter trustfulness, but whenever he touched her he knew consciously, as he had not done before, what the attraction of cruelty is, why the strong torment the weak. And therefore—though he could not have said why "therefore" —he also understood something that had never made much sense to him, or interested him at all: parental feeling. It gave him a most extraordinary pleasure when Pilun called him "tadde."

He sat down on the bed platform under the window. It was a good-sized room with two platforms. The floor was matted; there was no other furniture, no chairs or tables, only a little movable fence that marked off a play space or screened Pilun's bed. Takver had the long, wide drawer of the other platform open, sorting piles of papers kept in it. "Do hold Pilun, dear Dap!" she said with her large smile, when the baby began working towards him. "She's been into these papers at least ten times, every time I get them sorted. I'll be done in just a minute here—ten minutes."

"Don't hurry. I don't want to talk. I just want to sit here. Come on, Pilun. Walk—there's a girl! Walk to Tadde Dap. Now I've got you!"

Pilun sat contentedly on his knees and studied his hand. Bedap was ashamed of his nails, which he no longer bit but which remained deformed from biting, and at first he closed his hand to hide them; then he was ashamed of shame, and opened up his hand. Pilun patted it.

"This is a nice room," he said. "With the north light. It's always calm in here."

"Yes. Shh, I'm counting these."

After a while she put the piles of paper away and shut
290

the drawer. "There! Sorry. I told Shev I'd page that article for him. How about a drink?"

Rationing was still in force on many staple foods, though much less strict than it had been five years before. The fruit orchards of Northrising had suffered less and recovered quicker from the drought than the grain-growing regions, and last year dried fruits and fruit juices had gone off the restricted list. Takver had a bottle standing in the shaded window. She poured them each a cupful, in rather lumpy earthenware cups which Sadik had made at school. She sat down opposite Bedap and looked at him, smiling. "Well, how's it going at PDC?"

"Same as ever. How's the fish lab?"

Takver looked down into her cup, moving it to catch the light on the surface of the liquid. "I don't know. I'm thinking of quitting."

"Why, Takver?"

"Rather quit than be told to. The trouble is, I like that job, and I'm good at it. And it's the only one like it in Abbenay. But you can't be a member of a research team that's decided you're not a member of it."

"They're coming down harder on you, are they?"

"All the time," she said, and looked rapidly and unconsciously at the door, as if to be sure that Shevek was not there, hearing. "Some of them are unbelievable. Well, you know. There's no use going on about it."

"No, that's why I'm glad to catch you alone. I don't really know. I, and Shev, and Skovan, and Gezach, and the rest of us who spend most of the time at the printing shop or the radio tower, don't have postings, and so we don't see much of people outside the Syndicate of Initiative. I'm at PDC a lot, but that's a special situation, I expect opposition there because I create it. What is it that you run up against?"

"Hatred," Takver said, in her dark, soft voice. "Real hatred. The director of my project won't speak to me any more. Well, that's not much loss. He's a stick anyhow. But some of the others do tell me what they think. . . . There's a woman, not at the fish labs, here in the dom. I'm on the block sanitation committee and I had to go speak to her about something. She wouldn't let me talk. 'Don't you try to come into this room, I know you, you damned traitors, you intellectuals, you egoizers' and so on and so on, and then slammed the door. It was grotesque." Takver laughed without humor. Pilun, seeing her laugh, smiled as she sat curled in the angle of Bedap's arm, and then yawned. "But you know, it was frightening. I'm a coward, Dap. I don't like violence. I don't even like disapproval!"

"Of course not. The only security we have is our neighbors' approval. An archist can break a law and hope to get away unpunished, but you can't 'break' a custom; it's the framework of your life with other people. We're only just beginning to feel what it's like to be revolutionaries, as Shev put it in the meeting today. And it isn't comfortable."

"Some people understand," Takver said with determined optimism. "A woman on the omnibus yesterday, I don't know where I'd met her, tenth-day work some time, I suppose; she said, 'It must be wonderful to live with a great scientist, it must be so interesting!' And I said, 'Yes, at least there's always something to talk about'. . . . Pilun, don't go to sleep, baby! Shevek will be home soon and we'll go to commons. Jiggle her, Dap. Well, anyway, you see, she knew who Shev was, but she wasn't hateful or disapproving, she was very nice."

"People do know who he is," Bedap said. "It's funny, because they can't understand his books any more than I can. A few hundred do, he thinks. Those students in the Divisional Institutes who try to organize Simultaneity courses. I think a few dozen would be a liberal estimate, myself. And yet people know of him, they have this feeling he's something to be proud of. That's one thing the Syndicate has done, I suppose, if nothing else. Printed Shev's books. It may be the only wise thing we've done."

"Oh, now! You must have had a bad session at PDC today."

"We did. I'd like to cheer you up, Takver, but I can't. The Syndicate is cutting awfully close to the basic societal bond, the fear of the stranger. There was a young fellow there today openly threatening violent reprisal. Well, it's a poor option, but he'll find others ready to take it. And that Rulag, by damn, she's a formidable opponent!"

"You know who she is, Dap?"

"Who she is?"

"Shev never told you? Well, he doesn't talk about her. She's the mother."

292

"Shev's mother?"

Takver nodded. "She left when he was two. The father stayed with him. Nothing unusual, of course. Except Shev's feelings. He feels that he lost something essential—he and the father both. He doesn't make a general principle out of it, that parents should always keep the children, or anything. But the importance loyalty has for him, it goes back to that, I think."

"What's unusual," said Bedap energetically, oblivious of Pilun, who had gone sound asleep on his lap, "distinctly unusual, is her feelings about him! She's been waiting for him to come to an Import-Export meeting, you could tell, today. She knows he's the soul of the group, and she hates us because of him. Why? Guilt? Has the Odonian Society gone so rotten we're motivated by *guilt?* . . . You know, now that I know it, they look alike. Only in her, it's all gone hard, rock-hard—dead."

The door opened as he was speaking. Shevek and Sadik came in. Sadik was ten years old, tall for her age and thin, all long legs, supple and fragile, with a cloud of dark hair. Behind her came Shevek; and Bedap, looking at him in the curious new light of his kinship with Rulag, saw him as one occasionally sees a very old friend, with a vividness to which all the past contributes: the splendid reticent face, full of life but worn down, worn to the bone. It was an intensely individual face, and yet the features were not only like Rulag's but like many others among the Anarresti, a people selected by a vision of freedom, and adapted to a barren world, a world of distances, silences, desolations.

In the room, meantime, much closeness, commotion, communion: greetings, laughter, Pilun being passed around, rather crossly on her part, to be hugged, the bottle being passed around to be poured, questions, conversations. Sadik was the center first, because she was the least often there of the family; then Shevek. "What did old Greasy Beard want?"

"Were you at the Institute?" Takver asked, examining him as he sat beside her.

"Just went by there. Sabul left me a note this morning at the Syndicate." Shevek drank off his fruit juice and lowered the cup, revealing a curious set to his mouth, a nonexpression. "He said the Physics Federation has a full-time posting to fill. Autonomous, permanent."

"For you, you mean? There? At the Institute?"

He nodded.

"Sabul told you?"

"He's trying to enlist you," Bedap said.

"Yes, I think so. If you can't uproot it, domesticate it, as we used to say in Northsetting." Shevek suddenly and spontaneously laughed. "It is funny, isn't it?" he said.

"No," said Takver. "It isn't funny. It's disgusting. How could you go talk to him, even? After all the slander he's spread about you, and the lies about the *Principles* being stolen from him, and not telling you that the Urrasti gave you that prize, and then just last year, when he got those kids who organized the lecture series broken up and sent away because of your 'crypto-authoritarian influence' over them—*you* an authoritarian!—that was sickening, unforgivable. How can you be civil to a man like that?"

"Well, it isn't all Sabul, you know. He's just a spokesman."

"I know, but he loves to be the spokesman. And he's been so squalid for so long! Well, what did you say to him?"

"I temporized—as you might say," Shevek said, and laughed again. Takver glanced at him again, knowing now that he was, for all his control, in a state of extreme tension or excitement.

"You didn't turn him down flat, then?"

"I said that I'd resolved some years ago to accept no regular work postings, so long as I was able to do theoretical work. So he said that since it was an autonomous post I'd be completely free to go on with the research I'd been doing, and the purpose of giving me the post was to —let's see how he put it—'to facilitate access to experimental equipment at the Institute, and to the regular channels of publication and dissemination.' The PDC press, in other words."

"Why, then you've won," Takver said, looking at him with a queer expression. "You've won. They'll print what you write. It's what you wanted when we came back here five years ago. The walls are down."

"There are walls behind the walls," Bedap said.

"I've won only if I accept the posting. Sabul is offering

294

to . . . legalize me. To make me official. In order to dissociate me from the Syndicate of Initiative. Don't you see that as his motive, Dap?"

"Of course," Bedap said. His face was somber. "Divide to weaken."

"But to take Shev back into the Institute, and print what he writes on the PDC press, is to give implied approval to the whole Syndicate, isn't it?"

"It might mean that to most people," Shevek said.

"No, it won't," Bedap said. "It'll be explained. The great physicist was misled by a disaffected group, for a while. Intellectuals are always being led astray, because they think about irrelevant things like time and space and reality, things that have nothing to do with real life, so they are easily fooled by wicked deviationists. But the good Odonians at the Institute gently showed him his errors and he has returned to the path of social-organic truth. Leaving the Syndicate of Initiative shorn of its one conceivable claim to the attention of anybody on Anarres or Urras."

"I'm not leaving the Syndicate, Bedap."

Bedap lifted his head, and said after a minute, "No. I know you're not."

"All right. Let's go to dinner. This belly growls: listen to it, Pilun, hear it? Rrowr, rrowr!"

"Hup!" Pilun said in a tone of command. Shevek picked her up and stood up, swinging her onto his shoulder. Behind his head and the child's, the single mobile hanging in this room oscillated slightly. It was a large piece made of wires pounded flat, so that edge-on they all but disappeared, making the ovals into which they were fashioned flicker at intervals, vanishing, as did, in certain lights, the two thin, clear bubbles of glass that moved with the oval wires in complexly interwoven ellipsoid orbits about the common center, never quite meeting, never entirely parting. Takver called it the Inhabition of Time.

They went to the Pekesh commons, and waited till the registry board showed a sign-out, so they could bring Bedap in as a guest. His registering there signed him out at the commons where he usually ate, as the system was coordinated citywide by a computer. It was one of the highly mechanized "homeostatic processes" beloved by the early Settlers, which persisted only in Abbenay. Like the less elaborate arrangements used elsewhere, it never quite worked out; there were shortages, surpluses, and frustrations, but not major ones. Sign-outs at Pekesh commons were infrequent, as the kitchen was the best known in Abbenay, having a tradition of great cooks. An opening appeared at last, and they went in. Two young people whom Bedap knew slightly as dom neighbors of Shevek's and Takver's joined them at table. Otherwise they were let alone—left alone. Which? It did not seem to matter. They had a good dinner, a good time talking. But every now and then Bedap felt that around them there was a circle of silence.

"I don't know what the Urrasti will think up next," he said, and though he was speaking lightly he found himself, to his annoyance, lowering his voice. "They've asked to come here, and asked Shev to come there; what will the next move be?"

"I didn't know they'd actually asked Shev to go there," Takver said with a half frown.

"Yes, you did," Shevek said. "When they told me that they'd given me the prize, you know, the Seo Oen, they asked if I couldn't come, remember? To get the money that goes with it!" Shevek smiled, luminous. If there was a circle of silence around him, it was no bother to him, he had always been alone.

"That's right. I did know that. It just didn't register as an actual possibility. You'd been talking for decads about suggesting in PDC that somebody might go to Urras, just to shock them."

"That's what we finally did, this afternoon. Dap made me say it."

"Were they shocked?"

"Hair on end, eyes bulging—"

Takver giggled. Pilun sat in a high chair next to Shevek, exercising her teeth on a piece of holum bread and her voice in song. "O mathery bathery," she proclaimed, "abbery abbery babber dab!" Shevek, versatile, replied in the same vein. Adult conversation proceeded without intensity and with interruptions. Bedap did not mind, he had learned long ago that you took Shevek with complications or not at all. The most silent one of them all was Sadik.

Bedap stayed on with them for an hour after dinner in the pleasant, spacious common rooms of the domicile, and when he got up to go offered to accompany Sadik to her school dormitory, which was on his way. At this something happened, one of those events or signals obscure to those outside a family; all he knew was that Shevek, with no fuss or discussion, was coming along. Takver had to go feed Pilun, who was getting louder and louder. She kissed Bedap, and he and Shevek set off with Sadik, talking. They talked hard, and walked right past the learning center. They turned back. Sadik had stopped before the dormitory entrance. She stood motionless, erect and slight, her face still, in the weak light of the street lamp. Shevek stood equally still for a moment, then went to her. "What is wrong, Sadik?"

The child said, "Shevek, may I stay in the room tonight?"

"Of course. But what's wrong?"

Sadik's delicate, long face quivered and seemed to fragment. "They don't like me, in the dormitory," she said, her voice becoming shrill with tension, but even softer than before.

"They don't like you? What do you mean?"

They did not touch each other yet. She answered him with desperate courage. "Because they don't like—they don't like the Syndicate, and Bedap, and—and you. They call— The big sister in the dorm room, she said you—we were all tr— She said we were traitors," and saying the word the child jerked as if she had been shot, and Shevek caught her and held her. She held to him with all her strength, weeping in great gasping sobs. She was too old, too tall for him to pick up. He stood holding her, stroking her hair. He looked over her dark head at Bedap. His own eyes were full of tears. He said, "It's all right, Dap. Go on."

There was nothing for Bedap to do but leave them there, the man and the child, in that one intimacy which he could not share, the hardest and deepest, the intimacy of pain. It gave him no sense of relief or escape to go; rather he felt useless, diminished. "I am thirty-nine years old," he thought as he walked on towards his domicile, the five-man room where he lived in perfect independence. "Forty in a few decads. What have I done? What have I been doing? Nothing. Meddling. Meddling in other people's lives because I don't have one. I never took the time.
297

And the time's going to run out on me, all at once, and I will never have had . . . that." He looked back, down the long, quiet street, where the corner lamps made soft pools of light in the windy darkness, but he had gone too far to see the father and daughter, or they had gone. And what he meant by "that" he could not have said, good as he was with words; yet he felt that he understood it clearly, that all his hope was in that understanding, and that if he would be saved he must change his life.

When Sadik was calm enough to let go of him, Shevek left her sitting on the front step of the dormitory, and went in to tell the vigilkeeper that she would be staying with the parents this night. The vigilkeeper spoke coldly to him. Adults who worked in children's dormitories had a natural tendency to disapprove of overnight dom visits, finding them disruptive; Shevek told himself he was probably mistaken in feeling anything more than such disapproval in the vigilkeeper. The halls of the learning center were brightly lit, ringing with noise, music practice, children's voices. There were all the old sounds, the smells, the shadows, the echoes of childhood which Shevek remembered, and with them the fears. One forgets the fears.

He came out and walked home with Sadik, his arm around her thin shoulders. She was silent, still struggling. She said abruptly as they came to their entry in the Pekesh main domicile, "I know it isn't agreeable for you and Takver to have me overnight."

"Where did you get that idea?"

"Because you want privacy, adult couples need privacy."

"There's Pilun," he observed.

"Pilun doesn't count."

"Neither do you."

She sniffled, attempting to smile.

When they came into the light of the room, however, her white, red-patched, puffy face at once startled Takver into saying, "Whatever is wrong?"—and Pilun, interrupted in sucking, startled out of bliss, began to howl, at which Sadik broke down again, and for a while it appeared that everyone was crying, and comforting each other, and refusing comfort. This sorted out quite suddenly into silence, Pilun on the mother's lap, Sadik on the father's.

When the baby was replete and put down to sleep,

Takver said in a low but impassioned voice, "Now! What is it?"

Sadik had gone half to sleep herself, her head on Shevek's chest. He could feel her gather herself to answer. He stroked her hair to keep her quiet, and answered for her. "Some people at the learning center disapprove of us."

"And by damn what damned right have they to disapprove of us?"

"Shh, shh. Of the Syndicate."

"Oh," Takver said, a queer guttural noise, and in buttoning up her tunic she tore the button right off the fabric. She stood looking down at it on her palm. Then she looked at Shevek and Sadik.

"How long has this been going on?"

"A long time," Sadik said, not lifting her head.

"Days, decads, all quarter?"

"Oh, longer. But they get . . . they're meaner in the dorm now. At night. Terzol doesn't stop them." Sadik spoke rather like a sleep-talker, and quite serenely, as if the matter no longer concerned her.

"What do they do?" Takver asked, though Shevek's gaze warned her.

"Well, they . . . they're just mean. They keep me out of the games and things. Tip, you know, she was a friend, she used to come and talk at least after lights out. But she stopped. Terzol is the big sister in the dorm now, and she's . . . she says, 'Shevek is—Shevek—' "

He broke in, feeling the tension rise in the child's body, the cowering and the summoning of courage, unendurable. "She says, 'Shevek is a traitor, Sadik is an egoizer'—You know what she says, Takver!" His eyes were blazing. Takver came forward and touched her daughter's cheek, once, rather timidly. She said in a quiet voice, "Yes, I know," and went and sat down on the other bed platform, facing them.

The baby, tucked away next to the wall, snored slightly. People in the next room came back from commons, a door slammed, somebody down in the square called good night and was answered from an open window. The big domicile, two hundred rooms, was astir, alive quietly all round them; as their existence entered into its existence so did its existence enter into theirs, as part of a whole. Presently Sadik slipped off her father's knees and sat on the plat-

299

form beside him, close to him. Her dark hair was rumpled and tangled, hanging around her face.

"I didn't want to tell you, because . . ." Her voice sounded thin and small. "But it just keeps getting worse. They make each other meaner."

"Then you won't go back there," Shevek said. He put his arm around her, but she resisted, sitting straight.

"If I go and talk to them—" said Takver.

"It's no use. They feel as they feel."

"But what is this we're up against?" Takver asked with bewilderment.

Shevek did not answer. He kept his arm around Sadik, and she yielded at last, leaning her head against his arm with a weary heaviness. "There are other learning centers," he said at last, without much certainty.

Takver stood up. She clearly could not sit still and wanted to do something, to act. But there was not much to do. "Let me braid your hair, Sadik," she said in a subdued voice.

She brushed and braided the child's hair; they set the screen across the room, and tucked Sadik in beside the sleeping baby. Sadik was near tears again saying good night, but within half an hour they heard by her breathing that she was asleep.

Shevek had settled down at the head of their bed platform with a notebook and the slate he used for calculating.

"I paged that manuscript today," Takver said.

"What did it come to?"

"Forty-one pages. With the supplement."

He nodded. Takver got up, looked over the screen at the two sleeping children, returned, and sat down on the edge of the platform.

"I knew there was something wrong. But she didn't say anything. She never has, she's stoical. It didn't occur to me it was this. I thought it was just our problem, it didn't occur to me they'd take it out on children." She spoke softly and bitterly. "It grows, it keeps growing. . . . Will another school be any different?"

"I don't know. If she spends much time with us, probably not."

"You certainly aren't suggesting—"

"No, I'm not. I'm stating a fact, only. If we choose to

300

give the child the intensity of individual love, we can't spare her what comes with that, the risk of pain. Pain from us, and through us."

"It isn't fair she should be tormented for what we do. She's so good, and good-natured, she's like clear water—" Takver stopped, strangled by a brief rush of tears, wiped her eyes, set her lips.

"It isn't what we do. It's what I do." He put his notebook down. "You've been suffering for it too."

"I don't care what they think."

"At work?"

"I can take another posting."

"Not here, not in your own field."

"Well, do you want me to go somewhere else? The Sorruba fishery labs at Peace-and-Plenty would take me on. But where does that leave you?" She looked at him angrily. "Here, I suppose?"

"I could come with you. Skovan and the others are coming along in Iotic, they'll be able to handle the radio, and that's my main practical function in the Syndicate now. I can do physics as well in Peace-and-Plenty as I can here. But unless I drop right out of the Syndicate of Initiative, that doesn't solve the problem, does it? I'm the problem. I'm the one who makes trouble."

"Would they care about that, in a little place like Peace-and-Plenty?"

"I'm afraid they might."

"Shev, how much of his hatred have you run up against? Have you been keeping quiet, like Sadik?"

"And like you. Well, at times. When I went to Concord, last summer, it was a little worse than I told you. Rock-throwing, and a good-sized fight. The students who asked me to come had to fight for me. They did, too, but I got out quick; I was putting them in danger. Well, students want some danger. And after all we've asked for a fight, we've deliberately roused people. And there are plenty on our side. But now . . . but I'm beginning to wonder if I'm not imperiling you and the children, Tak. By staying with you."

"Of course you're not in danger yourself," she said savagely.

"I've asked for it. But it didn't occur to me they'd ex-

301

tend their tribal resentment to you. I don't feel the same about your danger as I do about mine."

"Altruist!"

"Maybe. I can't help it. I do feel responsible, Tak. Without me, you could go anywhere, or stay here. You've worked for the Syndicate, but what they hold against you is your loyalty to me. I'm the symbol. So there doesn't . . . there isn't anywhere for me to go."

"Go to Urras," Takver said. Her voice was so harsh that Shevek sat back as if she had hit him in the face.

She did not meet his eyes, but she repeated, more softly, "Go to Urras. . . . Why not? They want you there. They don't here! Maybe they'll begin to see what they've lost, when you're gone. And you want to go. I saw that tonight. I never thought of it before, but when we talked about the prize, at dinner, I saw it, the way you laughed."

"I don't need prizes and rewards!"

"No, but you do need appreciation, and discussion, and students—with no Sabul-strings attached. And look. You and Dap keep talking about scaring PDC with the idea of somebody going to Urras, asserting his right to self-determination. But if you talk about it and nobody goes, you've only strengthened their side—you've only proved that custom is unbreakable. Now you've brought it up in a PDC meeting, somebody will have to go. It ought to be you. They've asked you; you have a reason to go. Go get your reward—the money they're saving for you," she ended with a sudden quite genuine laugh.

"Takver, I don't want to go to Urras!"

"Yes you do; you know you do. Though I'm not sure I know why."

"Well, of course I'd like to meet some of the physicists. . . . And see the laboratories at Ieu Eun where they've been experimenting with light." He looked shamefaced as he said it.

"It's your right to do so," Takver said with fierce determination. "If it's part of your work, you ought to do it."

"It would help keep the Revolution alive—on both sides —wouldn't it?" he said. "What a crazy idea! Like Tirin's play, only backwards. I'm to go subvert the archists. . . . Well, it would at least prove to them that Anarres exists.

302

They talk with us on the radio, but I don't think they really believe in us. In what we are."

"If they did, they might be scared. They might come and blow us right out of the sky, if you really convinced them."

"I don't think so. I might make a little revolution in their physics again, but not in their opinions. It's here, here, that I can affect society, even though here they won't pay attention to my physics. You're quite right; now that we've talked about it, we must do it." There was a pause. He said, "I wonder what kind of physics the other races do."

"What other races?"

"The aliens. People from Hain and other solar systems. There are two alien Embassies on Urras, Hain and Terra. The Hainish invented the interstellar drive Urras uses now. I suppose they'd give it to us, too, if we were willing to ask for it. It would be interesting to . . ." He did not finish.

After another long pause he turned to her and said in a changed, sarcastic tone, "And what would you do while I went visiting the propertarians?"

"Go to the Sorruba coast with the girls, and live a very peaceful life as a fish-lab technician. Until you come back."

"Come back? Who knows if I could come back?"

She met his gaze straight on. "What would prevent you?"

"Maybe the Urrasti. They might keep me. No one there is free to come and go, you know. Maybe our own people. They might prevent me from landing. Some of them in PDC threatened that, today. Rulag was one of them."

"She would. She only knows denial. How to deny the possibility of coming home."

"That is quite true. That says it completely," he said, settling back again and looking at Takver with contemplative admiration. "But Rulag isn't the only one, unfortunately. To a great many people, anyone who went to Urras and tried to come back would simply be a traitor, a spy."

"What would they actually do about it?"

"Well, if they persuaded Defense of the danger, they could shoot down the ship."

"Would Defense be that stupid?"

"I don't think so. But anybody outside Defense could make explosives with blasting powder and blow up the ship on the ground. Or, more likely, attack me once I was outside the ship. I think that's a definite possibility. It should be included in a plan to make a round-trip tour of the scenic areas of Urras."

"Would it be worthwhile to you—that risk?"

He looked forward at nothing for a time. "Yes," he said, "in a way. If I could finish the theory there, and give it to them—to us and them and all the worlds, you know —I'd like that. Here I'm walled in. I'm cramped, it's hard to work, to test the work, always without equipment, without colleagues and students. And then when I do the work, they don't want it. Or, if they do, like Sabul, they want me to abandon initiative in return for receiving approval. They'll use the work I do, after I'm dead, that always happens. But why must I give my lifework as a present to Sabul, all the Sabuls, the petty, scheming, greedy egos of one single planet? I'd like to share it. It's a big subject I work on. It ought to be given out, handed around. It won't run out!"

"All right, then," Takver said, "it is worth it."

"Worth what?"

"The risk. Perhaps not being able to come back."

"Not being able to come back," he repeated. He looked at Takver with a strange, intense, yet abstracted gaze.

"I think there are more people on our side, on the Syndicate's side, than we realize. It's just that we haven't actually done much—done anything to bring them together—taken any risk. If you took it, I think they'd come out in support of you. If you opened the door, they'd smell fresh air again, they'd smell freedom."

"And they might all come rushing to slam the door shut."

"If they do, too bad for them. The Syndicate can protect you when you land. And then, if people are still so hostile and hateful, we'll say the hell with them. What's the good of an anarchist society that's afraid of anarchists? We'll go live in Lonesome, in Upper Sedep, in Uttermost, we'll go live alone in the mountains if we have to. There's room. There'd be people who'd come with us. We'll make a new community. If our society is settling down into politics and power seeking, then we'll get out, we'll go make an Anarres beyond Anarres, a new beginning. How's that?"

"Beautiful," he said, "it's beautiful, dear heart. But I'm not going to go to Urras, you know."

"Oh, yes. And you will come back," Takver said. Her eyes were very dark, a soft darkness, like the darkness of a forest at night. "If you set out to. You always get to where you're going. And you always come back."

"Don't be stupid, Takver. I'm not going to Urras!"

"I'm worn out," Takver said, stretching, and leaning over to put her forehead against his arm. "Let's go to bed."

Chapter 13

Before they broke orbit, the view ports were filled with the cloudy turquoise of Urras, immense and beautiful. But the ship turned, and the stars came into sight, and Anarres among them like a round bright rock: moving yet not moving, thrown by what hand, timelessly circling, creating time.

They showed Shevek all over the ship, the interstellar *Davenant*. It was as different as it could be from the freighter *Mindful* From the outside it was as bizarre and fragile-looking as a sculpture in glass and wire; it did not have the look of a ship, a vehicle, about it at all, not even a front and back end, for it never traveled through any atmosphere thicker than that of interplanetary space. Inside, it was as spacious and solid as a house. The rooms were large and private, the walls wood-paneled or covered with textured weavings, the ceilings high. Only it was like a house with the blinds drawn, for few rooms had view ports, and it was very quiet. Even the bridge and the engine rooms had this quietness about them, and the machines and instruments had the simple definitiveness of design of the fittings of a sailing ship. For recreation, there was a garden, where the lighting had the quality of sunlight, and the air was sweet with the smell of earth and leaves; during ship night the garden was darkened, and its ports cleared to the stars.

Though its interstellar journeys lasted only a few hours or days shiptime, a near-lightspeed ship such as this might spend months exploring a solar system, or years in orbit around a planet where its crew was living or exploring. Therefore it was made spacious, humane, livable, for those who must live aboard it. Its style had neither the opulence of Urras nor the austerity of Anarres, but struck a balance, with the effortless grace of long practice. One could imagine leading that restricted life without fretting at its restrictions, contentedly, meditatively. They were a meditative people, the Hainish among the crew, civil, considerate, rather somber. There was little spontaneity in them. The youngest of them seemed older than any of the Terrans aboard.

But Shevek was seldom very observant of them, Terrans or Hainish, during the three days that the *Davenant*, moving by chemical propulsion at conventional speeds, took to go from Urras to Anarres. He replied when spoken to; he answered questions willingly, but he asked very few. When he spoke, it was out of an inward silence. The people of the *Davenant*, particularly the younger ones, were drawn to him, as if he had something they lacked or was something they wished to be. They discussed him a good deal among themselves, but they were shy with him. He did not notice this. He was scarcely aware of them. He was aware of Anarres, ahead of him. He was aware of hope deceived and of the promise kept; of failure; and of the sources within his spirit, unsealed at last, of joy. He was a man released from jail, going home to his family. Whatever such a man sees along his way he sees only as reflections of the light.

On the second day of the voyage he was in the communications room, talking with Anarres on the radio, first on the PDC wave length and now with the Syndicate of Initiative. He sat leaning forward, listening, or answering with a spate of the clear, expressive language that was his native tongue, sometimes gesturing with his free hand as if his interlocutor could see him, occasionally laughing. The first mate of the *Davenant*, a Hainishman named Ketho, controlling the radio contact, watched him thoughtfully. Ketho had spent an hour after dinner the night before with Shevek, along with the commander and other crew members; he had asked—in a quiet, undemanding, Hainish way—a good many questions about Anarres.

Shevek turned to him at last. "All right, done. The rest can wait till I'm home. Tomorrow they will contact you to arrange the entry procedure."

Ketho nodded. "You got some good news," he said.

"Yes, I did. At least some, what do you call it, lively news." They had to speak Iotic together; Shevek was more fluent in the language than Ketho, who spoke it very correctly and stiffly. "The landing is going to be exciting," Shevek went on. "A lot of enemies and a lot of friends will be there. The good news is the friends. . . . It seems there are more of them than when I left."

"This danger of attack, when you land," Ketho said. "Surely the officers of the Port of Anarres feel that they can control the dissidents? They would not deliberately tell you to come down and be murdered?"

"Well, they are going to protect me. But I am also a dissident, after all. I asked to take the risk. That's my privilege, you see, as an Odonian." He smiled at Ketho. The Hainishman did not smile back; his face was serious. He was a handsome man of about thirty, tall and light-skinned like a Cetian, but nearly hairless like a Terran, with very strong, fine features.

"I am glad to be able to share it with you," he said. "I will be taking you down in the landing craft."

"Good," Shevek said. "It isn't everyone who would care to accept our privileges!"

"More than you think, perhaps," Ketho said. "If you would allow them to."

Shevek, whose mind had not been fully on the conversation, had been about to leave; this stopped him. He looked at Ketho, and after a moment said, "Do you mean that you would like to land with me?"

The Hainishman answered with equal directness, "Yes, I would."

"Would the commander permit it?"

"Yes. As an officer of a mission ship, in fact, it is part of my duty to explore and investigate a new world when possible. The commander and I have spoken of the possibility. We discussed it with our ambassadors before we left. Their feeling was that no formal request should be made, since your people's policy is to forbid foreigners to land."

"Hm," Shevek said, noncommittal. He went over to the far wall and stood for a while in front of a picture, a Hainish landscape, very simple and subtle, a dark river flowing among reeds under a heavy sky. "The Terms of the Closure of the Settlement of Anarres," he said, "do not permit Urrasti to land, except inside the boundary of the Port. Those terms still are accepted. But you're not an Urrasti."

"When Anarres was settled, there were no other races known. By implication, those terms include all foreigners."

"So our managers decided, sixty years ago, when your people first came into this solar system and tried to talk with us. But I think they were wrong. They were just building more walls." He turned around and stood, his hands behind his back, looking at the other man. "Why do you want to land, Ketho?"

"I want to see Anarres," the Hainishman said. "Even before you came to Urras, I was curious about it. It began when I read Odo's works. I became very interested. I have—" He hesitated, as if embarrassed, but continued in his repressed, conscientious way, "I have learned a little Pravic. Not much yet."

"It is your own wish, then—your own initiative?"

"Entirely."

"And you understand that it might be dangerous?"

"Yes."

"Things are . . . a little broken loose, on Anarres. That's what my friends on the radio have been telling me about. It was our purpose all along—our Syndicate, this journey of mine—to shake up things, to stir up, to break some habits, to make people ask questions. To behave like anarchists! All this has been going on while I was gone. So, you see, nobody is quite sure what happens next. And if you land with me, even more gets broken loose. I cannot push too far. I cannot take you as an official representative of some foreign government. That will not do, on Anarres."

"I understand that."

"Once you are there, once you walk through the wall

with me, then as I see it you are one of us. We are responsible to you and you to us; you become an Anarresti, with the same options as all the others. But they are not safe options. Freedom is never very safe." He looked around the tranquil, orderly room, with its simple consoles and delicate instruments, its high ceiling and windowless walls, and back at Ketho. "You would find yourself very much alone," he said.

"My race is very old," Ketho said. "We have been civilized for a thousand millennia. We have histories of hundreds of those millennia. We have tried everything. Anarchism, with the rest. But I have not tried it. They say there is nothing new under any sun. But if each life is not new, each single life, then why are we born?"

"We are the children of time," Shevek said, in Pravic. The younger man looked at him a moment, and then repeated the words in Iotic: "We are the children of time."

"All right," Shevek said, and laughed. "All right, ammar! You had better call Anarres on the radio again—the Syndicate, first. . . . I said to Keng, the ambassador, that I had nothing to give in return for what her people and yours have done for me; well, maybe I can give you something in return. An idea, a promise, a risk. . . ."

"I shall speak to the commander," Ketho said, as grave as ever, but with a very slight tremor in his voice of excitement, of hope.

Very late on the following ship night, Shevek was in the *Davenant*'s garden. The lights were out, there, and it was illuminated only by starlight. The air was quite cold. A night-blooming flower from some unimaginable world had opened among the dark leaves and was sending out its perfume with patient, unavailing sweetness to attract some unimaginable moth trillions of miles away, in a garden on a world circling another star. The sunlights differ, but there is only one darkness. Shevek stood at the high, cleared view port, looking at the night side of Anarres, a dark curve across half the stars. He was wondering if Takver would be there, at the Port. She had not yet arrived in Abbenay from Peace-and-Plenty when he last talked with Bedap, so he had left it to Bedap to discuss and decide with her whether it would be wise for her to come out to the Port. "You don't think I could stop her even if it wasn't?" Bedap had said. He wondered also what

kind of ride she might have got from the Sorruba coast; a
dirigible, he hoped, if she had brought the girls along.
Train riding was hard, with children. He still recalled the
discomforts of the trip from Chakar to Abbenay, in '68,
when Sadik had been trainsick for three mortal days.

The door of the garden room opened, increasing the
dim illumination. The commander of the *Davenant* looked
in and spoke his name; he answered; the commander came
in, with Ketho.

"We have the entry pattern for our landing craft from
your ground control," the commander said. He was a
short, iron-colored Terran, cool and businesslike. "If
you're ready to go, we'll start launch procedure."

"Yes."

The commander nodded and left. Ketho came forward
to stand beside Shevek at the port.

"You're sure you want to walk through this wall with
me, Ketho? You know, for me, it's easy. Whatever happens, I am coming home. But you are leaving home.
'True journey is return. . . .' "

"I hope to return," Ketho said in his quiet voice. "In
time."

"When are we to enter the landing craft?"

"In about twenty minutes."

"I'm ready. I have nothing to pack." Shevek laughed, a
laugh of clear, unmixed happiness. The other man looked
at him gravely, as if he was not sure what happiness was,
and yet recognized or perhaps remembered it from afar.
He stood beside Shevek as if there was something he
wanted to ask him. But he did not ask it. "It will be early
morning at Anarres Port," he said at last, and took his
leave, to get his things and meet Shevek at the launch
port.

Alone, Shevek turned back to the observation port, and
saw the blinding curve of sunrise over the Temae, just
coming into sight.

"I will lie down to sleep on Anarres tonight," he
thought. "I will lie down beside Takver. I wish I'd brought
the picture, the baby sheep, to give Pilun."

But he had not brought anything. His hands were empty, as they had always been.

THE BEST IN SCIENCE FICTION AND FANTASY FROM AVON ▲ BOOKS

URSULA K. LE GUIN

The Lathe of Heaven	43547	1.95
The Dispossessed	44057	2.25

ISAAC ASIMOV

Foundation	44057	1.95
Foundation and Empire	42689	1.95
Second Foundation	45351	1.95
The Foundation Trilogy (Large Format)	26930	4.95

ROGER ZELAZNY

Doorways in the Sand	49510	1.75
Creatures of Light and Darkness	35956	1.50
Lord of Light	44834	2.25
The Doors of His Face The Lamps of His Mouth	38182	1.50
The Guns of Avalon	31112	1.50
Nine Princes in Amber	36756	1.50
Sign of the Unicorn	30973	1.50
The Hand of Oberon	33324	1.50
The Courts of Chaos	47175	1.75

Include 50¢ per copy for postage and handling, allow 4-6 weeks for delivery.

Avon Books, Mail Order Dept.
224 W. 57th St., N.Y., N.Y. 10019